YRSA SIGURDARDÓTTIR
Translated from the Icelandic
by Philip Rughton

◆

SOMEONE TO
WATCH
OVER ME

Complete and Unabridged

CHARN
Leic

First published in Great Britain in 2013 by
Hodder & Stoughton
London

First Charnwood Edition
published 2015
by arrangement with
Hodder & Stoughton
An Hachette UK company
London

A catalogue record for this book is available
from the British Library.

ISBN 978–1–4448–2242–7

Published by
F. A. Thorpe (Publishing)
Anstey, Leicestershire

Set by Words & Graphics Ltd.
Anstey, Leicestershire
Printed and bound in Great Britain by
T. J. International Ltd., Padstow, Cornwall

This book is printed on acid-free paper

This novel is dedicated to the memory of my grandmother, Vilborg G. Guðjónsdóttir (4 November 1909 — 24 July 1982).

— Yrsa

Preface

Saturday, 8 November 2008

The cat was keeping a low profile, concealing itself in the darkness behind the dense but leafless bushes. It crouched there, motionless, the only movement its yellow eyes flickering back and forth; its defences were up against whatever else shared the night. The humans who used to feed it had long since forgotten it, and the cat knew there were things hidden in the dark that didn't come out in daylight. It always made itself invisible as the hush of night descended, when people let down their guard as the shadows either vanished or took over, depending on your point of view. The cat still hadn't made up its mind which it was, and it didn't care: it liked this time of day, even though its hackles rose from time to time in anticipation of the unexpected, of whatever bad thing was just around the corner. Everything that hated the light was now set free; the dark corners merged with their surroundings, all around was darkness and solitude.

A dull cracking sound made the cat flex its claws into the damp, cold soil. It couldn't see anything but still it resisted drawing attention to itself, breathing more shallowly and pressing its scrawny body as flat to the ground as possible. The cold air, which moments before had felt so refreshing after a day sleeping on the sofa,

1

became oppressive, and each inhalation left an unpleasant flavour on the creature's rough tongue. Inadvertently, it hissed low in its throat, and frantically tensed itself to spring away from the terrible thing that was there somewhere but invisible, like the owners of the voices on the radio of the people it shared the house with. Suddenly the cat turned, darted out from under the bushes and ran as fast as its feet could carry it, away from the house.

★　★　★

Berglind sat up in bed, wide awake. When she woke in the middle of the night it usually happened gradually, while she tossed and turned in search of the perfect sleeping position. But this time she'd seemed to jolt awake from a deep sleep, feeling as if she hadn't slept at all. It was completely dark in the master bedroom and outside was a pitch-black, starless sky. The illuminated hands on the alarm clock revealed that it was just gone three thirty. Had she been woken by crying from the child's room? Berglind listened carefully, but heard only the low ticking of the alarm clock and her husband's heavy breathing.

Berglind pushed back the duvet, taking care not to wake Halli. He'd had enough to put up with these past few months and the last thing she wanted was to disturb him. Although the holy men seemed to have done their job well, she didn't dare to hope the matter was settled so soon after their visit. But she couldn't express that to her husband, or to anyone else, in case people thought she was doing it for attention and ended up doubting her word — or rather, doubting it even more — over what had happened recently. Even Halli, who had experienced it all with her, had tried to find rational explanations, but most of them were so unlikely as to be ridiculous. He had never fully accepted her theories, although over time he stopped objecting to them, since nothing else seemed possible as the strange events kept multiplying. Still, it was to Halli's credit that he had held back and tried his best to support her, despite the cracks that had formed in the foundations of their marriage. They weren't on the home straight yet; their problems were far from over, although at least one of their biggest issues seemed to be behind them now. At work Halli's hours had been cut back and seemed unlikely to be reinstated, and although Berglind's job as a civil servant was supposedly secure there were financial issues there, too. Who knew, perhaps she would be next to suffer from the cutbacks.

Berglind's eyes adjusted quickly to the darkness and she got out of bed carefully. There was no point lying back down yet. She would have a glass of water and check Pési was sound asleep; hopefully then she would be tired again. Otherwise she would play a couple of hands of solitaire on the computer or surf the Internet until her eyelids started drooping. Long ago she'd mastered the art of distracting herself with pointless and repetitive tasks in order to restore

3

her peace of mind. Otherwise she would never have been able to stay in the house so long. Berglind shut the bedroom door behind her, trying not to let the hinges creak. They had been planning to replace all the doors when they bought the house, but they'd never got round to it. The hallway was cold as ice; the chilly tiles made the soles of her feet tingle and she regretted not having stopped to look for her slippers. In her heart she knew she never would have; it would be a long time before she could bring herself to poke around in the darkness under the bed. Hopefully it would happen. No, not *hopefully*, it *had* to. Otherwise she would lose her mind.

The water in the kitchen tap was lukewarm so she let it run for a while as she stared out at the familiar street and the houses opposite. The road was shrouded in darkness, although it looked like someone had forgotten to turn off the light in the garage directly opposite. Presumably a window had been left open as well, because a bare light bulb swung there slowly, as if in a gentle breeze. Otherwise the row of houses was dark. The yellowish gleam from the streetlight did not spread to the front gardens, but died out at the edge of the pavement where the shadows took over. Berglind looked downhill, across rooftops, ignoring the running water as she let her eyes wander along to where Vesturlandsvegur Road turned up towards the suburb of Kjalarnes. She let go of the tap and rubbed the goose bumps on her upper arm. A car drove along the main road and she thought she could hear its engine whine as it splashed through

4

the rain-filled tyre ruts. Had they been there since the accident? The weather hadn't been like this, that night. The road was in need of repair, but it wouldn't happen any time soon. Berglind dragged her gaze away from the window and stuck a glass under the stream of water.

If only they'd turned down the invitation to the Christmas buffet. She didn't ask herself if she was only thinking this in hindsight; in her mind they had never wanted to go in the first place, but they had let friends persuade them. If this hadn't been the case, she didn't want to admit it; it was easier to deal with the consequences if it was someone else's fault that they had dressed up, asked Magga to babysit, and gone along. They hadn't used a babysitter since then, and didn't intend to. Their social life was now restricted to their home or places where they could take their four-year-old son.

She just couldn't imagine enjoying an evening out knowing he was at home with a babysitter, not since that terrible night and everything that had happened since. For the thousandth time she thought to herself that everything would have gone differently if they'd skipped the Christmas buffet altogether, or at least if they hadn't decided to have a drink at home to avoid having to buy one at the restaurant. But thinking that way only rubbed salt in the wound. They had accepted the invitation, and they had made childcare arrangements. Berglind's eyes automatically went back to the window and she stared at the black tarmac of Vesturlandsvegur Road, which ran like a dark, currentless river

5

along the edge of the neighbourhood. She closed her eyes and immediately saw the image she'd been faced with that fateful night. The flashing lights of the ambulance and the police cars had eclipsed both the Christmas lights on the roof of the house opposite and the heavy snow that was falling. The tiny white lights, which should have stood for peace on Earth and the hope of a new year, could not compete with the bright colours flashing from the vehicles. With the same hindsight she had used to convince herself they'd initially planned not to go to the dinner, Berglind now told herself that at the time she had immediately connected the accident on Vesturlandsvegur Road to their babysitter Magga, who hadn't yet shown up.

She opened her eyes and gulped down the water. It was still a bit warm and she regretted not having let the tap run even longer. Recently everything she did seemed tinged with regret, not that one could compare the temperature of drinking water to the death of a young girl, and not that the accident had been her fault. Nevertheless she felt terribly guilty. Magga's parents, who they'd met several times after the accident, had been devastated, and the look on their faces would haunt both Berglind and Halli for the rest of their lives, if not longer. Of course no one blamed them for the accident, at least not openly, but Berglind thought she could see in the mother's anguished eyes the belief that they were responsible in some way — if they had to go out, why hadn't they gone to pick Magga up? If they'd just made the effort to come and collect her, the girl wouldn't have been crossing the road, and would still be alive now. But because they had let themselves be persuaded to go out, Magga had been in the wrong place at the wrong time and some heartless bastard had run her over. He probably hadn't even looked back, let alone stopped to help the child crumpled in the street. Neither driver nor car had been traced; there had been no other traffic on that part of the road when the accident occurred, and no witnesses came forward despite repeated requests in the media. So Magga died alone, abandoned on the icy tarmac; she had stopped breathing by the time the driver of the next car spotted her and stopped. It was lucky he hadn't run over her as well, since a thin layer of snow had already covered her small body. Berglind squeezed her eyes shut again and rubbed them with her damp fingers. How wide was a car? Six feet? Nine? The girl had been at least half a mile away from their house, if not a mile. Such a random twist of fate, to have been on that exact spot in the road when that despicable driver showed up. She was too tired to try to calculate the odds but knew they must be tiny. When you thought about it, the odds of bad news always seemed to get exaggerated more than good, no matter how unlikely the event; hardly anyone won the lottery, but loads of people contracted rare, fatal diseases in unlikely ways.

Berglind opened her eyes again and drained the glass of water. Although the accident still haunted her, the hardest part hadn't been dealing with the tragic death of a girl who'd had so much to live for. That part of it was logical, at least: when a girl weighing not much more than seven stone meets a ton of steel travelling at over sixty miles an hour, there can only be one outcome. Of course it was a terrible tragedy, but the possibility of sudden death was part of the human condition. It had been harder to come to terms with what had happened next: Magga — or rather some sort of projection of her spirit — seemed to have resolved to keep her promise to take care of Pési, and came to watch over him whenever dusk fell. Perhaps the violence of her death had left her spirit unable to rest in peace? As far as Berglind could glean from the few horror movies she'd seen, people returned as ghosts if their deaths were unresolved. At first she and Halli hadn't understood what was going on, assuming when Pési said Magga was with him that he had been affected by hearing them talking about the accident. He was too young to understand death, so it seemed probable that he was trying to make sense of her disappearance. It was only natural that Pési missed her; she'd been babysitting for them since he was one and he was very attached to her. But alarm bells rang for Berglind when the boy began repeating over and over that Magga felt poorly and that everything was *all hurty*. That's when Berglind first started listening to him properly, trying to overcome the numbness that had consumed her since the accident. With all the inexplicable and frightening things that had happened since the accident, she no longer doubted what was going on.

It had grown colder in Pési's room, with condensation forming on the windows as soon as darkness fell. Turning up the thermostat had made no difference, and the plumber they called stood and scratched his head for an hour before leaving them in exactly the same boat but with a hefty bill. An old mobile that hung over the boy's bed, one they'd meant to get rid of long ago, moved even when there was no breeze, and there were continual electrical disturbances just in that one room: the light flickered constantly, no matter how often they changed its bulb. The air in the room would begin to feel dense and heavy towards the end of the day, even if they opened the window. It was as if all the oxygen had been sucked out of it, and every breath left behind a disagreeable metallic taste. Of course, this could all have had a logical explanation that time and patience would help them discover. The house was old and needed a lot of work. However, some of the phenomena couldn't possibly be attributed to that: Pési's pile of cuddly toys was always arranged in a neat row in the morning; they'd find his clothing folded on a stool in the corner, even if it had been lying in a heap on the floor when he went to sleep. Pési often woke up in the night, but now they didn't need to fetch him a drink, take him into their bed to sleep or go to his room to calm him down, because when they went to check on him they would find him smiling in bed, saying: 'You didn't have to get up, Magga is looking after me.'

This sometimes led them to take him into their own bed, but the girl's spirit seemed not to like this. The family frequently woke to find the duvet slipping slowly off them and down onto the floor. A scraping sound would come from under the bed; it always started quietly, then suddenly intensified into violent scrabbling. The sound would cease when Halli peered under the bed, muttering sleepily about the bloody mice, although they had never seen a single mouse. The chill they had noticed in Pési's room was now manifesting in the master bedroom, along with the condensation on the windowpanes and the electrical disturbances. On top of this, little dark puddles had started forming in the doorway; they looked like blood in the semi-darkness, but turned out to be water when the lights were turned on. Twice they called carpenters to search the roof for leaks; neither of them found anything.

It was incredible, really, how long they had suffered all this with only tradesmen to help them. One morning Berglind announced that she couldn't take it any more; the house would be put up for sale immediately, never mind the recession and the declining property market. That morning they'd woken to find some of their clothes hanging on the outside of their wardrobe. And not just random items: Halli's smart suit, a shirt and tie inside it, and one of Berglind's dresses, with a matching bolero jacket. The outfits they had been wearing the evening of the Christmas buffet. There had been nothing there when they had gone to sleep. Berglind's fear was intensified by the fact that for the first time since this had all started, Halli seemed as frightened as her. Instead of trying to sell the house at the worst possible time, they decided to bring in a medium to try to get rid of the ghost — or whatever this was. As Halli had pointed out, they couldn't even be sure that selling the property would help, since the ghost seemed to be haunting Pési, not the house.

They hired a medium who said that he could sense a tormented and unhappy soul hanging around Pési, but that he didn't know how to free them from its presence. The same went for the psychic woman they called next, who came with an enthusiastic recommendation from Berglind's aunt. Neither of them reached this conclusion free of charge, and the household's finances weren't robust enough for Berglind and Halli to work their way through the relevant column in the classified ads. Their last resort was the parish priest, whom they hadn't seen since Pési's christening. At first the man was reluctant, perhaps suspecting he was the butt of some sort of joke. However, Berglind's helpless terror must have been clear as soon as he saw her; the priest's attitude changed, though he told them he couldn't promise anything. Over the course of several visits he experienced the cold that seemed to surround Pési at dusk, and the static electricity in the air around the child. The priest called in the bishop, and together they performed Iceland's first exorcism in over a century. After going from room to room, the bishop had announced to them ceremoniously that the spirit of the girl would no longer enter their home. And by some miracle, it seemed to have worked.

As if a magic wand had been waved, it was immediately different in the house, though it was hard to pinpoint what exactly had changed.

11

The atmosphere at home felt like it used to. Of course it would be difficult to rid themselves of the constant fear that something was about to happen, and it would doubtless take time for their hands to stop trembling. But time healed all wounds, and Berglind thought to herself now that she would settle for a slow but steady recovery.

The parquet creaked upstairs, in Pési's room. Berglind put down her glass and turned around slowly. The sound continued, as though the boy was walking around. Her mouth went dry and her goose bumps sprang up again. She was ridiculous, still jumping at shadows. With measured steps she climbed the stairs, and when she reached the door to her son's room she could hear his muffled voice inside. She wanted to put her ear to the door and listen, but instead she opened it calmly. Pési was standing on tiptoe at the window, looking out. He stopped talking and turned around when he heard the door open, and Berglind's hand flew to her mouth when she saw the condensation on the windowpane.

'Hello, Mummy.' Pési smiled at her sadly.

Berglind hurried to her son and pulled him forcefully from the window. She held him close and tried at the same time to wipe the windowpane. But the haze couldn't be wiped away. It was on the outside of the glass.

Pési looked up at her. 'Magga's outside. She can't get in. She wants to look after me.' He pointed at the window and frowned. 'She's a little bit angry.'

12

1

Monday, 4 January 2010

The building looked quite ordinary from the road. Tourists probably assumed it was just another farm where men toiled and sweated happily, at peace with God and the world. Perhaps they thought it was an unusually large and imposing family home, but either way they wouldn't have dwelled on it too long and probably wouldn't have looked back once they had passed it. Actually, it was just as likely that Icelanders thought much the same, but the place hardly ever came up in conversation; the rare times it was mentioned in the press, it was usually because something tragic had happened to one of the poor unfortunates inside. As they always do, readers would have skimmed over the general details in search of the juicier parts that described the most shocking and bizarre aspects of the residents' behaviour, then skipped ahead in the hope of finding something more positive. After closing the paper it was unlikely they would retain much information about the place or its inhabitants; it was easier to forget about people like them. Even within the system there was a tendency to sideline the unit; certainly people understood the value of the work they did there, but there seemed to be a silent consensus among government officials to have as little to do with it as possible.

Thóra was sure that if they'd had more work at the law firm right then, she might have turned down the case that had brought her here. Of course, it was possible that her curiosity about the vaguely worded assignment would have made her take it on even if she were busy — it wasn't every day that an inmate of the Secure Psychiatric Unit at Sogn requested her assistance.

Actually, the history of the SPU was short; until 1992 prisoners with mental health problems had either been placed in institutions abroad or simply kept among the general population at Litla-Hraun prison. Neither option was ideal. In the first eventuality the language barrier must have caused patients untold hardships, not to mention the distance from their family and friends; and in the second, the prison was not an adequate healthcare facility. Thóra didn't know how well the prisoners considered to be of sound mind would interact with those suffering from mental illness, and she couldn't imagine how the harsh conditions of prison life could possibly be conducive to the treatment of the criminally insane. All seven places at Sogn were always occupied.

The turn was sharp and her car's wheels skidded on the slippery gravel. Thóra gripped the steering wheel more tightly and concentrated on getting up the short driveway. She didn't want to start her visit by driving off the road and having to be towed up out of the shallow ditch — today was going to be weird enough without that. The woman she'd phoned to put in her request to see

14

the inmate had been quite pleasant, but it was clear from her tone that such enquiries were anything but commonplace. Thóra thought the woman had also sounded nervous, as if she was worried about the purpose of Thóra's visit. Not that that was surprising, given the background of the man she was there to meet. This was no run-of-the-mill inmate, no nervous breakdown, drug addict or alcoholic. Jósteinn Karlsson had been firmly on the road to perdition since his youth, despite numerous interventions by the system.

Thóra had acquainted herself with his record after deciding to assist him, and it hadn't made for pleasant reading. She had only had access to two of his cases — the details of the crimes he'd committed as a juvenile were off-limits — and in one of them, from twenty years ago, Jósteinn had been charged with false imprisonment, actual bodily harm and sexual offences against children. He was alleged to have lured a nearly six-year-old boy into his home from the street, for a purpose that thankfully never became clear because the man in the flat next door called the police. The vigilant neighbour had long distrusted Jósteinn and insisted that he was responsible for the disappearance of his two cats, after the animals had been found in poor condition directly below Jósteinn's balcony. But although Jósteinn had been caught red-handed in his home with a child unknown to him, and in spite of the existence of a character witness without a good word to say about him, Jósteinn escaped from the affair relatively unscathed. The child couldn't be persuaded to testify, either in court or elsewhere. A psychologist had attempted to speak to him, but to no avail. The child clammed up as soon as the topic was broached. It was the opinion of the psychologist that Jósteinn had scared the boy into silence by threatening him. This, he said, was a common technique of abusers, to buy the child's silence with threats before violating their innocence, and nobody was easier to frighten than a young child. It was impossible to get the boy to tell him how Jósteinn had threatened him, or anything about what had occurred before the police arrived, which made it impossible to prove beyond doubt that Jósteinn had abused the child in the apartment. The prosecution's allegation of sexual assault and bodily harm did not get far, since the boy had no injuries. Yet no one in the courtroom could have believed Jósteinn's claim that he'd thought the child was lost and wanted to help him find his parents. Due to the lack of evidence, Jósteinn received a suspended sentence of six years for false imprisonment.

Twelve years later Jósteinn sexually assaulted a teenager, and this time there was no vigilant neighbour. The parents of the little boy who'd escaped relatively unharmed must have offered up heartfelt prayers of thanks when the media began to report the details of what Jósteinn had done to the second boy. Thóra remembered the case well — though almost a decade had passed — but this was the first time she had read the verdict itself. It seemed clear that Jósteinn had intended to kill the boy, and only pure chance had prevented him; the woman who cleaned the

16

hallways had come to work a day earlier than usual that week, as her daughter was due to be confirmed the next day. She probably wouldn't have noticed anything if she'd only vacuumed the communal areas as usual, but some kid had spilt his ice cream on the wall right next to Jósteinn's front door, meaning she stopped there for longer than she usually would. When she turned off the vacuum cleaner she could hear the victim's muffled cries for help, and after a moment's hesitation she decided to phone the police instead of knocking on the door. In her call the woman had told the emergency services operator she'd never heard anything like the sounds coming from the apartment, and she was unable to describe them in detail. All she could say was that it was the sound of terrible suffering. The police broke into Jósteinn's flat again, and this time he was caught red-handed.

As she read through the ruling Thóra noticed a strange detail that piqued her curiosity. During the investigation, the police had received an anonymous tip telling them exactly where in Jósteinn's flat to find certain photographs; these photos had been taken over a number of years and showed clearly how many children he had abused, and in what ways. The photographs had raised the level of the investigation; had they not been found, the individual offences Jósteinn would have been charged with might have only seen him sentenced to a few years. The discovery of the pictures allowed the police to obtain a search warrant for Jósteinn's workplace, a computer workshop, to which they had not

17

previously had access. An enormous amount of child pornography and other hardcore material was found, which gave the investigators enough evidence to bring the case against him. Shortly thereafter it went to trial and Jósteinn was ordered to undergo psychiatric evaluation, following which he was found guilty but declared not criminally liable due to insanity. This meant he was acquitted of the criminal charges, but sentenced to detention in the Secure Psychiatric Unit at Sogn, where he was to remain until the courts ruled that his treatment was complete and that he no longer posed a threat to those around him.

Thóra could glean little more except that Jósteinn seemed to have fared rather better than his victim, who was still recovering in Reykjavík City Hospital's rehabilitation unit when the sentence was passed. In her peculiar phone call with Jósteinn he'd hinted that he wanted to discuss an old case, but it was unclear whether he meant the first one or the second. To reopen either seemed preposterous; he had received a ridiculously light sentence first time round, and the more recent case was so clear-cut that she couldn't see what there was to challenge about the verdict. Was Jósteinn hoping to overturn the ruling of insanity and have his incarceration transmuted to an ordinary prison sentence, after which he might be able to gain his freedom? From the short conversation they'd had it was impossible to assess his mental condition; he'd sounded completely normal, if a little brusque and arrogant. He was probably just as ill as the day that he'd arrived; the verdict had included a summary of the psychiatrist's diagnosis, stating that Jósteinn suffered from acute schizophrenia and other personality disorders that could mostly be kept in check with drugs and therapy but that would be almost impossible to cure fully. Thóra had noted that the same psychiatrist suggested the possibility be explored of housing Jósteinn in a secure psychiatric ward abroad, one better equipped to handle such a severely damaged individual; the doctor thought it unlikely that any Icelandic unit would be able to cope.

Thóra got out of the car and took her briefcase from the back seat. It actually didn't contain anything other than printouts of the two Supreme Court verdicts, along with a large notebook. Not that she expected to take many notes; she was almost sure she'd turn down the case, conjuring up some imaginary work as an excuse. The details of how Jósteinn had abused the teenager still haunted her, and she did not intend to hasten this man's release from custody. In fact, she wished she'd just said no from the outset. She shut the car door and walked to the entrance. She was in no position to assess the man's mental health and was unsure what she would be confronted with: had Jósteinn recovered his sanity? Was he now so overcome with remorse that he wanted a second chance? Or was he incurably evil, desperate to be released and find his next victim?

Thóra rang the bell and looked around while she waited. She watched two men walk slowly towards a little greenhouse and go in, each

19

carrying a bucket. One of the men looked like he had Down's syndrome and was possibly an inmate, while the other appeared to be a staff member. Her attention was directed back to the house when the door opened to reveal a woman in a white coat, which she wore unbuttoned over jeans and a tatty jumper. The coat looked just as well worn as the jumper, and repeated washing had all but erased its National Hospital logo.

The woman introduced herself as the duty nurse. She ushered Thóra in and showed her where to hang her coat, making small talk about the traffic and the weather, then led her further into the house and opened the door to a shabby but cosy sitting room where she said the interview would take place. Large windows looked out on a garden and the little greenhouse, inside which the two men Thóra had seen a couple of minutes ago were now busily tending some impressively lush plants. The nurse volunteered the information that the green-house's construction had been funded by a generous donation from an elderly woman who more than sixty years before had lost her two-year-old daughter; a man with severe mental health problems had woken one day with the desire to kill someone, not caring who. He had chosen the little girl, though she was a perfect stranger to him. Her mother's benevolence after all these years showed great strength of character, thought Thóra, though this didn't make her any less nervous about the security situation in the sitting room if Jósteinn should decide to attack her. Ideally, she would have preferred them to sit on opposite sides of bulletproof glass. 'Am I safe here?' She looked around at the chairs with their embroidered cushions.

'I'll be in the next room.' The woman looked unruffled. 'If anything happens just shout and we'll be right there.' Realizing Thóra was still unsure, she said: 'He won't do anything to you. He's been here for nearly ten years without hurting anyone.' After a slight hesitation she added, 'Well, any human beings, anyway.'

Thóra frowned. 'What do you mean — has he hurt an animal?'

'That's not an issue any more. There are no animals here now, because of how the most acutely ill inmates reacted to them. But of course we are in the countryside, and animals from the nearby farms do sometimes wander into the grounds.' The nurse didn't give Thóra the chance to pursue the subject. 'Please have a seat and I'll go and get Jósteinn.' It seemed that the man hadn't earned himself a nickname during his detention. 'I know he's excited to meet you.'

The woman left, and Thóra pondered where it would be safest to sit. The last thing she wanted was to end up too close to him. A worn armchair positioned slightly off to the side appeared to be the best option, and Thóra went over and placed her briefcase on the coffee table in front of it. She decided to stand there until the man came in, having read a long time ago about the importance of standing when wishing to gain the upper hand. The person sitting was forced to look up at the other, which — so the theory ran

— tipped the balance of power.

The nurse brought Jósteinn in, introduced him and reminded Thóra that she would be within earshot if they needed her. Thóra saw a grin flicker across Jósteinn's face at this, although the nurse had been careful to word it as if she were offering to bring them coffee if they called for it. He clearly realized that Thóra was nervous, so the balance of power was irrelevant. It was no use letting it get to her, so Thóra collected herself and calmly invited him to sit. Refusing to meet her eye, he accepted her invitation with the same sarcastic smile as before, choosing the sofa across from her chair. She followed his example and sat. Jósteinn was slim, and although the clothes he wore were not at all fitted, Thóra could tell from his sinewy neck and hands that he was strong. He appeared to have dark hair, but it could have been the gel or wax he'd applied making it look darker than it was. It looked almost as though he'd just been swimming, and in one place the clear substance had run down his cheek, leaving a shiny streak on his bony, rat-like face. He still hadn't looked directly at her.

'Are you comfortable?' he said. Although the question was courteous, his tone was faintly mocking. 'I hardly ever have visitors, so I want your visit to be as pleasant as possible. They wanted to put us in a meeting room, but I thought it was too formal so I asked if we could meet here.' He narrowed his grey eyes at the coffee table between them and pursed his thin lips. 'I hardly ever have visitors,' he repeated, then smiled unconvincingly. 'Never, in fact.'

'It might be easier if you got straight to the point.' Thóra was generally much politer to people she met through work, but Jósteinn made her so uneasy that she was going to find it hard to avoid being downright rude to him. 'I've acquainted myself with your case as best I can, but I don't know what it is you expect of me. Naturally, I would prefer it if you just told me.'

'*Naturally?*' Jósteinn looked up at her now. 'What's natural? I've never been able to figure that out.' He sniggered nastily. 'If I had, we wouldn't be sitting here.'

'No, probably not.' Thóra opened her briefcase. 'You've been here at Sogn for eight years or thereabouts. Is that right?'

'Yes. No. I'm not too sure. Numbers and I don't mix. They lay traps for me, then I fall in and can't get out.'

Thóra didn't want to know what he meant. She had all the evidence she needed: he was still ill. Whether he was still dangerous was another matter, although Thóra felt fairly confident that he was. 'Trust me, it's been pretty close to eight years.' She regarded him as he nodded apathetically. 'Do you miss your freedom?'

'I've come to consider myself just as free here as anywhere else.' Jósteinn waited, perhaps expecting Thóra to contradict him, and continued when she said nothing. 'Freedom is multi-faceted, it's not just about locked doors and bars on the windows. The kind of freedom I long for doesn't exist, in my opinion, so I'd never be completely free anywhere. Here is no worse than anywhere else.'

Thóra had no idea how to get the conversation on to a more even footing. 'Do you have anything to occupy you? Do they have recreational activities, arts and crafts, anything like that?' She couldn't envision the man with scissors and glue, unless he were gluing someone's lips shut to stop them screaming as he stabbed them with the scissors.

Jósteinn laughed woodenly, like a bad actor auditioning for a comedy. The laughter stopped as abruptly as it had begun, and he straightened in his chair. 'There are activities, yes. One guy embroiders pillows, and as you can see he's been here quite a long time. I work on repairing broken computers that we get for free from the government. The work suits me fine. It's what I did before I came here.' He pointed out of the window. 'And Jakob works in the greenhouse, growing herbs and lettuces.'

Thóra turned and watched the two men come out of the little greenhouse, their buckets appearing much heavier now than when they'd gone in. It was clear now that the chubbier one did have Down's syndrome. 'Very practical.' She very much wanted to ask what Jakob had done; as far as she knew, people with Down's were usually peaceful and good-natured. Of course this went for most people, and it was the exceptions to the rule who ended up here.

'He's my friend. A good friend.' For the first time Jósteinn seemed to be speaking sincerely. It didn't last long. He turned away from the window. 'Is it possible to reopen old cases? To

24

overturn a conviction and get an acquittal, if you're innocent?'

Thóra was prepared for this question, and had in fact been waiting for it. 'Yes, if there is strong enough evidence of wrongful conviction.'

'I've recently become a rich man. Did you know that?'

Thóra shook her head. Was he delusional? 'No, I haven't looked into your finances. Have you made a profit from your computer work?' Perhaps his definition of 'rich' was different to hers.

'I inherited money from my mother. Now everything I am *and* everything I own comes from her.' His features softened into a dopey smile and Thóra recalled reading about his difficult childhood and the genetic nature of his condition. He had probably been raised by an unfit mother, a female version of himself.

'She was hit by a car, you see, and because she was paralysed she got benefits. She died soon after, and now the benefits and everything else she owned are mine. I'm getting rid of all her personal belongings but the money, I'm keeping.'

'Do you have a trustee?' asked Thóra. She was pretty sure he wouldn't be allowed control over his own finances.

'No. But I do have a supervisor. He's never been to see me; I've not even had a phone call.' Jósteinn spoke dispassionately, as if unaware of the significance of this. 'I want to use the money to reopen an old case. I don't have much use for it otherwise. Luckily, too much time has passed

25

since I was convicted for the boy I messed with to sue me for damages. Or rather, for his relatives to sue me — I heard he lost his marbles.' Jósteinn grinned, seeming to find the idea amusing.

There was a sudden knock on the window. Thóra couldn't conceal her shock, and Jósteinn looked delighted. 'It's just Jakob, wanting to know who's come to see me. As I told you, I've never had a visitor.' He smiled again. 'Which is understandable, of course.'

Thóra stared back at the beaming face with thick-lensed glasses pressed up against the window. Jakob ran his muddy hands down the pane, leaving brown smears, before waving enthusiastically at Thóra. She waved back. 'Why is he in here?' The question slipped out before she had a chance to stop it.

Jósteinn did not seem rattled. 'He killed five people in an arson attack, just like that. It was amazing.'

'Yes, an extraordinary case.' Thóra remembered it, as it wasn't an everyday occurrence for people to burn to death in Iceland. It had been overshadowed by the financial crash, which had happened at the same time. 'Was it about eighteen months ago?'

'I think so.' Jósteinn flapped his hand dismissively, as if the timing of the fire were an irrelevance. 'He's only about twenty, and he'll probably spend most of the rest of his life in here. People like him often have weak hearts, so he might die before he ever gets out.'

They seemed to be getting off-course again. Thóra said, 'I think I ought to tell you that I don't believe there's much to warrant reopening your case. You were caught red-handed, so to speak, and I can't see how you could come up with a new explanation for what happened without very compelling new evidence. The verdict looks bulletproof, and I can't see that there was anything untoward in how the case was tried.'

Jósteinn laughed again, louder this time. An unpleasant waft of halitosis drifted over to Thóra and she screwed up her face involuntarily, as she did whenever a change in the wind gave her an unwelcome update on the state of decay of her neighbours' compost heap. His hilarity was short-lived, and Jósteinn let his expression go blank once more. 'Not *my* case! Jakob's. The fire.' He ran his hand through his greasy hair and then wiped it on the arm of the sofa. 'He didn't do it. I know more than you can ever imagine about what it takes to do bad things. Jakob didn't set light to anyone or anything, and I want you to prove it.' He suddenly leaned forward and grabbed Thóra's hand, which had been resting on the coffee table, with both of his. His eyes met hers for a brief moment, but then moved back down to their joined hands. She could feel the sticky hair gel, like thick sweat, on his palms. 'Sometimes a child who's had his fingers burned still wants to play with fire . . . '

2

Wednesday, 6 January 2010

Her name was Grímheiður Þorbjarnardóttir, and
if she had a nickname she chose not to reveal it
to Thóra. She seemed on the defensive, and had
firmly declined to take off her slightly tatty coat,
sitting there still bundled in it despite the
warmth of the office. She had, however, quickly
removed her hand-knitted shawl, matching hat
and lined leather gloves and placed them in her
lap. The hat and shawl were a similar colour to
the coat, but not close enough to match.
Grímheiður had probably not been wearing the
coat when she bought the wool, and the result
was a little jarring. The woman's swollen red
fingers fiddled with the shawl's fringe as her eyes
searched for a place to put it.

'Are you sure you don't want me to hang up
your coat for you?' Thóra held out her hand
hopefully. It was one of those winter days when
the cold north wind fights the sun for control
and neither appears to be winning. As long as
the battle was raging Thóra could not open the
windows; the winds were hitting the building
square-on, and the slightest chink in its armour
would immediately turn her little office into a
walk-in fridge. Keeping them closed was only
marginally better, because the merciless sun
made a furnace of it. Over the years Thóra and

28

Bragi, her business partner, had somehow never got round to buying curtains, which made it nigh-on impossible to be in the office on cold, sunny days like this one.

'No.' Grímheiður's reply was curt, bordering on rude. She appeared to realize this, because her cheeks, already red from the heat, darkened even further. 'I mean, no thanks. It's okay.'

Thóra nodded, let her outstretched hand drop and decided to get down to business. 'As I mentioned on the phone, I've been asked to look into your son's case, on the grounds that he's been wrongfully imprisoned.' She paused to allow Grímheiður to respond, but the woman neither spoke nor reacted. 'Since you are your son's legal guardian, I don't wish to accept this case without your consent. Of course I could take it on without consulting anyone, but I'm unwilling to do so without the full cooperation of you and your son. I will also speak to the lawyer appointed by the Supreme Court as Jakob's supervisor; as you know, he is responsible for ensuring that Jakob doesn't stay at the institution any longer than necessary. Obviously any move to reopen the case would concern him.' Grímheiður was staring impassively at the table, and Thóra couldn't be sure if she was actually paying attention. 'Since your son's development is . . . ' Before the meeting began Thóra had tried to come up with the right terminology to describe Jakob without offending anyone. Now that the time had come she couldn't remember what she'd decided on, so she'd have to wing it and hope for the best. 'Since Jakob has Down's syndrome your opinion holds even more weight than it usually would, although of course I will discuss it further with him if you wish us to proceed with the case. I would like to reiterate that this is free of charge for both of you, so your consent does not affect Jakob's finances, for which you are the legal executor.' Jakob, unlike Jósteinn, had been deprived of control over his finances and the court had appointed his mother as his legal proxy. 'As I told you on the phone, your son has made friends with this Jósteinn, who is adamant that he wishes to cover the cost of the investigation. I feel I should say that I don't fully understand why he's doing this and am finding it hard to shake off the feeling that he has some motive beyond pure philanthropy, but that's not for me to judge at this stage.'

'I've met him.' The woman's thin lips tightened, causing them to almost disappear. 'I don't like him. But Jakob seems to consider him a great friend, and he's a good judge of character despite his learning disability.' Grímheiður fell silent and resumed smoothing out the fringe of her shawl.

Thóra didn't know what she could add to this without embarrassing herself by revealing her ignorance of mental disabilities. She knew little about people with learning difficulties, or at least those that were as severe as Jakob's, and it made her feel stressed and uncomfortable. No doubt there was plenty of information out there, but Thóra hadn't had much time and had decided to wait until she was sure the case would be ongoing. And that all depended on the woman who now sat before her, melting. 'But leaving aside the question of the purity of Jósteinn's motives, what's your opinion on this? Do you see any sense in it? What effect do you think it would have on your son, given that there's no guarantee of it changing anything? I can't predict how he'd react if his case was reopened — let alone how disappointed he'd be if it didn't do any good.'

Grímheiður stopped fiddling with the fringe and clenched her fists until her knuckles whitened. Then she relaxed them and let her shoulders droop. 'When I found out I was pregnant with Jakob, my husband and I had long since lost all hope of having children. We were both already in our forties, and of course we were delighted. When I underwent an amniocentesis, as I was advised to due to my age, we also found out what sex the baby was.' She inhaled sharply and sat up straighter. 'Well, anyway. I was steered towards aborting the foetus, not explicitly, but quite emphatically. Neither I nor my husband could bear to contemplate it, despite everyone saying it would take over our lives completely; on the contrary, that was precisely why we wanted a baby. It made no odds to me that I'd have to stop working, though we certainly enjoyed having two wages. Neither of us made a huge amount of money; we barely hit an average wage. But either way, an abortion was out of the question. He was our child, no matter how many chromosomes he had.'

Thóra couldn't help but be impressed. She was sure that faced with the same dilemma her choice would be different, but that was irrelevant since she already had two children. Perhaps the decision hadn't helped the woman's marriage; she was the only one registered to the telephone number Thóra had called. 'Are you still married to Jakob's father?'

'He died when Jakob was ten. Another victim of nanny-state bureaucracy. He was a plumber, and he was sent east to Hveragerði to do a small job for a contractor. It was early May and they'd put summer tyres on all the company cars, but their regulations don't control the weather and he hit black ice. He flipped his car over on Kambarnir and died instantly.' The woman looked away and gazed out of the window. 'He hadn't liked the look of the weather, so he'd called the police to see if he could put on winter tyres. They said no.' She paused. 'When Jakob turned twenty the system went to work to put him into a sheltered community. The social worker who handled his case felt it best for him to move away from me, since in her infinite wisdom she thought I was overprotecting him and inhibiting his development. I'm still not sure quite how it was all sorted out, since I know that at the time there was a long waiting list for the community. For some reason the others on the list were turned down and Jakob was squeezed in. If you ask me, their so-called support was just the opposite: you never got what you wanted, and you never wanted what you got.'

'Were you opposed to him living in a sheltered community?' It was a ridiculous question given what the woman had just said, but Thóra always preferred to have everything spelled out to prevent any misunderstanding.

Grímheiður didn't seem to mind. 'Yes, I certainly was. He was too, but that just made it more of a challenge for the system, and in the end they won and I let myself be persuaded. But my doubts didn't arise from any fears about his future; if I'd had a crystal ball, obviously I would have fought harder. I just wanted to have my son with me; I thought I could care for him better than complete strangers, off somewhere in the middle of the city. And his benefits made a difference, too. It's very hard to run a household alone. After he moved out, the residence received the lion's share of his monthly allowance and what little was left wasn't even enough to keep him in clothes and shoes.'

'How long had Jakob been living there when the centre burned down?' Thóra was careful not to say *when he set the centre on fire*.

'Nearly six months. Not long.'

'And was he happy there, or did he not have the chance to settle in properly?'

'He was terribly unhappy, really depressed. Maybe not as bad as he was after the fire, or when he was transferred to the Secure Psychiatric Unit at Sogn, but still miserable. Jakob needs stability, not turmoil.'

'Then you think it might be inadvisable for me to take on this case? It will inevitably be a disruption for him.'

The woman gave Thóra a look of fierce determination. Her face bore the marks of a difficult life; deep wrinkles fanned from the corners of her eyes to her temples, like the sunbeams Thóra's daughter drew in the sky in all her pictures. Even deeper furrows lay across her forehead, but although her face was lined with signs of stress her eyes were like a teenager's, the whites clear and the demarcation of the irises sharp. 'Someone called me today from Sogn and advised me to ask you to leave it, for Jakob's sake. I was having a few doubts, but after that call I made my decision and I won't change my mind.'

'So you're against it?' Thóra was both relieved and disappointed. She had wanted to take the case, but also felt compelled to refuse it. Sometimes it was good to let others make decisions for you, but she was a little irritated that someone had tried to influence Jakob's mother, even if it had been done with good intentions.

'No, absolutely not. I want you to take the case, and spare no one in your investigation. Neither me nor Jakob. I'm done with following the advice of people who think they know best. It's my decision now.'

Thóra smiled weakly. 'Nevertheless, I feel that you should think it over a little longer. Those are not strong grounds for such an important decision. There are other factors you need to consider; the few advantages would be hard-won, and the disadvantages could be considerable. You should think through all the possible outcomes.'

'I've already done that, and my decision is the same: I want you to take the case. I would be a fool if I refused it on Jakob's behalf; I would never be able to afford the cost of reopening his case myself.' Grímheiður stared at Thóra, her blue eyes wide like a child's. 'Jakob is innocent and his name should be cleared, sooner rather than later. I don't have many years left, I'm sure, and when I'm gone there won't be anyone to look after him. So it's now or never. I would give anything to spend whatever's left of our lives together, but not the way things are now. Not like this.'

In Thóra's experience family members usually thought their loved one was innocent; she had seen them react as if the accused were a cute little bunny rabbit that by sheer bad luck had ended up in the talons of the legal eagles. She thought back to the guileless young man she'd seen at Sogn and decided that a bunny wasn't such an absurd metaphor in this instance. 'Before I make my final decision I'd like to see the evidence you've brought.' She watched Jakob's mother reach for an old-fashioned briefcase made of cracked plastic.

'I've not thrown any of it away; I just couldn't.' The woman put the briefcase on the desk with a solid *clunk*; it was heavy. 'You'll read this differently from me, but hopefully you'll see what I think is obvious.' She started to stand but had forgotten the shawl, hat and gloves in her lap. They dropped to the floor and the woman bent down, red-faced, to pick them up. After straightening back up she spoke again. 'Jakob didn't set the home on fire, so he didn't kill anyone. He deserves to come home.'

'I hope so,' was all Thóra could say. What the poor boy deserved remained to be seen.

* ★ ★ ★

Thóra's eyes had gone dry from squinting at the computer screen. She hadn't opened the briefcase, as clearly it would take a while to go through its contents; she also feared she'd find images or descriptions of charred corpses, and needed to prepare herself mentally. So she had decided to write a few e-mails and then read up on Down's syndrome. Thóra didn't know much about it, but maybe the condition had been known to cause aggressive behaviour or psychotic episodes that could explain why Jakob had turned to arson, if indeed he did have anything to do with the attack.

Despite extensive online searches and a lot of reading, she found nothing conclusive. She did, however, find herself much better informed about the syndrome. She learned that it was caused by an extra chromosome, and that various disorders were associated with it including learning disabilities, heart defects, poor muscle tone and a below-average life expectancy. The average life span of a person with Down's syndrome was said to be around fifty years, but most of the articles pointed out that this was an extraordinary improvement compared to half a century ago, when it had only been twenty-five. Various other characteristics were mentioned: facial features were markedly different from the average western appearance and the tongue was often too large for the mouth, as a result of which it often protruded. The palms of the hands had only one transverse line instead of two like most people. Other features were listed, most of them unlikely to be relevant to the case and many too technical for Thóra to understand them fully. She assumed she would find an analysis of Jakob himself in the briefcase, and that it would include his IQ score, though these were generally held to be highly subjective; the IQ of individuals with Down's syndrome was usually around 35–70. This was a broad range, so the generalizations she was unearthing told her little about Jakob.

Thóra also took some time to familiarize herself with the laws and regulations that might apply to Jakob specifically as an intellectually disabled person, and quickly noticed the change that had occurred in society's attitude towards this group. The names of older laws, which had been dropped before current legislation on issues pertaining to the disabled, revealed an attitude that no longer existed: a bill from 1936 was named the *Law on Idiot Asylums* and one from 1967 the *Law on Institutions for Imbeciles*. In a report accompanying the bill for the latter law Thóra found this era's definition of intellectual disability, which was then called 'feeble-mindedness'. This term applied to a number of different categories: people who had IQs lower than 50 and were either 'morons', if their IQs were between zero and 24, or 'imbeciles' if their IQs went from 25 to 49; and 'idiots', whose IQs were between 50 and 70 or 75. The words were like needles in Thóra's eyes and the scant resources that had been available to these poor people were equally painful; at the time there was no choice apart from placement in an institution, regardless of an individual's age or gender. No respite care or assistance was available, meaning that the parents of a severely disabled or hard-to-control child had no other choice than to send it away. This had changed, thank goodness, but there was no doubt a long way to go before everyone's needs could be accommodated.

She also found a report on the number of developmentally disabled people in Iceland: it was around half a per cent of the population, which was not small. Thóra also looked specifically for information about sheltered community residences and discovered that the implementation of this form of living had begun in 1980, so there had been time to gather some experience regarding how they could best be run. According to the information she found, these units were homes for small groups of disabled people, generally not more than six, all aged sixteen or older and each under the one-on-one supervision of at least one staff member. The staff's responsibility was to provide support and therapy, with a view to advancing the residents' independence and life skills. The administration and setting up of these homes was at the expense of the state, although the money came from various of its budgets: construction costs were paid out of the Disabled Investment Fund, staff salaries from the Treasury, and communal expenses were taken from the residents' insurance benefits, accounting for up to seventy-five per cent of the amount.

All in all there were almost ninety such establishments in Iceland, totalling around four hundred and fifty residents.

The telephone on the desk emitted a peculiar sound, startling Thóra. The ring tone was very loud and high-pitched — their secretary Bella must have changed the setting, probably just to annoy her. Thóra suppressed her anger and lifted the receiver. 'Yes?'

'Your parents are here to see you; should I show them in, or tell them you're not here?'

Thóra knew her parents were standing in front of Bella as she spoke. The girl was a lost cause. 'Show them in.' There was no point telling her off, if only because once Thóra started she wouldn't be able to stop.

Her parents appeared in her office doorway, and after greeting them she invited them to sit down. They seemed ill at ease, and small talk about the weather did nothing to loosen them up. Finally her father got to the point, and the reason for their agitation became clear.

When he had finished explaining, Thóra stifled a sigh and took the paperwork her father was holding out to her. 'So you don't think you'll be able to pay back the loan? Did this eventuality never occur to you when you bought the house?' The property her parents had financed with a massive foreign-currency loan was a rather grand summer home in Spain; the purchase price looked high to Thóra, even without the doubled exchange rate of the euro. 'The monthly payments would be crippling, even if you weren't retired.'

'We were advised that we could let it out, and the rent would cover the mortgage payments. The former owners said they were going to take care of it for us,' said Thóra's father, as her mother nodded vigorously beside him.

Thóra ground her teeth. 'Of course they did.' She flipped to the clause in the agreement that specified the payment amounts. 'According to this, the property was purchased entirely on credit. A one hundred per cent mortgage is pretty risky, whatever the exchange rate, and I doubt that the rent would ever have covered the payments, even without the global financial crisis and a decline in the Spanish tourism industry.' She looked up at them. 'So you started renting it out? Did the rent pay off the mortgage, initially?'

They both looked sheepish, shifting in their chairs. 'Well . . . ' said her father.

'How much of the monthly payment did it cover? All of it? Half? A third?' She hardly dared go any lower. 'How do you think I can help you with this? And why didn't you tell me that you'd bought a house in Spain? You're in a very tight spot; it's almost impossible to default on a mortgage.'

'We didn't want to get you involved at the time, but we were hoping you might know a way to get it converted to a bullet loan?' He smiled weakly, clearly realizing this was not a viable option. Thóra's mother still seemed hopeful, though, and was nodding her head even more energetically than before.

'That can't be done.' Thóra didn't want to waste their time pretending to entertain the idea.

'Your position is even worse than it was, since you haven't paid anything for several months. It's probably been flagged as a bad debt at the bank, and if you don't make a payment very soon you could wind up bankrupt.'

'Is there nothing that can be done? Some sort of legal trick?'

'Nothing I can think of. The lawyers who draw up these mortgages are no fools, and the bank loaned you the money in good faith. The sellers who conned you into buying this place also seem to have protected themselves pretty well, since it states quite clearly here that they offer no guarantee that you'll be able to rent it out.' Thóra gently laid the papers on her desk and tried to keep her composure. 'This is a very tricky situation, and I'm sure you've tried to come up with a solution. The house is up for sale, which is good, but I doubt it will sell quickly and you're very unlikely to make your money back on it. Whatever you *do* make should shrink your debt, at least. But the property market is as dead there as it is in Iceland, so the house is unlikely to sell any time soon.' Thóra sighed. Her parents weren't the first to show up in her office looking for a magic solution to insurmountable financial difficulties. 'How were you planning to get yourselves out of this?'

'Well, we do actually have an idea,' said her father. Her parents exchanged a glance. 'We can't rent out this bloody place in Spain, except for a week here and there, but what we have done is put our house here in Iceland up for sale, and we've had a good offer that will allow us to pay off the other mortgage monthly until we can realistically put that house on the market. We've also found a nice flat we can afford without endangering the Spanish payments. The thing is, we'd have to hand over the house immediately, but we can't move into the flat for two months. That is, if we decide to do it.'

Thóra's mother had stopped nodding along with her husband and was watching her daughter's reaction closely.

'And where would you stay until your flat is ready?' Thóra swallowed hard, just resisting the temptation to cross her fingers. She was an only child.

'Well, we were thinking maybe we could just bunk in with you.' Now they were both smiling eagerly. 'We wouldn't be any bother, and we'd even help out with the housework.'

Thóra was struggling to stay calm. Of course she wanted to help her parents out of the financial hole they'd dug for themselves. They had been very good to her throughout her life and she was more than grateful for that. Her problem with the idea stemmed from her own domestic situation. Her house was a decent size, but there were quite enough people living there already. Besides herself, there were her two children, ten-year-old Sóley and nineteen-year-old Gylfi; Gylfi's girlfriend Sigga; and their son Orri, now two and a half. Thóra's partner of several years, Matthew, had also recently moved in. The addition of a fourth generation to the household would eat away even more at their limited amount of private time. 'I see,' was all she could say.

'It won't be for long, probably not even the full two months,' said her father cheerily. 'I'll find work and then we can go to a hotel or get another short-term rental somewhere.'

Clearly nobody had broken the news to him about the unemployment figures. She didn't want to discourage him by pointing out how much had changed since he'd retired, or that right now the one thing the market didn't need was a career banker, even one who had ended up as a branch manager. As far as she knew his only saleable skill was managing other people's money, which made it even harder to understand how they'd been duped. In fact they'd been doubly cheated: tricked into putting their savings into equity funds which, according to the sales patter, made you a handsome risk-free profit on the interest; and then advised to take out loans against their property portfolio to buy everything their hearts desired. The original amount her parents had put into this fund would have covered the bulk of the price of the summer home when they'd made the decision to buy it, but now it had been whittled down to a third of the size and things looked dire for them. Their life savings were as good as gone, and their debt to the bank — the same one that ran the stock exchange — had been too much for them even before the crash of the króna had doubled the size of the loan.

Now that she understood this depressing situation, Thóra could see why her parents had been so embarrassed. At first she'd thought they'd come to write their wills and were unsure how to broach the subject. That seemed a rather comical thought now that it was clear how little they had to divide up.

'I'm sure we'll sort something out,' she murmured, forcing out a reassuring smile.

'I know it's crowded at your place, but maybe we could stay in the garage,' said her father brightly. 'I think I could make it quite cosy. I bet Gylfi would help me, and maybe also your . . . friend, the German.' Thóra's parents weren't overly fond of Matthew, which she thought stemmed from two things in particular: firstly, they spoke no German and rather patchy English, and secondly, Thóra was pretty sure they were convinced he'd take their daughter, grandchildren and great-grandchild back to Germany with him. Maybe it was this that had pushed them into buying a summer home abroad. They were even less impressed when Matthew wasn't offered work in the new bank that was built on the ruins of the old one; he was a foreigner, and was considered too expensive to retain. He still hadn't found suitable work and his prospects were looking less than rosy. Actually, he was in pretty much the same boat as her father.

Her father smiled again, this time with more conviction. 'As I say, it won't be for long. I have complete faith that the króna will get stronger, and then maybe we can go to Spain and spend some time at the house. But as things stand right now, we can't afford it.' In other words, when he found a job he planned to celebrate by going on holiday.

Thóra smiled back at him, trying to put her heart into it despite her mixed feelings. 'And even if it doesn't happen and you're with us the whole time, that's fine. Of course you're welcome to stay.' She decided that for now she'd stop nagging them about making a payment on the mortgage. There would be plenty of time for that. 'It gets quieter every other weekend, when the kids go to their father, so there will be more room for us.' As she said this she realized how much she'd miss the few days a month she spent alone with Matthew. She certainly wasn't looking forward to breaking the news to him.

Bella barged into the office, and Thóra wondered, not for the first time, whether it wouldn't be wiser to lock the door when she had clients or visitors. She always came to the same conclusion — that Bella probably wouldn't let it stop her.

'Have you taken my stapler?' Bella planted her hands on her hefty hips, glaring at Thóra.

'No, Bella, I haven't,' replied Thóra calmly. 'Why would I do that?'

'It's been stolen, and you're the most likely culprit.'

'Well, legally you can't steal your own possessions. I own this firm, which means I can't *steal* anything here.' Thóra met Bella's narrowed eyes levelly. 'Please knock before entering next time, and shut the door behind you when you leave. Now.' Thóra hoped the girl would leave before she spotted the stapler on Thóra's desk. She had borrowed it that morning before her secretary arrived and forgotten to return it, though she had no intention of admitting this.

Bella turned on her heel without another word, but left the door open behind her by way of getting in the last punch. Thóra's parents had watched the whole thing open-mouthed, and when the secretary had stomped out of earshot her mother whispered, 'Can't you get rid of that girl? She's terribly rude.'

Thóra shook her head. 'It's complicated.' The firm was stuck with Bella because she was the landlord's daughter and her employment had been part of the terms of the lease.

'That's most unfortunate,' tutted her mother, picking up her handbag and holding it tightly as if Bella might sneak up and pluck it off the back of her chair.

'Well, Thóra, we can't stay.' Her father stood up. 'You've probably got enough to do and we've got to get over to the estate agent to finalize the paperwork on the offer.'

Thóra gulped. 'Of course.' She followed them out and said goodbye, and when they were gone she hurried back to her office to call Matthew and tell him about the latest additions to their household. He would be so pleased. As she was dialling, her mobile beeped, indicating she'd received a text. Curious, Thóra hung up the landline and reached for her mobile. The message was from the Internet message service *ja.is*, so it could be from anyone. She opened it, thinking either the contents or the sign-off would identify the sender, but the one-word message didn't make any sense to her; perhaps it had come to the wrong number?

Pregnant

She felt a sudden surge of panic. Was Gylfi's girlfriend pregnant again? She hurriedly called her son, who thankfully had no clue what was going on and reassured her that Sigga was neither pregnant nor planning to be. Thóra was relieved, but something about the mysterious text still made her uneasy.

3

Wednesday, 6 January 2010

It was no wonder the briefcase Jakob's mother had left was falling to bits. One more Post-it note would probably have finished it off, it was so full. Thóra would probably need to transfer the contents to a new case when she returned them to Grímheiður; it would be easier than stuffing all the files back into this one. But for the moment it was empty, the papers that had previously stretched it to bursting point scattered across the desk. Thóra leaned back in the top-of-the-range office chair she'd bought when the company's fortunes had finally appeared to be looking up, about a month before the economy imploded. There was simply reams of information here, and she obviously wouldn't have the luxury of going through all the files before deciding whether or not to take on Jakob's case. She would have to pick out the ones that seemed most likely to contain useful information. She started two piles on her desk, sorting the papers by apparent relevance. Admittedly, her criteria were governed mostly by her desire to keep the 'yes' pile under half the height of the 'maybe' one. By the time she'd sorted through most of the papers, her plan seemed to have worked.

Although Thóra had only skimmed the files,

she was filled with dread. She didn't need a long-winded report to tell her that the events of that night had been horrific. Five people had died tragically; four residents and a night watchman. The centre admitted disabled people aged eighteen to twenty-five, and residents were not moved to another facility when they hit the maximum age. It was a new build, meaning all the residents who perished were young, which made the whole thing even sadder. And to make matters even worse, the watchman unlucky enough to be working that night, one of twelve staff members, was just as young at twenty-three. Fire can be merciless, and in the residence it appeared to have burned out of control and rendered everything and everyone in its path unrecognizable. Thóra couldn't believe somewhere like this hadn't had a decent fire alarm fitted, which might have saved some, if not all, of the victims. She also found it odd that neither the residents nor the night watchman had been able to escape and raise the alarm. Maybe the fire had spread too fast, but that seemed unlikely.

Thóra gathered the remaining papers, put them on top of the larger 'maybe' pile and turned her attention to the smaller pile. As soon as she started reading the first file, she regretted not having put them in any particular order, either by date or likely relevance. She set aside the file — a report about technical aspects of the fire — and flipped down through the rest until she found the verdict in Jakob's case. Soon most of her initial questions were answered, and she could see a clear sequence of events.

Shortly after 3 a.m., petrol that had been spilled that night along the corridors and into the living quarters was set alight. The fire doors had been propped open with chairs and other objects, but only the ones leading to occupied apartments; the rooms with no one inside had been left alone. It would be difficult to argue that this had been an accident; it was a clear example of malice aforethought. The report stated that the night watchman, Friðleifur, had been attacked and struck at the base of the skull. Although the autopsy and other evidence could not be conclusive, he was probably unconscious before the petrol was trailed through the building. His body was found melted onto a chair in the duty office, and there was nothing to suggest that he had moved or tried to escape. The cause of death was listed as suffocation from smoke inhalation. So Friðleifur had been unable to keep his charges safe, and the building's electrics had failed them too; because the home was so new a few of its systems, including the fire alarm and sprinklers, were yet to be connected. This had been raised as a concern, but with the work so behind schedule the excitement of moving everyone in overcame common sense and the residents were installed before all the loose ends were tied up. The concerns raised were quickly forgotten and the sensors — which would have saved lives — sent their messages into space instead of alerting the sprinkler system.

In a further twist of fate, a second watchman who should have been covering the night shift had called in sick at short notice, and no one could be found to replace him. In his statement he said that Friðleifur had called him at home an hour before the time the fire was estimated to have started. At that point there had been nothing much to report; the other man was only calling to ask about a key he couldn't find. The files also mentioned another phone call, but this one to the centre, not from it. This call, which was brief, had occurred just before Friðleifur called his sick colleague. The caller, a young man not named in the files, claimed to have been drunk at the time and to only vaguely remember making the call; it must have been a wrong number, as he did not know anyone at the residence. His explanation was not questioned, since the other staff testified that drunk people often seemed to accidentally call the centre on weekend nights. They had always assumed the home's telephone number must be one digit off the number of a club or bar, although they hadn't looked into it as it hadn't seemed that important.

The care home had been located in a new estate right next to Reynisvatn Lake, where the fully paved and tarmaced streets wound around plots that still stood empty. No one could afford to build houses any more. The building was some way away from its nearest neighbour so the fire burned unnoticed for quite a while. Eventually some of the neighbours were woken by the stench of smoke, called emergency services and had four fire engines despatched. It was immediately obvious to the fire-fighters that there was no point entering the blazing building, so all their efforts were directed at controlling the spread of the fire.

Once they had the fire more or less under control, they began searching in what was left of the building and found the bodies of four residents, as well as that of Friðleifur. Contact was made with the facility's director, Glódís Tumadóttir, who was roused from a peaceful sleep into a living nightmare. She managed to stammer out that there ought to have been six people in the building, five residents and the watchman, and a hunt for the missing resident was initiated immediately. It was impossible at that stage to identify any of the bodies, which hindered the search. Still, the police managed to find Jakob within an hour; he was wandering the streets of the Grafarholt neighbourhood, reeking of petrol and scared out of his wits. He fled when the two policemen who had spotted him got out of their car, but the physical restrictions of his extra chromosome stopped him outrunning them. His attempt to flee the scene was what swung the court's ruling against him, along with his fingerprints on a twenty-litre petrol can found at the scene and his inability to explain what had happened. There was nothing in the ruling or court records to suggest that his disability hadn't been taken into consideration. His unwillingness to move to the centre was described at length as a possible explanation for his actions. It was concluded that he had set fire to the home, thereby killing those inside. However, the ruling went on to say that it accepted the expert witnesses' assessment of Jakob as not being criminally liable due to his functional disability. Therefore he was acquitted of criminal charges. The doctors who had assessed him also advised the court that he should be considered a risk to others, so measures should be taken to prevent him from doing further damage by housing him in an appropriate institution. Hence his current confinement in the Secure Psychiatric Unit at Sogn.

There should have been six residents at the community residence. Only four had died in the fire; Jakob was the fifth. Thóra was unable to find anything in the long document regarding the fate of the missing resident. There must be an explanation elsewhere in the stack, and she made a note to look out for it. She also scribbled down that she needed the names of everyone who'd testified and given statements; in the court documents almost everyone was identified only by a letter. 'X testified that . . . ; B felt . . . ' and so on. If she came across anything that might indicate a mistrial, she would have to speak to some of them. Although some time had elapsed since the fire, there was a slim chance one of them might remember something — some small detail that hadn't seemed important at the time but that could now help prove Jakob's innocence.

Thóra found it hard to make sense of Jakob's testimony, both in court and in the countless interrogations he'd endured. She had never read a testimony that was so garbled and confused. It read more like the words of a child, which in a way was not far from the truth. Jakob's intellectual maturity was completely at odds with his physical age. She found a reference to his IQ, which turned out to be just under 50, though all that meant to Thóra was that he would have been classed as an 'imbecile' in 1967. It was an ugly word, but useful in helping her recall what she had read about IQs; 100 was the average, which meant technically Jakob had half an intellect, whatever that meant. She made another note, this time to remind herself to find out what that score of 48 signified. Did he have a mental age of five? Or two, or twelve? Was it even possible to make such a comparison? If she could put Jakob into a familiar context, it might help her understand his behaviour.

Jakob had given several conflicting accounts of his movements that night. His explanation for not having been found at the scene seemed to change with each interrogation: he had been on his way to see his mother; he was hungry and wanted to buy ice cream; he didn't remember anything; he'd been scared, but he hadn't been fleeing the scene. He had no explanation for why his fingerprints had been found on the petrol can, but since doubts were quickly raised as to whether he understood the question, the can was produced and shown to Jakob. His response was immediate and violent; he screwed his eyes shut and refused to open them until the can was taken away. This had only served to add weight to the case against him, as it seemed the can reminded him of what he'd done. But Thóra wasn't sure this held water. If he'd had nothing to do with the fire, the can could still have frightened him because it was connected with the fire. Perhaps he had even seen someone else starting it. That could also explain why he had reeked of petrol; he may have fled the scene after it was poured on the floor. It was a long shot, especially given that Jakob himself had at no point claimed this to be the case. He'd have no reason to keep quiet about it . . . unless he was afraid of the guilty party? Thóra smiled to herself. She was speculating too much; it was far more likely that Jakob was unable to distinguish between reality and fantasy when he was stressed.

Thóra put down the court ruling and pulled the 'yes' pile closer. Flipping through it, she chose another document at random. Time passed as she went through the whole stack, but she felt no closer to determining Jakob's guilt or innocence. She replaced the final document on the pile and reached for the notes she'd scribbled down. Irritated that her efforts had borne no fruit, she sighed heavily as she skimmed back through her notes. Who would do something like this? If Jakob was innocent someone else was guilty, and that person might be impossible to track down. The act bore all the hallmarks of psychosis; what else could make someone murder five people who had done no one any harm? It was possible the arsonist had specifically targeted the night watchman, but surely there would have been a simpler way to kill just one man?

Thóra stared at the names of the four young residents who had died. Next to each she had jotted down what she'd learned about their disabilities. She had hoped to determine whether one of them could possibly have started the fire but been trapped inside by accident, or even have wanted to die. They had all been found in or near their beds, so it seemed unlikely but not inconceivable. This was not a viable explanation for either of the young women on the list, though. One of them, Lísa Finnbjörnsdóttir, had been comatose; she'd been unable to walk, speak or do anything else, and thus had had neither the strength to set a fire herself nor the ability to coerce someone else to do so. The other woman, Sigríður Herdís Logadóttir, had been both blind and deaf, and also severely mentally impaired, so she seemed equally unlikely to have been the culprit. The same went for one of the two male residents, Natan Úlfheiðarson. He'd been severely epileptic and heavily medicated at night, so he couldn't possibly have been up and about. Unless, of course, he had skipped his medication for once, but that seemed unlikely; she would check the autopsy. The other man, Tryggvi Einvarðsson, had been physically capable of committing the crime, but not mentally. He had been severely autistic and never left his apartment on his own.

She looked up from her notes. It was ludicrous to work on the assumption that these people were in any way responsible for their own deaths, and if she was hoping to prove that someone other than Jakob had done it, she'd have to look

56

elsewhere. Actually, if she didn't find anything else in the files she might not even take the case. Everything seemed to have been done by the book, as you would expect in such a serious case, even one in which the trial had been brought forward and held as quickly as possible. Thóra pulled over the other pile of papers, which she'd been hoping she wouldn't have to go through. The crime scene photographs gave her goose bumps. Although they were low-resolution, poor quality black and white images, she could almost smell the smoke and ash, which must have been overpowering when the photos were taken. The police had captioned each photo, which given the extent of the fire damage was very useful in identifying what each image showed. She thanked God the photos had been taken after the bodies had been removed; she wasn't sure she'd have had the stomach for those pictures. Even looking through these ones made her feel a bit nauseous, and her throat was dry. She wanted to gulp down so much water that her entire body would be waterlogged, so fire couldn't harm her.

She gathered together the autopsy reports. First Natan, the medicated epileptic. Posthumous blood tests showed that Natan had indeed taken his medicine, which meant he had died in his sleep of smoke inhalation. It was clear from the position he was found in that he'd made no attempt to escape or even defend himself against the fire. Thóra felt relieved, but her hopes that the others had also slept through it were short-lived. The deaf-blind woman, Sigríður Herdís, had been found next to her bed; she had probably been trying to crawl underneath it. Her cause of death was not smoke inhalation, but burns. Thóra wished she hadn't read this; the thought of a girl who couldn't see or hear dying this way horrified her. To make matters worse Sigríður Herdís had been the youngest in the home at only eighteen.

Thóra turned to the next autopsy reluctantly, afraid of what she might find. The report was on Lísa Finnbjörnsdóttir, the paralysed coma patient. Her cause of death could only be smoke inhalation; Thóra could imagine nothing worse than the poor girl lying there unable to move while fire swept over her body, regardless of whether or not she was conscious.

Thóra didn't get as far as the cause of death; when she was nearly halfway through the report she realised something didn't fit. She flipped back to the first page to make sure that she was reading about the right person, then put down the papers and rubbed her eyes. This changed everything, and left her with no doubt that Jakob's case ought to be re-examined. The ruling hadn't contained a single word about the realization she had just come to, but it seemed inconceivable that everyone had overlooked it. She opened her eyes again and began scrutinizing the documents in the large pile, this time with more attention.

A sheltered community should be a safe haven for the unfortunate, like a fortress to protect the most needy and vulnerable members of society. But that was clearly not the case. What had actually happened there?

4

Wednesday, 6 January 2010

Thank God there were only ten minutes of the programme left. Margeir couldn't recall ever being so desperate for a broadcast to end, however bored he usually was by the end of the day. The host of the next show hadn't arrived yet, but that didn't matter: Margeir was going off air on the dot. He would just rerun an old show and hope no one complained. He doubted anyone would; already about half their output consisted of repeats, as it was the only way to keep such a small private radio station going. The number of listeners decreased throughout the evening anyway, and it was unlikely that the few who were still listening by this time would make a fuss. Margeir's show was hardly keeping its head above water; it was based on listeners phoning in, so when he didn't have any callers, there was no show to speak of. For far too long he had put off asking the station manager to get it moved to an earlier time slot, to the extent that now he'd got sick of it; it showed in his performance, which in turn made it less and less likely that his wish would be granted. Margeir couldn't pinpoint the precise moment when his interest in his job had started waning, nor did he understand what had caused the decline, but suddenly he was plagued by apathy — and it showed.

A red light blinked, indicating that a listener was on the line. Margeir turned down the volume on the music he played to save having to come up with the inane babble he resorted to between callers. His producer was on holiday and there was no budget for a temporary replacement, so Margeir had been forced to relearn all the technical details he'd been taught years before: how to play advertisements, cue up songs and answer phone calls. Others had lined up the more complicated elements before he went on the air, and he'd been told on the phone that all he had to do was turn up, wait for the pre-recorded show ahead of his to finish and jump in at a designated time. On his way to work he had wondered what he'd do if the preceding programme had stopped before he got there. He decided that rather than try to get help he'd just go home, allowing the screeching of the broken equipment — or just silence — to be sent out across the ether.

The light blinked faster and Margeir cursed inwardly for not having had caller ID transferred over so that he could see who was on the line. When the producer was on duty he was told in advance whether the caller was a 'friend of the station', one of the ones who called every show to talk for the umpteenth time about their interests — or rather, their obsessions — with an enthusiasm that bordered on mania. Their complaints were never original, and none of them was interested in having their views refuted; they considered the station their private soapbox. It was precisely these people that had drained away all the pleasure from his job; every recycled word eroded the happiness and expectation that had characterized his first month at the station. Originally, the focus of his show wasn't meant be politics; the idea was to broach lighter subjects, and by doing so reach a younger audience. It hadn't worked. The people who called in had no interest in movies or new music, and even less in the lives of actors and pop stars. The same group that listened during the day listened during the evening, and all they wanted to do was hold forth on political topics. The light was still blinking; apparently the listener hadn't given up. Margeir didn't even need caller ID, he could see that this was one of the obsessives; any ordinary person would have hung up after holding for so long.

The song ended, abruptly; now he had a dilemma. Either talk about something random, or fight to get a word in edgeways amid the ramblings of God-knows-who. Margeir could think of nothing clever to say, so he took the call. 'Good evening, you're through to Margeir, what's on your mind?'

'I've been listening to the show and I wanted to say that I think my friend Gunnbjörn, who called in earlier, is getting stupider every day. What's he got against the European Union? Is he scared, or something?'

Out of old habit Margeir defended the person being attacked. The stream of nonsense continued, and whenever he tried to interrupt, the caller raised his voice. Soon he was practically screaming, which had the desired effect because

Margeir stopped interjecting. In the end, however, he'd had enough, and by raising his voice to a volume he didn't know he was capable of, he managed to overwhelm the ranter. 'Well, it's time for a commercial break, so unfortunately we'll have to say goodbye for now. Thanks for calling.' He hung up, not caring if it caused offence, and quickly ran an ad. He knew he'd started resorting to this as a means of escape too often, and as the station manager had once pointed out when giving him a dressing-down, while the sponsors might initially be delighted that their advertisements were heard more often, it wouldn't take long before they realized the number of listeners was decreasing for that very reason. Unfortunately, people didn't actually tune in to hear commercials.

There were only five minutes left of the show when the final advert on the tape finished. Instead of giving in to his desire to put on another song, he decided to talk about a newspaper article on cycle paths. He actually had no opinion whatsoever on this area of transport policy, and it amazed him how good he was at discussing a topic without meaning a word of what he said. This had started to affect his private life; the women he met weren't impressed when he automatically switched to bland DJ patter every time there was an awkward silence. Lately even his parents had started rolling their eyes when he joined in conversations at family gatherings.

The light had started blinking again. This time the call was a godsend; the show was about to end, so it didn't matter what dickhead was on the line — he wouldn't have long. 'Good evening, you're through to Margeir, what's on your mind?' He winced as a screech of feedback pierced his eardrums. 'Could you please turn down the volume on your radio, caller?' This wasn't one of the regulars, that was certain. They had learned long ago to turn off their radios when they got through. The noise stopped and Margeir repeated his greeting, which had become so hackneyed that he could say it backwards without any problem. 'Good evening, you're through to Margeir, what's on your mind?'

'Good evening, *Margeir*.' He didn't recognize the voice, and the emphasis on his name sounded sarcastic.

'To whom am I speaking?' Margeir had been so busy grumbling to himself about the regular callers, he had forgotten how difficult first-timers could be.

'To me.'

Margeir looked at the clock in the hope that just once, time had sped up at the right moment, but he was disappointed. Four minutes left. 'Well, my friend.' The man must be drunk; sometimes heavy drinkers called the evening show just to have someone to talk to. Yet another reason to want an earlier slot. 'Our time is running out, so you'd better hurry up if you want to share something with the listeners.'

'I called to talk to you. Just you.' The voice was not slurring at all; on the contrary, every word was clear and seemed loaded with hidden meaning.

'Well, that's too bad, my friend. You're on air. Don't you want to share something with the listeners?' The damn clock must be broken. Time simply refused to pass.

'Do you want the listeners to hear what I have to say?' The caller paused. 'I'm not sure you do.'

Margeir wasn't used to letting listeners throw him off balance. He couldn't deny he often found them tiresome, but he always kept his composure. This call, however, was nothing like the ones he was used to; the voice was calm and level but somehow unpleasant, as if the man was about to burst into mocking laughter. 'Hey, I think our time's up. Karl will be on in a minute, so if you're lucky you can call back and have a chat with him.' Margeir should have just said 'goodbye' and hung up, but he paused long enough for the eerily composed man to speak again.

'Be careful.' The voice sounded odd, and Margeir suddenly wondered if it was a woman, or even a child, pretending to be a man. 'Soon there will be a reckoning and it won't be pretty. Did you think this was over?'

'This? What do you mean, 'this'?' Again Margeir knew he was being unprofessional; he should be cutting the caller off, not encouraging him.

'You should know.' There was a quiet chuckle, which stopped as suddenly as it had started. 'What do you do when you get too drunk, these days? Things aren't going that well, are they, one way and another?' The man's breathing got heavy and ragged, then he said: 'I'm so hot. I'm burning up.'

Margeir had had enough. 'OK, thanks, pal.' He disconnected the line. 'That's it from me. I'm leaving you now, listeners, but I hope we can meet here tomorrow evening at the same time. Good night.' He tore off his headphones and played the programme's theme music, then stood up, his knees weak. He ran back through the brief conversation in his mind but couldn't put his finger on exactly what had caught him off balance unless it was the voice itself, which had been impossible to read. It was unusually calm, completely at odds with the voices of the other listeners who called in. That must be it. He was tired and bored and fed up with everything at the moment. He moved down to the other end of the table, where the producer usually sat, and lifted the little handset that displayed the callers' numbers. He checked the most recent one, but the little screen showed only the letters: *P.No* for Private Number. Margeir gnawed the inside of his cheek and stared at the screen. The flesh was bumpy there, scarred by the nervous habit even though he hadn't done it for many years. Now his teeth caught on the scars.

'Hi! Sorry I'm late. Damn car was playing up again.' The next DJ in the schedule had arrived without Margeir realizing. The man's loud greeting startled Margeir and he had to take a deep breath before answering.

'I was just going to put on a pre-record.' Margeir put down the caller-ID gadget. 'My outro music is still playing, so you have a few seconds.'

'Who was that nutjob at the end? I was

listening to it in the car. Man, I hope he doesn't take your advice and call me too.'

Without knowing why, Margeir felt sure that wasn't going to happen. His instinct told him the caller thought he had business with him, not the other hosts. He felt uneasy as he walked out to the dark car park. In his mind the abhorrent thought took hold that he knew exactly what the caller had been talking about, and as soon as he was in his car he quickly locked the door.

$$\star \quad \star \quad \star$$

'Is she asleep?' Svava put down the pen and took off her reading glasses, happy to be able to take a break from peering at the small print. She had chosen the glasses at random in a petrol station and their strength was not right for her at all. She couldn't put off making an appointment with the optician any longer.

'Who?' The young woman was one of the temps who moved from department to department, covering sick leave and holidays, so it was hardly surprising she didn't know who Svava meant.

'Room 7, the girl who was just admitted.'

'To be honest, I didn't look in on her. I was checking the drip in Room 3. It was running out, so I changed the bag.'

'No problem.' Svava stood up. 'I guess I'd better check on her.' She placed her glasses on her forehead in case she needed them; they didn't make that much difference, but they were better than nothing. She smiled at the temp; it actually didn't matter whether she'd checked on the patient, as Svava liked to keep an eye on the new patients and try to learn a bit about them. Often you could detect when a patient was about to go downhill, through signs you wouldn't necessarily notice unless you knew them. Only by learning what was normal for a patient could you identify abnormalities.

She walked from the staffroom down the corridor to Room 7. Her route took her past several rooms, and from each open door she could hear slow breathing and the electronic beeps of monitors and other equipment. Everything seemed normal, or as normal as could be expected, and as she approached Room 7 she heard nothing to make her quicken her pace. Assuming the girl was asleep, she tiptoed into the spartan white room, almost empty apart from the huge bed. No attempt had been made to disguise the hospital bed as something more homely; the chrome frame was clearly visible.

Svava had never given it much thought until this young woman was admitted, since there seemed little point. Most patients weren't in the department for long, and their illnesses ended with them either going home or being carried out in a coffin, which would at least be spruced up with a satin lining. It was a different matter for this girl, who was a young woman really. She had spent many years of her short life in hospital beds, and would be in one until it ended. She was completely paralysed, which confined her to the bed for the larger part of each day. The only change came when she was moved — with great effort — into a specially modified wheelchair and allowed to go out for a breath of fresh air with an orderly. This was not a service provided by the hospital; she was seriously ill and it was not considered safe to move her. Svava wished the room could be made more comfortable somehow, but she thought any attempt to do so would be like hanging Christmas lights on a shotgun. The girl wouldn't be in the room for long no matter what, so it was futile to make any kind of effort doing it up; Svava's role, like the others' in the department, was to nurse and heal, not to play interior designer.

As Svava entered the room she noticed something odd. The sterile smell that generally overwhelmed everything was contaminated with what smelt like body odour. She went to the girl's bedside and saw that her forehead was damp. Grabbing a flannel from the bedside table, she wiped off the girl's brow before laying her hand across it to check whether she might have a temperature. This didn't seem to be the case; the girl was rather cold to the touch, if anything. Still, there was something wrong, because the girl's eyes were wide open and moving back and forth as if she were having some kind of attack. Maybe she was suffering from cramps, though of course her body lay motionless, as her muscles were no longer under her brain's control. Her EKG showed a rapid pulse, far *too* rapid, although her systolic and diastolic blood pressure readings appeared normal. If the girl was simply feeling off colour she might be a bit panicky. Svava had plenty of experience in dealing with the physically disabled, but it was rare to see someone this seriously affected, who was unable to express herself except with her eyes.

'Did you have a bad dream?' Svava leaned closer to the girl's face and followed her eyes closely. She thought she'd been told that the girl would blink once for yes and twice for no but had never tested this out, so it could very well be the other way around; Svava couldn't remember. The girl blinked twice and Svava decided to stick to her first instinct. 'Are you thirsty?' Again the girl blinked twice. Svava hoped she'd guessed correctly; it would have been awful if the girl had woken from a nightmare dying of thirst and was given nothing to relieve it. 'Are you . . . are you awake?' A ridiculous question, but it was the only one that Svava could think of to test out the answer. The girl blinked once. So Svava *had* got it right: one blink was yes and two was no. But although she had worked this out, they'd be here all night if she didn't ask the right questions.

'You can use the cards.' She looked up and saw the locum nurse in the doorway. 'I've worked in departments that take care of people as acute as her, and I learned a bit about communicating with them. There's computer equipment that's a lot more sophisticated, but nothing like that seems to have come with her, if she even knew how to use it.' She looked at the girl, then back at Svava. 'Not that I know how to use that kind of thing myself, so I wouldn't have been much help. But I'm pretty good with the cards, which should be here somewhere . . . '

'What cards?' Nobody had told Svava.

The girl walked in and looked around. She bent down to the bedside table and picked up some plastic cards, each of which was divided into a number of squares with pictures or symbols. She positioned one of them directly in front of the girl's face and started pointing. The girl used her eyes by blinking or looking left or right, seemingly directing the nurse to the right square. After doing this for some time and working through several cards, the girl suddenly shut both eyes and didn't open them again. Only then did Svava dare to say anything — she hadn't wanted to disturb this primitive, almost alien communication. 'Did you make any sense of that?'

The woman shrugged and looked puzzled. 'I'm no expert at this so I may have misunderstood her, but what I did get wasn't exactly helpful.'

'What did she say?'

'Hot. Burning.' The woman shrugged apologetically. 'Something like that.'

'Burning?' Svava didn't think the cards were much use if this was the result. 'She doesn't seem hot to the touch; but maybe I need to change her duvet for a lighter blanket.' She put her hand on the motionless girl's leg; yes, if anything, it felt rather chilly. 'I guess the best thing would be to advise the morning shift to get a developmental therapist in to speak to her. Someone who can communicate with her properly.' She looked at the young woman, who appeared to be sleeping — though that wasn't very likely

— and noticed that she had an earphone in one ear, plugged into the radio. She pulled it out carefully and held it up to her own ear. It was set to one of the talk-radio stations; she recognized the theme music that was playing. 'Wouldn't it be nicer for her to listen to something a bit lighter? Although whatever's playing, it's not ideal to sleep with that in your ear. Maybe she just wanted to block out the noise.'

After putting the plastic cards back in their place, they both walked out. Svava turned in the doorway and looked back at the young woman's pale face and lank hair.

Hot. Burning.

What did she mean?

5

Thursday, 7 January 2010

The residence stood on the edge of the neighbourhood — if it could be called a neighbourhood. Paved streets lay between empty plots that were still waiting for houses to be built on them. At one junction after another the street signs served as uncomfortable reminders of the area planners' broken dreams. It would be a long time before any happy families drove down Mímisbrunn, Friggjarbrunn or any other 'brunn' to their new homes. If anyone was thinking about building there, they would either have to have a lot of spare cash or a loan at favourable terms, neither of which was available these days. It was as if Iceland's castles were no longer in the sky but had crash-landed there on the outskirts of the city to remind them to be more cautious next time around. The roundabout that was meant to keep traffic flowing smoothly now did nothing more than complicate the route of anyone who strayed there by accident. Thóra stared out of the window while Matthew sat at the wheel, just as dumbfounded as she was by what they saw. As they turned a corner a single house appeared at the end of a cul-de-sac, but instead of lessening the surreal atmosphere, this solitary building only underlined it.

'I guess the people who first noticed the fire

must live there?' Matthew nodded towards the house, which disappeared from view as they exited the roundabout. Thóra had told him all about the case before asking him to accompany her on this tour. She was more comfortable having him along; she didn't know her way around the area, least of all in darkness and with a light snow falling. This way she could concentrate on finding the place without having to worry about driving. Also, it was just nice to have company.

'Probably,' she replied. 'I don't remember the name of the street, but there aren't many houses to choose from.'

'Are you going to pay them a visit?' Matthew's voice suggested he sincerely hoped not.

'No. There was nothing unclear about their testimony, at least nothing that has any bearing on the verdict. They didn't see anyone, they didn't hear anything, they simply went to sleep and then woke to the smell of smoke when it was already too late. Who knows, maybe something will come to light that'll change my mind, but I don't think I have anything to discuss with them.' Thóra squinted in order to read the sign ahead of them. 'I think we should turn here.'

Matthew took his eyes off the road briefly and smiled at her. 'You don't say. It's either turn here or drive off-road onto the open moor.'

'Well, you never know,' said Thóra. 'According to the map I looked at, we should almost be there. We drive to the end of this road and from there a little dead-end street should lead off to the home.'

'If it's still standing,' said Matthew. 'Maybe it was demolished. The way you described the fire made it sound as if it was practically destroyed; there can't have been much to restore.'

But the house had been neither demolished nor restored. A large concrete shell stood exactly where the map said it should, at the end of a short road that had probably only been built to serve this one house. That it should have been allocated a name was rather generous, since it looked much more like a driveway. A low fence marked the boundaries of the large plot surrounding the centre and a wide gate swung gently back and forth as if it wanted to invite them into its solitude.

'Well, now.' Matthew drove slowly up to the building's entrance. There he stopped the car and glanced at Thóra. 'Are you happy to look at it from here or do you want to walk around the house?'

Thóra had already buttoned her coat up to her chin to keep out the cold. 'We're getting out, of course. I'm hoping we can get inside.' And with that she quickly climbed out of the car, so as not to have to listen to Matthew's objections. As soon as she shut the door she noticed two things: the bracing cold, that would be unbearable if the wind were blowing, and a vague smell of smoke, despite the considerable amount of time that had passed since the fire. Thóra took a deep breath to convince herself that she wasn't imagining it, and although the smell was faint it still made her nose prickle. She pulled the collar of her coat right up under her eyes to keep out the unpleasant odour. She saw Matthew wrinkle his nose too as he stepped out of the car, but he only shuddered slightly before pushing his repulsion aside. He wasn't the kind of person who would hold his nose, but Thóra knew him well enough to realize that was exactly what he was longing to do.

They walked around the house, surveying the damage. The windows were boarded up from the inside with plywood panels, and around them the white paint of the exterior walls had turned black, especially near the top, where you could almost make out the shadow of the flames that had blazed up into the sky.

'The glass probably shattered in the heat.' Matthew shone his torch on one of the frames. 'I'm no fire expert, but I doubt the residents who died broke the windows themselves.' He lowered the beam. 'Or the fire-fighters might have done it when they were trying to rescue them.'

Thóra bent down and picked up a large piece of glass she'd stepped on. 'I don't think so, as the glass has fallen out here — the windows must have been smashed from inside.' She let it fall. 'Anyway, I have a report from the Fire Prevention Unit that I'm sure will explain. It looked too complicated to read when I first went through the files.' They came to a side door, which led through to the garden behind the building. It had a large board nailed across it, and beyond it stood a garden table with two broken legs and no accompanying chairs.

There was a large gap at the lower edge of the board. 'The catch has come off.' Thóra pushed carefully on the hastily attached fastening and it gave way. 'We can go in if we want.'

'Er, yeah — no thanks.' Matthew looked unimpressed. 'You can see it isn't safe. The roof is probably hanging by a thread and it could collapse on top of us. I don't care about me, but you're not going in there.'

'Come on.' Thóra took a torch, pushed again on the board and shone her light on the ceiling of the side passage. 'The ceiling here is made of concrete, so it's not going anywhere. Have a look.' Matthew seemed grudgingly convinced about the sturdiness of the structure but continued to try to dissuade Thóra. Even as he was using all his strength to enlarge the opening so that they could slip through, he carried on warning her about all the dangers that might await them. Then they were inside the building.

The torch wasn't much use in the pitch-black. All the windows were covered, preventing the dull gleam of the streetlights from filtering in, yet a layer of water glistened on the floor. 'I didn't realise we would ruin our shoes.' Thóra felt the ice-cold water leak through the seams of her canvas trainers.

'We're not the first unauthorized visitors to come here.' Matthew aimed his torch at a corner, where several beer cans lay, along with a cigarette packet and some other paper rubbish. 'This could hardly have been here when the house caught fire.'

'No, I suppose not.' It looked to Thóra as if it had been a kind of living room, although the furniture had been removed. On a wall, empty

76

shelf-brackets jutted out forlornly. Shards of broken pottery were scattered in the water on the floor but it was difficult to work out where they had come from; probably vases, or pots for houseplants. 'Shall we try and go further into the house? It's divided into various apartments and it would be good to have a look at them. Our shoes are ruined anyway.'

Matthew pointed the light down at her feet. 'You're not kidding.' He then shone it back into the house to check what lay ahead. At the end of the room a corridor led in two directions. 'We can have a look around, though I don't quite understand what you think we'll find. There's nothing here that's going to make any difference. It's an empty shell and it's been inspected plenty of times before — and under better conditions.'

'I'll feel better having seen it with my own eyes. The descriptions I read only tell half the story — they give a two-dimensional view of the situation instead of the three-dimensional one that will help the witnesses' testimonies really make sense.' She was grateful that it was too dark in the building to see Matthew's expression. She doubted he'd think much of this justification and it was imperative that she set off before he could protest and drag her out. She walked in the direction of the corridor. 'It won't take long.'

They set out cautiously; they had no idea what might be hidden in the shallow water and neither of them was interested in falling into it — the fact that it had soaked their feet was quite enough. The water deepened a little when they entered the corridor, enough to cover the edges of their shoes at the ankles. They both shivered, and Thóra recalled the old saying that as soon as the cold gets hold of your feet, you're cold all over. Once they'd passed the little kitchen, the doors of the apartments began. They were all open, and Matthew pointed out that they were obviously flame-resistant fire doors, because the only damage visible on them was a layer of soot. Then he pointed his torch up at the ceiling, and they both stared at the little sprinklers running the length of the corridor.

'This shouldn't have been possible.' Thóra felt as if the smell of smoke had intensified just at the thought of how horribly the residents died, and how they'd been screwed over both by other people and by fate. 'It was a total fuck-up; maybe that's why they were in such a rush to close the case. I'm sure there's a reason it was wrapped up so quickly, though I suppose it didn't help that they couldn't keep the suspect in a normal detention cell.'

She followed Matthew into the first apartment. They quickly took stock of everything inside it. Most of the furnishings had been removed. They called them 'apartments', but this tiny space barely deserved the name; the sleeping area, kitchen and sitting room were all in one open-plan area, with the bed in a nook next to the bathroom, the only part of the apartment that could be called spacious. They peeked into it and saw that it was tailored to the needs of a severely disabled resident; the shower area alone was at least twice as large as the one in Thóra's house, and needed to be to accommodate the various handles and supports fastened to the walls. A shower-curtain, once cheerfully decorated with pictures of colourful fish, hung in tatters from the ceiling, sooty, crumpled and partially melted. Thóra was careful not to touch the remains for fear of getting even filthier than she already was, and she wondered whether they'd have to install a shower area like this once eight people were living in her house, which currently had only one shower. Matthew still hadn't been anything but positive about the prospective changes to the household, but Thóra knew he was only being polite; he must be dreading it as much as she was, if not more. Now that his job at the bank was a thing of the past, he'd be the one who'd have to sit at home most of the day with her parents. She'd have to take him with her whenever she could, otherwise everything would fall apart. She was even considering having a Brazilian wax, which a girlfriend of hers had raved about, in order to surprise him. Even though she'd heard that the first time it was like being skinned — without anaesthetic.

'Do you know who lived where?' Matthew tried to shut the charred wardrobe nailed to the wall next to the bed. It was empty apart from shelves that lay, black with soot, at its bottom.

'I don't know precisely but I remember that the most physically disabled ones lived in the apartments, opposite the shared bathroom. I read that somewhere. Where the others lived was probably listed in the files, but the information was scattered about and I still have to piece it all together. It will be easier now that we've been here, because now I have a clearer mental picture of it all.' They moved through the next few apartments. When they came to the fourth, it was immediately obvious that it was intended for a severely disabled individual. A track was fixed to the ceiling, branching in several directions — over into a small side room with an imposing toilet, across to the place where the bed had probably been standing, and out into the corridor. They followed the track out and saw that it led to a large bathroom, ending over the largest bathtub that Thóra had ever seen. On the ceiling above the tub was some sort of apparatus, attached to the track. There was a sturdy steel hanger, upon which were fastened two chains ending in hooks. 'What primitive contraption is this?' Thóra pushed one of the chains slightly. It emitted a soft creak as it swung slowly back and forth. 'This could hardly have been used for transporting people between rooms, could it?'

Matthew stopped the chain from swinging. 'Actually, that's exactly what it must have been for. They wouldn't have been transporting water in buckets to the bathtub. I suppose there must have been ropes or something else at the bottom of this that got burnt in the fire.' He tried to drag the contraption along the track but it appeared to be dented, because he could only move it a few centimetres. 'I think this must have been used to move people, no matter how weird the idea might seem.'

'Jesus.' Thóra felt a sharp pang of pity. How did disabled people tolerate so much? Maybe it was better to have been born that way and not know anything different. But who was she to judge? No doubt she'd have to steel herself against what she'd be seeing and hearing in connection with this case. They followed the track on to the next apartment, which looked much like the previous one. The only difference was that on the wall next to the bed was a box with connective tubes, which she recognized from intensive care rooms in hospitals. The plastic labels beneath them were no longer legible.

'This is probably for oxygen.' Matthew, who had bent down to the box, straightened up again. 'I expect the person who lived here needed oxygen during the night.' In the dim light Thóra saw him frown. 'I wouldn't have wanted to be near the oxygen tank when the fire spread. Oxygen feeds fire and if it was in every other room here, that might explain why the damage was so extreme. The fire would have intensified and become uncontrollable in a split-second.'

It was clear that Thóra would have to go through the fire report. She hadn't previously considered the oxygen, although she realized Matthew was right as soon as he mentioned it. She looked around in search of evidence of damage other than that attributable to the fire itself. 'Might the fire actually have been caused by an explosion?' she asked, although she didn't see any evidence of one. 'I mean, if the oxygen supply somehow ignited? Shouldn't there be a tank somewhere in the house connected to these tubes in the wall?'

'I would have thought so.' Matthew looked underneath the box but there was nothing. 'There's no visible connection to a tank here, though there are lines behind the box. There must be an equipment room somewhere where it's stored. I expect we'll find it if we look through the whole place.'

They completed their tour of the apartments without discovering much more. They were all very similar and had long ago been stripped of anything personal or individual, first by the fire and then by the clean-up. The very few things left behind told Thóra and Matthew nothing: broken window shutters on the floor, a pot lying on its side in the kitchen. Thóra hadn't really expected to find anything of much significance, but they continued inspecting the house. In the night watchmen's duty room they found nothing but an open key cabinet and a dirty whiteboard that was surprisingly undamaged compared to everything else they'd seen. They also looked in a large, empty room whose function was difficult to determine. The floor material seemed different to elsewhere in the house, and by dragging her toes along the surface Thóra noticed regular stripes that indicated it was tiled; the floor elsewhere had been smooth, probably carpeted. 'Maybe this was a storage room.'

Matthew moved around the space, examining the walls. 'Well, it wasn't the equipment room. There aren't any sockets here besides two standard ones.' They left the building without working out what the room had been for, and looked into a few rooms which were accessed from outside: a cleaning cupboard with a bent steel basin that hung at an angle on the wall, and another smaller storage room.

It was still snowing, and they continued their circuit of the outside in a hurry. But they were forced to slow down when they came to three doors at the front of the house that had not been closed. One of them turned out to lead to the rubbish room, and another to an exterior storage area where a rusty, dirty lawnmower stood in one corner along with some broken garden tools, also rusty. The petrol had no doubt been stored here, and Thóra took a moment to examine the lock on the door, which appeared not to have been tampered with. It wasn't locked, although that didn't mean anything given that a long time had passed since the fire.

The third door led to what was indisputably the equipment room. On the wall were connective hoses with melted labels, and steel frames that could have supported canisters or tanks. Matthew shuffled his feet to preserve the tiny bit of warmth left in them. 'Of course, this wouldn't have been accessible from the house due to the risk of fire. Maybe other, more dangerous materials were stored here.'

'This door has taken a real hit.' Thóra tried to nudge the heavy steel slab that stood half open. It was so twisted that one of the four powerful hinges had broken and it wouldn't budge. 'Could this indicate an explosion?'

'Yes, I would have thought so. Also, you can see that the plaster has fallen off in several places in here.' He shone his torch on a large cracked patch of wall where the bare concrete showed through. 'This could be from a canister that exploded.'

'That must have made an incredible noise.' Thóra stood up on tiptoe to see how close they were to the family home they'd driven past. She thought she caught a glimpse of its roof. 'Why didn't those people hear anything? Is it possible to sleep through an explosion but wake up to the smell of smoke?'

'Who knows?' Matthew turned off the torch. 'Shall we get back to the car before our toes drop off from frostbite? I'm sure you'll find out something about this explosion in the case files. There's nothing more we can do here.'

Thóra nodded. They turned away from the house and walked towards the car. 'I forgot to tell you a little detail I found in the reports.' She looked sadly back at the ruins of the house. 'One girl who died in the fire was pregnant.'

'And?' Matthew didn't seem surprised. 'Bad things can happen to anyone.' He gave her a puzzled look. 'You mean you find that strange because the woman was disabled? People are people, Thóra, regardless of whether or not their bodies are fully functioning.'

Thóra rolled her eyes. 'Oh, for goodness' sake, do you think I'm that easily shocked?' She exhaled irritably, but her annoyance quickly turned to sadness again. 'The woman — or girl, rather — was comatose. That's not what I call consensual sex.'

Matthew said nothing. He opened her door and Thóra climbed into the car. He hurried to the driver's side, started the engine and turned the heater all the way up, then scrunched his fingers together and blew on them. When the warm air blowing from the heater started to inch its way over Thóra's feet, it created a burning sensation that was almost worse than the cold. 'Did the files say who the father was?'

'No, it never came out and there wasn't a single word about it in the verdict.'

'Do you think whoever got the woman pregnant started the fire to cover it up?' Matthew sounded highly sceptical. 'That's pretty drastic.'

'I don't know, damn it. But it could have been Jakob who did this.'

'Started the fire? Or had sex with the woman?' Matthew started backing out of the car park.

'Either. Or both.' Thóra leaned back in her seat and stared at the building in her wing mirror until it disappeared from sight.

6

Friday, 8 January 2010

Thóra put down her pen and proudly looked over her drawing of the residence's floor plan. It certainly wouldn't win any architectural awards but she was enormously proud of the outcome all the same, since what mattered to her was to mark each apartment with the name of its resident. That had proved extremely difficult, because more often than not she'd been forced to use the testimonies of many different individuals to place each one. She would find out in due course whether her hard work would be of any use. Contemplatively, she ran her index finger along the plan of the house, through all the apartments, vaguely feeling the tiny indents that the pen had left in the paper. Rather like the tracks those young people had left behind, she thought — tracks in the memories of those who loved them, that would become less and less noticeable over time and would disappear completely as the residents' relatives died. Thóra lifted her finger from the paper and cleared her mind. These melancholy thoughts would be of no help to her in solving the case and she had already spent more time on the drawing than she could afford. This wasn't the only case that she was working on; of course it was highly unusual, but it was complicated enough without her losing herself in its emotional aspects.

One of the things that troubled her was that Jakob had occupied the apartment next to Lísa Finnbjörnsdóttir, the young pregnant woman. Although even the furthest-apart flats weren't that far from each other, Thóra still felt this was a bad omen; Jakob would have been able to get to the woman's apartment in a matter of seconds. To make matters worse, there were very few other residents who could possibly have been the child's father; five out of six apartments had been occupied, with only three men: Jakob, Natan Úlfheiðarson and Tryggvi Einvarðsson. Natan had been the heavily medicated epileptic, and Tryggvi had been severely autistic and, according to the court records, generally never left his room. Neither seemed likely to have had intercourse with the girl, although Thóra knew this assessment might be completely wrong. Hopefully someone would be able to answer this question unequivocally. Perhaps the paternity had been determined but not mentioned in the records out of respect for the deceased and her family; perhaps she'd had a boyfriend; perhaps she'd been impregnated by someone who came to visit her. The possibilities were endless; what mattered was to find the right explanation and pray that it had nothing to do with Jakob.

Before Thóra had started her drawing she'd spoken to one of the centre's neighbours, the one who had reported the fire, but hadn't gleaned much from their conversation. The woman had answered her questions and Thóra had had to listen to her complaints about how awful it was to live in such a ghost town; construction of the proposed preschool had been postponed indefinitely, forcing her and her husband to find one in town for their two children. The snow was rarely cleared and when it was, it was done badly; the same went for the bin collections. The woman went on like this for some time before Thóra finally got the chance to bring up what she'd come to discuss. She was relieved when she eventually said goodbye to the woman, convinced by then that the couple's testimony was credible; they'd simply been fast asleep and had probably been woken by the reverberations of the explosion, though neither of them had realized what it was. The only peculiar thing about the woman's testimony was that she had specifically pointed out that the couple was used to sleeping through noises, such as loud traffic. Sometimes gangs of kids had been known to hang around the neighbourhood at night, especially at the weekends, but luckily that was now a thing of the past. They hadn't seen anyone that night, and had noticed nothing unusual.

Now Thóra resolved to get down to business. She looked up the name of the centre's director: Glódís Tumadóttir, which Thóra thought sounded a very bright and cheerful name. When she finally managed to get hold of the woman through the Ministry of Welfare, her voice sounded entirely at odds with the image that her name evoked. Glódís frequently sighed heavily, as if she bore all the sorrows of the world on her shoulders. After listening for half an hour to her complaints about the bustle of the Regional Office for the Disabled in Reykjavík, Thóra eventually managed to persuade her into a meeting, although the discussion was accompanied by a long and detailed report on how Glódís couldn't give her more than about fifteen minutes, since naturally she'd have to get back to thanklessly slaving away at her understaffed workplace. Thóra wanted to scream when she finally hung up. She'd met far too many of these kinds of people, who felt that their wages didn't match their great talent and who wallowed constantly in self-pity. She couldn't be the only one who wanted to give them all a good smack in the hope of snapping them out of their self-appointed martyrdom. But that would have to wait for another time. In retrospect, she realized that underneath all the moaning, the woman had probably been worried or agitated about her call. Perhaps all the waffle about the unfairness of her job had been caused by nervous anxiety; after all, it couldn't have been pleasant for Glódís to have to discuss the case again. She could have something to hide, but it might not be anything unnatural or suspicious; the young people who died had been her responsibility and although the home hadn't been in operation for long, she must have had emotional ties to those who died. No doubt everything would become clearer when they met face to face.

Thóra's mobile phone beeped, telling her that she'd received a text. The message was entirely unfathomable, and had again been sent from ja.is. She hoped it wasn't some idiot who'd entered a friend's number wrongly, and was now using her number by mistake. If that was the case, then someone somewhere was asking an extremely important question: *How did Helena get burned as a child?* She felt momentarily spooked, given that the message mentioned fire, but she dismissed it as coincidence and shut her phone.

Bella hadn't arrived yet though it was nearly ten o'clock, so Thóra scribbled a note to her to remember to order more paper for the photocopier. The chances of the secretary actually doing it were slender, but Thóra refused to let the young woman have the upper hand so she added hurriedly underneath: *Can't pay your salary if I can't print out a payslip*. Then she put on her coat and left. It was still snowing outside but now it was coming down faster and thicker, not at all like the gentle flurries of the previous evening. She'd have to hurry if she was going to scrape the ice and snow off her car and make it to Síðumúli in time for the short interview window Glódís had so kindly granted her.

A thick, heavy layer of snow covered the car and the slush underfoot made it difficult for her to stand close enough to be able to clear it off properly. This made her hand motions clumsy and Thóra was more or less covered with snow when she finally got behind the wheel and drove off. Along the way, ill-equipped cars caused endless delays as they spun their wheels and slid back and forth across the road while irritated drivers honked their horns.

Thóra decided not to join in the horn concerto and instead took the opportunity to call home and speak briefly to Matthew. He turned out to be on his way out for a run, which he did every day of the week except Sunday, whatever the weather. Thóra found this totally incomprehensible — the only time she might consider running would be away from a crazed murderer, in the unlikely event that one was after her. She hadn't said as much to Matthew, however, since it seemed so important to him. She simply smiled to herself every time he suggested that she come with him, although her smile had faded somewhat when he gave her a pair of top-quality running shoes as a Christmas present. For the moment she could still use the weather as justification, but when spring came, the fear of breaking her leg on the ice would no longer be a viable excuse; instead she would have to admit that she had no interest in unnecessary physical labour or else come up with some other reason. She hadn't been able to think of anything better than an allergy to bees, but it was still a long time until spring and she might come up with more credible ideas as the days got slowly longer. Thankfully, she didn't need to go to the gym to keep her figure trim; she was slim by nature as well as tall, which meant that the extra kilos that occasionally came — and went, without any special effort — distributed themselves quite easily over her frame without being too noticeable.

She was very close to being late. When she finally pulled up in the car park, which was half buried in snow, her mind drifted to what Matthew had said before hanging up: that she

91

should proceed carefully with her questions about the home. He hadn't wanted to elaborate other than to say that handicaps and illnesses were sensitive topics and it was easy to hurt people, even if no harm were meant. He said that he suspected that those who took care of disabled individuals were even more sensitive to the way things were phrased than the individuals themselves. This did nothing to improve Thóra's feelings of uncertainty on precisely this subject; despite having read through the case's countless documents, she realized how poorly informed she still was about which terms were considered inappropriate when referring to the former inhabitants of the community residence and their circumstances. Despite Matthew's warnings, she was relieved to speak first to a woman who had no blood connection to the residents; it was less likely that Thóra would offend her than a family member. Perhaps she could learn from this conversation and take in concepts and terminology that were thought appropriate. But she wouldn't be able to avoid speaking to the relatives of the dead residents — if, in fact, they were willing to meet her — because most other sources of information about the centre had burned to ashes. They were under no obligation to speak to her, of course, and the fact that her client was the man whom they believed to be responsible for the deaths of their children didn't exactly go in her favour. She didn't need to go offending people with inappropriate comments on top of all that.

After clambering out of her tilted car, which

was partly perched on a snowdrift, Thóra hurried inside. There a young woman received her very warmly; she was the complete opposite of Bella, and told her that the wait would be brief. Shortly afterwards, the same smiling girl announced to her that Glódís was available. She directed Thóra in and in a moment Thóra was seated in a chair in the woman's extremely unassuming office.

'My schedule has opened up a bit so we're not quite so pressed for time.' As she spoke, Glódís removed some completed application forms from her desk and stuck them in a folder. 'The people that I was expecting cancelled their appointment. It happens often when the roads are like this. Which means, of course, that I'll be absolutely swamped when the weather improves again, but there's nothing we can do about that.' The woman was about the same age as Thóra, but was even more tired-looking than Thóra considered herself to be. Her two-toned, off-blonde hair with black roots did little for her puffy, excessively made-up face. Overall, she looked like one of those women who'd been the prettiest girl in her class as a teenager, before the unkind ravages of time had set in. 'So, how can I help you? You said that you were working for Jakob. I don't quite know what I can do, exactly; my acquaintance with him was rather limited, as you know.'

Thóra nodded. 'I was asked to investigate the case thoroughly, since there seems to be some doubt that Jakob was involved. I'm gathering evidence and information with a view to the case possibly being reopened by the Supreme Court.'

The woman's expression hardened and she struggled to keep her tone pleasant. 'What do you mean? What sort of doubt?'

Thóra decided not to tell Glódís who had instigated the new investigation. She knew that if she mentioned the paedophile, their conversation would be finished. So she worded it as vaguely as she could. 'After reviewing the testimonies and other matters related to the verdict in the case, it appears to me that it was poorly prosecuted. It's also possible that Jakob's disability wasn't fully taken into account. He appears to have been rather erratic throughout his testimony, probably not comprehending the seriousness of the case.'

'All of the protocols were followed to the letter.' Glódís's lips had thinned disapprovingly. 'The police sought our advice and we sent them a developmental therapist who assisted in the interrogations and everything relating to Jakob's special circumstances. I don't believe that it could have been handled any better.'

'Maybe not; but nonetheless, the doubts that I mentioned do exist. It may well be that later on it will become clear that everything was concluded precisely as it should have been, but until then I must acquaint myself to the best of my ability with everything that might suggest the existence of reasonable doubt concerning Jakob's guilt.'

'I don't see why.' The woman was obviously offended and made no attempt to conceal it. 'Jakob started the fire and killed those people. He has the intellectual maturity of a child, which means it isn't possible to blame him for malicious intent, but he still should have known better and not done it. People with disabilities are not exempt from the obligations that human society lays on our shoulders, nor do they wish to be exempt. They want to live their lives on an equal footing with the rest of us, and they should be bound by the laws of our country.'

'Then have you formed an opinion as to why he did this? Had he displayed violent tendencies before, or other behaviour to suggest that he was dangerous?' Thóra was very keen to avoid allowing the conversation to get too general. If she allowed it to stray off the main subject, it would deteriorate into a monologue on the woman's pet topics, which were of little interest to Thóra.

'He wasn't outwardly violent, perhaps, but he was angry and scared and completely opposed to any changes in his circumstances. Almost all the other residents were delighted with the care they received, but he was the odd one out.'

'It's my understanding that his mother was completely opposed to him moving there. Maybe that was the reason for his unhappiness?' Perhaps there was more to it; something that Jakob's mother didn't know or wished to hide.

'Yes, true. He was unhappy about having to move but he wasn't given the chance to express his opinion. In the end he would have been just as satisfied as the others, once he realized how much better it was to be out from under the protective wing of his mother.'

'Weren't there a lot of people wanting to move into the residence? Why was so much pressure

95

put on his mother to admit him?'

Glódís ran her hand through her two-toned hair. 'I don't see what difference that makes. Are you trying to say we're responsible? That this would never have happened if he'd been allowed to continue living at home?'

'No, that's not what I meant.' Thóra kept her composure, telling herself not to rise to any provocation. 'My intention is to demonstrate that he had nothing to do with the fire. If this turns out to be the case, it certainly matters where he was living.' She allowed Glódís a moment to consider this and saw her tense shoulders relax slightly. 'From the little interaction that you say you had with Jakob, do you think it's possible that he took this desperate measure to get what he wanted? That he perhaps considered it the only way for him to return to his own home, by burning the place to the ground?'

'I don't know.' Glódís was clearly being cautious. By far the best response, of course, was to say as little as possible. 'My dealings with him were limited and I decided not to burden myself by going through the case any more than my job dictated was necessary. The whole thing hit me very hard; as director of the centre it caused me enormous professional shock.' She hurriedly added: 'As well as emotional shock, of course. I'd known many of those young people for a long time. The most disabled ones had been regular visitors at a short-term community residence for children where I worked for many years. You form relationships with your clients, even though you're paid to supervise them.'

96

Thóra nodded, her expression sympathetic. 'Naturally.' She smiled warmly at the woman. 'Then you'd probably agree with me that it's important for us to remove all doubt as to who the guilty party is? I'm sure you wouldn't want the criminal to be walking free while an innocent man is locked up.'

'Of course not.' Once again the woman clamped her lips shut, this time until they nearly disappeared.

'If we let ourselves believe for a moment that Jakob is innocent, could you imagine who else might have done it? I'm not thinking exclusively about the residents; what about an outsider or a disgruntled employee who felt he had a score to settle?'

Thóra had to give Glódís her due: she did appear to think this over before she replied. As she opened her mouth, her lips turned from white to pink again as circulation was restored. 'I must insist that I believe Jakob started the fire. Just so we're clear on that.' She hesitated before continuing: 'The young men and women who died that night weren't like ordinary people, who might have someone who wished them harm for whatever reason. They hurt no one and offended no one, except perhaps the kind of bigots who can't tolerate anyone different from themselves. In other words, they had no enemies; there's no list of people who bore grudges against them.'

Thóra decided to wait a little before dragging the pregnancy into the conversation, although she greatly longed to throw it in the face of this rather rude woman. She feared it would be difficult to pursue the subject, and that the conversation might end there and then. 'Fine. What about their families, though? It's not unheard-of for a relative to resort to drastic measures when things get tough, and might it not be conceivable that one of them started the fire so as not to have to witness his or her child suffering? Perhaps someone who might even have been breaking down under the strain and not had the strength to care for their loved one any longer? Unemployment and uncertainty sap some people of all their strength; maybe this was an act of desperation on the part of someone who had lost all hope and wasn't in his or her right mind?'

'It sounds as if you're describing Jakob.' The woman smiled for the first time, but it was a smile completely devoid of joy, and full of spite and sarcasm. 'He meets both criteria. Dashed hopes, not in his right mind.'

Thóra ignored this remark. 'So all of your employees were happy at work and had no complaints?' She paused to allow Glódís to digest this. 'That must be rather unusual.'

'I will neither discuss individual employees with you, nor the group as a whole. None of them has anything to do with this; they chose to do a selfless job on low wages because they wanted to do good. They would never have hurt those whom they had under their dedicated care.'

'It wouldn't be without precedent,' said Thóra cautiously. 'But you mustn't take it the wrong way when I ask. I'm not just fishing for information, and I'm not accusing your employees or anyone else. I'm simply trying to exclude as many people as possible so that I can use my time on what matters.' Then Thóra let the bomb drop. 'For instance, finding the person who made Lísa Finnbjörnsdóttir pregnant. It must have been important for someone to cover that up.'

The woman paled. 'What do you mean?' There was no doubt that she knew precisely what Thóra meant.

'Surely it must have been obvious to you that this young woman in your care was expecting a baby?' Thóra pressed on, striking while the iron was hot. 'The only thing I need to know is who the father was, and whether the child was conceived with her consent.'

After a short silence Glódís spoke up again. Clearly she wasn't about to be intimidated. 'I don't know who he was.' Instead of spinning a story about not having known, she seemed to want to address the issue openly. This was shrewd of her, since it must have been clear that Thóra wasn't going to give up, but would keep returning until she was able to speak to someone who could provide her with answers. It would be much better if this person was Glódís and not her immediate superior, or even the person one rung further up. She'd be wise to tie up this unpleasant discussion while she could. 'That was another terrible shock; it caught me completely by surprise when I was informed of the autopsy results. I swear that I thought it must be some kind of mistake.'

'But then?' pressed Thóra. 'You must have carried out some sort of internal investigation of the matter. Her parents at least must have demanded that much.'

'Obviously, they were distraught when it came to light. And although they were too upset by her death to pursue it very rigorously, of course they asked a lot of questions about it. We did everything we possibly could to get to the bottom of it, but without success. None of the employees we spoke to had any idea how it could have happened on their watch, and it's hard to understand how such a thing could have taken place without them noticing. In the daytime there are at least three staff members on duty and the rooms are always open. Apart from the permanent employees, there are also nurses' assistants and developmental therapists who aren't there all the time but still spend hours on the premises. I just don't see how it could have happened.'

'Did she ever go home or leave the centre at all? Did she go to the hospital, or visit friends or relatives?'

'No; why would she? She was comatose, which meant there was no reason to disturb her apart from in exceptional circumstances. She was fed intravenously and needed oxygen, and you don't get that kind of equipment in ordinary homes. She was actually sent to hospital twice during the course of her time with us, but neither occasion was around the time that she would have conceived. She was four months into her pregnancy when she died, and all our investigations into who the father might have been were based on that timescale.' Glódís rubbed one of her temples, looking pained. 'Lísa wasn't actually a permanent resident at the home, but we were asked to take care of her while another solution was sought. The department she'd been in for many years had closed and we weren't full, so it made sense. She was actually due to have been moved soon after the time of the fire, but of course that never happened.'

'Which could indicate that the culprit wanted to take the opportunity to do it before she was moved.'

'As I said, we have no idea who the father was, so any theories are nothing more than that — theories. The care home was full of people and it's impossible to imagine how Lísa's pregnancy could have happened.'

'You say that there were always a lot of people around in the daytime, but what about at night? There was only one person on duty the night of the fire, and perhaps not only that one time. The night shift must have been under suspicion.'

'There were always two staff members on duty at night, with two exceptions. On the night of the fire, and once during the first week after we opened. The timing of that particular occasion doesn't fit with Lísa's pregnancy, and in any case, it's clear that the night watchmen had nothing to do with it. There were four of them in total, two different shifts, two on each shift. They worked every other week and were off in between. It's difficult to invert your body clock like that at regular intervals, and it's certainly true that only a particular type of person chooses to do such work. But none of them was the perpetrator in this dreadful case.'

'Why not? Because they said so?'

'No.' Glódís looked slightly annoyed. 'The coroner demanded that their DNA be compared to that of the foetus, and the analysis cleared all four of them — including the one who died.' She shut her eyes. 'I'd give a lot to know who did it, and how. It makes me furious to think something like that could happen somewhere where I am responsible.'

'Were others tested? What about the male residents?'

'Yes, but it ended there. Each individual test costs around two hundred thousand krónur, I understand, so it was never going to be possible to test every male who had ever set foot through our door. But as far as my boys go, neither Natan nor Tryggvi nor Jakob turned out to be the father. I should mention, perhaps, that I haven't seen their results myself, although I did get a copy of the test results on the night watchmen sent to me because I was their boss at the time. But I heard from someone in this office that the other results were negative, and I don't see any reason to doubt that. In any case, the bastard who forced himself on Lísa has yet to be found.'

'So you agree that it's impossible for her to have given consent?'

Glódís looked up quickly. 'Of course it's impossible. She was comatose; she was never conscious. It's out of the question that she consented to intercourse. This was a criminal act, however you look at it.'

'Wasn't the matter referred to the police, then? You can't look past the fact that this was rape, and under the most appalling circumstances.'

'No, it wasn't reported.'

'Why not?'

'It wasn't me who didn't want to. But when it came down to it, her parents didn't want the police to know about it and they got help to prevent them finding out. They said they didn't want to see newspaper articles discussing their daughter in this context, and they knew the details would get splashed everywhere. It was too late for her, in any case, and sentences for sexual offences aren't heavy enough to amount to any real justice. Even if the guilty party had been found, they thought it would be just as likely that he would receive a paltry sentence that they would have found hard to accept.'

'But what about public institutions? The police or prosecutors? Didn't they carry out a proper investigation? Rape is not a private matter, once it's discovered.'

'No.'

This all sounded most odd. 'How can that be? It's a serious violation of criminal law. Her parents shouldn't actually have had any say in how the case was handled.'

'They got help, as I told you. The father of Tryggvi, the autistic boy at the residence who died that same night, is high up in the Ministry of Justice and they turned to him. He prevented the matter from going any further.'

'I see.'

Glódís nodded. 'After that, our hands were tied.'

7

Friday, 8 January 2010

Thóra had an appointment with a client back at the office that afternoon. The man was divorcing his wife; the process had begun before the financial crash but had been delayed because the couple had had second thoughts in the middle of it. In the wake of the disaster, they had cosied up to each other in search of the good old days when everyone in the banking and business world had been honest and the authorities respectable. This sudden affection, however, turned out to be merely the death throes of youthful love, and after two months of renewed intimacy they came to the conclusion that nothing had changed — they weren't made for each other after all. The divorce was put back on the agenda but now under entirely different conditions; their rather sizable assets had gone up in smoke, leaving only their debts to divide up. Their civility seemed to have evaporated along with their assets and the couple, who'd previously seemed to get along quite well, had changed into ravenous vultures in each other's presence. Thóra and the woman's lawyer had their hands full preventing them from coming to blows in their joint meetings. Fortunately the husband was meeting Thóra alone that afternoon.

The hot dog Thóra had bought for lunch was on the large side and the last bite went down with a bit of difficulty. She licked mayonnaise off her lower lip and took a gulp of the flat fizzy drink that came with the lunch special. She was feeling quite pleased with herself after her conversation with Glódís. She ran her eyes down a printout of the names of all those who had worked at the centre; the former director had given her the list after Thóra had informed her that she could just as easily find the staff members' names in the court records. That was perhaps not entirely true, since such a list was unlikely to be exhaustive and there would be no easy way for Thóra to fill in the gaps. From Glódís's list she saw that there had been fourteen full-time staff and a total of ten substitutes and specialists, which meant that, in truth, even finding all the names in the police reports would have proved a Herculean task. It would be impossible to speak to each and every one of these people, but with insight and a good measure of luck she could hopefully filter out those who she most needed to speak to. Glódís had also let her have the names of the residents' parents, which would doubtless have proved simpler to find, but it spared Thóra the trouble of going through all the obituaries and death notices from the period following the fire. She was certain that some of these people, staff or family members, must know how Lísa's child had been conceived, but the name of the father was probably not on either list.

Although Lísa's rape was a vile act, it wasn't

unprecedented. Thóra had read on the Internet that morning about necrophiliacs, people whose fetish was to have sex with the dead. Nor was this sort of repulsive sexual deviance anything new. The 'father of history', the Greek Herodotus, told of how Egyptians let the corpses of beautiful young women rot for three to four days before they were handed over to those who were to anoint them, to prevent them from being disgraced in this way. Of course, Herodotus was also called 'the father of lies', so Thóra didn't know how much this story could be trusted. It was clear, however, from other articles that she skimmed over, that this was a not uncommon modern-day fantasy. Around seventy per cent of those who suffered from this fetish said that they dreamed of sex with people who neither resisted nor gave any sign of rejecting them. A comatose person would certainly fit into this category.

Thóra dug her mobile phone out from her overflowing handbag and called directory enquiries. She decided to utilize the time that she had before meeting with her client to speak to Jakob's former defender, the lawyer also appointed by the Supreme Court as Jakob's supervisor. She had tried several times to reach Ari Gunnarsson since starting her investigation, to no avail, and he hadn't responded to her messages. But Thóra had no other choice but to keep on trying, since Ari's insight into the case was sure to aid her investigation. It was also more appropriate to let him know of her intentions formally, rather than simply through messages left on his answering machine. His role as supervisor was to ensure that the individual deemed not criminally liable remained in residence at the designated institution for no longer than necessary, although this particular issue would have no influence on the reopening of the case.

Thóra had immediately recognized Ari's name in the dossier. His details were often given to people who'd been arrested when they asked for a lawyer. He was a decent guy, as far as she could tell; not exactly a genius, but no idiot either. She recalled a rumour which had circulated in the legal world that he had come dangerously close to being disbarred due to being bankrupt for many years, but had somehow escaped this punishment. The man appeared not to have particularly good references, which made Thóra curious about who had selected him to supervise Jakob and why. Had Jakob himself been made to point at a name on a police list, or had his mother done so? She supposed that if you didn't know any lawyers, that was no worse a way than any other to choose one.

Ari answered on the second ring, apparently in the middle of lunch. He mumbled to her to definitely drop by — he had an hour free, and it would give him an excuse to put aside the boring job he was working on. He apologized for not having responded to her messages; he simply hadn't got round to it. After swallowing his food in a dramatic fashion, he stopped mumbling and gave her the address of his law office more intelligibly. As she'd expected, it was close by;

few lawyers set up shop in the suburbs. When she got there, she discovered that his firm shared a corridor with a few other unassuming offices, including several small wholesalers and a dentist. The latter seemed not to be taking a lunch break, judging by the whine of the drill that came from behind his closed door as Thóra walked by.

Ari's office was a mess. He was obviously self-employed, because there was only one desk set up in the spacious room. Bookshelves lined the walls and were loaded with rubbish that seemed to have been dumped there at random. A sofa that had seen better days stood under the window, but she could hardly see it for the papers, files and books that were scattered all over it. Even the floor was being used as a filing cabinet and Thóra had the feeling that it wouldn't take long for a narrow path to form from the door to the table and the worn-looking visitors' chair. After Ari showed her in, she took a seat. He was on the phone when she arrived and appeared to be negotiating a car purchase, with Ari wanting more for the vehicle than the buyer was willing to pay. A half-eaten sandwich in a rustling plastic wrapper moved back and forth when Ari wanted to place particular emphasis on his words. A piece of lettuce flew out from between the slices of bread and landed on the computer screen in front of him. It slid down lazily as Ari wiped away the mayonnaise streak that it left behind. Finally he hung up, without having concluded the car deal, and smiled at Thóra.

'Sorry, I didn't realize that you were so close by.' Thóra started muttering politely that that was all right, but she didn't get to finish her sentence before Ari interrupted her. 'But enough about that. What can I do for you? You said that you're working on reopening Jakob's case. How come?' He took a big bite of the flimsy white-bread sandwich, which was now falling apart after its vigorous shaking.

Thóra told him the entire story of her new assignment before turning to the business at hand: ' . . . and since you were Jakob's lawyer, I wondered if you had any useful information, or if you could remember anything about the case that struck you as odd or unusual.'

Ari laughed curtly. He was on the chubby side and it made his cheeks wobble. 'The oddest thing about that case was the client. He was completely ga-ga. I won't be defending any more retards, or whatever you're meant to call them now. It was like dealing with an ugly, overgrown child. And as if it wasn't bad enough defending him, they appointed me to be his supervisor.'

Thóra tried not to be too offended by what he said, hoping it was just a reflection of his insecurity. She doubted many clients found their way to this den of chaos. 'Of course the young man is developmentally disabled, so I can completely understand that communication between you must have been difficult. But I was thinking of something related to the investigation or to the case itself. I'll make my own judgements on him as a person.'

'Such sensitivity!' That nasty laugh again, but

109

thankfully it ended abruptly. 'You know, I'm actually relieved they didn't consult me about the reopening of his case. I should be insulted or pissed off, but I'm not at all, not in the least. It was one of the worst cases I've ever taken on, and I've seen a lot in my time. But it all seemed pretty clear-cut to me: those who died were better off dead, to call a spade a spade, and Jakob is best kept institutionalized for life. If you really believe he's innocent, all I have to say is: 'Good luck with that'.'

Thóra didn't know quite how she should respond to this extraordinary statement. It was probably best to let it go unremarked; otherwise there was a risk that this would end in an argument. She now seriously doubted that this man had handled Jakob's interests with anything resembling professional integrity. 'So you saw nothing in the case that might suggest someone else had a hand in what happened? I'm aware that Jakob's testimony was contradictory, to the point where at times his guilt didn't seem to be in question, but as you said yourself, he behaves like a child, and they've never been considered reliable witnesses. If full consideration wasn't taken of his disability, it's equally likely that something was accidentally missed that might point the finger at someone other than him.' As she spoke, Thóra marvelled to herself at Jakob's bad luck in getting Ari as his lawyer. The man was probably great at wrangling with the judicial system on behalf of petty criminals, but he was the polar opposite of what was needed for this case.

'No, I don't think so.'

Thóra wasn't convinced. 'So there was nothing that came to light regarding the running of the home, or anything else suggesting that someone other than Jakob had reason to want to destroy it?'

'No, nothing.'

'What about the young paralysed woman who was pregnant, Lísa Finnbjörnsdóttir? Do you think it stretches credibility to say that the father would have been anxious to conceal the pregnancy?'

'What?' Ari seemed genuinely surprised. His lower jaw slackened and his half-open mouth formed a black hole in his otherwise pale face. 'Where did you get that idea?'

'It's in black and white in the girl's autopsy report. She was around four months pregnant when she died. The father is unknown, but it's clear that conception took place at the centre. She didn't get out much, so I understand.' The black hole opened even wider and Thóra caught a glimpse of the pink tip of the man's tongue.

'I wasn't remotely aware of this, and nor was anyone else as far I know. It was never mentioned in the hearings, or the interrogations, or anywhere else for that matter.'

'It's untrue that no one was aware of it, although it was never discussed, out of consideration for her family. You could easily have found out about it, but since you failed to do so, everyone was able to breathe easier.'

Ari was quick to recover his composure. He shut his mouth again with an audible snap and

111

spread out his hands dramatically. His shirt cuffs were threadbare and the pinstripe material of his suit shiny with wear at the elbows. He clearly wasn't raking it in defending burglars.

'Well now. I doubt that it would have changed anything. Who would kill a whole lot of people just to hide such a thing? I can see it must have been awkward and all that, but I mean . . . ' He let his hands drop. 'Why not just kill *her*? Cram a pill or two into her mouth, end of story.'

Thóra thought she might cram a thing or two into him if he went on like this much longer. 'Of course it's impossible to understand how or why it happened; I'm just pointing out that something was going on that someone wanted to keep hidden, and there might be more to the case that I'm not aware of. Might you not have come across something but maybe considered it irrelevant to the defence case?'

'No, I swear I don't remember anything. I would tell you if I did.' His chair creaked as he leaned back. 'I should tell you that I was swamped with work when this case was handed to me. Looking back on it, I might not have taken the time to go over every small detail. But that's another matter; what's more important is that it wouldn't have made a difference. All the evidence indicated that Jakob started the fire, and the court would hardly have been receptive to vague theories about other culprits.' He turned to the slightly sloping bookshelf behind him. 'I can do one thing, of course, which is lend you the files. I still have them here somewhere.' He looked around and smiled mischievously at

Thóra. 'I'm not one for throwing things out, as you might have guessed.' She didn't return the smile.

'I've already had most of the material from Jakob's mother. She saved everything she got her hands on.'

'That's just a small proportion of it. She can have this if she wants it.' He pulled one file after another from the shelf. 'She was an old woman who wouldn't have benefited from seeing it. In case you're easily shocked, before you read it you should know that there are aspects of this case that are a little . . . unsavoury. Another reason why I couldn't get properly involved in it. There was far too much going on; it was too weird and fucked-up to get my head round.'

'How so?' Thóra didn't understand where the man was going with this. Considering his previous statements, it could well be that he'd been so repelled by the descriptions of the disabled residents and the work of the residence that he'd had to put aside the case.

'These people were all weirdoes — the residents, of course, but the staff too. These so-called professionals testified in court one after another and the stuff they were coming out with was so mental that I wasn't the only one who'd had enough by the end of it. According to them we should all leave our jobs and start doing something noble, like caring for the disabled. People may say the work they do is incredible, but I don't think it was all done out of the kindness of their hearts, if you catch my drift. There was something funny going on.'

113

Thóra cleared her throat loudly, mostly to stop herself from shouting. Ari was saying something about these people only being fit to go in a meat grinder, but she wasn't really listening now. Had someone who felt the same way as Ari burned down the home, out of hatred towards those less fortunate than himself? A lot had gone on since the nation's money evaporated, and some people must have resented the fact that funding was being allocated to these causes. Though admittedly it did take more than a foul mouth and a narrow mind to do something as drastic as killing five people. 'Was there anything else, besides the specialist carers, that pissed you off about the case?'

'Plenty.' The look of outrage over the arrangements at the unit faded slowly from Ari's face and was replaced by a more serious expression. His eyes flicked to the side and he stared at the rubbish on the floor by his desk instead of meeting Thóra's gaze, as he had done until now. 'I think what frustrated me most is that it seemed like money had been poured into the construction of this centre, but not into other comparable enterprises. I looked briefly into whether this was normal, to throw equipment and employees at an establishment as if we were a wealthy oil empire, and it wasn't. The only reason that place had as much put into it as it did was because one of the prospective residents had connections in high places. He was accepted instead of others on the waiting list, and that's just the tip of the iceberg. Corruption is everywhere, as you no doubt know.' The sudden

114

look of horror on Ari's face, which he immediately tried to hide, suggested that he'd accidentally said something he'd been trying not to mention.

'Who do you mean? Which of the residents?' asked Thóra.

Ari threw up his hands. 'Sorry, I don't remember. I'll look it up later and send you an e-mail.' He didn't ask her for her e-mail address, so clearly this e-mail would never be sent. She would have to find out by other means.

'Could this corruption, or whatever it was, have been the reason behind the fire?' Thóra had no idea how that might be the case, but who knew, maybe someone whose child hadn't been admitted had lost it when it turned out that the offspring of someone better-connected had queue-jumped the waiting list.

'No.' Ari shook his head. 'I've told you that Jakob is the guilty party. He started the fire and that's the end of it. Maybe he didn't realize the consequences it would have but he did it nonetheless. Isn't he doing OK at Sogn? It can't be all that different to living at the residence.'

The image of Jakob's face as he'd pressed up against the window when Thóra visited the Secure Psychiatric Unit flashed across her mind. 'I think he's having a terrible time there. Really terrible.'

'Aw . . . ' Ari's expression of sympathy was entirely devoid of sincerity. 'Well, at least the people there are more like him. That care home was a bag of mixed nuts, get it? Those poor fuckers had nothing in common. Another shitty idea dreamed up by the bureaucrats.'

'Oh?'

'Someone had the genius idea of trying to run an institution for individuals who have totally different disabilities. It was supposed to be a great master-plan for some reason, though I'll never understand why. It was because they put so much pressure on Jakob's mother that he moved in. They needed a mongoloid; they're generally all aborted these days, which meant there weren't many of them in his age group to choose from when the admissions selections were made.'

'Down's syndrome.' Thóra had to correct him. He was clearly unaware of the proper terms when it came to discussing people outside his narrow definition of normality. And to think she'd been worried about her own use of language.

'Whatever.'

'But didn't the person he leapfrogged at the top of the waiting list also meet a requirement for a particular type of disability, one that others didn't have?'

Ari waved his hands as if he were being pestered by an invisible fly. 'What's that? No — he was autistic and they're a dime a dozen. It doesn't show up on the ultrasound, you see.' He winked at Thóra conspiratorially.

'Right.' Thóra tried hard not to frown; she had no desire to encourage any more of these comments, but she also didn't want to shock the man into refusing to lend her the files. This whole encounter was excruciating, but she would have to put up with it until he handed her the stack of papers that was on the verge of falling over onto the rubbish on his desk. One thing was clear, at least: the person who had jumped the queue must have been Tryggvi, the autistic resident.

Ari suddenly stretched out one hand, nearly knocking over the stack of papers. 'Just so you know what to expect . . . ' He unfastened the buttons on his shirtsleeve and rolled it up, revealing a fat pink arm that clearly hadn't done a scrap of physical labour in years. In the middle of it a large, shiny, horseshoe-shaped scar was clearly visible. 'Jakob, your current client, did this. That's how sweet and innocent he is.'

Thóra couldn't take her eyes off the unsightly, uneven skin. 'What happened?'

Ari pulled his sleeve back down. 'He bit me. Just took a piece right out of me.'

'Unprovoked?'

'Of course — what, you think I deliberately made him angry?' He refastened the button. 'He simply bent me over the table where we were sitting and took a bite.'

'What were you discussing?'

'Just some stuff about the case. I don't remember precisely, but it wasn't anything upsetting or significant.'

Ari pushed the files carefully an inch closer to Thóra. 'I didn't even report it, so no one can say I didn't protect my client's interests. I should have bowed out of the case, of course, but we were about to go to court and like a fool, I felt uncomfortable about the idea. You, on the other hand, can still quit — and that's what I'd recommend you do. A scar like this would doubtless do you more harm than me. And I wasn't the only one he hurt; he often attacked the people who lived with him, staff as well as residents. This isn't the only scar that he has on his conscience. He's prone to violence, as well as being guilty. That's all there is to it.'

'You don't remember how you came to be chosen to defend Jakob? I can tell from what you've said that he's not exactly the kind of client you like to work for.'

'No, hardly. He's the worst client I've ever had.' He seemed contemplative, but it wasn't convincing. 'But how I ended up defending him . . . I just can't remember. Probably the police suggested me.' He smiled and patted the stack of files. 'It was a huge mistake for you to take this case, but as I said, you can still back out. My bloody arm still hurts now.'

Thóra took the files. She didn't think she would withdraw from the case, but she was certain that she would be very careful around Jakob. 'Thanks for the warning.' She had arranged a meeting with her client the next day at Sogn, and she was definitely taking Matthew with her. She wouldn't be alone with Jakob, that much was clear.

8

Friday, 8 January 2010

The meeting with the lawyer had gone worse than Glódís could have imagined. In truth, before their encounter she had given little thought to what they might discuss; had thought that it would be smooth and easy work to convince this Thóra of Jakob's guilt, and subsequently to persuade her not to dig any further into the case. To her mind there was no doubt about his part in the horrific deed, so this should have been a piece of cake for Glódís, but she hadn't reckoned on the woman being so well prepared and their conversation taking such an unexpected turn. How could she have known that the lawyer had access to all of the court documents on the case? Glódís had assumed they would have been locked up after the sentence was pronounced. In retrospect, she had no idea why she had thought this to be the case, but she'd been dead wrong. This was a bloody mess. She couldn't afford for this case to be reopened. She'd suffered enough because of it in her career, and only now was the fall-out from it finally starting to dissipate. Glódís had lost count of all the meetings she'd been called to because of everything that had come up during the investigation and the trial. That whole time she'd felt like an outsider in her workplace; no one spoke to her voluntarily for fear that her unpopularity with the higher-ups was infectious. She didn't know how she'd get through it if it happened all over again.

A familiar feeling of depression washed over her. How could it all have gone so wrong? It had always seemed like a good idea to her, no matter what anybody said afterwards. Overnight she'd become a kind of rising star within the organization. Before she'd suggested a unified community residence, disabled housing issues were like matching socks after doing the washing. The blind over here, the paralysed there, and autistic people somewhere else. Oops, one with severe dementia — oh well, he's the only one, can't do anything for him. In the end her proposal had been welcomed eagerly and was implemented with great speed: Iceland was experiencing a boom, people were enthusiastic, and there was plenty of money. If the experiment worked, more of these kinds of centres would be built when budgetary resources allowed. When she was then informed that she was being considered to run this innovative unit, it seemed fate was smiling on her, especially after she'd been an assistant director for ten years and obliged to take on all the most tiresome and difficult cases by a boss who took only the agreeable ones for himself. Now it was Glódís's chance to allow herself that luxury. But her bliss had been short-lived.

Jakob, that damn Jakob. If only she hadn't pushed so hard to have him admitted, right now she would be in her little office in the nice new residence, casually tallying up receipts with supermarket bills or taking a bit of time out to browse sunny places to visit for her summer holiday. But no. Now she was sitting at the Regional Office for the Disabled, answering phone calls from family members whose only role in life appeared to be to irritate her. When will a space become available? The wheelchair's got too small. Isn't it possible to extend my daughter's day-care hours? Endless demands that she could hardly ever meet, with very little thanks for her trouble. Now, since they'd been preaching bloody cutbacks and savings, it looked as though the few positive conversations that she'd had with the agency's clients or their relatives had become a thing of the past. It had given her monotonous days some colour to be able to fulfil people's wishes from time to time. Yes, her life had undergone a complete transformation. All because of Jakob.

She felt a painful throb in the small of her back, which ran up her spine and stopped at her neck. Glódís moaned softly and reached behind her head to rub the sore area. It did little good, as she'd known it wouldn't. She still hadn't managed to rub away her headache. The doctor had informed her that it was a consequence of injuries she'd received when she'd been struck heavily with a broom on her lower back. Two vertebrae had been pressed together and there was little that could be done about it apart from a major operation that had no guaranteed outcome of success. Again, all Jakob's fault. He had attacked her from behind, completely unprovoked, and the blow had sent her crashing into a wheelchair in the corridor. The blow had been so hard that she hadn't felt the initial impact at all; the fear of being paralysed had overwhelmed everything else and she'd wept with relief when she realized that her legs hurt. Luckily other workers had happened to come along and had removed Jakob, because otherwise he would probably have continued to hammer her with the broom. In any case, he was standing over her when she opened her eyes, staring at her with his familiar sheepish expression. And then this idiot lawyer thinks the man is innocent. She'd change her opinion pretty sharpish if she got hit like that herself. Glódís found herself hoping that that would happen.

'There's a quick meeting in ten minutes. We're going to continue discussing the cuts.' The fact that the woman in the doorway had come to notify her of this meeting was one more sign that the business about the fire was slipping into the coma of oblivion. If it were just allowed to be left to rest, like Sleeping Beauty, everything would be good again.

'Thanks. I'm coming.' Glódís put on her most pitiful expression and continued to rub her neck. 'I'm dying of pain. This is never going to go away.'

'Take a painkiller.' The woman vanished from the doorway without showing any sign of empathy. Glódís had further to go than she had hoped, particularly if this lawyer started raking everything up again. Glódís had to ensure that this wouldn't happen; she was afraid she would just be fired. Cuts inevitably meant a reduction in staff and she would probably be among the first to go. And what then? There were few jobs available in the recession and unemployment benefits were low and didn't last long. She knew the requirements for disability benefits well enough to be able to take advantage of her back injury and receive them, but they were next to nothing. She did have a few contingency plans, though; for example, knuckle down and perform so well that she made herself irreplaceable, contact the union and get them on her side, or play the trump card she was saving until all other avenues appeared closed. That time could very well be approaching.

For the moment, however, she had to make an urgent decision. Should she tell her superiors about the lawyer's visit and the possible reopening of the case, or keep quiet? It would of course be worse if they found out about it later, worse still if they discovered she had kept it secret from them. On the other hand, any hope that this could turn out to be a flash in the pan would be gone if she opened her mouth. Glódís had trouble concentrating due to the pain in her neck. She let her head roll onto her shoulder and shut her eyes. With a concentrated effort she emptied her mind of worries. This self-consolation didn't help much, however, since it merely cleared the way for other more troubling thoughts and memories. *Look at me. Look at me. Look at me.* This repeated itself continuously until she opened her eyes.

Glódís wiped away a tear that had slowly

formed. It made a tiny wet spot on the back of her hand, which disappeared quickly but left behind a grey mascara streak that would have been almost invisible if she weren't aware of it. This reminded her uncomfortably of her job as the centre's director: it had lasted only a short time, but had managed to leave behind a black smudge on her soul. She straightened up and went to the meeting.

* * *

The nurse knew he was forgetting something, but couldn't think what it was for the life of him. His shift was ending and this wasn't the first time that he'd had this nagging feeling at the end of the day. His job was hectic and it was impossible for him to finish everything; more often than not he had to put off visiting patients and spending quiet time speaking with them, as he would have preferred to do. The strictly necessary tasks had to take precedence, and in recent days the lack of staff had meant that these were divided between fewer pairs of hands. He wasn't actually worried that he'd forgotten something important; he'd administered all the necessary medications and those who'd been scheduled for examinations or x-rays had gone and returned. No, this was something different.

'How's your stomach?' He bent down to an old man hunched in a wheelchair at the edge of the corridor. The man had obviously embarked on too long a journey and not made it to his destination, wherever that was.

'What time is it?' His pink gums shone. His dentures lay in his lap. Every word was accompanied by a wet smack.

'It's almost four o'clock, my friend.'

'Are you the doctor?' More wet smacking, and the final word was such an effort that a tiny bit of saliva ran down the man's chin.

'No, I'm the nurse, remember? I took your blood pressure earlier.' He positioned himself behind the wheelchair. 'Shouldn't I help you back into the lounge? Then you can watch TV before dinner or enjoy the view outside.'

The old man's sinewy neck cracked when he attempted to turn his head around to look at the nurse, but he could only move it far enough for one eye to briefly meet his gaze. His expression was one of doubt and mistrust, but the young man had long grown used to this from very elderly patients. These people were from a different time when nurses had all been female. In any case, his number was diminishing, and the nurse had never been offended by their suspicion or let it get on his nerves. Sometime in the distant future he would probably be sitting in an advanced version of the same wheelchair, looking with yellowed eyes at new, changed times that he didn't understand. He rolled the man's chair into the lounge and positioned him so that he could choose between watching television or gazing at the life that passed by outside without him.

The duty room was in order, so it wasn't the tidying or finishing up of paperwork that had been bothering him. A medical record rested on the table and he picked it up to put it back in its place. No one could say that he left his work behind for the next shift. The file fell open and a piece of paper slipped out. He grabbed it as it fell and at the same time as he noticed the female handwriting he realized what he had forgotten; he didn't need to read what was written there to remember it. He had forgotten to call a developmental therapist to speak to the poor young girl in Room 7, as his colleague Svava on the evening shift had requested. He hurriedly dialled the internal number, but there was no answer. That was not a good sign. It was almost four o'clock and developmental therapists didn't provide round-the-clock service. Damn it.

There was nothing for it but to pay the girl a visit and see whether he could do anything himself. As far as he knew, no doctor was expected until after his shift ended and in any case there was no guarantee that a doctor would be able to accomplish any more than he could. He would at least have to try to communicate with the girl so that he could mention this at the shift change later — if in fact there really was a problem. The note had mentioned a rapid heart rate and anxiety that might have been due to a nightmare, but it was necessary to find out whether something preventable was troubling the girl. It was extremely tricky to deal with patients who communicated with difficulty or not at all; only they could describe the majority of their symptoms, which made any diagnosis a thousand times more difficult than usual, if not impossible. This girl was the worst example of

126

this problem that he had ever encountered, and the department was not properly equipped to handle these kinds of cases. So he couldn't rely on previous experience to communicate with her, and he had to admit to himself that he'd spent as little time with her as he could get away with. There was something about her complete lack of mobility that disturbed him. He hoped for her sake that he was alone in feeling this way, but deep down he knew that this wasn't the case.

Inside the room a faint beeping sounded from the EKG machine, which the girl had been hooked up to after the incident yesterday evening. The day's readings had already been collected for the doctor, who would look in on her after dinner. Someone else would have to go over the information that was currently trickling out, but for the moment he was grateful for the monitor because the diligent needle that moved continuously across the paper showed that there was still life in the girl. There was hardly any other evidence to confirm this; her slender body lay virtually motionless beneath the blanket and you had to concentrate to notice the feeble movement of her chest, which barely moved when she breathed. The girl stared up at the ceiling and appeared not to have noticed his arrival, though he knew that she could hear perfectly well.

'Hi, Ragna, how are you doing?' He walked up to her and took her pale, bony hand. A needle had been inserted into a cannula in the back of it and he suspected that half the weight that now rested in his palm belonged to its pink plastic casing and the large bandage that held it in place. The bandage must have been bound round the cannula as automatic procedure, because there was no risk of the girl bumping her hand or knocking the needle against things that she touched. Her hand didn't move unless it was moved. He stroked her hand carefully around the edge of the plastic, knowing that she had full feeling. What an awful, awful existence.

The girl's eyes moved and she blinked. He leaned closer to her and smiled. 'I have a confession to make: I forgot to ask for a therapist to come and speak to you today. But I promise I won't forget again, and you can tell me off if he doesn't come and see you tomorrow. First thing in the morning.' He smiled again, overcome by how unreal she seemed. A life-size, living doll that couldn't move. He continued to smile but now his smile was sad, even though it was meant to cheer her up. Of course, the girl couldn't return the smile, and instead just stared at him with her big, frightened eyes. He wasn't sure why he felt that her eyes were fearful; maybe because her gaze reminded him of a sick kitten that he'd once cradled in a feeble attempt to play veterinarian at the request of the middle-aged woman in the next-door apartment. She'd come to him because she knew that he worked at a hospital and asked him to take a look at the little scrap, which was sickly and hot. He had protested and explained that he knew nothing about animals, but to little avail. Still, it hadn't been the opinion of his neighbour that had bothered him, but the eyes of the kitten, staring at him as its heart beat erratically in its tiny breast. The poor thing had realized that it depended entirely on the man who had it in his grasp; he could throw the creature down, crush it or cuddle it — as he did, of course. The girl was in the same situation; she was so helpless that her entire existence depended on others. If they didn't nourish her, give her water, care, and everything else that a person needed, her days would be numbered. It must have been a terrible feeling, especially in a new place where she knew no one.

'Are you expecting any visitors this evening? Your mother or father?' They at least could make contact with the girl, even if most of the staff couldn't do so. She blinked twice and he knew that meant no. They hadn't been taught more than yes and no, any more than they'd been taught sign language when a deaf person was admitted.

'I'll let the evening shift know that they should ask you how you feel, whether you're in any pain. Okay?' She blinked once. 'Are you in pain?' She blinked twice but he was no nearer to knowing how she really felt. Her parents would have to get more information out of her, preferably about exactly what was wrong. He got goose bumps on his arms as once again he couldn't help thinking about how it would feel to live only in your mind, your body a lifeless shell.

To prevent her from noticing how uncomfortable he suddenly felt in her presence, he quickly turned his back to her and pretended to be checking the IV drip. 'Maybe you want to watch

TV? There are movies until six on the hospital channel and I'm sure there'd be something you'd enjoy.' He bent down to tilt her up in bed slightly, then fastened her securely beneath her arms with a specially designed harness, to prevent her from slipping back down. He pulled the television closer, turned it on and switched to the movie channel. On the screen appeared two American actors he recognized, although he didn't know their names. He didn't know which movie it was and could only hope she would like it. 'There you are. My shift is almost finished, but I'll see you tomorrow morning.'

He turned in the doorway to look back at her. Up until then he had avoided her gaze, and he was startled to see that she was now following him with her eyes and blinking at him over and over. 'See you tomorrow.' He went into the corridor, half ashamed for not going back in. She probably had something on her mind but he felt so uncomfortable in her presence that he didn't trust himself to try to ask her what it was. What was left of his shift would be put to better use writing a note to her parents. They could speak to her and find out what was bothering her. Once he had decided on this, he felt a bit better.

How was he to know that no one ever visited her?

9

Saturday, 9 January 2010

The drive to Sogn seemed as if it would never end. Conditions were awful — drifting snow and black ice — and it felt like her destination was getting ever more distant. The awkward atmosphere among the passengers didn't help: Matthew drove, while Thóra made repeated attempts to carry on a conversation with Grímheiður, Jakob's mother. Thóra felt that they should have her with them at this first formal meeting with Thóra's client. The woman was quiet and seemed to be terrified in the back seat, holding the handle above the window with a death grip. She told Thóra weakly that she didn't have a driving licence, which made her feel rather anxious when the road conditions were so bad. She added that this was the reason she so rarely came to visit Jakob during the winter, though even in the summer she had difficulty finding a lift. She didn't have many friends and of course her relatives had their hands full with their own lives; it wasn't really on to ask them to drive her all the way out to the countryside east of Reykjavík. It had been easier when Jakob had been in the community residence, even though she'd had to walk a considerable distance from the bus stop. She concluded this short speech by thanking Thóra sincerely for wanting to bring

131

her along; it had been more than a month since her last visit. Thóra was silent after hearing this; the situation between Grímheiður and her son was sadder than she'd imagined. All the same, she hoped the woman didn't have too high hopes that this would be a completely normal visit.

En route, Thóra asked her tactfully about her and Jakob's relationship with the lawyer Ari Gunnarsson, and received the answer she'd expected, that it had been rather strained. They'd been incredibly unlucky with the choice of Jakob's supervisor; Thóra had gone through all the files he'd given her and there was scarcely any sign that he'd looked at them. There was nothing scribbled in the margins, no page corners turned down, and considering how messy the man seemed to be, this was unlikely to stem from any inclination to keep the files neat and tidy. Grímheiður said that Ari didn't have any understanding of Jakob's condition and that he'd constantly expected things from Jakob that Jakob was incapable of: taking notes, reading over depositions and criticizing them, and so forth. He'd also been rather rude to both Jakob and his mother and didn't seem to put much effort into the defence, though Grímheiður stressed that she knew nothing about these things and was in no way qualified to judge. Thóra pursued this by asking her how Ari had come to be chosen as Jakob's attorney, to which Grímheiður replied that the man had called her the morning after Jakob had been found wandering around after the fire and the process to formally arrest him had begun. This process

132

wasn't easy, since Jakob was underage and numerous people had to be summoned, including his mother, as his guardian. She didn't know where Ari had got her number, but she believed that the police or someone else involved in the arrest must have given it to him. She had no idea how such things worked and accepted the man's offer to defend her son. At that point it simply hadn't occurred to her that this was anything other than a mistake that would soon be fixed. When this had turned out not to be the case she hadn't wanted to take the trouble to change lawyers — she'd even thought that it was too late, since they were going to try to speed up the case as much as possible.

Thóra remained silent throughout Grímheiður's account, though she found it all rather odd. The fire had occurred on Saturday evening and the formal arrest was made the next morning. Lawyers weren't in the habit of calling people and offering them their services, least of all on a Sunday morning. How had Ari heard about the case? She'd never heard of the police getting in touch with lawyers to give them unsolicited, insider tips about possible clients, which made her think Grímheiður's explanation was unlikely. It was of course possible that in all the fuss surrounding Jakob's developmental level and his legal position, unorthodox procedures had been followed, but Thóra was dubious about this theory. If anything, the authorities would have wanted to do everything by the book.

The wind had dropped and the snow had more or less stopped drifting by the time they finally drove up to the Psychiatric Secure Unit. The sun pushed its way up from the horizon and cast its merciless rays on the crust of snow. They shielded their eyes while waiting for a moment on the doorstep for someone to answer the entryphone. They made a great fuss about Matthew, since Thóra had neglected to inform them of his attendance. After a bit of wrangling he was allowed to accompany them as her assistant. They were also delayed by Grímheiður having come with two full plastic bags of groceries for her son. The old woman had to hand in everything that she had with her and the contents reminded Thóra of what a terrible cook she herself was. Out of the bags came a Mackintosh tin containing doughnuts, a mountainous stack of flatcakes, half a glazed ham wrapped in cling-film, rhubarb pie and all manner of other cakes and breads, all home-baked. The woman must have been up all night preparing it. The food was put back in the bags, which were then placed in a back room somewhere before they were finally taken to meet Jakob, in the same homely, worn-out sitting room where Thóra had met Jósteinn. She would have liked to use this trip to have a few words with him regarding the cost of the investigation, but she couldn't help feeling that it would be better if he were otherwise engaged. She didn't particularly want to see him again.

They sat down on the sofa and tried to make themselves comfortable, even though the seat was pretty saggy. Grímheiður chose to sit at one end of the sofa, clearly hoping that Jakob would

134

be allowed to sit next to her, because she pulled a large easy chair over before sitting down. Thóra said nothing; the better mother and son felt, the more relaxed Jakob would be, and thus the greater the chance he would be persuaded to talk. By the time he finally appeared, accompanied by a staff member, his mother had rearranged the embroidered cushions at least four times in the seat that she intended for him. They gave each other a long hug before he plonked himself down in the chair. He hurriedly gathered the cushions one by one from underneath him and let them fall to the floor. Thóra and Matthew stayed quiet as his mother asked him how he felt, whether he was eating well and whether he always brushed his teeth for two minutes every morning and evening. He answered all of her questions in the same way: 'I want to go home.' In the end Grímheiður introduced Thóra and Matthew, to whom Jakob had paid no attention.

'This is Thóra, Jakob. She's a lawyer. Like Ari, but much better. She's good, and maybe, just maybe, she can help us so that you get to come home.'

Jakob looked at them both in turn and frowned. He appeared to have slept badly, his hair was dishevelled and there were noticeable white marks at the corners of his mouth from saliva or toothpaste. His trousers were too short and his frayed sweater too large. Why wasn't it possible to keep people properly presentable in these places? You could be sure that those who worked on disabled people's issues wouldn't go

135

round in used or the wrong size clothing. 'I want them to leave. I want to talk to you, Mummy. Just you. Why can't you move here if I can't go home?' His sentences all ran together, as if he were pushed for time. Perhaps he thought the chances that his wish would be granted would increase if he spoke so fast that it would be difficult to distinguish the words.

'Hello, Jakob.' Thóra interrupted him and extended her hand. When he didn't take it, she withdrew it. 'It would certainly be much better if you could move back home. As your mother said, I'm going to see whether that's possible, but you've got to help me a little bit.' His expression was still sceptical, and now seemed even a touch angry. 'I need to ask you some questions and you must answer me truthfully and correctly. This won't be like when other people have been speaking to you, because you can tell me everything and I'll never get angry. I want to be your friend and you can trust your friends.'

'What's your name?' It wasn't a good sign that he couldn't remember her name for more than a second. How could he possibly be expected to remember things from over a year ago? Hopefully he just hadn't been listening.

'My name is Thóra and I want to try to help you. I'm actually not at all certain that you started the fire. Do you remember the fire?' He shook his large head but his fearful expression suggested otherwise. 'Yes, Jakob, you remember it, don't you?'

'Fire is hot and it burns and hurts. I definitely know that.'

'Exactly.' Thóra smiled. She had to be careful, especially not to ask leading questions. 'Did you maybe see how the fire damaged the home and hurt the people there?'

'The home hurt the people too.' Jakob looked at his mother. 'A lot of them started crying. But not me.'

'Did they start to cry when the fire was burning the house?' Thóra wasn't sure whether he was speaking generally and referring to how unhappy he'd felt at the centre or whether he meant the cries of those who died in the fire.

'Then as well. I didn't start crying.' He looked proudly towards his mother. 'I was good like you told me to be.'

'So you saw the fire?' Thóra did her utmost not to be too aggressive, but she needed to work this out.

'The fire was bad.' He turned to his mother again. 'I don't want to talk about the fire and I don't want to talk to this lady. She's just like the bad man.' Thóra assumed he meant Ari.

'Did you know that I brought raisin cakes for you?' Grímheiður took her son's large hand in hers. 'If you're good about talking to Thóra, I'll see whether you can have one afterwards. I made them for you in the big pot. Do you remember it?' He nodded and turned slowly back to Thóra.

It was probably better to start with something other than the fire. 'Do you remember Lísa, Jakob?' He nodded and didn't appear thrown by the mention of her name. 'Was she your girl-friend?'

'No, she couldn't talk. She was still good, though.'

'How was she 'good'?' Thóra prayed that he wouldn't answer this by saying anything romantic or sexual.

'She never cried. She was always just tired and sleeping.'

'Was there ever anyone in bed with her?' Jakob looked in surprise at Thóra. 'No. Never. That was just her bed.'

'Did you ever get into bed with her?' She felt she had to just ask straight out, although Grímheiður's look of astonishment suggested that she didn't know why Thóra was asking the question. 'Or did you see anyone else do that?'

'No,' Jakob half shouted. 'There was no room and I had my own bed. Everyone had their own bed.' He paused before adding: 'Mine burned but that was okay. I didn't want it. I have a room at Mummy's house. No one is bad there.'

'Who was bad at the home?'

'Lots of people. One woman was very bad and I hit her.' He frowned. 'She deserved it. She was bad.'

'You should never hurt people, Jakob. You know that.' His mother stroked the back of his plump hand. 'Do you remember how angry everyone was?'

'No one was angry when *she* was hurting . . . ' he tailed off.

'Are you talking about Glódís? Who did she hurt?' Thóra hoped that it was only the director that Jakob had beaten. With the bite on Ari's upper arm, that made two assaults, which was two too many. She'd seen Glódís's testimony about this incident the second time she'd looked

138

through the court documents, but had hoped that it was an exaggeration or a misunderstanding, that Jakob hadn't intended to hurt the woman. It appeared that wasn't the case.

'She hurt . . . a lot. I don't want to talk about it.'

'Did she hurt *you*? Was that why you hit her?'

'No, she took the picture that Tryggvi gave me. It was mine but she took it from me and said that I couldn't have it. I got angry and hit her with the broom. She deserved it. You can't take what belongs to other people. That's stealing.'

Thóra hurried to speak before Grímheiður chipped in with some motherly guidance and reprimanded her son for this long-past deed. 'Did you get the picture back? What was it of?' Perhaps Jakob had nicked a report or some other document from Tryggvi's apartment; according to the descriptions given of him in the court papers, Tryggvi hadn't communicated with other people.

'Glódís never let me have it back. And I wanted to have it, it was a picture of a man shouting. And letters that I didn't understand.'

'Did Tryggvi give you the picture? Did he say anything to you?'

'No, he just handed it to me. That's just as much giving as if he'd said something. He couldn't talk.'

This conversation appeared to be leading nowhere. Jakob's attack on Glódís had apparently been prompted by frustration and irritation at the injustice that he thought he'd been done; first he'd been deprived of his home, and then his picture. 'So Tryggvi was your friend. That's nice.'

'Poor Tryggvi.' Jakob shut his eyes tightly and murmured something incomprehensible. Then he opened them wide again and stared at Thóra. 'Look at me. Look at me.'

Thóra, who had hardly taken her eyes off him since he came in, held his gaze. 'I'm looking, Jakob. Did you want to tell me something?' The young man's energy suddenly flagged and he seemed to go limp in his chair.

'I want cake.' His tone was a classic child's whine. 'I'm not answering any more questions.'

'Just a little longer, Jakob. Then you can have cake.' Thóra hoped she was right. She had no idea what rules they had about eating here; there could very well be a ban on eating between meals. She hoped not. 'Who do you think set the centre on fire, Jakob? You can tell me and I won't tell anyone. It would help me so much if you told me what you think, because you knew everyone.' There was no need for her to put so much effort into this question, because the answer came immediately and categorically.

It was just a pity that it couldn't be taken seriously. 'It was an angel. An angel with a halo. A broken halo.'

'Did you know this angel?' Thóra hoped that he simply meant a good person, maybe someone he'd had a good experience of.

'No, I don't know any angels. They all belong to God.'

'If an angel set the residence on fire, then it wasn't an angel from God.' Thóra shook her

140

head to make this clear to him. 'Angels are good and those who are good don't start fires and hurt people. How do you know it was an angel? Did it tell you that?'

'No, I just know it was. I almost saw it completely and it was completely good. It wanted to make people stop crying.' Despite the confusion about this character, Thóra was finally on track. Perhaps Jakob had seen who was responsible after all — if there was any truth to his words. 'And what was the angel doing when you saw it?'

'It was walking. With a suitcase. In my room. There was a bad smell, then it left.'

'Where did it go, Jakob? Did it go up to heaven?' Thóra wanted to know how crazy this story was. If he replied that the angel had ascended to God, it would be very difficult to take his story seriously. If not, there was a good chance that the glow from the fire or another illusion had caused the arsonist to appear to Jakob, in his drowsy state, to be an angel. Perhaps the suitcase had been the petrol can, for instance.

'It just went. To the others.' Jakob suddenly leaned over to his mother. 'Then it got incredibly hot.'

'Why didn't you tell the police about this, Jakob? Then they could have punished the angel instead of you. They think you started the fire.'

'I told them about the angel but they didn't want to hear about it. They said I mustn't lie.'

'Wasn't anyone nice to you when you were talking to the police?' Thóra knew a therapist had been present during the interrogations, the transcripts of which she'd skimmed over, though she didn't remember the person's name. Of course, it could be that this angel story had come out in an interrogation that hadn't been recorded, in which case the investigation couldn't exactly be considered exhaustive.

'No one was nice. Not once. They were all so angry with me.' He shut his eyes and burrowed his head into his mother's shoulder. Grímheiður's face was awash with grief; going over the story again was clearly taking it out of her.

'Were there only policemen with you?'

'I don't want to talk about this. I want to go home.' Jakob didn't open his eyes, and instead pressed closer to his mother, which pushed her head completely to the side.

'Maybe you'll get to go home, Jakob, if you keep being so helpful. I think you're doing a very good job talking to me and I'm sure you'll get some cake soon.' She decided to leave further discussion of the interrogation for a better time. She still had to go through the files Ari had given her and the interrogation about the angel might be in there somewhere. 'Was the suitcase green? Green like grass?'

'I know exactly what colour green is,' Jakob replied crossly, straightening up. His mother's head immediately sprang back into its proper position. 'But I don't remember. It was so dark.'

'But was it really big, or just like this?' Thóra held her hands out to what she thought was the right size for a petrol can.

'Like this. Not huge.' He suddenly grinned

broadly. 'Mummy and I went to Spain once and we bought a suitcase. It was huge — like this, see.' Now it was his turn to hold out his hands and he stretched them out as far as he could without falling off his chair. His poor mother — if Jakob was right about the size, the bag could have fitted both of them in and a few more people besides. Thóra sighed. If this was an indication of how many errors the young man's statements might contain, he would never be a great witness.

'Jakob. Tell me one thing. You must promise to be completely honest. Cross your heart.' Thóra traced a cross over her heart, and he followed her example. 'Did you set the residence on fire, maybe by accident?' He shook his head. 'Did you have a lighter or matches, or did you find any in the home?' He shook his head again. 'You're not fibbing?'

Jakob shook his head a third time and now with such force that his hair stood out as he did so. 'No. No. No. No. I was afraid of the angel and I left. I didn't want him to take me with him to heaven. I wanted to go to Mummy.'

'But did you take the suitcase with you?'

Jakob hesitated and looked at his mother. She continued to stroke his hand. 'Just tell the truth, darling. You remember, the true stories are always the best ones.'

'I took it. The angel had lost it and I didn't want the fire to damage it. God might get angry at the angel and that wouldn't be good. I put it outside so it wouldn't burn.'

Bingo. Thóra believed him, despite all this talk

143

of divine beings and other peculiarities in his story. 'Good, Jakob. Thank you.' She smiled at him and he returned the smile faintly, his slanted eyes crinkling above his chubby cheeks. 'Did you hear the angel say anything, Jakob? To you or anyone else?'

'No, but I couldn't hear very well. There were so many people screaming and then there was an explosion. I think the angel left because of all the noise. Angels don't like noise very much. That's why it wanted to take people to heaven. They always cry so much on Earth.'

★ ★ ★

Thóra and Matthew stood in the corridor. She was happy with the outcome of the meeting. After asking Jakob about life in the centre but not learning anything new, they'd left the sitting room to give mother and son some time alone before the three of them had to return to town. No doubt all the things he'd told her had already been recorded in the case files and in court, but now that she'd spoken to him in person she believed his story, even if it was childishly expressed. The verdict had stated that Jakob's explanations were far-fetched and were found to be in accordance with his impaired intellect, but it had not gone into any more detail. Was it somehow beneath the dignity of the court to put his full testimony in print? Obviously people were only allowed to spout bullshit if they were considered to be of sound mind. Thóra had read plenty of testimonies made by people who seemed hardly any more advanced intellectually, even if they were considered to be better connected to reality. 'I'm certain he's innocent, but I'm well aware that that isn't enough to get the court to reopen the case. We need more, and not just the truth about what happened with this pregnant girl.'

'Well . . . ' Matthew didn't appear as convinced as she was. 'You know, you're pretty impressionable, Thóra. I understood most of what he said, but I wouldn't trust myself to make a judgement of guilt or innocence if I only had his statements to go on.'

'No, but I think I trust *myself*. You don't raise two and a half children without learning a few things; I know how kids lie. Jakob is simply a big child, and I had the feeling that he was answering honestly. He might be confused, but he's honest.'

'He's an adult, Thóra. A man. Not a child, even if he is intellectually impaired. Don't forget that. Your children certainly weren't lashing out with broom handles or biting chunks out of people.' Thóra had no answer to this. Once Gylfi had pushed his friend out of a swing at preschool, and Sóley had pulled a girl's hair in a supermarket, but there had been no other violent incidents. And Gylfi's son Orri had never hurt a fly. Matthew was right, developmentally impaired adults were not children.

The man who'd brought Jakob and his mother raisin cakes when Thóra and Matthew had left the room reappeared. With him was Jósteinn, and Thóra felt the hair rise on her arms. 'Jósteinn

145

heard that you were here and he wanted to have a few words with you. I understand you're doing some work for him, and you've already met. Is that all right with you?' Thóra didn't quite see how she could say no with Jósteinn staring over the staff member's shoulder, so she said yes and the man left them standing awkwardly in the middle of the corridor. 'I'll be in earshot if you need me,' he said before leaving.

'I'm so pleased that you took on this case.' Jósteinn smiled. He seemed to be staring at Thóra's stomach. 'So pleased.' His sour-smelling breath nearly made her gag, and she stepped back involuntarily, hitting the back of her head against the wall.

'Yes, well, I don't know yet whether it will have the intended result, but I believe there's reason to continue.' Her head hurt so much that she felt like crying. 'Actually, I feel I must inform you that due to your and Jakob's special circumstances, there's a limit to how much I can update you on the progress of the case. Many elements of what I find out will remain confidential between me, Jakob and his mother. That's non-negotiable.'

Jósteinn smiled, revealing his yellow teeth. His gaze had shifted to her arm now. 'I wouldn't suggest anything different.'

'How can I get a budget to you? It would be best for you to approve it before we go any further. I can also send you a breakdown of the time that's already been spent on the investigation. Do you have an e-mail account, or access to a fax machine?'

146

A dry rattle that was probably meant to be laughter emerged from Jósteinn's throat, and again his bad breath overwhelmed her. 'No chance. We don't have Internet or phone access. You'll have to ask them out front whether you can send a fax to me via the office. I think they could manage to waste one single sheet of paper on me.'

Thóra didn't like his sarcastic tone, or anything else about him. Once again he had too much gel in his hair. He really seemed to have gone to town with it. 'OK, I'll get them to agree to that.' Thóra hoped his isolation from the outside world didn't apply to banking matters. Perhaps he couldn't pay her after all; maybe he had never even intended to do so.

As if Jósteinn had read her thoughts, he announced, 'I'll get my supervisor to sort out all the payments, although that might not be within his official remit.' He pulled out a folded piece of paper and handed it to Thóra. 'This is his name and phone number. You can call him when you want to get paid.' He smiled again, now with his eyes closed. 'Or to reassure yourself that I have enough money.'

Thóra looked at the handwritten details. Each letter was drawn with great care and it looked as if Jósteinn had used an old-fashioned fountain pen. But she wouldn't need to keep the piece of paper because she was very familiar with the name, and even the number. *Ari Gunnarsson.* What a strange coincidence.

10

Sunday, 10 January 2010

'I hope Grandma and Grandpa will always be with us.' Sóley grinned happily and put down her toast, which was sagging beneath the weight of the jam slathered on it. 'It's much nicer having *them* in the garage, instead of a load of old boxes.'

Thóra returned her daughter's smile as she took the last plate from the dishwasher. The machine had been in constant use, apart from at the dead of night, since her parents had moved in the previous evening. Once the household was at full capacity the washing machine would be going every waking hour as well. 'Yes, it's a nice change, isn't it?'

'Orri speeterman!' Three members of the household were awake: Thóra, Sóley and Thóra's grandson, who was two and a half. Ever since someone had given him a Spiderman T-shirt, he thought he was a superhero. The boy still had some way to go before he could be considered a great orator, but he was starting to speak more.

Sóley opened her mouth to correct her nephew, but stopped and took a bite of toast instead. 'Oh, yeah. You need to help me find a costume. It's Kolla's birthday tomorrow and we're supposed to wear fancy dress.' It was doubtful that many people besides her mother would have understood her with her mouth full.

'When's the party?' Thóra knew it had to be today or tomorrow; Sóley had made it her speciality to let her mother know about such things with the smallest possible amount of notice.

'Later today.' Sóley swallowed her huge mouthful dramatically.

Although Thóra was sorely tempted to suggest that she go as the Invisible Man, with her costume being that she didn't turn up, she decided not to. 'Maybe Grandma and Grandpa can help you.'

Sóley agreed to this, beaming. 'When is everyone going to wake up, anyway? I think they've slept long enough.'

'Everyone's tired after last night. We'll just let them sleep.' All working together, Thóra and Matthew, her parents, Thóra's son Gylfi and his girlfriend Sigga had made space in the garage and set up a bed and other essentials for the newest members of the household. While they worked, Sóley had looked after Orri, but the toddler had kept trying to help with the move, which was met with limited enthusiasm by the movers. The garage had been crammed with stuff, and they hadn't had time to sort through everything that had been shoved in there. Instead, some of it had been put in the basement and the rest out in the shed in the garden. The shed hadn't been used much up to that point, but now it couldn't hold another thing. 'They'll be up before we know it, demanding coffee and cakes.'

'Speeterman.' Orri looked down at his chest, enraptured by the costumed man on his shirt. His breakfast lay untouched on the table in front of him, since he couldn't take his eyes off the superhero for long enough to eat.

'Spi-der-man, not speeterman.' Sóley had finally tired of the endless repetition. 'He's called Spi-der-man.'

'Speeterman.' Orri neither looked away from the image nor let his language coach distract him.

'Why can't he talk better, Mum?' Sóley's frustration didn't surprise Thóra; her daughter had long been comparing Orri to her best friend's sister, who was the same age, and the little boy was far behind her in terms of language development.

'He can say quite a few other things, so don't worry about it. He'll be chattering away before you know it, and then you'll miss the time when he hardly said anything.' Sóley obviously disagreed with this, so Thóra quickly changed the subject. 'Did you feed Mjása this morning?' Unexpectedly, the family cat hadn't shown itself when Thóra came into the kitchen; usually it was the very first one to demand food in the morning, and feeding it was how she started most of her days.

Sóley nodded and swallowed the last bite of toast. 'She couldn't wait for you. I think she was dying of hunger.'

'As always.' The cat ate several times a day and didn't appear any the worse for it, since despite its apparently bottomless appetite, it always stayed quite slim. If it was indoors and someone so much as walked past the kitchen it would be there, mewing pitifully in the hope of getting fed. 'It wouldn't have wanted to wait for sleepy old me.' Thóra hadn't been able to find her mobile phone when they were all finally able to go to bed, and she hadn't felt like calling it to locate it. As a result, she hadn't set an alarm and had slept late. Now she caught a glimpse of the phone under a crumpled tea towel on the kitchen sideboard. She reached for it and saw that while she was sleeping she'd missed a phone call, and received a text. That was unusual. No one ever called her at night nowadays; the time when she could expect messages from tipsy girlfriends downtown, telling her about late-night parties was long gone, and although she recalled those days fondly, she didn't miss them. Perhaps the same wasn't true of one of her girlfriends, who simply had to tell Thóra about some cute man she'd just met. The screen said *Number withheld* when Thóra tried to view the details of the call. She could see that it had been around three o'clock, long after she'd vanished into dreamland. The text had come five minutes later. It was sent from ja.is, which meant that there was no way of knowing whether it was from the same person as the missed call, although that seemed likely. If so, the person in question had been at a computer or accessed the Internet through their phone. Several of her friends had smartphones that they bragged about at every conceivable — and inconceivable — opportunity. She opened the text, though she thought she could guess what was in it: *Leave your man at home and come to the party* or *Guess who I went home with?* In fact the only thing that she couldn't predict was how many smiley faces would follow the message.

When she read the text she was so surprised that she dropped the phone into the sink with a *thunk*. Sóley looked at her inquisitively and even Orri tore his eyes from Spiderman for the first time since being put in his chair. Thóra reached for her mobile phone, which was lying between two coffee cups, thankfully dry and intact. The screen was still backlit and the black letters blared provocatively at her: *Who raped Lísa? Whose child is it?* Both very good questions, but the one uppermost in Thóra's mind was: 'Who sent this message?'

★ ★ ★

Matthew put down the phone, let himself fall back onto the pillow and yawned. 'Is the shower free?'

'The *shower?*' Thóra grabbed the phone back. 'Who cares about that? Don't you think this is weird? It's the third time I've got this kind of message; I received two the other day, but I ignored them because I thought they'd come to me by accident. One of them just said *Pregnant*, but the other was *How did Helena get burned as a child?* You have to admit it's pretty strange. I have them here if you want to see; luckily I didn't delete them.'

'Okay, no, no need. It is very odd, I'll certainly

152

admit that.' Matthew closed his eyes. 'I'm just not really awake yet.'

'No, obviously not.' The light of the phone's screen faded, although the text was still visible through the grey. 'The thing is, not many people know that I'm investigating this case. In fact, I can only think of two: the lazybones lawyer, Ari, and the woman who used to run the centre, Glódís. I'm fairly certain Jakob's mother didn't know where I was going with the questions about Lísa, and Jakob had no clue. And besides, he doesn't have access to either the Internet or a phone.'

'But why would Ari or Glódís send a message like this?' Matthew was starting to perk up, though he sneaked in a deep yawn. 'What's the purpose of these questions? To get you to dig around to find out who the father is? I wouldn't have thought either of them would want to draw attention to that. He admitted how he only skimmed through the files, and she was very open about how little she thought of her clients.'

'Well, I don't know, maybe one of them was drunk and wanted to stir things up.'

Matthew pushed himself up onto one elbow. 'Isn't that a bit far-fetched?' He cocked his head to listen, then smiled when he realized that the shower was free.

'Yes.' Thóra put her phone in her pocket. 'But it simply couldn't be anyone else. I can't think of anyone, anyway.'

'I don't suppose the woman, Glódís, discussed it with someone at work, and they then took it personally? Maybe a former employee of the centre who was unhappy with the outcome of the case?'

'Maybe.' Thóra relaxed her forehead and her worry-lines disappeared. 'I also had another idea. Sóley's going to her friend's birthday party where the kids are supposed to wear costumes, and it made me think of a possible explanation for the angel Jakob mentioned. The home burned down in October — the month of Halloween. It's becoming more and more popular and there may have been a fancy dress party in the neighbour-hood, even though the fire didn't occur on the thirty-first.'

Matthew looked unconvinced. 'I seriously doubt it.'

'But it wouldn't hurt to check.'

Matthew got up, put on a bathrobe and headed to the shower, and Thóra took out the centre's employee list and sat down with it in front of the computer. First she attempted to find any reference to a fancy dress party somewhere in the vicinity of the residence on the night of the fire, but she found nothing, not even when she widened the search parameters to include the entire city. The idea was probably too far-fetched, as Matthew had said. Sóley and Orri were staring transfixed at a cartoon on TV, so she had total peace and quiet, for the moment at least. Disappointed at not having got anywhere with her idea about the costume party, she decided to investigate whether any of the people on the list still worked for the Regional Office. This proved easier than she'd hoped. The office maintained a website that listed the names of its employees, although it didn't specify who did what, so she couldn't determine whether a particular person worked with Glódís at the main office or in a community residence in town. The office managed a total of twenty-eight homes, but only their directors were named on the site. Thóra recognized only one name from the list of former employees: Elías Þráinsson, who had been promoted, which must have been painful for Glódís to witness. Thóra suspected that despite her bitching and moaning about her workload, Glódís had it pretty easy where she was; at least, her phone hadn't rung once during her meeting with Thóra. Other phones in the office had hardly seemed to shut up. The fire must have been a blow to Glódís's career, even if only for the revelation of Lísa's pregnancy and the fact that the security system hadn't been set up yet. Of course Glódís couldn't be blamed for the fire, but someone had failed in their duties.

She saw that approximately half of those people on the list still worked in the Regional Office. Except for Elías, Thóra couldn't find out what jobs they did, despite searching everywhere, and she wondered whether it actually mattered. Since the person sending the messages was in the habit of covering their tracks, they'd hardly be likely to admit sending the messages or say what was on their mind. It might be more useful to stop trying to track down this mysterious texter and focus instead on what the former employees of the centre had to say about its operations. In this regard, Thóra strongly suspected that those who no longer worked for the Regional Office would speak more openly. On the other hand, she had no idea how she would track down these particular employees, most of whom had rather ordinary names, because she didn't have any other information about them except for what was stated on Glódís's list. She couldn't think of anything else but to turn to the Internet telephone directory. She was able to rule out a high proportion of the names from their job titles, which were listed in the directory.

She had just one name left when Matthew came up behind her and stroked her hair. She could smell his aftershave. She took hold of his hand and brought it to her lips, but as she turned to him she spied her mother, wearing a dressing gown that Thóra remembered from her childhood home. Even the belt, which was tied tightly around her waist, was showing signs of wear. In places the material had worn through to little more than threads, revealing a red, full-length velvet nightdress that looked as if it could melt icebergs. The effects of the aftershave instantly vanished.

'How's it going? Should I make us some coffee?' Thóra's mother smiled at them and walked purposefully into the kitchen without waiting for a reply. Shortly afterwards they heard her humming a tune that sounded familiar, but impossible to place. From the garage came the sound of Thóra's father whistling the same melody.

This was going to be an interesting living arrangement; maybe now wasn't a bad time for

her to make an appointment for that bikini
wax . . .

★   ★   ★

Margeir woke up miserable and thought at first
that he was hungover. His mind struggled to
orient itself. He felt as if he must have drunk an
enormous quantity of something — a whole box
of cheap white wine, maybe even two. But then
his head cleared and he remembered that he
hadn't drunk a drop. His headache was caused
by something else. He opened his eyes carefully
and avoided lifting his head from the pillow. He
lay like that for a few moments, staring at the
bedroom window, which was shut tight. The air
in the room was thick and heavy and even
though he should have long been impervious to
it, his nostrils burned with each inhalation,
forcing him to breathe through his mouth. In
order to do so, he had to push away the thought
of the poisonous grey cloud slipping past his
teeth and tongue before running along his soft
palate and down into his lungs. He felt nauseous
and tried to gather the strength to stand up and
open the window. Why was it closed, anyway?
Margeir always slept with it wide open, whatever
the weather. If he could have, he'd have removed
the outer wall during the night and allowed the
clear, cold air to waft around him. He must have
either forgotten to open the window or shut it
sometime during the night.

He reached for his alarm clock and turned it
towards him. It was the clock radio his brother

had given him as a Christmas present, thinking it appropriate since Margeir worked at a radio station. It was now nearly 9.30 a.m., which was about what he'd expected. He felt so rotten that he couldn't even tell if he was still tired. But the fog in his head was starting to clear and he could finally remember when he'd gone to sleep and what he'd been doing. There had been no drinking involved. He had rented a film from the corner shop, and when that had finished he had sat for two hours watching trashy TV. He hadn't gone to sleep until nearly three, which was not that late for him. Most single men his age were probably awake longer than he was on weekends, and the thought bothered him. This winter had been different to all the previous ones, and his desire to go out and have fun had vanished slowly but surely. All the good feelings alcohol used to stir in him now seemed so hollow and false; smiling and laughing ran completely contrary to how he felt. His job undoubtedly contributed to his misery; he had the whole disappointed, disillusioned nation on the line. When he felt this crappy, he simply had no desire to try to enjoy himself. He felt nothing but relief the first time he declined to go out on the town with his friends, and from that point on there was no going back; it became easier and easier just to stay at home. They had long since stopped calling him.

The alarm on the bedside table suddenly went off and Margeir stared at the device as his own voice blared out of it. It was a repeat of his show from the day before. For a second he felt as if he'd turned on the radio with his mind, but then he realized what had actually happened. He knew it was pathetic, but until things got better and he found a day job he didn't want to get into the habit of sleeping late. So he got up and attempted to occupy himself with something, every day of the week. Eight o'clock on weekdays and nine thirty on weekends.

His head felt lighter and the throbbing pain in his neck had dulled. He raised himself onto his elbows and sat up. The sooner he opened the window, the better. With the same technique that he used when jumping into a cold pool, he got to his feet without thinking or hesitating and took the two steps to the window. The latch was stiff but he finally managed to wrench the window open and suck in the pure, ice-cold air.

'Who is this?' His voice sounded lifeless in the worn-out mono radio behind him. 'Don't call if you're just going to breathe into the receiver.'

Margeir felt a chill run through his body but he didn't know whether it was because his lungs were now full of fresh, cold air or whether the repeat of the telephone call from the previous night's show was making him uncomfortable.

'Just wait. Just wait.' If he sounded a bit lacklustre on the radio, the voice of the person he was speaking to was completely lifeless. Hearing it now, he was certain it had been tampered with, probably via some sort of program that could be downloaded from the Internet. There was a particular mechanical tone to the voice that was even more apparent on the little radio than it had been through the station's telephone the previous evening. His own voice sounded again and his agitation was obvious to him, although others would hardly have noticed it . . . hopefully. He sounded arrogant and offhand: 'For what? For you to get to the point? What's on your mind, friend?'

'The reckoning.'

'What reckoning?' Now the fake toughness was gone from Margeir's voice. It had become clear to him that this was the weirdo who had started calling in on almost every show. If this continued, it could be called harassment, but Margeir wasn't certain the police would agree, nor could he see how a telephone restraining order would be implemented. Especially since Margeir would never involve the police in this. Not if the nutter on the telephone was insinuating what Margeir suspected he was.

'You know perfectly well what I mean. Justice finds everyone in the end.' Loud inhalation, long exhalation. 'And there's no escape.' The caller hung up and a loud dialling tone followed, until the engineer realized Margeir wasn't going to add anything clever and put on a song.

His headache was growing steadily more intense. Margeir sat carefully back down on his bed. Sinking slowly into his pillow, he turned off the radio, though he actually longed to push it off the table. As he did so, he spotted his mobile phone lying next to the radio and reached for it thinking perhaps he remembered the phone having woken him in the night. As he fiddled with the buttons in search of calls that he might have missed he suddenly remembered what had

160

happened: he had received a text, a message from ja.is that had disturbed his pleasant sleep and troubled him enough to make him get up, go to the window and shut and lock it. Although he was in no mood to read the message again, his fingers ran over the keys and opened the text, completely against his will.

The reckoning is coming. Is there someone outside?

11

Monday, 11 January 2010

Monday mornings were frequently chaotic at the office. It was as if they all had difficulty registering that the weekend was over and a new work week was starting. They wandered in and out of their offices as if they were trying to remember what they were supposed to be doing, or hoping that one more cup of coffee would get their brains in gear. Thóra was no exception, least of all this Monday; work was the last thing she wanted to do.

She had realized when she started awake at the sound of the alarm that she was alone in the bed. That hadn't particularly surprised her; generally Matthew woke long before she did, went out for a run and was nearly halfway through it by the time she came to her senses. Today, however, he had not only already returned but had also taken a shower and was neatly dressed and ready for the day. He stood at the end of the bed, staring pleadingly at her. 'You have to take me with you to work. I'll do anything. I'll even help Bella.' Thóra rubbed the sleep from her eyes and muttered something garbled that could have been interpreted as neither yes nor no. 'I simply cannot bear another minute of your father's whistling. I'll get used to it, I know, but right now it's driving me nuts.'

She let him come with her to work. Thóra's parents saw to getting the kids up, giving them breakfast and sending them to school, so she managed to get ready more quickly than usual. The expansion of the household did have its advantages, and Thóra bid her parents goodbye with a kiss, feeling exceptionally happy with life despite the whistling that drifted out after them as they left the house. It didn't hurt that Matthew had already got the car ready. This was one of Thóra's least favourite jobs, maybe because she usually ended up with her arms full of snow. Although the garage had been full of boxes and there had been no immediate plans to tackle the clearing-out project, she'd always held onto the notion of parking the car in it one day. This distant dream, which frequently popped into her head on cold winter mornings, was now a thing of the past — for the next two months at least.

Thóra's restlessness couldn't, therefore, be attributed to the morning having started badly. She simply hated the fact that the weekend had somehow unexpectedly turned into a new work week. Until she could properly get into gear, she would just have to occupy herself with something; the only question was what that might actually be. She couldn't get started on any of the cases awaiting her so she scrolled through her e-mails in search of messages that she'd forgotten or had left to answer later. But even that was problematic and in the end she gave up and shut down her e-mail altogether. She still had to go over the firm's unpaid bills, but that would have to wait until the afternoon, or even tomorrow morning. She needed to do something more creative, or more exciting, until midday, by which time she would have regained her vigour.

Thóra turned away from the computer and the stack of bills. Matthew lay on a little sofa at the other end of the office, his feet hanging over one of the arms and a laptop on his knees, doubtless reading the news from home. After the weekend, it had crossed Thóra's mind that perhaps they should shut themselves in the office in order to have a little time to themselves, but looking at how Matthew's frame filled the sofa, the idea seemed suddenly less feasible. Besides, the lock on the door would never keep Bella out if she were in the mood to disturb them.

Thóra crumpled an empty, torn envelope into a ball and threw it gently at Matthew to draw his attention away from his computer. 'How would you like to pop up to the Ministry of Justice with me to check whether the father of the autistic boy can be persuaded to tell me something? We can stop off at a café and have a restorative drink.'

Matthew caught the ball and looked as though he was considering tossing it back, but eventually decided against it. 'Coffee sounds wonderful. That swill you serve in the lobby is completely undrinkable.' Matthew grimaced at the cup resting on the coffee table in front of him. It had stopped steaming soon after the first sip. 'If I didn't know any better I might have thought you'd used the grounds twice.' He stood up. 'Not

164

that that would be completely unheard of in this office.' He tossed the crumpled paper at Thóra, hitting her on top of her head. 'One-all.'

★　★　★

The ministry was located on Skuggasund Street — from *skuggi*, 'shadow' — and it was impossible not to wonder how the street had got its name. The area didn't look particularly dark or shadowy, and besides, the street had been given the name before the buildings were put up. Maybe the namer had had the foresight to realize that the buildings on both sides of the street would shed prominent shadows across the site where the ministry stood. Or perhaps the name had been given because the street had been condemned to stand in the eternal shadow of the National Theatre. In any case, as soon as they entered the ministry's interior, things brightened up, but as they moved further into the building, a peculiar sensation descended on Thóra again; now it felt as if they'd gone back many decades in time, since the building's architecture bore such strong witness to the middle of the previous century. However, this feeling vanished when they were shown into the office corridor after the boy's father had told the receptionist that he would see them. In the corridor, they could have been standing in absolutely any contemporary building; they walked past one office after another, all kitted out in the same style: a desk with a computer and a clunky telephone, the walls lined with stuffed IKEA bookshelves. When they reached the right office they expected it to be like all the others, but they were wrong; this one was much larger and more luxurious.

'Please come in.' Einvarður Tryggvason rose from his massive office chair and walked over to them. His voice was gentle and deep, his handshake firm and his hands soft. His whole appearance was spotless, in fact: his dark, elegant suit appeared to shine and it was as if he'd just got up from the barber's chair after a haircut and a close shave. His smile revealed white teeth that weren't completely straight, but which gave him a character that defined the difference between a good-looking 'real' person and a model. Strange as it might have seemed, it was precisely this imperfection that made him appear perfect. It struck Thóra how well this man would fit into politics and she wondered why he'd chosen the bureaucratic system rather than parliament or a ministerial position.

'I was extremely glad when they told me you wanted to see me,' Tryggvason continued, 'because I'd heard that Jakob's case was being reinvestigated, and your name was mentioned in connection with that.' He smiled politely at Matthew. 'But I've heard nothing about you.'

Thóra introduced Matthew by saying that he assisted her with various assignments and was bound to the same confidence as she was. She then added that in both their cases, however, that confidence came with the caveat that if anything came to light demonstrating or supporting Jakob's innocence, it would be used in the report she'd submit with her petition to reopen the case. The man's expression didn't change and he said he had no objections to that; everyone surely wanted the case to be resolved and for the right man to bear the responsibility. Thóra did notice a shadow cross his smooth face when he spoke of the criminal and realized that behind the formal, polished courtesy lay an individual who, naturally, felt anger, happiness, sorrow and all the other emotions that shape a personality. 'Have a seat and I shall answer whatever I can, as long as the questions are within the bounds of propriety.' He followed this with yet another Colgate smile, but his eyes were no longer twinkling. 'I've requested coffee for us, but if you would rather have tea I can fix that.'

It was Monday morning, so it had to be coffee. Einvarður sat carefully, making sure not to sit on his jacket, and gave the knot of his tie a slight tug, as if to assure himself that it was still centred and tightly secured. 'Before we begin I'd like to ask you one thing that is understandably of great importance to me: do you think there's a real chance that Jakob has been wrongfully detained?' Einvarður stared into Thóra's eyes as if he had a lie detector in his own dark blue ones.

'Yes, I do.' Thóra didn't need to pretend. The more she considered it, the less likely it seemed that poor, simple Jakob had been responsible. 'I have significant doubts about the statements he made during his interrogations and in court, and I also feel that he's very unlikely to have been able to conceive of and carry out such a complicated deed.'

167

'It really wasn't that complicated, surely?' Einvarður's expression was suddenly fierce. 'You just pour out some petrol and light it.'

'It required a bit more than that, if you think about it: you'd have to get hold of the petrol and leave all the fire doors open, and I would seriously question whether Jakob even knows what a fire door is. If his version of events is viewed with his disability in mind, my hunch is that he saw the perpetrator, but without being able to identify who it was. And there's another detail that raises questions, which is too complicated to go into here. But in a nutshell, I feel that he doesn't have the mental ability to have pulled this off without succumbing to the fire himself.'

Einvarður had listened to Thóra attentively without giving any visible indication of what he thought of her explanations. 'The police, the prosecution and two different courts disagree with you.'

'I'm aware of that,' Thóra replied without any irony or irritation. She hadn't expected the man to have anything but doubts about her investigation and was actually extremely surprised that he'd even agreed to meet her and Matthew. 'That doesn't change the fact that this is my conclusion after studying the case, and that's why I have decided to look into more than just the files that form the basis of those parties' opinion. This visit is part of that.'

'Who do you believe did start the fire, if it wasn't Jakob?' The man's voice was devoid of any feeling as he said these words, which

168

somehow gave them more weight than if they'd been spoken in anger.

'I haven't formed an opinion on that yet, but obviously I hope to do so. In a petition to reopen a case, there's no stronger position than being able to categorically identify the guilty party.'

'And am I to understand from this visit that you believe me to have been involved?' Einvarður smiled jovially.

'As I said, I haven't formed an opinion as to who might have been responsible. I don't yet have enough evidence to do that.' Thóra smiled back at him, but Einvarður paled slightly. He had clearly expected Thóra to laugh off this ridiculous notion. 'But no, I haven't come here because I think you're responsible. I was hoping that you could give me a better insight into life at the home, and whether there was anything about it that seemed off-kilter, not as it should have been.'

Einvarður seemed to have regained his composure and was now as slick as before. 'Well, that's a difficult question, I must admit. We just visited our son and didn't really follow the goings-on at the residence very closely; after all, the idea was for the residents to have their own place of refuge, one they could look on as their own apartment.'

'When you say we, do you mean you and your wife?' Thóra assumed that the man was married; he was wearing a rather broad gold band. There wasn't a scratch to be seen on its highly polished surface.

'Yes.' He reached for a large framed

photograph on the shelf behind him. 'And our daughter.' He handed Thóra the photo. 'This is Fanndís, my wife, and our daughter Lena. And this is Tryggvi.' He pointed at the photo, leaving a fingerprint over the face of his deceased son on the otherwise spotless glass. 'No one should have to experience such a thing.'

Thóra took the photo and didn't know whether he meant having such a sick child or losing him under such tragic circumstances. She assumed he meant the latter. The family photo had been taken indoors, and in fact the background suggested that they were in their son's apartment at the centre. Father and son sat on a little sofa, while Einvarður's wife leaned on the sofa arm next to her son and the daughter stood straight as an arrow at the other end. They were all strikingly beautiful. Einvarður appeared relaxed even though he was dressed in an even smarter suit than the one he had on now. His arms were around the shoulders of his wife and son. Fanndís, also dressed stylishly in a salmon-pink shift dress, smiled radiantly at the camera. Their daughter was wearing a white full-length dress with a yellow headband, which made her look rather like a Roman priestess. The children each resembled one of their parents; the daughter looked like her blonde, exceptionally beautiful mother and the son like his dark-haired father. They all looked as if they could work as models, except perhaps the son who, although very good-looking, was lacking a little in concentration. The other three were looking straight at the camera and smiling, but he looked a bit off to the side, staring at something outside the frame that was attracting his attention more than the photographer. His hands were also in an unnatural position, the fingers of both tangled together as if in a peculiar prayer. In addition, his fingers seemed to be slightly less in focus than everything else in the photo, as if they'd been moving quickly. Unlike the rest of his family, he was dressed in casual clothing.

'Excuse my rudeness,' said Thóra. 'I should have started by expressing my sympathy. I'm not going to pretend to understand how you feel; I just can't imagine it. It must have been horrible.' She handed Matthew the photograph. 'Your son was really very handsome.'

'Yes, he was.' Einvarður took the photo from Matthew, who had had a good look at it. 'But that was the only good card fate dealt him. Mentally, he was in his own little world, and none of us who cared about him could access it.' He put the picture back on the shelf, making sure to position it so that it faced straight ahead.

'Did he never express himself — never speak or use any kind of sign language?' Thóra wanted to know whether there was any point in asking whether the boy had told his parents anything useful about life at the care home.

Einvarður shook his head. 'No, he never said a word. He understood what people said, or so we believe, but he never communicated. He was extremely interested in illustrated educational books but we never knew for sure whether he read them or just looked at the pictures. Sometimes he stared at the same page for a long time.'

'But do you think he was aware of his environment?'

'No, I doubt it. At least, I don't think he understood or noticed what happened around him in the way that we would. My wife disagreed with me, of course. In the twenty-two years that we had Tryggvi, we never could decide about that, which is maybe the best indication of how incomprehensible his life was, at least to those of us who are supposedly normal.'

'So your wife thought it was possible to reach him?' Maybe she was better informed than Tryggvi's father.

Einvarður placed his palms flat on the desk and leaned forward conspiratorially. 'She thought so, and she never gave up on the idea that it might be possible to find a way of treating Tryggvi as, or training him to become, a fully functional member of society — or close to it, at least. It seemed impossible to me, but obviously I didn't want to dash her hopes. Of course, secretly I shared her dream — I even had modest hopes of my own. Stranger things have certainly happened.' He leaned back in his seat. 'We'll never find out whether or not it would have worked.'

'But you must have visited him and been inside the home, even though he didn't live there long. How did you find the facilities and the staff's treatment of your son? According to Jakob, the residents were miserable, but I don't know whether that view is coloured by his own unhappiness at having to move there.'

Einvarður raised his dark eyebrows, which, were it not for one or two stray hairs, would look

172

almost as if they'd been shaped. 'I certainly wasn't aware of that and I visited my son every other day, usually. Even though the place was off the beaten track, I tried to go after work at least twice a week, and we also went both days on the weekends. Fanndís and Lena visited him even more than I did. His mother went virtually every day.'

'But you didn't notice anything? Nothing that struck you as odd, or that might have suggested that the residents were unhappy?'

'Well, many of them clearly didn't feel great, but that had nothing to do with the residence itself. Several of them were either in pain or had difficulty expressing themselves, and Jakob probably took this as evidence of distress. He'd only lived with his mother before he moved to the home, if I remember correctly.'

Thóra nodded; she'd come to a similar conclusion herself. She considered telling him about Ari's insinuation that Tryggvi had jumped the queue when it came to the admissions procedure, but decided to leave it alone. There was probably something in it, but she couldn't see what it might have to do with the case. 'But your son — did he seem content?'

'As far as I could tell. At first he was fairly agitated and unhappy at being in a new environment, but he'd started to recover and become his old self again. You said you'd read through the case files, which means you probably know that Tryggvi's high-level autism made him extremely sensitive to change. He can't . . . ' The man corrected himself, embarrassed. 'Excuse me — he couldn't, I meant to say. But anyway, he couldn't bear unexpected noise, movement in the corner of his eye, strangers, changes in diet; he hated being in the car and was even worse about boarding planes, so our dreams of taking him on a nice beach holiday were unrealistic, to say the least. He wanted everything set in stone, and he reacted to change very badly, whatever guise it came in.'

'Did Tryggvi ever go to the others' apartments — did he visit the other residents, or decide to have a look around? Maybe not at first, but after a bit of time had passed?'

'Absolutely not. He never took the initiative as far as human interaction was concerned, and in fact he avoided it as much as possible; he always stayed in his own apartment unless he was forced to leave it. The staff definitely weren't doing their jobs properly if they were allowing him to go visiting — and I very much doubt that was happening. Who says that Tryggvi visited other apartments? Jakob?' His expression hardened. 'Are you trying to pin this on my son?'

Thóra shook her head. 'That wasn't why I asked. Although their circumstances were different, your son was in the same boat as Jakob, in the sense that starting that fire required organizational abilities that neither of them possessed. We're not trying to blame Tryggvi. On the other hand, he was male, and I'm currently trying to draw up a list of men who can be exonerated from having fathered the child that was conceived at the care home. I don't know whether you were told, but Lísa Finnbjörnsdóttir, the young comatose girl, was pregnant.'

A crack appeared in Einvarður's polished appearance, revealing a glimpse of the man beneath. 'You're joking.'

'No. My jokes are generally in slightly better taste. Actually, I'm surprised that you're surprised, because according to my information, you were fully informed of it.'

The man grew agitated, raking his fingers through his hair, his eyes wide. 'I didn't mean that. I was so surprised that it came out wrong.' He dropped his hand. 'I heard about it after the fire occurred and the investigation started. I just haven't been able to absorb it still. My apologies for how ridiculous that sounded.'

'You do know that there's DNA from the foetus, or at least there was, but they need genetic material from the father to compare it with.'

'You're welcome to take a sample from me to rule me out. I personally suggested that the same be done with my son — I even paid for it out of my own pocket.' He flushed slightly at his hairline. 'The girl's parents asked me to help them put a stop to any further investigation of this case and I pulled a few strings. In order to prevent any possible suspicion later on that I'd done something out of line, I wanted it to be quite clear that what I was doing had nothing to do with trying to cover Tryggvi's tracks. The results of my son's test also effectively ruled me out as the child's father; there was too little correspondence between Tryggvi's DNA and that of the foetus. But as I say, if you want to run another test I'm happy to cooperate.'

This ruling-out made sense as long as Tryggvi was definitely Einvarður's son; Thóra decided not to raise the possibility that he wasn't. 'But why did you take it upon yourself to do such a thing for the girl's parents? It's an odd thing to propose in a matter that serious.'

'I just wasn't completely myself at the time. That's really all I can tell you. Well, that and maybe the fact that the girl's parents were grief-stricken and pursued it so insistently. I feel I must mention that I didn't act in isolation; the police knew all about it, as well as the prosecutor. We all agreed unanimously that I should grant their request. Her father had already been cleared of any suspicion.' Einvarður appeared very keen to convince them that he had been guided purely by the parents' wishes, and it was indeed difficult to imagine what other reason he might have had. Unless he'd been trying to ensure that Jakob's investigation and trial should proceed as quickly as possible. 'Believe me, I'll do anything I can for you if it helps uncover who abused this young woman; and indeed if it reveals that someone other than Jakob started the fire. I didn't connect these two appalling incidents at the time, but I can completely see where you're going with this investigation and why.'

'All and any help is much appreciated, of course. If you happen to think of anything, now that you've had a bit of time to distance yourself from these events . . . '

'Is it all right if I tell my wife about Lísa? She spent more time there than I did and she might have noticed something or be able to think of something. She took the death of our son very badly and it didn't do anything to help her condition; my wife is terribly sensitive.'

'I don't see why not, as long as she keeps the information to herself. If your wife is willing to speak to me herself, that would also be very much appreciated.'

'That's easy. She's generally at home. She stopped working when Tryggvi was born and our daughter still lives with us, so that arrangement still suits her even though things are easier and calmer for her than when Tryggvi was alive. I'll ask her to call you.' He took the business card Thóra handed him. 'Have you spoken to the filmmaker?'

'Which filmmaker?' Thóra had seen no mention of a filmmaker either in the court documents or in anything else she'd read.

'There was a young man gathering material for a documentary about the centre's work. It was all approved by the Regional Office and was going well, I think. The man was there all the time and I'm sure he has a lot of material you might be able to access. Who knows — maybe there'll be something of use to you buried in there somewhere. And what's more, I bet he got a good sense of what it was like there in relation to other similar homes. I'm sure he could reassure you that everything was just fine.' With this, Einvarður skilfully avoided any further discussion of what might have happened to Lísa. No doubt he realized how callous this seemed because he quickly added, in a graver tone: 'I

177

hope you find the person who did this to Lísa, and if Jakob is innocent of starting the fire, I would be the first to celebrate if you find the bastard responsible. On the other hand, if Jakob is guilty, I sincerely hope that he's locked up in Sogn until the day he dies.'

12

Monday, 11 January 2010

Thóra left their meeting with Tryggvi's father feeling reasonably pleased. Not much new information had emerged, of course, but Einvarður had promised to be ready to assist her, which was something of a step forward. If she needed data or information, he'd see that she got it. Thóra reflected that it must be nice being part of that mysterious elite who always seemed to get their own way. Einvarður's offer wasn't subject to any provisos that this information would depend on others' consent, nor was it an offer to explore whether he could help in some way. He simply intended to help them out, and appeared convinced that he'd be able to do so. Thóra was unused to this level of cooperation and thought for a moment that she'd misunderstood him — not because of his being so certain that he could get hold of what she needed, but because he appeared to be prepared to hand the material over unconditionally. Useful information went hand in hand with power, which people were seldom keen to share with others. Thus it could be difficult to extract it from certain people, and it was rare to hear of it being served up on a plate. The more usual scenario would have been for the man to make her chase him before he reluctantly shared the information in order to emphasize his own importance. Maybe Einvarður's amenability was the reason he hadn't tried to claw his way up the ladder in politics.

In an additional act of collaboration, before saying goodbye to Thóra and Matthew, Einvarður had called his wife and informed her that she should follow his example and provide Thóra with all the assistance she might need. Thóra sat listening but adopted the expression of someone who, though forced to be in earshot of a couple's conversation, is so distracted that it goes completely in one ear and out the other. Of course, she heard everything that Einvarður said as well as the faint sound of his wife's replies, though she couldn't distinguish the individual words. The message was clearly delivered as an instruction, yet it was completely free of any unpleasant or bullying tone. Nevertheless, it was abundantly clear that Einvarður expected his wishes to be followed. He then informed Thóra and Matthew that Fanndís could meet them whenever it suited them, scribbled her mobile number on a slip of paper and handed it to Thóra. As she took hold of it, instead of releasing his grip on it, he looked resolutely into her eyes. 'We all want the right man to be convicted — in fact I insist upon it.' Once he'd made his declaration, he let go of the paper and Thóra sat there unsure about whether his comment was meant generally, or was directed at her alone. As they parted, she muttered something about that being fair enough.

Matthew hadn't understood much of what had transpired at the meeting, but he was slowly but surely putting together the main details of the case. 'What do you suppose it's like to have such a severely disabled child?'

'Difficult, no doubt.' The snow crunched beneath Thóra's feet. In more heavily populated areas, the layer of white had probably already turned to slush, but here few people had been out and about, even though it was nearly noon. 'Difficult, and sad — but it must be rewarding, too. Small victories become big ones, and it's amazing how people can adapt to different circumstances and accept their lot in life.'

'You're sounding quite philosophical.'

'That's your question making me think that way.' They crossed the street towards the car. 'To be honest, I actually have no idea — I can't even get my head around it.' This was the honest truth; since accepting the case, Thóra had frequently, if unintentionally, found herself wondering what Orri's life would be like if he were trapped inside an undeveloped body or mind — though she always pushed away these thoughts as soon as they appeared. She'd also wondered whether some subconscious prejudice was clouding her vision, but she was pretty certain that that wasn't the case. In her opinion, prejudice fed on hatred, and in this case she felt quite the opposite: she found it unbearably sad to think about these young, severely disabled people who missed out on so much of life. It was also perfectly clear to her that they must be hurt by this kind of attitude; not to be considered as individuals, but instead defined by their disability. She resolved to cultivate a more informed manner of thinking and was sure this would help her with her investigation. 'I could really do with something proper to eat.' She looked up along Hverfisgata Street, hoping to spot a restaurant. 'I don't know whether I'm depressed or starving, but I need some sustenance.'

They went over to a little café-restaurant nearby and when Thóra saw on the menu hanging in the window that bacon and eggs were on offer, that settled it. Matthew wasn't quite as excited. The place was decorated with old books on shelves that appeared even older and on the verge of collapsing. There were very few tables inside. Thóra found the place cosy, but Matthew disagreed, quietly muttering that he doubted very much if the dust was regularly wiped off the books. Thóra hoped for the employees' sake that this was indeed the case — besides, it would hardly be great from the diners' perspective if the staff were constantly stirring up dust that could otherwise have lain on top of the old tomes, troubling no one. However, she said nothing, having long ago realized that Matthew preferred the places where he ate to maintain the same standards of hygiene as an operating theatre. 'Just be sure you don't bite the books,' she told him. He gave her a dirty look before studying the menu in search of something boiled to eat.

'I think we should contact Fanndís, Einvarður's wife, straight away. Strike while the iron's hot.' Thóra watched the girl at the counter pour them two cups of coffee. 'They might change their minds if we wait.'

'Do you want me to go with you?' Matthew didn't seem too thrilled at the prospect. 'I don't

182

have much to add, and she might find it disturbing, me just sitting there silently between you.'

'It didn't seem to bother her husband. He spoke freely even though you didn't say anything.'

'Women are different. I'm absolutely certain she'll trust you with more information if you go on your own. I don't quite know where to put myself when these disabilities are discussed. Unfortunately I seem to understand everything that's said about them, even though I'd prefer not to.'

The coffee was placed on the table in front of them and they remained politely silent as the waitress served them. When she was finished, Thóra spoke up again. 'It'll be fine. You get used to the topic quickly. And maybe she's the kind of woman who gets all aflutter when there's a handsome man in the vicinity and says more than she meant to.' She took a sip of the aromatic coffee. 'Besides, I don't want to go alone.'

They finished their food, which had been served at remarkable speed and had disappeared just as quickly into their bellies. Thóra felt much better afterwards, and it didn't hurt that the food had been particularly good. Matthew had even cleared his plate, after a cautious start. 'They won't have to wash up after us,' said Thóra, looking at her gleaming plate, 'so maybe they'll have time to dust off the books.' She smiled at Matthew as she dug out Fanndís's number.

★　★　★

Lena watched her mother put down the phone and stare into space. She had rubbed her ear continually as she spoke. After Lena's brother Tryggvi had died, her mother's nervousness had increased so much that one ear had turned almost permanently crimson from all the rubbing. 'Who was it?' Lena tried to appear uninterested.

'Huh?' Her mother looked at her in surprise and for a moment Lena had the feeling she didn't recognize her.

'On the phone. Who was calling?' Lena bit into the apple she'd chosen from the fruit drawer in the fridge and let the large steel door fall shut.

'Oh . . . ' The pout her mother's mouth made to form this pointless word lasted longer than necessary. Her lips, painted a pale red, formed a circle around the cavity of her mouth as Lena waited for more words to tumble out. 'Yes, you mean that . . . It was a woman your father wants me to meet.' Her fingers reached for her scalp and started fussing with her perfect hair. 'You should wash apples before you eat them, Lena. They're sprayed with pesticides and you don't want to swallow that stuff.'

Lena ignored the advice and swallowed a bite of apple. 'A woman that Dad wants you to meet? Who is she? And why?'

'She's a lawyer. And it's nothing that you need to worry about.' Her mother twisted her mouth into a smile that was anything but convincing. 'Aren't you going to spend the day studying? You don't have many days left until your exams.'

Lena shrugged. 'Later. There's no hurry.' She went over to the kitchen island and sat on a high stool opposite her mother. 'Are you two talking about getting divorced?' She tried to say this nonchalantly, as if she didn't care. Her father was always at work these days, which was kind of unusual and suggested that something wasn't right, though Lena hadn't actually suspected there might be anything to worry about until she'd heard her parents arguing about a woman at the ministry who her mother wanted him to send on leave. Her mother had never involved herself in matters concerning her father's employees, and it suggested something was up. What did it matter to her mother if one woman was at the ministry or not? The part of the argument she'd heard before they became aware of her presence also suggested that this wasn't just about work: her mother had said that the woman had made a fool of her, was laughing at her; that her father was a complete idiot to believe her story. No, there was no question that the woman was some slut her father had fallen for, maybe precisely because of how different she must have been from Lena's perfect mother. Lena couldn't actually blame her father for seeking out a less frosty embrace.

'Of course not. Come on.' Her mother let her hand fall away from her bright red ear and put both her palms on the granite worktop between them. Lena could sympathize; the surface was cold to the touch and she'd often done the same thing to steady herself — sometimes with her palms, although several times she'd laid her cheek to the surface. 'It's to do with Tryggvi. Something that your father thinks is important but that I don't completely understand.'

'What about Tryggvi?' Lena's mouth went dry. Did she have to open old wounds? 'I thought that was finished. You promised.'

Her mother pressed her hands so firmly against the stone that they turned white, and the bones stood out even more than usual. 'Well, it's not directly about Tryggvi, it's about Jakob.'

'Jakob?' Lena put down the apple. It was no longer delicious, but heavy and awkward in her hand. 'Are you joking? Jakob who started the fire?' What was wrong with her father? He could behave oddly sometimes, but this was weird even for him. He knew exactly what her mother had gone through when Tryggvi had died, and now he was going to risk setting that all off again.

'Your father says that this lawyer is investigating whether Jakob is truly guilty. She's quite certain that there is some doubt.'

'She said *some* doubt? Not serious doubt?'

Her mother shut her eyes and it looked to Lena as if she were counting to ten. Then she opened her eyes and stared past her daughter. 'I don't know, Lena. Maybe there really is serious doubt over his guilt.'

'Who started the fire if it wasn't that sicko Jakob?' Her voice sounded screechier than usual. A new trial and rehashing of Tryggvi's death would send her mother over the edge and cause her father to retreat behind a protective wall of silence. This time the idea of divorce wouldn't eventually drift away like it had before. Last time, their marriage had hung by a thread and it wasn't until recently that they'd begun to resemble their former selves again — except that

186

now family life no longer revolved around Tryggvi's difficulties. Lena felt a bit guilty. She'd been terribly fond of her brother, maybe not quite as much as her mother, but probably just as much as her father. The problem was only that he'd displayed no affection in return, which had adversely affected the relationship between father and son but appeared to have had no effect on her mother. Maybe what had kept her going all that time was her steadfast belief that it would one day be possible to draw Tryggvi out of his shell. Lena felt sad at the thought that this might actually have happened if her brother had lived longer. 'Who else could have done such a thing?'

'She didn't say.' Her mother was growing annoyed and clearly didn't want to discuss the subject any further. 'She's coming here soon and maybe then things will become clearer. It's probably just some nonsense that your father took seriously.'

'Why does this lawyer want to talk to you? Can't they just leave you in peace?'

'You'd have thought so, but apparently not. I have no idea why she wants to meet us. Maybe she's speaking to all the parents.'

'Maybe she thinks Tryggvi started the fire.' Lena regretted her words as soon as she'd spoken them, but now there was no turning back. 'Maybe she knows he liked fire.'

Her mother opened and shut her mouth twice before saying: 'Finish your apple. You don't have to waste the whole thing for one mouthful.'

Lena wondered whether she should let her

mother get away with this, or whether she should repeat the question. 'I'm not hungry.' Nonetheless, she picked up the apple, brought it to her lips and sucked juice from it. 'When is this woman coming?'

Her mother glanced at her watch, which hung loosely from her wrist. She'd always been slim, but Tryggvi's death had deprived her of her appetite for several months and she still hadn't regained her former weight. 'In half an hour. You should get dressed.'

Lena looked down at her checked pyjamas. 'Me? I'm not going to meet any lawyer,' she retorted, then immediately regretted it, because of course she was dying to know what the woman had to say. It was unlikely that she'd be able to persuade her mother to tell her anything about what they discussed, and if their home life was about to turn to shit again, she wanted to know why. The sooner the better.

'Don't be silly. Of course you're not, but she doesn't need to come to the house and see a teenager hanging around here in her pyjamas in the middle of the day.'

'I'm almost twenty-one, Mum. I finished puberty several years ago, in case you hadn't noticed.'

'Of course I noticed. Everyone noticed.' Her mother grew angrier with every word. Lena was well aware that it had nothing to do with her; she was simply a conversational punchbag her mother used to calm herself down. When Fanndís spoke again she was calmer; her ear was even almost a normal colour again. 'Seriously,

Lena. Change your clothes.'

'Jesus.' Lena stood up and took the apple with her. She'd been planning to jump in the shower and get dressed anyway, but had been stubbornly putting it off just because of her mother's pushiness. Lena had long since grown used to the fact that everything had to look good, no matter how much grief or anger might be simmering underneath. When she was seven she'd dropped a full tin of biscuits on her foot on the Feast of St Þorlákur and crushed the nail of her big toe, but she'd still had to wear patent leather shoes on Christmas Eve even though the pain made her eyes water with every step. Tryggvi had always been well dressed and groomed even though it hadn't mattered to him. Once Lena had suggested that she and her mother go to the Kringlan Shopping Centre and buy Tryggvi a tracksuit, which he'd find so much more comfortable than stiff blue jeans. Her mother had got extremely annoyed with her — tracksuits were for gymnastics, she'd said, not for everyday wear. Maybe her mother had been completely different before Tryggvi had come into the world; Lena didn't know, because she was younger than him.

The shower perked Lena up; she'd made it slightly too cold to be comfortable. Her lethargy was washed away, leaving behind a clear, alert mind in a body that broke out in goose bumps when she emerged from the shower — every-where except on her calves, where she'd had a skin graft. The patch was just as smooth and shiny as when the skin had been fixed there.

She'd been ten years old at the time. She didn't know whether it was because the new skin didn't react to cold or whether goose bumps simply didn't form there. Maybe it was a combination of both. Lena hurried to dry her calf. She didn't want to remember it, didn't want to relive being burned, didn't want to think that because of it she wouldn't ever be able to wear a short dress on a night out like her friends. And least of all she didn't want to remember how Tryggvi had liked fire; fire that had hurt her so badly. Her parents had forbidden her ever to mention his fascination with it. That ban must still be in place. It had been introduced when the community residence caught fire.

Downstairs the doorbell rang. Lena hurriedly wrapped a large, full-length towel around herself. Of course the lawyer couldn't see through the ceiling, but any protection was good. The woman mustn't find out about this. For Lena's sake, and for her parents', but most of all for the sake of their memories of Tryggvi.

13

Monday, 11 January 2010

Margeir tried hard to hide his desperation but it was difficult to rein it in, and the tiny beads of sweat he could feel forming on his forehead weren't helping. 'But might you be making changes soon? A new schedule for the spring, which could open up the possibility of moving the show?'

The station manager's face showed no sign of sympathy. Behind him hung a poster that declared: *It's never too late to become the person you could have been.* Underneath the text smiled a toothless old man, a thick textbook in his arms. Even though it would be a few decades before Margeir was anything like as old as the subject of the picture, he felt compassion for the old man nonetheless. It would probably be simpler to take a college course than to deal with his boss; at school at least you dealt with lots of different teachers, not one person who controlled everything. The small, private radio station had a monarch, who now sat before Margeir and didn't seem inclined to do him any favours. If his proposal found no favour with the manager, there was no higher court to which he could appeal.

'You were offered an earlier time slot when I hired you. You didn't want it then.' The manager shrugged. 'The early bird catches the worm.'

'I certainly *did* want it. I just couldn't take it, because I had another job besides the radio show. But I gave that up ages ago, so things have changed now. It would make such a difference if I could have a morning or afternoon slot. Since I was offered as much last winter, I thought I'd ask whether the offer was still open.'

The manager scowled. 'It's not quite that easy, mate. Things have changed a lot since you started.'

Margeir knew he meant the recession, which had swallowed everything in its path. But it was unfair to use it as an excuse; unlike other industries, radio had actually been positively impacted by the financial crisis. 'Listenership is up. Advertising sales have increased.'

'Exactly.' The scowl was gone, replaced by a contented smile. 'That's exactly what I meant. People listen to us now because we offer independent talk radio. National issues keep us afloat. Your show is more like . . . ' The manager stared at the ceiling as he searched for the right words. 'Gossip, froth, pop songs. These days people want to quarrel and fight, not sing along.'

'Have you listened to my show recently?' When it looked as if the manager wasn't going to answer him, Margeir continued hurriedly. He didn't need the humiliation of hearing him say no. 'The show might have started off on a lighter note, since it was primarily music, but it's completely different now. I do exactly the same as the others during the day — take calls from listeners who are furious about the country's situation. So the schedule is more or less the same all day and all night. People are just as angry at night as they are in the daytime.'

'Precisely.'

Margeir hadn't expected this reply. Was the manager agreeing with him? His tone of voice suggested otherwise. 'What do you mean?'

'From what I've heard, your show is practically a variation on what we've got on during the day. A lamer version of the primetime shows. I'm not about to reshuffle my most popular DJs to make room for someone who doesn't have the same spark.'

'What do you mean, spark?' Margeir knew exactly what he meant, but he couldn't think of a way to defend himself. He'd often thought the same thing. His passion was disappearing, his enthusiasm waning. He answered calls out of a sense of duty and took the path of least resistance, saying as little as possible instead of expressing strong opinions or deliberately dis- agreeing with the caller. In fact, he often agreed with them, which usually put them off. The people who called in were more used to being contradicted and provoked, and didn't know how to respond when the radio host simply said: *Yes, you're right, I see your point.*

'You know what I mean. I heard a repeat of your show the other day and it was crap. You could almost feel how bored you were with your listeners. I was this close to calling you and telling you not to bother showing up again.' As he said this, the manager brought his index finger to his thick thumb until they nearly

193

touched. 'Luckily for you, I didn't want the hassle of having to find a stand-in, so it's thanks to my laziness that you still have your job. But as long as you go on like this, you can forget about me moving your show up. Daytime hosts need to be sharp and motivated. Not half asleep or bored out of their skulls. Who do you think would advertise for that kind of host?'

'If I just had the chance to try out an earlier slot, maybe I could convince you that I'd do really well with it? I'm very interested in engaging with national issues, even though they weren't originally meant to be part of my show.' Margeir was lying; he found all the nonsense going on in Iceland these days deathly dull: just endless incomprehensible political entanglements and lunatic bank and business magnates. Why waste your energy wailing on about greed and dishonesty? 'I read every newspaper I can get my hands on and I'm always online, so the show you heard wasn't a typical one. I must have been under the weather. Everyone has off days.'

'I don't.' His boss wasn't joking, even though everyone at the station knew that he was no better than the rest of them; he always seemed to get the wrong end of the stick with the callers he spoke to, and ended up getting irritated by them: Maybe it was easy to think you were perfect if you were a dictator. 'But it doesn't make any difference; I see no need to mess with something that's working fine. *If it ain't broke, fix it.*'

Margeir was itching to correct him, but let it go for fear that it would bring this brief visit to a premature end. 'How about as a sidekick to another DJ? I don't mind playing a supporting role.'

The manager stuck out his lower lip and wrinkled his nose at the same time — quite a feat. 'Nah.' He thought for a moment, but then repeated: 'Nah. It's all running so smoothly right now that there's no chance. All the shows that need two hosts already have them, and it would be crazy to have three. There wouldn't be room for guests in the studio. Do you want to stand behind them, shouting to be heard?'

This didn't merit a reply. 'How about as a temp? Emergency cover, for when people get ill or go on holiday?'

'What's going on, Margeir? Have you got yourself a woman who wants you home at night?'

'No.' If only.

'What is it, then? Until now you've been quite happy with your time slot, or am I mistaken?'

'Yes. No.' Margeir squirmed in his seat. Soon he would be politely shown the door. It was only ten minutes until the manager's own show was due to start. 'I mean, yes, up until now I've been satisfied and no, you're not mistaken. It's to do with something else.' His mouth suddenly filled with saliva, and he swallowed hard. 'This real weirdo has started phoning in and the idea that he might be the next caller is putting me constantly on edge. I think he'd be less likely to call during the day.'

The laughter this provoked was loud and hearty. 'Dream on! Haven't you learned anything? The loonies call whenever the lines are open, it doesn't make a blind bit of difference what time of day or night it is. It's just part of the job; most callers are all right, but there are always a couple that are . . . how shall I put it . . . different. You can't take it personally.'

'It's not just a run-of-the-mill nutter. There's something really disturbing about his calls, even though he doesn't say much or stay on for very long.'

'Then don't answer. Simple.' The manager raised his hands and moved them in circles above his head, as if conjuring ideas from the air. 'I don't know . . . put on a song, read from the newspaper, find something funny on the Internet for your listeners. Play some commercials.'

'He calls from an unlisted number. But others do too, so there's no way of weeding him out; if I don't answer him when he's still trying to get through, no one else can be put through either. It would help if we could just screen our callers.' Margeir knew that it had long been in the pipeline to buy a machine that would make this possible.

'Hmm, yes.' The manager dropped his hands to his lap. There wasn't much evidence of the station investing in anything; one of the studio headphones had been in need of new foam since September. 'That's something I've been planning on sorting out, of course, but with the krona the way it is, it would be well worth waiting, even just a few months. You must understand that, surely — your finances can hardly be in great shape.' This was below the belt and the manager seemed to realize it, hurrying on. 'But why does it bother you so much? We all get strange phone calls and they mean nothing, at the end of the day. They're either from wannabe comedians or shrinking violets who don't dare to speak once they're on the air and just breathe into the receiver instead. I don't know why you let it get to you.'

'These calls are different. He's not a joker or a breather.' Margeir wanted to explain himself without going into precise detail. 'This listener seems to know me. He says things that he knows will bother me.'

This was getting too personal, and the last thing the manager was known for was his powers of empathy. 'What? You're not going to let that get under your skin, are you? It's just some coward who gets his kicks from knowing he's got to you. Laugh at him and hang up.' He leaned back, satisfied with his latest solution. 'There's no need to get worked up over nothing.' It was clear he'd had enough of this topic. 'Do you think you can manage that?' He didn't need to add, *Or should I start looking for someone else?*; it was clear to Margeir which way the wind was blowing.

'Uh, yes, of course. No problem.' But this was far from the truth. His words rang hollow in his ears. He had a *big* problem, but if he told the manager the whole story, he might as well quit. 'Well, keep me in mind if anything changes, but until then, no problem.' Margeir stood up and left the office, taking care to walk out with his head held high. As he went through the door it crossed his mind to turn around and get down on his knees. Maybe that was the way to get into the manager's good books. But his hesitation was momentary and he let the door click shut behind him. It was just as pointless to humiliate himself that way as it was to imagine that carrying on with his show would be *no problem*. Nonetheless, he allowed himself to hope that his fears might not come true after all.

★   ★   ★

It had been a difficult morning, and this was reflected in the atmosphere in the little duty room, where they were sitting dismayed and frustrated after hearing about the hospital's latest cutback plans. In short, they meant more work and less pay at the end of the month — a deadly combination. 'How come Bjarni in Room 2 hasn't been discharged? The x-rays show that he's fine to go home, and we need the bed. I made that clear yesterday.' The senior consultant was rarely happy, and always liberal with his criticism. He was due to retire soon and the recent organizational changes to the hospital and to his department had done nothing to improve his moods. 'How could I have been misunderstood?'

Silence fell over the group as each hoped that one of the others would come up with an explanation. The senior consultant tried in vain to make eye contact with them, until a nurse finally spoke up. 'His wife refuses to have him at home. A social worker is trying to find a solution, but until then we were told to leave him where he is.'

'And nobody said anything? This isn't our problem; the man is completely healthy. Healthy enough, anyway.' Again no one said anything; the patient had barely recuperated and his wife had just undergone a hip operation herself, making it difficult for her to look after him at home. 'We're expecting two new admissions this afternoon; what do you recommend we do with those patients? Send them home to this man's wife, perhaps?'

'Bjarni still being here isn't the problem — even if he'd gone, we could hardly put both the new patients in the same bed. Admissions have to be organized better. It doesn't make any difference whether it's one patient or two that end up in the corridor — it ought to be none.' The doctor who answered was widely tipped to take over from the senior consultant when he retired. He was a quiet, unassuming man, although recently he'd done more to make his presence known.

The senior consultant didn't look impressed. He crossed his arms, pushing his striped tie — which was noticeably too wide to be fashionable — to one side. 'This isn't the only thing that went wrong here yesterday. I see from the report on the paralysed girl in Room 7 that she still hasn't been seen by a therapist. May I remind you that this could provide an invaluable insight into her condition and therefore help us to diagnose her.'

'She came yesterday.' The nurse who said this flushed a little as she spoke, regretting having attracted the attention of her ill-tempered superior. 'The therapist. Someone might have forgotten to record it, but she was here and she sat with the girl for at least half an hour.'

'And? They could hardly have just been having a pleasant chat. Didn't she tell anyone what conclusions she drew from the session? Did she simply disappear without speaking to anyone?'

The young nurse became even more embarrassed and fiddled distractedly with a pen in the breast pocket of her scrubs as she spoke. 'She talked to me a bit on her way out. Said she was going to get in touch with us today about it.'

'Why the delay?' The senior consultant tightened his arms across his chest, pushing his crumpled tie to an even more ridiculous angle. 'Doesn't she know we've been waiting for this?'

'I don't know.' The young woman blushed even harder and looked pleadingly out of the corner of her eye at the doctor who'd spoken up first, but to no avail. 'She said she was going to write up her notes about what she got out of the patient and go over them. If I understood her correctly, she thought she might have misunderstood or misinterpreted what the patient was trying to say.'

'Misunderstood? Misinterpreted?' The sarcastic tone was completely unjustified but the senior consultant didn't care; it felt good to have an outlet for his irritation. He'd had enough of not being able to do his job properly. The hospital's quality controls were diminishing, but that wasn't the staff's fault; constant changes and lack of funding made things very difficult. 'How is it possible to misunderstand? Have you seen the cards they use for communication? It's not like there are many words to choose from.'

'I don't know exactly what she meant, but I imagine she'd be able to draw more conclusions from their conversation than we could.' The nurse had stopped fiddling with her pen. Her mood was beginning to darken. 'According to you she could, anyway.'

The senior consultant unfolded his arms. 'Well, we can't wait for this for another whole day, so I suggest you get in touch with the therapist immediately and figure something out.' The nurse merely nodded. Inside, her anger grew, but now it was directed at her colleagues, who had kept silent and made no attempt to help her. Of course she'd often done the same, but this was the first time she'd found herself playing the role of sacrificial lamb. She hoped she had enough integrity to learn from this and come to others' aid next time instead of keeping quiet. However, she knew deep down that she probably wouldn't.

After the meeting, alone at the duty station, she reached for the hospital phone directory. Just as she had given up all hope of the therapist answering, she heard a breathless voice on the other end of the line.

'Hi, sorry, I haven't forgotten you — I was called unexpectedly to the children's hospital and I've only just got back. I still have to go through my notes one more time, but I should be able to come over in half an hour or so.'

'That would be great. We're keen to know whether she has any complaints about anything, or if she's in pain. We're having a hard time determining the root cause of the symptoms she's displaying.'

'Oh, I doubt I'll be able to help you with that. I actually need to ask her a few more questions; yesterday she didn't want to say anything about how she felt physically. But it won't hurt to try again.'

'Really? What *did* she say, then?' The nurse wanted to know as much as possible in case she ended up being questioned again.

'If I understood her correctly, she's unhappy — or frightened, to be more accurate. But I wasn't able to clearly determine what of. That's why I'm going to try and communicate with her again today. It's an extremely primitive means of communication, although she's much better equipped for it than many others are, since she's literate and she can spell what she wants to say. It just takes an awfully long time, and on top of that it's very easy to end up in the wrong square. She was tired and impatient, so it didn't go very well. Hopefully it'll be better when I see her today.'

'What can she be afraid of? Us?'

'I'm not sure. She spelled 'oxygen' again and again when I asked, but I have no idea what she meant. Maybe she's having trouble breathing, although I didn't notice any signs of that. She also spelled the word 'man' more than once, and 'bad man' when I asked her to explain it better. I have no idea who she means, and by the time we reached that point I couldn't get her to continue. Plus, there are other things I don't quite understand, but I need a little more time to go over them and try to sort out the context.'

'Can you go into any detail?'

'I think the less I say right now, the safer we are. Let me just go over it a bit and speak to you properly after I meet up with her again. Maybe it's all just nonsense — a bad dream she had, or some kind of delusion, but I still feel it's worth checking to see whether I can get to the bottom of it, if possible. Her heart rate went through the roof when she mentioned this man, so it may be that her fear is causing symptoms that are confusing you guys.'

'I see.' The nurse tried to think of anything else she'd wanted to ask, but nothing came to mind. 'See you later, then. My name's Svava, I'll be here until four.' They said goodbye, and the nurse stared at her phone for a few moments before standing up. Maybe she should start by looking in on the poor girl; apparently she enjoyed listening to the radio, so maybe that would relax her and lessen her fear. Mind you, the girl's heart rate had actually increased when she stuck the ear phone in her ear the other day, and for a second Svava wondered whether it was the country's financial crisis, which was all they ever discussed on the radio now, that was scaring her. No, it couldn't be. It must have been a coincidence.

14

Monday, 11 January 2010

Each storey would have housed a family of three quite comfortably. The house was so overwhelming that it was actually difficult to appreciate its architecture; its overall appearance made it look as if the blueprints had been done to the wrong scale and the building was now a distended version of the original idea. It was the same story with the next house. They were all crowded together, and none had windows at the sides because of the proximity of their neighbours. Either the residents were well off or they'd received a good discount from the builders' merchants. Thóra had had considerable trouble navigating them to the northern part of the suburb of Grafarvogur, where she never normally had any need to go. Most of the driveways leading up to these enormous homes were empty of any cars, since maintaining these palaces required two breadwinners, but there were snow-mobile trailers in many of the driveways, and the odd camper trailer here and there, covered with a tarpaulin. Einvarður and Fanndís's driveway contained no trailers, however, and Matthew pulled up next to a newish family car that made it clear that the owner wasn't rolling in money, but didn't want it to look as if that were the case.

On a copper plate beneath the doorbell were the names of all the members of the family — Tryggvi included. She saw Matthew raise his eyebrows when he saw the son's name, but he said nothing; his only experience with children was with Thóra's son and daughter and her grandson, and he seemed to realize his limitations when it came to understanding parents. He rang the bell and after a few moments Fanndís opened the door. She was just as elegant as in the photograph at her husband's office, although she'd aged since it was taken. Tiny wrinkles stretched from the corners of her eyes to her temples and a vertical line lay at either side of her mouth. Otherwise her face was smooth and healthy-looking. The woman extended a slender hand adorned with rings and smiled warmly as they introduced themselves. The clothes she was wearing were not the kind that Thóra would have chosen if she worked at home; it looked as though Fanndís was going out to lunch at the golf club. But maybe she'd simply dressed up especially for her guests, and if that were the case, Thóra regretted having dressed according to the weather that morning.

They followed the woman through the beautiful foyer and into a large but tasteful living room that felt cosy despite its size. A small number of attractive paintings hung on the walls and family photos stood on shelves and on nests of tables. In all the photos showing the family dressed in their Sunday best, the daughter wore a long dress that looked Spanish to Thóra. 'Your daughter's clearly a strong character,' she said, pointing at the same photo that Einvarður had shown them in his office. 'Sometimes I think young people all dress alike, but that's not the case with her, I see.'

Fanndís stopped and looked at the picture. She blushed slightly and rubbed her ear. 'Yes. Lena has good taste and she always wants to look nice.' She smiled sadly and looked away from the photo. 'That was the last time we saw Tryggvi alive. My husband and I were on our way to the ministry's annual ball, which was held in Selfoss, and we gave Lena permission to invite her friends to a party. I can't begin to describe how we felt on the way home, knowing what had happened. I will never go to that ball again; I'm afraid it would stir up too many painful memories.' She cleared her throat and let go of her ear, which was now slightly red. 'But you don't want to hear about that. I was brewing some coffee; it'll be ready in a moment.' Fanndís waited until Thóra and Matthew had taken a seat before she sat down herself. 'Are you hungry, maybe? I can get you something to have with your coffee, if you haven't eaten yet.'

'No, thanks.' Thóra was sure she was declining something delicious but the bacon was like a lead weight in her stomach and there was no way she could eat another bite. Matthew followed her lead and declined, although no doubt he could easily have eaten more.

They chatted for a few moments about the weather, then Iceland's financial situation, but Fanndís's comments about the situation seemed practised and carefully neutral. Thóra was impressed — she still had no idea of the woman's real opinions by the time Fanndís decided to turn the conversation to her guests' business. 'I understand from Einvarður that you're investigating the fire at the community residence. I don't know how I can help you, but I'll try my best.'

'Thank you. Your husband was very generous to us and I should start by thanking you for agreeing to meet us. I understand that it's painful to have to relive this tragic event, and the last thing we want is to cause you any distress. We'd just like your opinion on what went on at the home, in case you know something that doesn't appear in the files.'

Fanndís pursed her lips before she spoke, but gave no other sign that she was uncomfortable with the topic. No doubt she disliked discussing private matters with strangers. 'I don't know what I can add to what I've already said. I was often at the centre and I didn't notice anything other than that the staff did a badly paid job diligently and selflessly. I don't really see the point in putting all my memories under a microscope in the hope of spotting some minor shortcoming.'

'That's not what I'm suggesting.' It was going to be much harder to discuss things with this woman than it had been with her husband. Fanndís had immediately put up a wall, and they were unlikely to break through it without changing tactics. Getting straight to the point obviously wasn't the way to go. 'Your husband showed me a photo of your son this morning. He was an incredibly beautiful young man.'

'Yes, he was.' Fanndís glanced out of the corner of her eye at the family photograph nearest her. 'As a newborn he really stood out from the other babies in the maternity ward. He had so much hair and he was so striking.'

'It must have been a shock when you discovered he was autistic?'

'Yes and no. There were definite signs from the start that we ignored. Deep down we knew that there was something fundamentally wrong, long before we admitted it to ourselves.' The woman stared at the photo of her son as she spoke. 'He never looked into my eyes as an infant. Even when he was breastfeeding he never looked at me. That was the first thing that struck me, although since he was my first child I didn't know much about how they were supposed to behave. He also hardly ever cried, but we thought it was just because he was an angel. Later the symptoms became more pronounced and by the time he was ten months old we had to admit that there was something wrong with him. He didn't make any baby noises. When we picked him up he didn't support himself; he was just floppy, helpless. He didn't like being touched, he didn't try to learn to talk and he didn't eat unless the food was put in exactly the same spot in front of him; the plate had to line up with the edge of the table and the plastic cup and spoon always had to be in the same place. I never worked out why he'd decided on this particular arrangement. Maybe I set the table like that the first time he tried eating by himself.

Everything had to be the same, always. He hated change, and he often became mad with fear when something unexpected happened. His life wasn't simple, in any case.'

'How did he take moving to the residence? Hadn't he always been at home until then?'

'It wasn't easy, but it had got better by the time the disaster happened. Moving brought so many changes that he was completely confused and he found it terribly difficult at first. We were there all the time to start with, to help him get used to it. No one knew him like we did.' The woman looked down, agitated, and rearranged her necklace. After she'd moved it to the centre of her chest she appeared to feel better. 'Tryggvi lived with us until he was twenty. I took care of everything for him during the daytime, apart from when he was in therapy or class; then I would take him there and pick him up. When he was offered a place at the centre, we accepted it, in the hope that it would help with his developmental therapy. It wasn't because we were giving up or didn't trust ourselves any longer to have him at home, as many people thought. We thought that perhaps he'd developed as much as he could under our care and that this change would help him make progress.' She paused before continuing: 'No one expected things to end as they did.'

'And did he make progress? Before the fire, I mean?'

Fanndís seemed surprised by the question, which was a bit odd considering how smart she seemed. 'No, not really, but the fire was only six months after he moved in, so he might have been about to show an improvement.'

The conversation was starting to flow now, which encouraged Thóra slightly. 'So did he attend therapy sessions and classes at the residence? I saw that the list of employees included developmental and physiotherapists.'

'Yes, the programme was a good one, if a bit old-fashioned for my tastes — though the director was very open to recent innovations. There's so much happening in terms of treatments for autism that has produced excellent results but that they won't try in Iceland, because of prejudice or some other reason, I don't know. Still, they worked hard and I don't want to sound ungrateful, but I would have preferred to see more ambition in such a supposedly progressive project. But of course, there was just so little experience in those who were running it.'

'I've heard that the residents were rather unhappy; did you notice that?'

'God, I forgot the coffee!' Fanndís pressed a hand to her chest and sprung to her feet. 'I'll be right back.' She hurried out of the room.

Matthew looked at Thóra in surprise.

From the kitchen came sounds of bustling activity, a cupboard door shutting and the chinking of crockery. Then they heard a voice, but it was difficult to determine if it came from a radio or whether Fanndís was speaking to someone, perhaps on the phone. Thóra listened carefully but couldn't make out what was being said or even whether it was one or two people speaking. She noticed a framed drawing on a low bookshelf next to the sofa, which intrigued her. She had to bend down to see the drawing properly and ended up taking it from the shelf. It was obviously not the work of a known artist, since as far as Thóra was aware they didn't tend to use crayons. So it was probably by one of the family's children, and it wasn't much of a leap to guess that it was Tryggvi. Thóra had no idea exactly what the artist had meant to depict, but in one corner large, clumsy characters spelled out *o8INN* or something similar. The picture was too carefully drawn to be by a toddler, and the subject too peculiar. In the foreground was a figure that was probably supposed to be a person, but it had neither eyes nor nose, only a gaping mouth that appeared to be screaming silently. Behind it was a building that seemed to be the community residence, drawn roughly, which was why the picture had drawn Thóra's attention. Although it bore a slight resemblance to the real thing there was something about it that didn't fit, but Thóra couldn't work out what it was that bothered her. There was also a second figure standing off to the side. Unlike the first, which was lying horizontally, this one was upright and had two eyes and a closed mouth. Its hands were raised and between them was a nearly perfectly drawn circle, divided into three sections by lines that met in the centre. There was something sinister about the figure, but it was difficult to pinpoint why; its facial features were unclear, apart from its fiery red mouth. If this was how Tryggvi had viewed people, and the world around him, no wonder he'd found life so difficult and been so afraid of change.

It was clear that the picture had originally been drawn in pencil, then coloured in. The thick, yellowish paper made it look older than it probably was. Thóra handed the picture to Matthew, who agreed that the building looked like the care home and drew her attention to what appeared to be fire burning in one of the windows. Thóra scrutinized the drawing more closely and wasn't quite convinced, although she could make out something reddish-yellow there. She was bending down to put the picture back when Fanndís appeared with coffee things on a tray. 'I was just looking at this drawing. Did Tryggvi do it?'

Fanndís put the tray on the coffee table and went over to Thóra. 'May I see it?' She took it and frowned. 'I'd forgotten about this. Where was it?'

Thóra pointed at the bookshelf. 'Did Tryggvi do it?' she repeated.

'Yes,' Fanndís answered distractedly, gazing at the picture. 'He had a real talent for drawing. It's not obvious in this one, because it was coloured in afterwards, but he drew all his pictures in one long movement — he never lifted the pen or pencil. He must have seen each one precisely in his mind before transferring it to paper, because there was no hesitation or nervousness once he started.' She put the drawing back in its place again, now so hidden behind the books that only one edge of the frame showed. 'I'd completely forgotten this picture. Our daughter had it framed and gave it to her father as a birthday present shortly after Tryggvi moved to the centre. I really don't know why she chose this picture, because there are so many other, much better ones. I find this one a bit creepy, which is why it's kept down there.'

'Is it meant to show the home?' asked Thóra. 'I feel like I recognize it, but it's not quite as I remember it.'

'Oh, yes. You didn't figure it out?' Fanndís smiled at Thóra as if she were a bit slow. 'It's a mirror image of the building. Tryggvi always drew mirror images; that was one of the symptoms of his autism. They tried to work out why and they decided that the scanner in his brain, if it can be called that, was calibrated wrongly. What he saw and wanted to convey in a drawing came out mirrored. Actually, we never discovered whether he did see life like that, because it turned out to be too difficult to test him, but there have been reported cases. People with this sort of disability can't learn to read clocks, for instance. Although it still seemed inconceivable when he died, maybe Tryggvi would have been able to do that one day.' She gestured towards the coffee. 'Please help yourselves while it's hot. The coffeepot is a bit worn out so it gets cold quickly.'

The coffee was indeed still hot and agreeably strong. Thóra placed her patterned cup on its saucer. She had poured herself too much and was afraid of spilling it. 'Did he draw a lot?'

'If a piece of paper and pen were put in front of him, he would start sketching immediately. As

213

I said, the pictures were always fully formed in his mind, so he never hesitated. He didn't speak, which meant he never asked for a drawing pad; he could have showed that he wanted one in some other way, but he never did. He didn't ever ask for anything, not even water when he was thirsty. For him, life just happened; he didn't try to influence its progress or change the course of events. I've often wondered what it must be like to live that kind of life, but I just can't imagine it. It's a shame, because it might have helped us understand him better. He had everything he needed in order to do what comes naturally to the rest of us: his vocal cords were normal and there was nothing wrong with his brain, based on the huge number of CAT scans and tests he underwent. There was just something undefinable missing, some connection or spark. I was told to think of it like a disconnection in a piece of electrical equipment; when two parts are uncoupled, nothing works the way it should, but when the connection's made everything starts running.' Fanndís raised her hand to her other ear and rubbed it. 'I hadn't given up on the idea that that might still happen.' She smiled, embarrassed, and looked out of the window, clearly not wanting to see the doubt in their eyes.

Thóra tactfully avoided commenting on the possibility of the boy's improvement; she knew little or nothing about autism, except that no one could be 'cured' of it, although remarkable progress was achieved in some cases. 'In the picture he drew someone screaming. Do you think that's a reflection of his feelings about where he was living? I asked you before whether the residents seemed unhappy; maybe this was Tryggvi's way of expressing it. The reason I'm so keen to discuss this with you is that you must be the person who spent the most time there, after those who were actually on the payroll. The employees would hardly tell me if the level of care was in any way substandard.'

'I don't know what to say. As I mentioned, Tryggvi hated change, which is a very common symptom of autism. Since he'd not long arrived there, it's hard to know how he would have felt over time. But it's still important to bear in mind that it probably wouldn't have been the place itself that caused him discomfort, but this aspect of his disability. Obviously I knew the other residents a little and they seemed to be doing okay, each in their own way. In general, I'd say the ones who were physically disabled seemed better off than the ones suffering mental disabilities. But perhaps that's to be expected.'

'So you never heard any shouting or screaming? Or any other noise that might suggest that something was wrong?'

'No. I mean, of course you did hear screaming, crying and everything in between. The residents were often upset about something. Sometimes no one could figure it out, but usually they could tell what the problem was. For example, some residents would kick up a fuss when someone was trying to help them, even though they were only in temporary discomfort. I believe the therapy could be uncomfortable; quite painful, even. I once injured my shoulder so I know this firsthand, though I had the self-control not to scream during physiotherapy.' Fanndís smiled at them. 'But any distress the residents felt wasn't down to the employees; on the contrary, they tried to make life as easy for them as possible. Of course they couldn't always manage it, because sometimes neither painkillers nor kindness can help. Some things hurt in a different way to, I don't know, hitting your thumb with a hammer.' She stopped smiling. 'Like the pain I experienced when Tryggvi died.'

'I can imagine it was terribly hard for you, and that it will continue to be so.' Thóra was keen to get the conversation back on track. 'If we assume Jakob didn't start the fire, was there any other resident you could imagine resorting to such a desperate act? Maybe without realizing the consequences of their actions?'

Fanndís grabbed her ear again. 'Not that I can think of. Everyone living there was either physically or mentally incapable of doing such a thing. Except for Jakob.'

'Well, you say that, but even with him I have serious doubts about the mental aspect. Starting the fire would have taken much more organizational ability than Jakob seems to possess.' Out of the corner of Thóra's eye she noticed Matthew staring at the doorway to the living room, although he was trying to hide it. He needn't have bothered, since all Fanndís's attention was on Thóra. 'What about the employees, or the other residents' relatives? Could they have been involved?'

Fanndís clearly found Thóra's question tasteless; her expression suggested Thóra had taken

216

some gum out of her mouth and stuck it underneath the coffee table. 'Of course not. The staff was composed of ordinary people who wouldn't have had anything to gain by committing such a crime — quite the reverse, in fact, since the fire meant their placement there was terminated and indeed several lost their jobs entirely. As for the other relatives, they weren't there as much as I was; most of them worked, which made it harder for them to visit. Most came on the weekends and I never noticed anything suspicious in their behaviour.'

'You'll have to excuse me.' Matthew stood up suddenly, smiling. 'I need to pop out to the car to make a phone call; I shouldn't be long.'

Thóra was careful not to let Fanndís see how surprised she was. She held off on any further questions until he was gone, then said, 'Has your husband told you that the girl in the coma, Lísa, was pregnant?' Fanndís nodded, and her hand crept back to her ear yet again and started worrying at the lobe. 'The man who made her pregnant would have had considerable motive to intervene. Isn't that right?'

Fanndís merely nodded again. The question was obviously unfair; you couldn't expect an ordinary person to put themselves in the shoes of a violent criminal, someone who would abuse someone who literally couldn't lift a finger in their defence. 'Well, hopefully the guilty party will be found; there's some DNA from the foetus and it's just a question of getting a sample from the right man.'

'Surely that means Jakob?' Fanndís glared at

Thóra. 'I would recommend that you send him for a DNA test. I don't know how he appears to you, but he's prone to violence and in my opinion he's entirely capable of doing that.'

'He's been ruled out,' replied Thóra. 'Whoever did it is still out there and may have even more on his conscience — like the fire, perhaps.'

★　★　★

Two cups of coffee later, Thóra and Matthew said goodbye. Matthew had reappeared just before Thóra decided that she'd got enough. When they heard the front door shut behind them, she nudged him with her elbow and asked where he'd really gone, but she couldn't get him to answer the question until they were actually sitting in the car. 'I noticed a young woman listening in as we sat in the living room. When she realized I'd spotted her she looked quite embarrassed, but she seemed to regain her composure and beckoned me through to speak to her.'

'And? What did she say?' The conversation was moving too slowly for Thóra.

'Her story didn't match her mother's, that's for sure.'

15

Monday, 11 January 2010

The garden was not a pretty sight; as the snow gradually disappeared in the day's unexpected warmth, the yellowing lawn and empty flowerbed were starting to peek through. The unkempt bushes in the borders were slipping out from under their melting burden and their last remaining leaves were falling to the ground. There was no reminder of the summer that Berglind longed for so passionately, except Pési's red plastic spade. She wrapped her dressing gown tightly around herself and slipped her bare feet into the rubber boots she'd fetched from the garage. They were icy and she felt her toes scrunch together in an attempt to gain warmth from each other. Of course she should have got dressed properly before going out, but she knew that if she'd given herself time for that she would have lost her bottle. The dead raven in the middle of the garden would have stayed there, right in her line of sight, until Halli came home, and she couldn't bear it. Berglind grabbed the handle on the sliding door and pulled it energetically before her courage deserted her.

She was met with cold, damp air and as she drew in a deep breath through her nose, what she smelled reminded her of the compost heap they'd tried to get going the previous year but had got rid of due to the stench. She hoped the smell wasn't coming from the bird's remains, though she knew that was impossible; the corpse hadn't been there the night before and there was no way it could have started to rot so quickly, especially not in winter. Nevertheless, she covered her nose with one hand as she walked across the wet grass, prepared for the worst. In the other hand she held a spade and a plastic bag so that she wouldn't need to touch the bird's body; her bravery had its limits. The stench grew stronger the closer she got, and her steps involuntarily grew shorter and slower. Perhaps the bird had been there longer than she thought; maybe it had emerged from the snow during the night when it had started to melt, but that seemed highly unlikely — there had been no noticeable hump where it now lay. Once Berglind had got close enough to reach for the bird she realized that the smell had nothing to do with the small corpse; it was simply in the air. But it was impossible to say what *was* causing it, because it seemed all-pervading, thick and repellent. She leaned the shovel against her body in order to free up both hands, and pulled the collar of her dressing gown up over her mouth and nose. By tilting her head and squeezing the dressing gown between her cheek and her shoulder she could protect herself from the stink. She knew she wouldn't be able to hold the dressing gown in place for long before the collar dropped back to her shoulder, so it was imperative that she get this over with quickly.

Berglind bent down carefully and arranged the

plastic bag so it would stay open. The sooner she got the remains into it and tied it off, the better. As if to make her life harder the wind blew the bag shut as soon as she opened it; the stillness that had greeted her when she'd first gone out into the garden had proved to be illusory. Berglind reached for a pebble lying close by to hold the bag in place. This on its own wasn't enough to keep the bag open, so she decided to grab some more stones from the gravel strip bordering the flowerbeds at the edge of the garden. Her collar fell from her face as she walked over, so she buried her mouth and nose in the crook of her elbow to block the odour, which the wind hadn't managed to disperse. She immediately felt better and by the time she reached the edge of the beds she could smell only a faint whiff of washing powder.

She couldn't see exactly where the gravel was, as in this shaded part of the garden the snow was still untouched by the sun. She rooted with her toe in the frozen white and after a quick search found what she was looking for. She cleared away the snow from a little patch and bent down to pick up the largest of the stones — at which point her hair became tangled on one of the bushes. Berglind became irritated that she hadn't pestered Halli enough in the autumn when he wriggled out of pruning them; if he'd given in to her nagging, this wouldn't have happened. Her scalp smarted as she tried carefully to untangle her hair; it was as though the bush was resisting. It wasn't until she took hold of all the hair that had wound itself round the branches and yanked with all her might that it came free, tangled and split from the struggle. A strand still hung from one of the branches, waving in the wind until it was gradually set free and blew away. Berglind watched it with annoyance and rubbed her sore head. She was really tempted to swear out loud, but didn't; people round here already thought she was a bit crazy, and she wasn't about to prove them right by talking to herself. She filled her hands with gravel and got ready to stand up, but was so startled by a hissing sound close to her ear that she lost her balance and fell back onto her arse in the wet snow.

Her heart pounded in her chest. She felt the cold sneaking in through her wet dressing gown as she stared into the yellow eyes peering at her through the hedge. The neighbour's cat stood bold as brass at the edge of their garden, its back arched. Berglind could feel that the hair on her arms had risen as well. 'Stupid animal,' she muttered, past caring now whether anyone heard her. 'What's the matter with you?' The cat responded with another hiss, louder than the first. 'Get out of here!' Berglind waved her hand in the hope of scaring it away, but it didn't move. She was even more irritated when she pulled herself up and wiped her dirty palms on her white dressing gown, but then sighed — it was due to go in the wash anyway. She looked around for the gravel but it had vanished into the snow where she'd dropped it, leaving behind a pattern of black holes that roughly formed the shape of a face: two eyes and a gaping mouth. Against her better judgement she shuddered at the thought of poking around in imaginary eye sockets or down a black throat, and decided to fetch some new gravel. This time she took more care to avoid the branches, as well as keeping a wary eye on the cat as she gathered together another handful. Considering how it had been acting recently, she was right to be on her guard. Usually the cat came to them and stood meowing at the sliding door in the hope of getting something to eat — often successfully — but now it never came any closer than the edge of the garden, from where it watched everything closely. Berglind could easily pinpoint the time this change had occurred, but had chosen to block out her certainty that it was related to the exorcisms that had briefly freed them from the spirit in the house. Maybe the cat was the only one that understood Berglind, as it seemed as sure as she was that this ghost, or whatever it was, was still hanging around outside.

Everyone else had turned their backs on her, even those who were initially shocked and sympathetic. This proved what she had probably known all her life but hadn't wanted to dwell on: that people's interest in the problems of others was finite. They might feel sympathy for a while if someone had suffered a traumatic life event, but then they would expect them to deal with it and move on as if nothing had happened. She had experience of this herself — as a child, she had been hit very hard by the death of her grandfather, and initially her other relatives had found the way she grieved for him very touching.

But as time passed, her tears were met with indifference or anger. 'What a terrible show-off you are! How long are you going to keep this up?' They whispered these things so her parents wouldn't hear, but they didn't seem concerned that she might still be upset. Now, twenty-five years later, she was again being accused of attention-seeking, and was even considered to be not quite right in the head. The same aunt who had hurt her with her callousness all those years ago had done it again when Berglind had bumped into her in the Kringlan Shopping Centre. She'd had to be honest when the woman enthusiastically questioned her about the haunting, and as Berglind began to walk away with Pési she had heard her aunt whisper conspiratorially to her friend: 'She's a queer fish — she always was, even as a child. But now it's like she's lost it completely. It's a wonder she hasn't been sectioned, or at least had the kid taken away from her.' Berglind was desperate to turn round and give her aunt a piece of her mind, but instead she tightened her grip on her son's hand and stalked away, her face burning and her eyes full of tears.

More goose bumps sprang up on her skin, not from remembering the old woman's spitefulness but because of what might be lying in wait behind her, whatever had scared the cat. She tried to conjure up the faces of those who had been good to her, in the hope of raising her spirits, but she could think of so few people that it just depressed her even more. She could actually count them on the fingers of one hand:

224

her sister, the couple next door and one supervisor at work. Her sister was on her side simply because she had to be; she hadn't actually ever said whether she believed Berglind or not, since in her opinion that was irrelevant. If Berglind was having a hard time, she was there for her and that was the end of it. The next-door neighbours and her supervisor, on the other hand, had never doubted the haunting; they'd wanted to hear all the details and to be updated on any new developments. Whatever the future held, Berglind was eternally indebted to them. It took a special sort of person to swim against the stream.

But none of these people was here right now, only this unknown horror behind her, and she had to get back inside on her own, whatever it took. She didn't have many options; she could hardly climb through the hedge and dash across her neighbours' garden to get back to her own house, not least because the outer door was locked and the only way in was through the gate behind her. Nor could she wait where she was for the thing to go away; the wind was picking up and her soaking wet dressing gown provided little protection against the chill. She had to turn around and walk through the garden, past the dead raven and the other thing that she didn't want to think about. She fixed her gaze on the cat, which looked straight back at her without blinking. It opened its mouth and hissed again, abruptly but loudly. There was no reason to hang around: *one, two, three, go!* Berglind raised herself up slowly as the cat continued to hiss deep in its throat. Now the animal seemed even more disturbed than when she'd been crouching down; its yellow eyes stared past her, as if at something behind her. Berglind stiffened. Why the hell had she gone out into the garden? She could easily have drawn the curtains if the dead bird was bothering her so much and tried to forget the ruffled black feathers and the wide-open beak screaming silently into the grey sky. Maybe the cat was just alarmed by the remains. Maybe the raven appeared to be alive and the cat was simply threatened by its size and was therefore trying to make itself as big as possible and warn the bird off by hissing. Had humans ever had a similar skill, it had long been forgotten, replaced by other abilities that were of more use to a civilized society but were no good at moments like this. Nevertheless, Berglind did her utmost to summon up something that would grant her strength, daring or fearlessness — but without success. There was nothing for it but to empty her mind, turn around and meet what awaited her.

The cat moved suddenly, interrupting Berglind's thoughts of escape. It pulled one of its front legs back in towards its body and appeared about to retreat into its own garden. Before it went, it looked up at Berglind and yowled piteously. Then it turned and fled, its long striped tail the last she saw of it. Now she was alone, and although the cat's presence hadn't exactly filled her with confidence, she'd been happier with some sort of living being nearby. Now as in her life generally, she stood alone against the unknown. Halli had grown tired of her jumpiness, and her endless speculation about solutions to the problem, though he'd tried to conceal it. He'd recently started working longer hours, even though the company had long since stopped paying overtime and projects were scarce. Since the attempted exorcism, her attempts to interest him in her theories had been less and less successful. He made no secret of the fact that he wanted her to pull herself together and stop obsessing. The more time that passed since the strange phenomena, the more distant his memory of them became, and the old, rational explanations began to surface again. These days Halli seemed not to remember half of what had happened before his very eyes, and the rest he put down to the house's structure. Any ideas about moving and starting again somewhere else were dead in the water; nobody could sell their house at the moment, and there was little hope that the situation would improve any time soon. When she mentioned that they could still live with her parents or some friends until the summer, when the long hours of daylight would drive away the darkness, he looked at her as if she were either stupid or crazy. She wasn't sure which was worse.

A surprisingly warm gust of wind blew like a breath down the front of Berglind's collar. Instead of warming her and making her feel better, it seemed to reanimate the stench, which had become less noticeable since she'd been forced to drop her arm away from her mouth and nose. Or maybe it had still been there and she'd got used to it, but the wind had suddenly made it stronger. Again it felt as if someone was breathing down her collar but this time from behind, and the hairs on the back of her neck stood up. The stench grew even stronger, as though a ghost was standing right behind her and emptying air from its rotten lungs down her spine. The memory of the compost heap returned once more and Berglind fought a wave of nausea. *One, two, three, turn around and walk briskly into the house. One, two, three!* She remained where she was.

The afternoon twilight cast a shadow over the toes of her boots which seemed to creep closer to her legs, growing larger with each passing moment. She wasn't going to stand there until darkness engulfed the garden, was she? She would have to go and fetch Pési from preschool in a minute. Even though part of her did want to stay put until Halli came home and rescued her, she didn't have her mobile with her, so she couldn't ask anyone to pick Pési up for her. There was nothing else for it but to go back in. *One, two, three.* Her feet were like lead. She was pathetic, absolutely pathetic. If she wanted to move she was going to have to get a grip on herself. Her state of panic was just making things worse, magnifying what the psychiatrist said were the consequences of a shock that she hadn't come to terms with; namely, the accident that had killed Magga. But then she heard a soft crunching sound behind her. A shock, even one as traumatic as Magga's death, couldn't conjure up noises out of nowhere. What if she really had

228

lost it? The psychiatrist would have a field day if he knew she was starting to think he'd been right. Maybe the sick leave he'd pretty much forced on her was to blame; if she were at work she wouldn't be standing here, terrified of something that might turn out to be nothing, in a dirty dressing gown with her hair all sticking up.

Again she heard a crunching in the snow. It didn't matter one bit whether it was her imagination or something real that was threatening her, she couldn't just stand there — but she couldn't move, either. *One, two, three.* She resolved to shut out her surroundings and think about something else entirely. Pési. What was he doing now? Drinking hot chocolate and eating an apple, as he usually was when she picked him up early? Berglind shut her eyes and remembered how sweetly he'd smiled at her when she'd picked him up yesterday. He'd been sitting off to one side against the room's back wall, while the other kids buzzed around the toy box. Their noise had subsided when he stood up and walked over to her; the children moving aside one after another as he walked through the group. Berglind had watched in surprise as they put down their toys, stood up and walked away. None of them said a word, and the rumpus that had met her ears on arrival seemed like a distant memory. Pési didn't appear to be startled by this, and acted as if the children weren't there. Berglind had been troubled; she'd been so preoccupied with her own problems that she hadn't given any thought to how he might be doing in preschool. At first everything had gone smoothly; he appeared to have playmates, friends even, but when she thought back on it, things had changed. He was always alone when she collected him. Alone on a swing, dangling his feet; alone pushing sand around absent-mindedly in the sandpit; alone kicking up snow at the edge of the playground. Alone.

The preschool teacher had smiled at Berglind as if there were nothing more natural than other children being frightened of her son, and Berglind had bent down to Pési and asked him to go and put on his snowboots. Then she asked the young woman straight out what was actually going on and whether Pési was being bullied. The teacher had given her another smile, a rather sickly one, and said that kids were sometimes like that without meaning anything by it. There was no reason for their behaviour; it had started some time ago, seemingly for no reason, and showed no sign of stopping. They'd thought about contacting Berglind and Halli but decided to wait until parents' evening at Easter, in case the situation should improve. *But don't worry, it'll get better. Just give it a little time.* Well, quite — this was exactly what she'd been told herself; she was going through a phase and just needed time to recover. When she pressed the teacher for answers, perhaps more zealously than she'd intended, the woman said that they'd tried to ask the brightest kids what was going on but hadn't received any sensible reply, just something vague about how they were scared of the angry woman who followed Pési. They

230

hadn't been able to explain in any more detail which woman they meant, but as the teacher spoke Berglind realized that she was putting two and two together and was about to come up with five. She thought Berglind was the angry woman the kids were afraid of. Instead of telling the teacher the whole story, Berglind thanked her politely and left. She knew from experience never to discuss the subject with anyone she didn't know well. Enough people knew about their misfortune as it was, and it was good to hold onto the faint hope that there were still a few who knew nothing about it.

Pési was waiting in the cloakroom, having put his left foot in his right boot and vice versa, obviously happy to leave preschool and go home. Never mind Berglind herself — her son deserved better. So instead of finding an outlet for her disappointment, she had bent down and smiled at him. *Let's go home; we can stop off at the baker's and buy some doughnuts.* He had shaken his head and said that he wanted to go straight back; he wanted to go to his room. Berglind knew why: home was his only refuge from the relentless and inexplicable bullying. As long as he didn't go to the window . . . *One, two, three.* For Pési's sake she had to go inside and get ready. The smell seemed to be subsiding again; it still lingered, but it wasn't as powerful as it had been just a moment before. Perhaps that was a sign that she wasn't in danger, and Berglind made her decision before she started having second thoughts. She turned around quickly.

231

The motion made the belt come off her dressing gown, which swung open. She stood there, exposed, facing the empty garden. Apart from the raven's corpse there was nothing to see; no one stood there shuffling from one foot to the other in the snow, making it crunch; no one was taking a deep breath, about to blow down her collar. She wrapped the dressing gown back around herself and took the first step in the direction of the garden door. When nothing happened her confidence grew, and before she knew it she was back at the house, past the dead bird, grabbing the door handle with a clammy palm. For the first time since they'd moved into the house the door wouldn't budge, and Berglind's courage diminished with every fumbling, unsuccessful attempt to open it. She didn't dare breathe through her nose in case the stench of decay had risen again, and the turmoil inside her as she scrabbled at the handle made her oblivious to the wind; she had no idea whether it was as warm as breath, or ice-cold. Suddenly the door came unstuck and opened just enough for her to squeeze inside. Panting, and with a pounding heart, she rushed into the warmth as she heard the crunching of the snow again behind her. With one movement she managed to slide the door shut again but she had to use all her strength, making the door slam loudly. Then she stood there for a moment trying to catch her breath, making sure to keep her eyes from the floor so that she wouldn't look into the garden.

Once her heartbeat had returned to something

resembling normality and the veins on the back of her hand had stopped trying to pop out of her skin, she reached for the floor-length curtain and pulled it shut. What was going on? Should she do something, say something? She hardly knew anything about Magga really, and even less about her death; her original theory, that the girl's confused spirit was trying to babysit Pési and complete the last task it remembered from its earthly life, didn't fit, because right now she was alone here and Pési was at preschool. So what did it want, then?

* * *

The air suddenly cooled and once again she was covered with goose bumps. The cold seemed to radiate from the sliding door, creeping up the curtain and drifting through the room like invisible smoke. Rage suddenly coursed through Berglind and she swept the curtain back, the expensive material ripping right up to the track as she did so. Under normal circumstances she would have yelped at the damage to the curtain, which now hung slackly from one hook; they almost certainly couldn't afford to repair it and would have to look out into the murky garden for what remained of the winter. But for the moment this thought was far from Berglind's mind; now she stared open-mouthed at the glass, which was covered, on the outside, with frost from top to bottom. Through it, it was as if she saw the shadow of someone outside, but then it disappeared. Traced on the frosty glass, she read:

O81NN. Or was it *OBINN?* She couldn't be certain. Neither meant anything to her and she retreated from the garden door without checking to see whether whoever had written it had left behind any tracks.

16

Monday, 11 January 2010

The snow on the windowsill had melted in the unseasonal afternoon weather, but turned into ice again after sunset. Although it was a short distance to Thóra's home from the law firm, she was apprehensive about driving on the ice and regretted having dropped Matthew off at home after their visit to Fanndís. She'd been expecting a client, which meant Matthew would have had to keep Bella company in reception for the duration, watching her perform her secretarial work with her usual good grace. It wasn't as if there was a shortage of work to be done at home; they still had to find space for some of the things from the garage and Matthew had offered to sort it out, though he knew he would be working to a soundtrack of his father-in-law's ceaseless whistling and his mother-in-law's endless questions about whether or not he wanted some cod liver oil. Matthew had managed to adapt to many aspects of Icelandic society, but taking cod liver oil was the exception. Thóra allowed him to skip it — he had enough to put up with from her friends, who had all come up with the same idea when Matthew and Thóra were invited to dinner or a party: to ply him with cured shark and brennivín. Now that he'd done the rounds of her friends and gamely played the naive foreigner, gaping in mock astonishment at these Icelandic delicacies, the invitations had all but dried up, as though it was unclear what else could be done with such an exotic guest.

Before they parted, Matthew had told Thóra everything he'd heard from the daughter, Lena, in the driveway. She was adamant that the truth concerning her brother's death should be brought to light, but feared her mother was trying to whitewash the image of the community residence, its staff and residents, damaging their investigation. She told him that her mother was fixated on everything being neat and pleasant and that she wore rose-tinted glasses. Of course it was impossible to judge whether either one of them was telling the truth; perhaps they'd had different experiences of the place, but Lena confirmed at least that the atmosphere at the home had been unpleasant, the staff quite unfriendly and the residents noticeably despondent. This was consistent with Jakob's admittedly slightly odd account, but Lena hadn't explained things to Matthew in any more detail, except to say that the residents didn't seem to want to live there, and few of them seemed happy. Lena did recall Jakob from the residence, and according to Matthew had shrugged her shoulders when he asked whether she thought he was guilty. *I don't know, he seemed all right, you know? I never saw him start a fire or even heard him talk about doing it*. She'd then tried to get Matthew to reveal why Jakob's guilt was now in question, and seemed very interested in whether any of the residents or staff were suspects. She said the latter had been incredibly strict and were capable of anything, apart from some of the younger staff members who'd been OK. Matthew thought he had skilfully deflected the girl's questions, while still encouraging her curiosity.

Another thing she'd mentioned was her parents' differing opinions about Tryggvi. They'd argued about how best to take care of him and had had different expectations of his improvement. Her father had long ago given up all hope, but her mother had been very interested in his therapy and was always reading about the newest miracle treatments. About a year before Tryggvi had moved to the centre, her mother had found some charlatan, transparent to everyone but her, who claimed to be able to cure autism. That had been the last straw, and her father had put his foot down and declared that things had gone far enough. They'd had a blazing row after this man's visit, which Lena didn't describe in any detail other than to say that it had been awful, and that afterwards her mother had started to succumb completely to her conviction that though trapped behind the bars of autism, Tryggvi was of completely sound mind. At the end of the argument her father had demanded that Tryggvi be placed somewhere where specialists could take care of him without her emotional state affecting his treatment. Six months later Tryggvi was moved into his new apartment. Lena had wanted to make clear to Matthew that her father was a good man. He had made the decision out of concern for Tryggvi's well-being, not a desire to get him out of the house. After her brother was moved away from home her parents' relationship had improved greatly and Lena had felt hugely relieved. *He wasn't a bad person, but he wasn't like, really alive, do you know what I mean? You couldn't tell that he had any feelings, he was just like a robot. You know, badly programmed.*

Lena hadn't said any more, as far as Matthew could remember, but before he went into the house he asked whether Thóra could call her to ask her a few more questions. *She mustn't call me,* Lena had told him, *but she can send me a text and I'll call her back. I really don't want my mother to know that I'm talking to you. She can be so weird.* Thóra wasn't sure whether she'd get in touch with the girl; she still had so many other people to speak to and she knew from personal experience that teenagers' viewpoints could be coloured by strong emotions. Of course, it could be that Lena was the only one who would speak to her completely honestly. Whatever the case, Thóra didn't need to make a decision about it tonight. It could wait.

After meeting her client, Thóra contacted the relatives of some of the other residents. She'd been apprehensive about these phone calls and had put off making them, but now that she'd visited Fanndís there was no sense waiting. There was a danger that Fanndís would get in touch with them before she did, since it seemed likely that the parents had all got to know each other while their children were living under the same roof, and had kept in touch in the wake of their shared tragedy. Ideally Thóra's calls would catch the relatives off-guard. People replied differently if they'd already mentally prepared themselves, even if it was only to make sure they came across satisfactorily.

★   ★   ★

No one seemed to have known about her or to have expected her to call. She actually spent a large part of each conversation rattling off the same spiel about the reason for her call, and convincing people that her aim wasn't to free a guilty man but an innocent one, but she'd expected that. Few parents would be overjoyed to hear from the lawyer of a man believed to have killed their son or daughter, and Thóra was actually surprised she'd been able to hold a conversation with relatives who were still grieving. Perhaps it was because Jakob had been acquitted of criminal charges, even though this was because he was unfit for trial.

Thóra had her work cut out digging up the right names of the victims' parents, because it transpired few of them had been questioned by the police or called as witnesses in court. But with the help of the obituaries she eventually managed to make a list of the requisite names. However, no obituaries appeared to have been written about Natan Úlfheiðarson, and of the three Úlfheiðars in the phone directory, only two were old enough for him to have been their son. In the end, Thóra found his mother by Googling the boy's name. Her search brought up a blog to which Natan's aunt had uploaded photos of a family reunion, and in one of them Natan, his mother, and his maternal uncle were named in the caption. Thóra spent some time looking closely at the young man in the photo, as well as at his mother. She couldn't escape the thought that perhaps this was a picture of the man who had had sex with Lísa, although in the photo he looked as innocent as could be. He and his mother sat at a cloth-covered table with white coffee cups and matching plates in front of them. Natan's mother, Úlfheiður, appeared slightly older than Thóra, and if the photo was anything to go by, she was quite a solemn person. Her brother didn't seem any livelier; neither of them looked like the life and soul of the party, and the empty chairs on either side of them seemed to confirm this. Perhaps the entire family was cast from the same mould.

Natan was more difficult to work out than his mother and uncle. The helmet on his head made him look a bit odd, even before you got to the huge grin that stretched from ear to ear — in marked contrast to his tablemates — or noticed that he only had one eye open. Thóra's understanding of epilepsy was limited, but the helmet was probably meant to protect his head if he suffered a seizure. The young man's expression suggested that he was also developmentally impaired, either as part and parcel of his epilepsy or yet another burden that he'd been born with. Of course it was also possible that the photographer had told a joke the boy found hilarious, then had clicked the shutter at an unfortunate moment. Natan's jolliness was incongruous, anyway, against the sadness on his mother's and uncle's faces.

Finally Thóra had drawn up a list containing the phone numbers and addresses of the relatives of the four residents who'd died in addition to Tryggvi. In one case it appeared that the parents were divorced, since the mother and father of Sigríður Herdís Logadóttir lived in separate locations.

The overwhelming feeling she experienced once she'd called everyone on the list was fatigue. Fatigue and sadness, though she wasn't sure why since none of the parents had complained about either their lot or that of their child, and they all seemed to be bearing up remarkably well. Their stories of painful struggles with the system as they sought decent housing for their child were without exception told with a complete lack of self-pity, and Thóra wondered whether rejection and obstacles strengthened people and helped them to deal with things more stoically. Úlfheiður, Natan's mother, was the only one who'd sounded rather cold. The photograph did indeed appear to have captured her character rather well. She didn't seem bothered that the wrong man might have been held responsible for her son's death, leaving the guilty party still on the loose. She described her son's illness to Thóra as if reading the text off a sheet of paper, betraying no emotion, but seemed happy to speak at length about him. At first Natan had appeared normal, but before he'd even left the maternity ward he had started having seizures and had remained behind in hospital when she went home. The nerve cells in his brain didn't work as they should have; they were overactive, according to his mother, and he was among those unlucky epileptics for whom medication wasn't very effective. He then underwent an operation, but it was unsuccessful, leaving him with the possibility of suffering a seizure at any time. He lost the sight in one eye when he was eight, after hitting his face on the edge of a table during a fit.

By this point in her story the woman sounded tired of going over it all again. She began to talk faster, telling Thóra how each fit had further damaged Natan's brain, and by the last one he'd been in a very bad way. Since Úlfheiður was a single parent and worked day and night to make ends meet, she couldn't afford to have him at home any longer, especially as the economy declined. He was subsequently moved to a facility for seriously disabled children, coming home only for occasional overnight stays, as well as two weeks in the summer. He'd lived there for around fifteen years, at which point he'd passed the age limit for that home, had moved to the new residence and died. Although Úlfheiður's account seemed callous, Thóra doubted that she'd always been like that; originally she must surely have been besotted with her child, like other mothers were. Obviously her circumstances had forced her to let go of her son and along the way her soul must have got damaged. Unless she was just naturally cold-hearted.

Úlfheiður had nothing much to say about the centre; she had rarely visited because she had no car and there were no buses — the area was a ghost town. She had met few people on the rare times that she'd gone, and actually only remembered one woman, who she described as stuck-up. The woman had given her a dirty look when in the course of conversation it came up that Úlfheiður was visiting the place for the first time, two months after it had opened. Úlfheiður snorted as she said this and for the first time Thóra detected a hint of emotion in her voice — she had been hurt by the other mother's reaction. *Of course she was always hanging around, even though her son didn't even know she was there*, she told Thóra. *At least Natan was aware of me and wanted me to be there.* Thóra had no interest in hearing more about the friction between her and Fanndís, and steered the conversation to Jakob, though she didn't find out much; Úlfheiður barely remembered him. She wasn't necessarily convinced that he'd started the fire; that could certainly have been someone else. But she couldn't be persuaded to name any names and Thóra got the feeling that she'd only really said it to please her.

At the end of the conversation Thóra asked cautiously about Natan's sex drive, but the woman said she knew nothing about that; she'd simply never thought about it. Before they said their goodbyes, Úlfheiður told her that she tried to think as little as possible about the fire; she'd long since come to terms with her son's death, as she'd known since he was born that he wouldn't live long. As Úlfheiður said this, Thóra stared at the image of Natan on the screen, smiling from ear to ear at the family reunion, happy with his life, unaware that some people would see it as simply a long, drawn-out fight to the death.

Although the conversation with Úlfheiður had been difficult, it was a walk in the park compared to the talk she had with Lísa Finnbjörnsdóttir's parents. Her mother had answered the phone but could barely be persuaded to say anything, except that they'd chosen to let the crime against their daughter be forgotten so that her name wouldn't be dragged posthumously through the justice system and her case sensationalised in the papers. She agreed when asked whether Einvarður had assisted them in putting a stop to further investigation of the case, but flatly denied that he or anyone else had influenced their decision. She'd then put her husband on the phone and made him finish the conversation, which mainly consisted of him trying to persuade Thóra not to name Lísa directly in the petition to reopen Jakob's case. There was no way Thóra could agree to this and a long time was spent bickering over the man's further attempts to persuade her to change her mind, which she deftly deflected. At the same time, she tried to coax out of him the names of those who could have raped his daughter. If he was telling the truth — and he appeared to be sincere in all of his answers — then he had thought about this a great deal, but Thóra could get nothing out of him. The call concluded with him begging Thóra one last time to allow his daughter to rest in peace. He sounded as if he were on his knees.

Other than this she didn't get much out of the

phone calls, though the investigation continued to make slow progress. For example, after speaking to the girl's parents, Thóra was fairly certain that Sigríður Herdís Logadóttir had had nothing to do with the fire; she had been both blind and deaf, as well as seriously mentally disabled. Lísa Finnbjörnsdóttir was also ruled out, which left only two other residents, Natan and Tryggvi, neither of whom seemed likely either. Nothing in the interviews with the parents suggested they had any information that might prove useful; the only new thing that came to light was that Tryggvi's unconventional therapy had been disruptive, since it seemed to have caused him unnecessary suffering. However, none of them wanted to go into this in any detail, as it hardly mattered given what happened later. Sigríður Herdís's mother said that she'd actually complained to the director that Tryggvi's wailing was causing her distress during her visits to her daughter. She believed her complaint had forced them to switch his therapy to a more conventional kind, because she hadn't noticed any noises on subsequent visits. Thóra asked her when she'd lodged this complaint, and she replied that it had been about three weeks before the fire. Neither she nor the other parents knew the name of Tryggvi's therapist, although Thóra assumed that he was on Glódís's list. She concluded her conversation with the woman and looked up Glódís's e-mail address, then emailed her to ask. The man must have known Tryggvi quite well and could hopefully tell her what he'd been capable of. It was getting late, so she didn't expect to receive a response from the director that day.

After speaking to the parents of all of the residents, she had nothing to indicate that the fire was connected to their offspring at all. Ultimately, it seemed more likely to have involved a member of staff, or someone else otherwise linked to the unit. There was no logical reason for any of the young people living there to have wanted to kill the others, and the more Thóra thought about it, the harder she found it to come up with any motive for such an evil act. If the aim was to hide Lísa Finnbjörnsdóttir's pregnancy, nobody could argue that this was the best way to do it; there had been no obvious attempt to make the fire look like an accident, and it would have been easier to suffocate Lísa, since she was confined to her bed. In fact, it was the very manner of her death that had precipitated an autopsy, so if somebody had killed her in order to hide her condition their strategy had been extraordinarily stupid. Perhaps the plan hadn't been to hide the deed, but rather to detract attention from Lísa by making all the residents and the night watchmen suffer the same fate as her. Still, what Thóra found most troubling was the fact that no one seemed to have known that the girl was pregnant, which in turn made it difficult to state in the petition that the fire might have been intended to hide this fact. Of course somebody may have known about the pregnancy, but Thóra had no way of proving it. According to Glódís the girl's periods had been irregular, to say the least, and her pregnancy was so recent when she died that she had no noticeable bump. So perhaps the question was how the perpetrator could have known about the pregnancy at all.

No matter what the reason for the fire, it was clear from the number of lives lost that it had been reckless and illogical. Potentially, then, the act of someone of limited intelligence, someone who didn't comprehend the consequences of their actions — unless the perpetrator had deliberately made it look that way. But why, and who could it be? There weren't many possibilities, but still Thóra's mind spun in endless circles.

Who had sent her the text messages, and why? Who had known that the fire alarm system was offline? Was it a coincidence that the same lawyer had defended both Jakob and his creepy friend Jósteinn? Did the words *look at me*, which Jakob had repeated to her, have any significance? Had the residents been unhappy with their living conditions, unbeknownst to their parents, and was that significant? Why had only one staff member been on duty, not two — and who had been aware of this?

But the complexity of the case was not Thóra's only problem. There were very few precedents for a petition to reopen a case, so other than the laws themselves, she didn't have much to go on; and although these were clear, they weren't particularly detailed. The case had to satisfy at least one of four criteria for the Supreme Court to approve the petition: new evidence that had come to light; an accusation that the police, the prosecution, the judge or other parties had prejudiced the case, especially through falsified evidence or false testimony; reasonable suspicion that the evidence presented in the case had been wrongly evaluated; or the discovery of substantial flaws in the prosecution of the case in court. Since any retrial required the prior authorization of the Supreme Court, Thóra didn't need to present a perfect defence immediately, but merely demonstrate unequivocally that one or more of these prerequisites was met. If the petition were approved, the case would move to the next level.

She still hadn't come across anything to suggest any element of wrongdoing on the part of the police, prosecutor or judge, though there was the question of whether Lísa's pregnancy should have been made clearer. As the autopsy report was part of the case files she couldn't present the pregnancy as new evidence, even though this detail hadn't come up in court. The third criterion, however — insufficient evaluation of the evidence — could be enough to reopen the case; she was thinking not only of Lísa's condition, but also of Jakob's description of the angel with a suitcase, which in her opinion had not been dealt with appropriately in court. If it was true that he had tried to inform the police of this detail, then his testimony had not been recorded; at least, Thóra couldn't find it in the reports or other files. She was also interested in the fourth requirement, the one concerning flaws in the prosecution of the case, and Ari's performance in this regard. Although it would be tough to prove that he hadn't acted in his client's best interests, Thóra was convinced of it. The best thing would be if she were to unearth new evidence. Then they could run the case back through the system, with a fairer outcome.

As Thóra considered these points, she couldn't avoid the most difficult question, the one really plaguing her: when all was said and done, was she sure Jakob wasn't guilty? Perhaps he was more cunning than she gave him credit for, and had had the sense to keep all the apartment doors open so the fire could spread freely. Unlikely though it seemed, it wasn't out of the question that Jakob had more organizational ability than they credited him with. His innocent appearance might be colouring her view of him, and it was conceivable that there was something in what Glódís and Ari had said about Jakob's violent tendencies. Perhaps it would help if she could see footage of a typical day at the home — if the filmmaker had such a thing and were willing to share it with her. She really had no firm grasp on what it had really been like there. She wasn't expecting to see someone scurrying around trying out the door mechanisms, or climbing a stepladder to inspect the sprinkler system, but maybe she would get a better feeling for the conditions that might have set the fateful sequence of events in motion. She didn't have any further evidence to suggest Jakob's innocence; for the moment, it looked as though she was relying on lots of small things combining to become greater than the sum of their parts.

She recalled Jakob's description of the angel with the suitcase and sighed heavily. She had no idea what he'd meant, but right now the 'angel' was just as likely to have started the fire as anyone else.

17

Tuesday, 12 January 2010

Thóra logged off the Internet in order to avoid the temptation to sit there reading the day's news. She needed to get to work, and besides, the news was always rather depressing. Foreign news had always been more exciting than domestic news, but after the bank crash, all that had been reversed. Icelandic drama — yes please! The more she read and heard in passing from better-informed colleagues, the more appalled she was by how events had panned out before the crash. In some ways, Thóra envied her parents, who must surely be the only ones who felt that this was all some sort of misunderstanding. Still, they were victims of the criminal masses and had lost more than most people Thóra knew, although everyone had been affected in some way. She missed the time when everything had been fine; when the nation had celebrated its handball team's medal in the Olympic Games and the Icelanders' successes in foreign markets had seemed unstoppable. Now that was all so unreal. She resolved to stop reading about the crash in the mornings; it was unhealthy for anyone to start the day on such a depressing note. It was bad enough having to look at Bella.

'The coffeemaker's broken.' The secretary

leaned against the doorframe. It looked as if she had an entire pack of gum in her mouth. 'It just stopped working.'

'Broken? Did it stop working and then break, or did it break first then stop working?' Thóra didn't know why she was even asking; she had heard something breaking out in the corridor but hadn't dared to go and see what was happening, since it was followed by Bella's colourful curses, which still echoed in her ears.

'It stopped working because it's broken.' Bella's face displayed no flicker of amusement. 'You've got to buy a new one, right now in fact. There's no way I can spend a day here without coffee.'

'Isn't there any instant? We have a kettle somewhere, and I haven't got time to go and buy a new coffeemaker.'

'Are you joking? Only wimps drink that stuff. Do I look like a wimp?'

Thóra couldn't help but answer in the negative. A wimp was the last thing her scowling secretary resembled. She had recently been experimenting with her hair colour and it was currently fluorescent green. This had left her hair extremely dry, which, coupled with its tendency to stick up vertically, made the effect even more alarming. 'You should have thought of that before you broke the machine. How exactly did you manage it?' The coffeemaker had stood securely on the table in reception. Maybe Bella had been practising gymnastics and run into it; such a thing wouldn't be unheard of.

'I threw my phone at it.' Bella said this without

blinking. 'The noise it was making was driving me mad.'

Thóra was on the verge of making a maddening noise herself, but she bit her tongue. 'Then I'm sure you'll enjoy the whistling of the kettle when you make some instant coffee. I'd put it in the same place — I think it will withstand your attacks better than the coffeemaker.' Thóra turned to her computer. 'Now leave me alone, please. I'm busy. Some of us actually do some work here, however alien the concept may seem to you.' She made a point of not ducking when she turned away; Bella didn't have anything in her hands that she could throw. Still, it was sensible to stay on your guard, so she watched her secretary out of the corner of her eye as she hovered in the doorway like a thundercloud before turning on her heel and vanishing. Thóra would have to remember to be careful when she left the office later. The filmmaker, Sveinn, had agreed to meet her and although she wouldn't be able to take any material away, she could watch the video he'd made at the residence. If she noticed anything particularly interesting, he was willing to negotiate with her about making her copies of the material. He had also explained at length that what he had filmed was pretty raw; he hadn't had a chance to edit it yet and it was unlikely that he ever would, since the project's financial backing had dried up. That actually suited Thóra fine; if the material was unedited, she was more likely to figure out what she was looking for. She planned to take Matthew with

253

her, since two pairs of eyes were better than one, and he would also be glad to get away from her parents for a bit. Hopefully he would get himself some coffee on the way to the office.

★ ★ ★

'Come in, I've got everything ready.' The man who welcomed them was unshaven and hollow-eyed, and was wearing an old tracksuit. Thóra had expected a studio or workshop but should have realized that was unlikely; the address was in a large apartment block in the Breiðholt suburb. At one end of the room all the furniture had been pushed together to make space for a dining table that held three computer screens arranged in a row. There was also a small keyboard and some huge headphones. Next to the table was an office chair on wheels, listing slightly to one side, as if it were as tired as its owner. 'I work from home, as you can see, so you'll have to excuse the mess. I would have tidied up if I'd had a bit more warning.'

Thóra briskly reassured him that they weren't put off by a bit of chaos, before the man could notice Matthew's look of horror. He couldn't bear dirt and untidiness, though his cleaning mania had had to relax slightly on moving into a household that included two teenagers and a toddler. Mind you, the mess in Thóra's house was mainly clothes, shoes, schoolbooks, toys and that kind of thing, strewn haphazardly as if the occupants had had to abandon the house in a great hurry. Sveinn was a different sort of slob altogether. Dirty dishes sat on a low coffee table with knives and forks placed carefully on top, side by side, as if he expected a cleaner to appear, clear everything off the table and ask whether anyone might like a coffee. Beneath the table were KFC buckets. A bath towel lay in a crumpled heap on the back of the sofa, and it also appeared that Sveinn liked to take off his socks in front of the television at the end of the day. A selection of single socks lay in front of the sofa, as if his feet had taken turns pushing a sock off while his hands were otherwise occupied, perhaps working their way through the fried chicken.

Thóra only gave the briefest glance in the direction of the shelving unit holding the television, but couldn't help noticing the Coke cans standing there as if on display. The rest of the junk on the shelves wasn't familiar enough for Thóra to distinguish what it was without looking for longer. 'Pull up some chairs; you're better off watching it on the computer when the material is this raw, as I said on the phone. The resolution is quite good, so it should be pretty clear.' Sveinn sat down on the office chair and started setting up the video. 'What sucks is that I'll probably never get to use this material.'

'Was the project killed off by the budget cuts?' Thóra had settled in next to the table but Matthew was still looking around for a passably clean chair.

'I'm pretty pissed off about it, though I know money is in short supply these days, and other things are probably taking priority.' The first frame appeared on screen and Sveinn adjusted the settings to sharpen the image. 'The project was green-lit in 2003, and I started working on it a year later. So I was shooting this material for several years — not continuously, of course. But still.'

'And what was the purpose of the film?' Thóra watched the man's tweaking and twiddling without any idea what he was doing.

'2003 was the Year of the Disabled Person and this project was the initiative of the Ministry of Welfare; it was supposed to have been a documentary about the situation of the disabled today, for those who knew nothing about them as well as those who already had an interest. Obviously I was pretty ignorant about the subject when I started, but I've become an expert now. In a hundred years' time they will be treated completely differently. There's some incredible stuff in here, but it's not like I came up with any magic solutions myself.' When Sveinn was finally happy with the settings he opened the media player. 'When it burned down, both television stations sought me out and I was offered a lot of money for clips of the place in action.'

'And did you let them use them?' Thóra didn't remember seeing any video clips in the news reports of the fire.

'No, I didn't get permission. It's all owned by the ministry and they prohibited its release. Of course the police were given a copy — without my being paid for it, naturally. It's fucking bullshit, because I could have used the money.

It's not a very profitable business, let me tell you.'

Thóra muttered vague agreement. 'You said you saw a lot of strange things while filming the documentary — was any of this at the home that burned down?'

Sveinn turned to her. 'Well, I don't remember exactly. I got my material from a variety of places, since the documentary was supposed to give an overview of the situation, and just one centre would never have been enough. It definitely wasn't the weirdest place I saw, even though the residents' circumstances were affecting. There are so many levels of disability, and the people at this place were among the most severely afflicted. Most of the people I met were just like you and me; completely capable of getting by in normal society, given the right tools.' He had moved the cursor into place to start the video, but the mouse appeared to be sticky, since he was holding the button down for a long time. 'Mental disability is so different from physical that I feel the two groups have little in common. It's one of the things I think will change over time; the boundaries between them will become clearer.'

Thóra was beginning to think he'd never start the film, but she didn't want to press him. 'So you didn't notice anything unusual there, compared to what you saw elsewhere?'

'Well, it was new, of course, and meant to be a kind of flagship, despite the way things turned out. Nothing was spared in the design of the centre, but as I understood it the finances ran

257

out and construction standards slipped. I felt as if the residents hadn't quite come to terms with being moved there and the staff hadn't settled in either. There was an almost amateurish feeling about the place, compared to the older units I visited.'

'Could you elaborate?'

'Oh, I just felt the staff were too young and sometimes kind of clumsy in the way they dealt with the residents.' Sveinn saw from Thóra's expression that she'd read more into his words than he'd intended and hurriedly added: 'Not that they bullied them or anything. They simply hadn't had time to learn how to deal with them. For example, I saw staff members standing right next to residents and discussing them as if they weren't there, which is extremely unprofessional.' He started the film, slightly embarrassed about it, or so it seemed. 'That might be in one of the clips, actually.'

The quality of the image that appeared on the three screens could have been better, though the cables on the floor in the opening shot suggested that it had been properly lit and sound-recorded. 'I'll fast-forward over the parts that aren't so important. Let me know if I should slow down or rewind.' They watched closely and Thóra pointed out Glódís to Matthew when she appeared. The director stood with crossed arms and watched from a distance as one of her staff attended to a young woman who sat in a chair, seemingly ignoring the transparent ball in her lap. The care assistant pressed one of the young woman's hands to her lips and placed the other one on the ball. 'Ball.' The woman squeezed the girl's hand, forcing her to tighten her grip on the ball. She then loosened her grip and folded her own fingers, then got the girl to feel them before moving the girl's fingers into the same position. 'Sign language?' asked Matthew.

Sveinn nodded. 'The girl was blind and deaf and had some sort of developmental disability to boot. The woman sitting with her is an occupational therapist or developmental therapist or something, but I can't remember her or the girl's names.'

'Sigríður Herdís Logadóttir.' Thóra had pretty much memorised the names of everyone at the centre and Sigríður Herdís had been the only deaf-blind one. She watched the girl handle the ball and various other things as the therapist handed them to her. Every time the woman handed her something new they repeated the exercise: one hand on the object, the other on the woman's lips while she told her what the object was called; then they practised making the sign with their hands. From time to time the girl realized what she was holding and was the first to make the sign, at which she received cheerful praise from her therapist. Glódís stood there motionless the whole time, watching. 'Is this the first video that you shot?'

'Yes, they run in sequence. Why do you ask?'

'I was wondering about the centre's director. She was obviously there to ensure that everything proceeded properly at the start, but surely she couldn't have followed everyone's treatment, all the time?'

'No, I agree, she couldn't. She was quite suspicious of me at first, but then she got used to my presence and I started seeing less of her. I would've expected the residents to find it difficult having me around, but not her.'

Over the course of the videos the stony-faced Glódís stopped appearing in every shot. At first they watched every clip to the end, but when there was little to see beyond the daily lives of the residents, they started asking Sveinn to go through them more quickly. There wasn't much to be gained from endless mealtimes and therapy sessions, and they found it uncomfortable to spy like peeping toms on the lives of these unfortunate people, now dead. In one of the scenes they spotted the young night watchman who had been on duty on the fateful night, and Sveinn paused the tape. 'This one died in the fire. It was sheer luck that his co-worker didn't die as well. He was off sick, or at least that's what I was told.'

'Is that significant?' Matthew looked at Thóra.

'I don't know.' She turned to Sveinn. 'Were there watchmen on duty at the residence during the daytime? Or was it just evenings and weekends?'

'It was staffed full-time on weekdays, so there was no need for a watchman except for the night shifts; but at weekends there were two of them working alone until noon, and then more people turned up to take care of lunch and receive visitors. I filmed there on several Sunday mornings because it was so quiet. That's how I know the arrangement. The one who died was a nice guy, very good with the residents and really laid-back, like all the night watchmen. Once his sister and friend came to visit and helped out, although the smell coming off them rather suggested they were just finishing off a long night on the tiles.'

Matthew couldn't hide his shock. 'Was that allowed?'

'Yeah, sure. They were fine really, and they weren't there that long. There was no ban on visitors to the centre, except of course at night, although I was never there then. I expect the same went for the staff as for the residents — that friends and relatives could pop in as long as they didn't get in the way. It wasn't *that* common, I don't think, but I probably have some footage of someone dropping in, somewhere amongst all this.'

In the event they didn't find a relevant clip, despite going through what felt like hundreds of them. It would complicate the case endlessly if they had to factor in unscheduled visits by friends and family of employees, and it made Thóra wonder whether the only way to find the person who impregnated Lísa would be to take a DNA sample from every man in Iceland. She tried to push aside this idea and focus on the screen. One resident after another appeared and she was able to identify them all, since they were so few and their disabilities so different. Jakob appeared several times and in one shot he looked very upset, muttering constantly that he wanted to go home and being told again and again that this was his new home and that he should stop complaining and find something interesting to do. The video stopped suddenly when he pushed the lamp off his bedside table as he stomped furiously around the room. In other segments he just looked bored, and when he did join in any group activity it was with his head hanging sullenly. Tryggvi featured the least often, which Thóra imagined was due to the antisocial aspects of his autism. He only appeared twice, sitting in his room, in one instance drawing something that appeared to be a face without eyes, but with a mask over its nose and mouth, and in the other staring into space and rocking slowly back and forth. The wall of his room was more or less covered with his pictures, which all had a similar subject: an eyeless figure, prostrate and with a gaping mouth, and another person in the distance holding up a ring divided into three. The same peculiar sequence, O8INN, appeared in all of them. However, the pictures weren't identical; when the camera panned slowly across the wall, prominent flames were visible in some of them. 'Do you know what the pictures are meant to show?' asked Thóra. 'For example, this figure lying down.' She had started to suspect that it might be Lísa. She must have always been in bed, and her eyes must have always been closed. Why the figure's mouth was gaping like that was another story; maybe it was one of those artist's secrets that would never be revealed.

'I have no idea, but he was extremely meticulous in his drawing. You should have seen how he went about it — I forgot to slow the film down to point it out to you before. He drew it all

262

in one movement without ever lifting the pencil.' They waited as Sveinn rewound to the shot of Tryggvi drawing, and stared silently at the screen as it demonstrated his peculiar method. The young man showed no sign of hesitation; he drew the pencil at even speed back and forth across the paper. 'I'd be willing to bet that if someone studied this, they'd find that he'd discovered a way to do it using the shortest line possible and with the fewest intersecting points. And he never stopped to think about it. Amazing.'

On the screen Tryggvi held out the picture behind him, in the direction of the camera, without looking up. 'Thank you,' a voice said, and a hand appeared to receive the picture, the video image wobbling slightly. 'He gave me the drawing, the poor thing. I expect he'd run out of Blu-Tack to stick up the pictures and didn't know what to do with them.'

'Incredible.' Thóra stared at the wall, which now filled the frame. 'I'm not sure I'd have wanted these pictures hanging in my room. They're just too sad — although he can't have been bothered by them, if he wanted to display them so prominently.'

'Well, I don't know. The next time I came they were all gone, and they'd taken all the boy's drawing implements. I never understood why, but maybe, as you say, the pictures *did* have a negative influence on him or something. He looked pretty sad after that, although he was hardly a bundle of joy before.' He fast-forwarded through some shaky recordings of the corridor

263

before letting the video play again.

Thóra's eyes were starting to hurt, but suddenly something caught her attention. The man had walked down the corridor taking brief shots of the interior of each apartment. 'Would you mind stopping?' The screen showed apartment number six. Inside, someone was lying in bed; the short, dark hair could have belonged to a woman or a man. 'Who's this?' Subconsciously, Thóra had been keeping count of the residents during the camera's trip into the apartments, and all five had already appeared.

'Oh, her. I don't remember her name. She was living there but got sick or something, so she was at home or in hospital, I think, when the fire occurred. And because of that, she's still alive.'

'What?' Thóra couldn't disguise her amazement. Suddenly, she remembered having made a note to find out why there were six rooms but only five residents, given the supposed demand for places, and she kicked herself for not asking Glódís during their meeting. 'Where is she now? Do you think it's possible to speak to her?'

'I have no idea where she ended up. At least, I didn't see her the few times that I went to other centres to do some filming after the fire.' He pointed at the equipment around her bed. 'She's seriously disabled and there's no way of communicating with her unless you know how — she only signals with her eyes. I'm not sure whether she's all there, mentally, but she seemed quite alert to me. Her eyes followed me every time I went into her room, though that might not mean anything.'

Thóra would have to dig around for information about her, from Glódís or someone else at the Regional Office for the Disabled. If that didn't work, she would go to Einvarður and remind him of his promise to assist them. But what would someone so severely disabled be able to add to what they already knew? She seemed unlikely to have any information Thóra wasn't already aware of, and she couldn't possibly have been present when Lísa's child was conceived. Yet it was incredible that this was the first they'd heard of her; up until now no one had said a single word about her, nor had Thóra seen her mentioned even once in the case files.

When Sveinn started the video again, Thóra was distracted and had difficulty focusing on what she was seeing and hearing. It was different for Matthew, who watched with great attentiveness; probably precisely because her own concentration had lapsed. 'Rewind just a bit.' Matthew had cocked his head sideways. 'Could you turn it up? I thought I heard something.' Sveinn did so, and they watched as an employee bent over a huge towel in a bathroom. 'Did you hear that?' Matthew looked at Thóra, who shook her head — she wasn't sure. 'One more time,' he said.

The man unfolded the towel with jerky movements as Sveinn rewound the tape. Then he began moving normally again, but Thóra's attention wasn't directed at what he was doing, but at what she could vaguely hear being repeated angrily in the background.

'*Look at me! Look at me!*'

18

Wednesday, 13 January 2010

The traffic on Skólavörðurstígur Street had started to build up again. The rumbling of the cars carried in through the half-open window and the exhaust fumes worked their way into Thóra's office. After one ill-advisedly deep in-breath she exhaled and grimaced, held her nose until she'd shut the window and then used the sheet of paper in her hand — which happened to be a list of the residence's employees and specialists — as a fan. That seemed to disperse most of the stink, but perhaps she had just grown impervious to it. Nonetheless, she felt a bit better when she sat down again. It was hard enough to form an opinion on who from the list she should speak to next, without suffering respiratory failure into the bargain. Glódís had included far too many people, fourteen full-time and ten part-time, and there was no way of knowing in advance which of them might provide any useful information. Thóra was still waiting for the director to answer her e-mail requesting the name of the man who had looked after Tryggvi. Thóra had also put a cross by one name: Glódís herself. And actually, she could also cross out Friðleifur Guðjónsson, the night watchman who had died in the fire. It wasn't as though she'd get anything from speaking to his gravestone, but Thóra still hesitated to cross out his name. Her pen hovered over the black lettering without touching the paper as she stared contemplatively at the letters. The young man had been hit at the base of the skull before the fire was lit. Was it to prevent him from helping the residents get out, or was there some other reason?

Thóra reached for the file containing the autopsy report in order to reassure herself that she'd remembered the sequence of events correctly. Indeed she had. The man had been hit from behind and died of smoke inhalation in the blaze, probably as he'd lain unconscious. She tapped her pen lightly against the edge of the table. Might the fire have been designed to kill the night watchman? The filmmaker had mentioned that Friðleifur had received visitors at the home, so it was possible that he'd fallen out with a guest that night. Nocturnal visits weren't permitted, but who was supposed to enforce that rule when the watchmen were alone on duty? It was also entirely possible that the criminal had thought he'd killed the night watchman and had set the place on fire in a desperate attempt to conceal the evidence. People in extremis can do the most unbelievable things, and what better way to conceal a murder than to make it look as though the violence had been directed at someone else? It could be that the same man had impregnated Lísa, which might have led to a fatal argument with Friðleifur. Thóra couldn't quite imagine it, since the watchmen could hardly have allowed their visitors to roam freely around the apartments at night, but it was just about conceivable. She knew nothing about Friðleifur Guðjónsson other than the little information contained in the testimony in the case files, and the good opinion of the filmmaker, although that was of little use. People rarely spoke ill of the dead, even though they might have cultivated less than flattering thoughts about them while they were still above ground.

On the other hand, it would be easy to speak to the man who shared shifts with Friðleifur, since his name was readily available in the files. Thóra looked up his mobile number and rang it, but he didn't answer and it didn't go to voicemail. Until she could reach him, the only way to determine whether she was on the right track was to speak to Friðleifur's relatives. She looked at the clock — almost five — and hurried to dig out the names of the man's parents from the files. No one answered the landline, and the mother's mobile was either turned off or out of range. However, Friðleifur's father Guðjón answered his at the second ring. It sounded like he was driving.

She introduced herself and offered to call later if it was inconvenient.

'Inconvenient? What do you mean?' The line was crackly, but she could hear his surprise.

'It's just that I can tell you're driving.'

'That's no problem. I'm about to park.' A moment later she heard the engine shut off. 'Did you say you were a lawyer? Are you from the bank?' Thóra explained carefully who she was and who she worked for. There was a long silence. For a moment she thought the man was going to hang up, but then he suddenly started speaking again, his voice now a great deal sharper. 'What the hell do you want from me?'

'I'm trying to get to the bottom of how this fire occurred and part of that process involves speaking to the employees of the centre and the families of those who died.'

'As if we know anything. You must be pretty desperate if you think that the family members are holding on to some sort of secret information. Do you really think we wouldn't have told it to the police when they were investigating the case?'

The man was going to be a tricky interviewee, that much was certain. 'A lot of what you discussed with the investigators back then didn't find its way into the reports. They don't include every little detail from the interviews. But just so you understand where I'm going, I have to rule out the possibility that the fire was directed at Friðleifur.'

'No one would have wanted to harm him. He was just an ordinary guy. He'd never got on the wrong side of the law, never even got into a fight.' The man's voice faded, but then he added sadly: 'Not even as a kid.'

After this the conversation went much better. The man's anger diminished and he appeared to realize slowly but surely that Thóra's intentions were good. She carefully formulated her questions so that it would be impossible to interpret them as being in any way negative towards Friðleifur. 'So he didn't hang around with anyone undesirable? Someone who might possibly have attacked him at work, and things might have escalated from there?'

'No, I don't think so. His friends were like him, easy-going, laid-back guys. Of course I wished he'd been a bit keener on the books, but I don't know whether that had anything to do with his friends; they were all the same, and most of them dropped out of high school. Actually, I think Friðleifur was planning to go back to school. It's just a hunch, but when I could finally bring myself to go through his room, I found a brochure of evening classes and some textbooks on pharmacology that he'd apparently bought. God knows he had enough time to study on the night shift.'

'He lived at home, in other words?'

'Yes — he didn't exactly make a fortune from that job, or from his previous jobs, so he couldn't afford payments on an apartment, and we weren't in much of a position to help out either. It's an incredible relief not to be stuck with an unsellable apartment on which you owe more than what you paid for it. Still, he was doing pretty well before he died; he'd become more sensible with his finances.'

Thóra's mobile beeped, and she read the short text message as she spoke. It was from Sóley, asking whether she was coming home. 'I don't imagine you and your wife ever visited the home, though I understand your daughter sometimes dropped in there?' She replied to Sóley as she waited for the man's reaction: *Soon.*

'Did she? I didn't know that. Why do you mention it? If she visited him, I don't see how

270

it'd be relevant here; he and his sister got on well, that's all.'

'I was just wondering whether she could maybe assist me. An outsider might have a clearer perspective and I can't see a statement from her anywhere in the case files.'

'No, there wasn't one; and as I say, I wasn't aware she'd visited him there. Are you sure?'

The phone beeped again. 'Well, I don't see why my source would have made it up, or indeed how he would have known that Friðleifur had a sister at all. I'm certainly not suggesting that anything untoward took place, but I'd still be interested to speak to her.' Thóra reached for her mobile to see the new message. Sóley still had to learn how to end these exchanges; every reply was always followed by another. Thóra had recently gone through it with her, but it didn't seem to have had any effect.

'I'd like to discuss it with her first. You don't think I'd let you loose on her without asking her?'

'No, no. Absolutely not.' She prodded the phone's keypad to see what her daughter had to say. On the screen she read *o2 short hose*, which meant nothing to her, but underneath it was a photo. 'Perhaps I could just get in touch with you again in a few days, or you could call me, and by then you might . . . ' Thóra lost the thread of the conversation. The picture on the little screen was a long way from the kind of thing Sóley usually sent. It was a black, charred corpse leaning back in the remains of an office chair. The deformed head hung over the

271

back of the seat as if the individual had been waiting to have his throat cut; his hands hung at his sides, black palms facing forward. She'd seen this image before. It was Friðleifur.

'Are you still there?' The man sounded concerned.

'What? Oh, yes. I'm sorry.' Thóra pressed the button to display the phone number and saw that the message was, of course, not from Sóley. 'Did you just send me a text message?'

He sounded surprised now. 'I wouldn't know how to — I'm not good enough with phones to be able to send a message during a conversation. Why do you ask?'

'Sorry, I just got a bit confused.' Thóra found it difficult to concentrate on speaking to Guðjón with the image on the screen filling her mind. Who had sent it, and why? She hurried to wind up the conversation. 'Will you speak to your daughter, then, and let me know? The sooner the better.' The man agreed he would and said goodbye. Who knew if he'd keep his promise? As soon as he hung up she turned back to the message on her phone. She was in such a rush that it felt like she had ten thumbs and she was afraid she'd deleted the message in her clumsiness. Luckily she hadn't. She checked the phone number from which the message had been sent, but now it appeared to have been sent from the phone company Telecom. After a rather lengthy call to the company, during which she was transferred twice to different departments, she was informed that it had probably come from the free SMS service that they offered on the Internet. When Thóra reported that she'd also received three strange messages from ja.is, the man on the line sighed and told her that the best thing would be for her to request that such messages be blocked from reaching her phone. It was very easy and could even be done online. When Thóra said that she wasn't keen on the idea, the man sighed again; clearly this wasn't the first time the messaging service had been misused, and he must be tired of having these conversations. When Thóra explained to him that her enquiry had to do with a court case, the man's tone changed and he told her that all messages sent from the Internet were actually registered and traceable, but that it took time to trace them. He pledged to look into it as soon as he could, but couldn't promise he'd find anything. He took down her mobile number and the time of the message, which he said was enough information, and they hung up.

Thóra took a closer look at the photo. It wasn't very clear on the little screen but she recognized the subject nevertheless. A similar photo had been included in the police records found in one of Ari's files, but not in the documents Jakob's mother had given her. The photo was one of several taken at the scene before the bodies of the dead were removed. They had all caused Thóra's hair to stand on end and each and every one of them had imprinted itself so strongly onto her mind that she didn't need to see them clearly in order to recognize them again. She called Matthew.

'How can I enlarge a photo that I received in a text message?'

'Oh, hi, Matthew. How are you, Matthew?'

'You'll get a hi later, when I come home. I seriously need to find out how I can view a photo from my mobile in an ordinary size. Do you know how?'

'Umm . . . ' Matthew clearly didn't relish admitting that this was beyond his knowledge, even though he was rather more technologically minded than Thóra. 'I don't know how you would do it on your phone but it must be possible to find out.'

'So you know how to do it on *your* phone?' Perhaps Thóra could forward the message to him.

'Umm . . . ' Matthew sucked his teeth. 'No, not exactly.' Before Thóra could say anything he added hastily: 'If you still have the cables that came with it, you should be able to upload the photo to your computer. If you've lost them, I'm sure Gylfi could help you with it.'

'Do we know anyone who keeps those cables somewhere they can actually remember?' As soon as she said this she remembered that they did: Matthew himself. She added hurriedly: 'Anyway, see you in ten minutes.'

Before Thóra left her office she looked up photos of the scene in order to confirm to herself that the little photo was of Friðleifur's body. Luckily it was among the first that she pulled out, so she was spared from having to trawl through the entire mess once more. It was quite clear that the subject of the photo was the same, and in fact it looked like exactly the same photo. Who the hell had access to the police photograph database, and why had they sent it to her?

★ ★ ★

'It's the murderer, and he's trying to frighten you.' Thóra's mother's face was creased with worry. 'You need to stop the investigation before he comes and sets *us* on fire.'

Thóra rolled her eyes. 'How about if we drop this subject while we're eating?' She smiled at Sóley and little Orri, who were gazing wide-eyed at her. Unfortunately, her mother had walked in on Matthew and Gylfi as Gylfi was working on uploading the photograph to her laptop — at the exact moment that the photo had appeared in all its glory on the screen. She wouldn't stop going on about it until Thóra had explained the situation, and was still fretting now.

'Is the murderer coming to kill us?' Sóley put her fork down. 'Wow, that's so cool.' Then she realized what she'd said and added: 'Isn't it?'

'Murrr-err.' Orri was still too young to understand what the word meant but was sensible enough to realize that it was something terrible, and therefore belonged in the same category as exciting things like dinosaurs and crocodiles.

'Of course not. Grandma's just joking.' She saw that Sóley didn't believe her one bit and added: 'Don't worry, there's no murderer on the way. Just finish your food, darling.' Thóra glared at her mother.

By the time the meal was over Sóley was her

usual happy self again, since the adults had all started talking with false cheer about something entirely different. Thóra waited until her daughter had gone to bed and her parents were sitting in front of the television before returning to the computer to take a better look at the photo. Matthew sat down next to her at the kitchen table and shook his head after peering silently at the screen for a few moments. 'It's very strange, I have to say. Could it be that the person who sent you this didn't realize that you have all the case files?'

'Good question. I can't think of anyone who could possibly be behind it. I mean, why would anyone send me this?'

'As I said, maybe the person who sent it doesn't know you already have the photos.' Matthew leaned back from the screen. 'But still, I don't understand their motivation. Maybe the aim is to frighten you, as your mother so helpfully suggested at the table earlier. Perhaps the first step is to try and figure out who has access to the photo. The quality suggests it may not have come straight from the camera, so it might have been scanned.'

'There are quite a few other possibilities. Apart from the policemen who worked on the investigation, the different parties involved in the case all received copies of the files: the judges, the public prosecutor's office and Jakob's lawyer, Ari. He let Jakob's mother have a copy of some of the material, but that didn't include the photo. I can't quite see why Ari would want to send it to me again like this. He could have drawn my attention to it by sticking a Post-it on it, or just pointed it out to me when I visited him.'

'Could someone in the justice system, the police or the prosecutor's office, have done it?'

'That's possible, but why should anyone there want to bother me with something like this? They'd be in serious trouble if it came out, and I can't see why anyone would take the risk. And whether the intention was to scare me or to help me, it seems like a weird way to send me a message. The police and the public prosecutor could easily summon me to a meeting if anyone there were interested in my investigation.'

'What about the victims' relatives? Were they given the files?'

Thóra shook her head slowly. 'I wouldn't have thought so. Usually, every attempt is made to protect the relatives from the unnecessary distress of seeing an image like this. In order to be given a copy, you'd need to have an extremely good reason. I can't imagine what grounds there might have been to turn over this photo to the parents or other relatives.'

'What about the people who ran the centre? Do you think they'd have been able to follow the investigation?'

'No doubt they would have, but not in any detail — and certainly not this kind of detail. This is just totally incomprehensible. The only thing I can think of is that someone within the system — someone who knows about my involvement and has access to this image — is losing their marbles.'

'Or had already lost them.' Matthew looked

Thóra in the eye. 'If Jakob *is* innocent, the criminal is probably on the loose. Maybe your mother was right. This photo is certainly enough to frighten someone off, but the message could have been clearer. I'd hazard a guess at 'mind your own business' or something along those lines, though.'

'But if that's the case, the real murderer would have to be a policeman, a lawyer or a judge. Or Jakob's mother. None of whom seem very likely.' Thóra lifted her phone. 'Speaking of the message, what could *o2 short hose* mean?'

'An apartment number? Weren't the residents' apartments numbered 01, 02 and so on?'

'Yes, actually they were.' Thóra exhaled. 'If I remember correctly, 02 was the number of Natan's apartment, but there was no hose there to my knowledge, long or short. Maybe the girl who's still alive might know what it means.'

'Isn't that a good enough reason for you to find her? Maybe this text isn't a threat at all, but a suggestion. She's the only one still alive who knows what it was like to live there. Maybe she was even involved in the case.'

'She's paralysed and she can't speak. I don't know how she could possibly have been involved.' Thóra shut her laptop. 'But I obviously do need to meet her. First I've got to find out who she is, and where she is.'

'That shouldn't be hard.' Matthew smiled. 'As far as I can see, your real problem will be how to question her.'

Thóra closed her eyes. 'Fantastic — this case just gets better and better.'

19

Thursday, 14 January 2010

The Secure Psychiatric Unit at Sogn had obviously not changed since Thóra had been there last; abandoned wheelbarrows still stood in the driveway and the same wooden boxes were stacked against the wall, a few work gloves on top. It looked as though the place had lain dormant since the doors had shut behind her several days ago and had come back to life just a few minutes before she rang the bell again; everyone appeared to be dressed in the same clothes and as far as she could tell the same outdoor shoes were still lined up in the foyer. 'It's really cold out,' Thóra remarked, handing her coat to the woman in reception. She couldn't think of anything else to say and she could hardly ask the woman whether she'd been waiting for her there since last time, even if that was how it appeared.

'Is it?' The woman draped the garment over her arm. 'Are you here to see Jósteinn? He was expecting a lawyer.'

'Yes, that's me.' Thóra glanced down at her shoes, which were wet from the slush in the car park, and looked around for a mat to wipe them on. 'I received a phone call from here this morning, saying he wanted to see me. That's all I know about it.' Although Thóra would have preferred to excuse herself from this meeting, pleading an enormous workload, that wasn't really on; the man was footing the bill for the investigation into Jakob's case, which meant that he had to be shown the minimum of courtesy.

'Please have a seat in the waiting room and I'll go and fetch him; do you remember the way?' Thóra nodded and stopped trying to clean off the bottoms of her shoes, since it was a hopeless task. Instead she made a show of taking them off, while the woman said, 'Hopefully we can get him to tear himself away from his workshop, since you've come specially.'

'Is he in there a lot?' Thóra had to pretend to take an interest in the man's daily labours, and in fact she was happy to make conversation with the woman, since it meant delaying the meeting. She wasn't exactly afraid of Jósteinn, but she wasn't looking forward to seeing him.

'Yes, he seems to feel at home around those broken computers; he achieves incredible results, in fact. We've lost count of the number of machines he's managed to cobble together from other broken-down ones. They've been given new lives in developing countries.'

'Do you think he gets something out of it, doing good deeds?' Perhaps Thóra needed to revise her opinion of Jósteinn. He seemed genuinely concerned about Jakob, and now this. Maybe there was a good soul somewhere deep inside that broken and damaged man.

The woman smiled pityingly. 'No, I wouldn't say that. He couldn't care less about those poor people in the Third World. He just likes the computers themselves; he says they're perfect, that it's impossible for them to make mistakes on their own. He enjoys giving them new life. He once told me that the great thing about computers was that they didn't have eyes or brains, which meant they couldn't tell how ugly he was, both outside and in. He's a very sick man, and the computers seem to bring him some kind of satisfaction, which he needs. As do we all.'

Thóra didn't know what more she could say, so she just nodded. She found her own way to the waiting room and when she opened the door to it she had the same feeling that she'd had when she walked into the building; the embroidered pillows appeared not to have moved a millimetre, and the puzzle on the dining room table looked equally untouched. Even the two puzzle pieces lying next to one of the table legs were still there, waiting to either end up in the vacuum cleaner or be spotted and picked up by someone eagle-eyed. Thóra considered gathering them up from the carpet herself, but decided not to. She wasn't going to be anything other than a spectator in this place; she wouldn't change anything. She didn't understand why she felt like this, but she didn't want to leave any trace on this sad little outpost of humanity, no matter how small.

Thóra turned her gaze to the window and looked at the empty, lonely greenhouse in the garden. The glass sparkled, but inside stood the empty spring pots, along with a bent watering can that may or may not have been full of water. Jakob was nowhere to be seen.

When Jósteinn appeared, accompanied by the woman from reception, Thóra felt her fists clench and she had an overwhelming desire to move all the way to the other end of the sofa. There was something about this small, skinny man that disgusted her. It didn't just come from what she knew he'd done to others; his thin hair was greasy and his scalp showed through the comb tracks; even his glasses were so dirty that it was hard to believe he could actually see through the grime. He made a failed attempt to smile and Thóra nodded in return. She couldn't bring herself to extend her hand, but it didn't seem to bother him.

'Can I just leave you two alone? I'll be nearby if you need something.' The woman from reception looked Thóra in the eye as she said this, and as before the subtext of her statement was clear.

'Yes, that's fine.' Thóra affected a breezy tone, as if this was no problem at all. 'We shouldn't be long. Isn't that right, Jósteinn?'

'Yes.' Jósteinn sat down in the chair opposite Thóra. He gazed in silence at his lap until the woman had disappeared. 'How's it going?'

'Do you mean Jakob's case?' Thóra caught herself staring at the closed door.

'Yes. Have you solved it?' Jósteinn's voice was hushed, as if he preferred not to be heard.

'No, I can't say I have, but it is progressing.' Thóra shifted on the sofa, which was too soft and too low. 'Why did you want to meet me? Just to find out how I was getting on?'

'Yes. Exactly.'

'Don't you think it's a bit unnecessary for me to come all this way to Sogn to tell you the little that I have to report? You could just as easily have called.'

Without looking up, Jósteinn smiled. His bottom lip split, leaving a bloody streak in the middle. He seemed neither to notice nor to be bothered by the pain that this must have caused him. Thóra couldn't take her eyes off his thin-lipped mouth and his stained teeth, which, despite their colour, were straight and beautifully even. His smile disappeared as suddenly as it had appeared and a little drop of blood ran slowly down his chin. 'I can't call. I don't have access to a telephone here, as you know.'

'Surely you can speak on the phone if you ask the staff to call for you, and if the call is supervised.'

He shrugged. 'I've never tried it. Haven't ever needed to call anyone before.'

'Look into it next time if you need to get in touch. This is a long drive out of town for me, and my time is better spent working on the case itself. Unless you wanted to ask me something specific, or tell me something? I totally under-stand if you want to keep track of the hours that are going into this or if you want to rethink your position regarding the investigation. That's not unusual when people realize how quickly it can start getting expensive.'

'No, that's not it at all. I was just worried that you haven't come back to speak to Jakob and I wanted to know whether it was because you were stuck.'

'Things are coming along, as I say.' The room suddenly felt unbearably hot. 'I'll speak to Jakob when I have a particular reason to, since there's no point confusing him with multiple visits. He has difficulty discussing what happened, naturally, and I'd prefer not to wear him out or mix up his ideas about what happened with endless questions.'

'So, this is a long way for you. It would be better if we were located in Reykjavík.' Jósteinn fell silent, looked up abruptly and then immediately back down into his lap. 'Don't you think so?'

'Yes, probably. But there's not much we can do about that.' Thóra decided to try to make good use of this trip by getting Jósteinn to say something about his acquaintance with Ari, who was one of the few people who could have sent the photo to her phone, though he was just as unlikely to have done so as the others who had access to it. 'Your legal supervisor was Ari Gunnarsson, the same man who defended Jakob. Is this a coincidence, or did it affect your decision to fund a potential reopening of the case? Do you have something against him, perhaps, and are you looking for revenge?'

Jósteinn shook his head, but Thóra thought she saw him redden a bit, even though his head was bowed. 'No.'

'So this *is* simply a coincidence?'

'Yes.'

Thóra didn't need a lie detector to work out that Jósteinn was hiding something, but she couldn't fathom how best to get the truth out of this strange man. She suspected coming down hard on him wouldn't achieve much. 'Did he do a good job with your case?'

'How would I know? I don't know how others would have done. I probably would have ended up here even if I'd hired every lawyer in the country. If you're sick, you're sick. You can't treat a damaged mind like broken bones. It might be possible if the brain were brittle, not soft. Repairs are always much more complex when you can't screw or hammer things together.'

'Yes, that's . . . a shame.' Thóra was keen not to stray any further into this topic. 'But you must have had a sense of whether he was working on your case wholeheartedly. Did he come to see you? Or did you never meet him?'

'We met several times during the preparations for the trial. I suppose he could have shown a little more interest, but he wouldn't be the first or the last person to find it difficult to stay focused in my presence. People don't understand me, but *I* understand *them*. Do you know what I mean?'

'No, I can't say I do.' Thóra took a deep breath before continuing. 'Did you ever meet Ari in connection with Jakob's case? Did he ever come here?'

'Yes, I saw him after Jakob was moved here. He still recognized me, even after all that time.'

Thóra didn't find that strange; she would be hard pressed to forget this man. 'But if you think that Ari botched Jakob's case in some way, and especially if you're sure he did, you should come out and say so immediately. I'm sure I'd discover it for myself in the end, but it would be less expensive for you to tell me straight away.'

'I'll never have the chance to spend all of my money, so a few hours more or less don't matter. Maybe I like watching you scurry around.' He didn't smile or alter his tone, so she couldn't tell if he was trying to be funny. 'But I can tell you that Ari puts just enough effort into his work to make it impossible to criticize. It's a talent some people have; you know they should be trying harder, but you can't put your finger on anything in particular. For example, one of the cleaners here. She makes the beds but the sheet isn't stretched well enough over the mattress, but it's not so baggy that anyone would think to say anything about it.' Jósteinn lifted his head slightly and stared at the embroidered cushion next to Thóra. He looked pale and didn't seem aware of the heat in the room. 'Anyone but me, that is. And why would they pay me any mind?'

Again Thóra chose to ignore the man's complaints and forged on. 'So you don't know for certain that Ari mishandled Jakob's case somehow?'

'Actually, I do.' Jósteinn didn't look up, his gaze locked on the cross-stitching on the flowery cushion.

'And would you consider sharing what you know with me?' Thóra tried to hide her impatience, but was almost ready to shake the information out of the man — once she'd put on some rubber gloves.

'I know that he didn't do his job properly, and I can prove it.' Jósteinn's expression became almost cheerful. 'He's related to one of the victims, and I bet he didn't tell anyone.'

'How do *you* know, if he kept it to himself?'

'Before I got into doing computer repairs I studied genealogy. I was looking through my own lineage for ancestors with whom I had things in common. I have distant connections to the family of my victim. When you have enough time to spend on your hobbies, you can make decent progress with them. When I'd run out of names to look up, I started on people I knew, and one day I searched for Ari's family. When Jakob came here and I heard about his case, I recognized the name of one of the victims. After reviewing my records I saw that the father of one of the young men who burned to death was related to Ari. It seemed rather odd, considering Ari had chosen to defend the guy accused of the murders. I found it intriguing. It's how I became interested in Jakob, actually.'

Thóra frowned. 'I learned in school that if you go back far enough almost all Icelanders are related somehow. What was the link between these two?'

'Ari and the father of the boy who died are first cousins. That's rather closer than usual. You and I, for example, are related seven generations back.'

Thóra was repulsed at the thought that the man had been looking her up in search of some kind of family connection. She hoped his information was out of date, and he didn't know about Gylfi and Sóley, or Orri. The thought that he'd so much as seen their names in print was unbearable. 'First cousins?' If this were true — and considering Jósteinn had a few screws loose, Thóra found it impossible to judge — it was most irregular. In fact, it was downright immoral.

'He hasn't really fulfilled his brief as Jakob's lawyer, has he?'

Thóra didn't reply, though she privately agreed. 'Which young man was it?'

'Tryggvi Einvarðsson. The son of Einvarður Tryggvason and grandson of Tryggvi Helgason; who is the brother of Gunnar Helgason, Ari's father. So you see, Ari and Einvarður are first cousins. If you want, I can go back and link their lineages to me. I've got a great memory.'

'No, thanks. That's plenty.'

★ ★ ★

On the way out Thóra spotted Jakob. His back was turned to her as he bent over a sink in a kitchen that seemed rather small given the number of people living there, washing up with gusto. 'Hello, Jakob.' He turned around at her greeting, displaying a giant white apron with large wet patches. 'How are you?'

Jakob looked at her and appeared not to realize who she was. Then a light clicked on and he beamed at her guilelessly. 'Have you come to get me? Can I go home to Mummy?'

'No, Jakob. Not yet, I'm afraid. I'm working on it, and I'll do everything I can to make that happen. Until then, you've got to be brave.' His smile faded and was replaced by a frown.

'I'm very brave but I still want to go home.'

'I know. Hopefully you can, but not today.'

'Tomorrow?' He cheered up again, and Thóra realized that she would have to choose her words more carefully, so as not to raise his hopes too much.

'No, not tomorrow, Jakob. Have you thought some more about the night we talked about when I came here the other day? Tried to remember it better?'

Jakob shook his head. 'I don't want to think about it. I just feel bad if I do.'

Thóra nodded. 'Tell me one thing — have you heard of a short hose? Something to do with the apartment that Natan lived in? Number 2?' Jakob stared at her blankly and shook his head. 'Okay, never mind. But you can probably tell me something else; what was the name of the girl who lived in the apartment at the end of the corridor? Do you remember?'

Jakob adopted a look of exaggerated bewilderment, squinting and frowning at the same time. 'No. I don't remember.'

'Try to think back a bit; she was always in bed and didn't speak.'

'I never talked to her. She always just stared at me. It made me feel uncomfortable.' He leaned forward a bit, his expression conspiratorial. 'I think she was called Ragga but I don't really know. She never did anything with us.'

'Ragga?' This could be short for Ragnhild, Ragnheiður or various other names. 'Do you know whose daughter she was?'

'No. Her mother and father had moved away.

They never came. Maybe she wasn't anyone's daughter and was just called Ragga.'

Thóra smiled. 'Maybe. Now, since I know you're so brave, I'm going to ask you something different, and that's how Ari, your lawyer, treated you. I know that you found him boring, but did he treat you badly? Was he ever mean, or angry?'

'He was strange. He was never happy and he always wanted to talk about boring things. He was boring.'

'But mean? Did you find him mean?'

'Yes, he's very mean. He . . . he kicks animals.' Jakob didn't meet her eye as he spoke and Thóra was fairly certain he had said it to try to please her. No matter what one might say about Ari and the bizarre situation he'd put himself in, she doubted he went around kicking animals in front of his clients.

'Let's just talk about what we know or have seen, and not what we think. Okay?' Jakob nodded sheepishly. 'Now, I know that you bit his arm, didn't you?'

'He was mean.'

'Maybe, but why did you bite him? Maybe he's mean but he must have said something that made you especially angry, mustn't he?'

'Yeah.'

'And what was that, Jakob? It would be really great if you could tell me about it.'

Jakob's tongue stuck out even further than usual and he licked his lips. 'He was mean; he said that I was lying to him and also that I was lying to the police. He said that he would have me put in prison if I didn't say that I started the fire and that I would never get to see Mummy. Never.'

Jakob's cheeks had turned red, so distressed was he by the memory. Thóra decided not to upset him any further, since it was quite clear what had happened. That bastard Ari had put the thumbscrews on Jakob and tried to get him to confess to the crime, which he obviously thought his client had committed. This was clearly unacceptable behaviour, but it would be impossible to prove. No matter that Thóra didn't doubt for a second that Jakob was telling the truth. She was filled with an even greater desire to secure his freedom. One of the things that had weighed most heavily against him was that he had confessed, withdrawn his confession, confessed again and then contradicted himself in his testimony. Perhaps this had been partly due to Ari's interference. How could Jakob have got so unlucky with his lawyer? 'We shouldn't talk about Ari any more. Let's talk about Friðleifur instead; do you remember him? He was an employee at the centre, and he worked a lot at night and early in the morning?' Jakob nodded again, but now he seemed wary. 'Was he nice, did he do his job well?'

'He was fun. He was funny.' Jakob smiled at some amusing memory that the night watchman's name seemed to have evoked.

'Did he sometimes have visitors at work? Did his friends come to see him?'

'Sometimes.' Jakob clamped his mouth shut again.

'How did they behave? Did they sometimes

291

argue with Friðleifur?' Jakob shook his head, surprised. 'So they were just calm — they didn't speak loudly or angrily or anything like that?'

'No.' Jakob looked puzzled and his eyes flicked around the room. Then he came closer to her, first appearing to peer past her and check whether anyone could overhear them. 'Can you keep a secret?'

'I'm really good at it.' Jakob bent to her and whispered.

'Friðleifur's friends came to visit to *breathe*. He told me that but he asked me not to tell anyone. Never. So you can't tell anyone, okay?'

'No, I won't tell, Jakob. But sometimes secrets stop being secret when the person who told them to you is dead. Not always, but sometimes.'

Jakob seemed uneasy with these new rules about something he'd obviously thought he clearly understood. 'You promised not to tell anyone. You promised.' He became more agitated with every word and Thóra remembered the stories of this small but sturdy man's violent tendencies.

'And I won't. I *do* promise.' She smiled, hoping to calm him down. Then, calling forth all the acting skills she possessed to seem conspiratorial enough, she whispered, 'Were they breathing smoke? From a pipe?' The best she could think of was that Jakob had come across the night watchman and his friends smoking hash and Friðleifur had tried to convince him of some nonsense about secret breathing.

Jakob's anger dissipated, and instead he looked shocked. 'No. They just came to breathe.

Not with smoke; they wanted *good* breathing.'

'Okay.' Thóra patted Jakob on the shoulder. An angel with a suitcase and good breathing. Clearly the boy was a mine of useful information.

20

Friday, 15 January 2010

There was nothing to worry about in the middle of the day, even one as grey and gloomy as this. Margeir inhaled the cool, humid air, filling his chest. A sense of well-being he hadn't felt in months washed over him and he shut his eyes. Maybe today would be a turning point in his life; a new start to a new life under new and more enjoyable circumstances. It was up to him to deal with much of what had tormented him lately and he had to stop beating himself up all the time. A bank of storm clouds filled the sky and a gusty wind blew snow from the handrail; winter wasn't going to relent until it had given its all. He brushed the snow off himself irritably. His coat rustled and the noise made him realize how quiet it was outside. There was no murmur of traffic, no whisper from the bare branches of the aspen; Margeir stared, captivated, at them, feeling as if he were watching a silent movie on television.

A muffled ringing came from his coat pocket, startling him. It was as if his hearing was suddenly jump-started; the wind whistling in the trees came through loud and clear, backed by the distant rumble of traffic. He recognized the radio station's number and despite his best-laid plans not to let the anonymous lunatic trouble him, he felt enormously relieved. The man had probably stopped calling, even though Margeir was still being bombarded with text messages that were bound to be from the same person. Margeir hadn't heard this coward's voice since looking up the address that had appeared in one of the messages. He suspected the weirdo lived there. Either the idiot regretted what he'd done after being found out, or he'd got bored of tormenting Margeir and had turned to someone else. Maybe it was the initial response that gave this guy his biggest kicks and it got boring to keep receiving *'Who is this?'* *'Leave me alone!'* and things like that in reply. Maybe the pervert had wanted to pester a girl, where he would doubtless get a more satisfying reaction. It was over. It must be over. It had to be over.

Margeir answered the phone cheerfully, certain that he was about to get some positive news; it wasn't often that work contacted him. But the weary voice of the station manager crushed his hopes. Advertising revenue was slow and the number of sponsors was decreasing steadily, so he wanted Margeir to find some legal party to sponsor his show in return for advertisements and good publicity from the station. He added that Margeir should think about it carefully, since his job depended on it; he shouldn't rule out any potential sponsors. Everyone was in need of publicity these days; times were hard and every customer and every penny was fought for. Nowhere could you find cheaper advertising that gave as much return, and the station's listenership was constantly growing. His sales pitch was so convincing that

Margeir was almost starting to consider advertising himself when the man said abruptly, 'You can do it, right? Otherwise I'll have to hire someone who *can* find his own sponsors. Times are tough, you know,' he continued, when Margeir didn't answer straight away.

'I'll see what I can do,' was all he could think of to say. 'Bye.' He hung up and exhaled slowly. The wind had changed; Margeir gasped when it proved to be colder than his lungs had anticipated. He cursed his complacency. How did unemployment payments work? He had no idea. He vaguely remembered his mother nagging him to sign on when he'd lost his job just over a year before, but he'd completely forgotten where to go and what to do. He wasn't particularly looking forward to bringing it up again, because he'd kind of implied that he'd already done it ages ago. He wouldn't be able to convincingly explain to her why he'd been so unmotivated, and he suspected he'd get only limited sympathy from her about it, even though she always took his side.

He fully expected his right to full benefits to have expired after all this time, but surely he was entitled to something. The government could hardly expect him to go begging on the streets, could they? Wasn't that against the law, too? He couldn't afford to lose any more income, and the money he'd saved up by doing two jobs at the same time was long gone. Plus he could hardly cut back any further on household expenses. The apartment was owned by his grandfather, so he'd never find lower rent anywhere else. He'd stopped making calls from his mobile phone and had cancelled his accounts for his landline and Internet, along with everything else that cost money and wasn't considered a necessity. His car was the only thing he was holding onto; no one would buy that piece of junk anyway, and it was good to have it for emergencies, even though the petrol tank leaked and he had to keep a can in the boot just to be on the safe side. He denied himself every other luxury and it was hard to think of further ways to reduce his expenses. He spent his money on little other than housing and food, and when you only ate noodles it was impossible to make cutbacks in that area. Pizza was a luxury he sometimes thought about but never allowed himself. The only proper meals he had were at his mother's, usually on Sundays. She earned a huge number of brownie points from her son for not mentioning his ravenous appetite and the quantity of food he devoured. Once she had asked him if he was still growing even in adulthood, but otherwise she acted as if she didn't notice anything unusual and simply started preparing bigger meals so that he could take the leftovers home with him. No, it wasn't like the good old days when he'd had enough in his wallet. Of course there hadn't been much left at the end of every month but he didn't recall ever having lacked anything. He hadn't had a clue about the hard times that awaited him.

He set off down the empty street, into the wind, and resolved to do the right thing. Nothing mattered any more but taking responsibility for himself and hoping people would see the truth.

Even though it would be hard to pin all the blame on him, you never knew; fate was unpredictable. As far as he could see it lulled people into a false sense of security, getting them to believe that everything would be all right and then knocking their feet out from under them when they least expected it. He remembered all the news stories about poor people winning lottery jackpots, only to fritter them away and be left with the knowledge of what they'd be missing for the rest of their lives. He had considered himself to be on the upswing; his life had felt as though it had direction, even though he didn't know exactly where he was heading or how he would get there. Now that feeling had disappeared and it was clear that his path lay along the baseline, not on an upwards trajectory. For the time being, at least.

Margeir pulled his hood up to protect himself against the cold. What was he whingeing for? There were loads of people much more unfortunate than he was and there was no reason to make things even worse than they actually were. If the worst came to the worst he could move in with his mother; unless, that was, he could actually find some sponsors. While he was pondering possible opportunities in that area his phone rang again and he pulled it hopefully from his pocket. Maybe the station manager had changed his mind, or maybe a sponsor had materialised and Margeir wouldn't have to come up with one any more. But this wasn't the case, and sponsorship was no longer Margeir's biggest concern.

Thóra was in a foul mood. She had returned to her office after her visit to Sogn and had made calls all over town to speak to those who were now most important to the case. But it seemed as though they'd all conspired to ignore her. Ari didn't answer — neither his office phone nor his mobile — and Glódís hadn't even replied to Thóra's first e-mail enquiring about who had been in charge of Tryggvi's therapy, let alone her second message asking for the name of the surviving sixth resident. Nor had she managed to contact the former director by telephone; the Regional Office said that Glódís was busy and refused to refer Thóra to someone else who could answer her question about the girl in Room 6. The woman on the phone defended herself by claiming client confidentiality, and there was little that Thóra could say in protest. The Ministry of Justice also informed her that Einvarður was busy in a meeting and would not be in his office for the rest of the day. Thóra had intended to go through the list Glódís had given her but when she attempted to do so, she either reached the voicemails of former employees or no one at all. Two of the numbers were out of service.

To make matters worse, Bella had seized her chance to wangle some time off after Thóra had left that morning, so reception was empty. The secretary had left a large note on the table, saying: *Gone to the dokter's.* Thóra and her partner Bragi had bought a spellcheck program as soon as they'd seen the first letters their secretary had typed up, and without a doubt it had been one of their best investments. Still, it was quite an achievement for Bella to have managed to squeeze two errors into the same word.

When her phone finally rang Thóra couldn't work out which of the numbers she'd been trying to reach was flashing up on her screen.

'My name is Linda, and I have a missed call from this number.'

Thóra reached for Glódís's list and looked up the name as she explained who she was and gave a brief summary of why she had been calling. It really didn't matter which of the employees it was, her sales pitch would always be the same. Just as she finished her final sentence she found the woman's name and her scrawled-down job title, which Thóra had found in the phone book. To her satisfaction she read that Linda was a developmental therapist. Judging from her voice she was older than Thóra, and she sounded calm and measured.

'I don't know whether I can be of any assistance, but if you want to drop by I'm happy to talk to you for a bit.' Then she added: 'I liked Jakob and I was never completely convinced that he was guilty, not looking back on it, anyway.'

Thóra accepted the woman's offer with thanks and scribbled down her address, a home for disabled children in the western part of town. She hurried off so as not to miss Linda before she went home, but nevertheless took the time to correct Bella's message, adding the word *brain* before *dokter's*. Hopefully the note would still be there in the morning.

★ ★ ★

The home Linda worked in was nothing like the one Jakob had supposedly burned to the ground. That building had been stylish and modern, but this one appeared to have been there since the very start of this well-established neighbourhood. It didn't look like a public building, except for the fact that the main door was unusually wide and there was a clearly marked parking space for the disabled in front of it. Thóra walked up to the ordinary-looking door and knocked, surprised that there was no doorbell. She immediately recognized Linda's voice again when the woman greeted her. She had guessed her age correctly; Linda appeared to be approaching sixty, in good shape and with a warm smile. Her salt and pepper hair was clipped into a short bob, but despite her sombre clothes and hair the woman gave off an air of warmth and equanimity. 'I'm not used to rushing to the door here but since I was expecting you, I was listening out. You don't need to take your shoes off; the cleaners will be here after supper and the floor is in a bit of a state after all the comings and goings today, anyway.'

As soon as Thóra had crossed the threshold, any similarity this place might have had to a traditional home ended. The hall was much wider than usual for such an old house, and it looked as though a sledgehammer might have been used on some of the panelling. The floor was carpeted and the woman wasn't exaggerating about how dirty it was. There were black streaks everywhere, probably from wheelchairs, and dirty shoe-prints trailed down the corridor before disappearing behind closed doors. 'I have an office here where we can sit down. There's often quite a lot of noise though it's calm at the moment, so it's better to be somewhere quiet if it all starts up again. Of course the building's not designed for the type of work we do here, so nothing's really what we might have hoped for. You get used to it.'

They walked past the open door of a large, bright room. In it were three children: a boy in a wheelchair who appeared abnormally bloated, as if from steroid use, a girl standing up in a kind of steel frame and another who sat upright at a table, staring fiercely at her plate, although it was difficult to tell what was bothering her. The other two looked in their direction as they walked by and smiled widely at Thóra. She waved and gave them her biggest smile in return, then had to hurry to catch up with Linda, who hadn't slowed down. 'Is this home like the one Jakob lived in?' She felt more comfortable coming at it from this angle than starting with the care home that had burned down, even though it sounded a bit artificial.

'No. This is a day-care centre, and it's only for younger children. They can't attend regular preschools or schools, but they still need education and stimulation that their parents can't provide.' Linda opened the door to a small but very tidy office. 'This building is one of several that have been given to the state or the city for a specific purpose. In this case, it was stipulated that it was to be used in the service of disabled children. The couple that lived here had a disabled daughter, so they recognized the need. They died many years ago but the situation isn't much better now than it was then. Not by a long shot.'

'Things haven't improved?'

'Not really, no, but they are bearable. The need is greater than the resources can cover. Every year more multi-disabled or seriously developmentally impaired children are born. It's impossible to provide them with all the assistance and intensive supervision they need, but of course we try our best. Unfortunately, some are neglected, but that's the government's problem, it's not up to us carers. In the old days everyone was piled into just a few places, and most of them into a kind of healthcare institution, the old Kópavogur Sanatorium. No matter how bizarre it might sound today, its official name up until 1980 was the State Central Sanatorium for Idiots; so some progress has been made there, at least. Now everyone's supposed to go to a community residence, but none of them are big enough in my opinion. When funds are scarce, many people are excluded. One person's needs are met exhaustively, while someone else gets nothing.'

'So it must have been a real blow when the centre burned down. I mean besides the fact that innocent people lost their lives there.'

'Yes, you can say that again. The government and the local councils don't insure their property, so no damages would have been paid. Given the current situation, there'll be no rush to build a replacement centre anytime soon, certainly not in the next few years. And in the meantime, the number of people needing help only increases.'

'It must be depressing to work under such conditions.' Thóra let her eyes roam over some photographs of disabled children on the wall behind the woman. They all appeared happy, like the ones Thóra had greeted as she'd walked down the corridor.

'Yes, if you can't look past the niggles and focus on what's in your power to change. I've been doing this for so long that I've developed a thick skin, and very few things get to me. And it's not all just sadness and misery here, like many people think. Most of the children here are fine; they're happy, despite having to battle with problems other children couldn't imagine. I'm confident they could even be described as happier than 'normal' children the same age. To a large extent it's about attitude, and computers have also narrowed the gap between disabled and non-disabled children a great deal. I know able-bodied kids who spend all day in front of a computer screen, making little use of the freedom their unimpaired mobility gives them. When it comes to disabled children, the main issue is how long it takes to change people's attitudes. Society in general has limited patience for those who aren't considered to be 'contributing'. Yet most of these people can work independently if they find a job that suits them, and you'd be hard pushed to find more diligent employees.'

Thóra nodded. She was sure an intellectually disabled person could perform secretarial work better than Bella. It had been naïve of her to think that the lives of these children revolved only around their difficulties. 'As I mentioned, I'm trying to get to the bottom of whether anyone other than Jakob, individually or collectively, could have been involved in starting the fire. I've uncovered certain details that are causing me some concern, although I haven't managed to prove any of them. Were your doubts about Jakob's guilt based on gut instinct, or something more substantial?'

'Unfortunately, they were purely based on instinct. Jakob had a difficult time at the residence, you know, but I just couldn't see him resorting to such desperate measures. He thought it would all end at some point, that he'd get to go home — it hadn't sunk in that he would be living there permanently. So that hardly ties in with the theory that he thought he needed to burn the place to the ground in order to get out of there.' Linda crossed her arms, her expression grave now; the smile that had seemed an intrinsic part of her appearance disappeared. 'While it was all going on, I was so grief-stricken that the sadness overshadowed everything; I felt so terribly sorry for the people who'd died, but also for Jakob. It was such an emotional rollercoaster that I couldn't focus on anything else. It never crossed my mind to doubt the investigation. I didn't explore my misgivings until later, but by then it was too late. Now I wonder whether the result would have been different if I, and others, had been more on the ball when Jakob needed us. It's not a nice feeling, I can tell you, and if I'm honest, I think I pushed it all aside. Probably to avoid having to deal with the thought that if it hadn't been Jakob, then someone else had been involved — and if so, who?'

'People aren't robots. Those are perfectly natural reactions to a crisis like this.' Thóra was happy to finally find someone apart from his mother who actually believed in Jakob's innocence. Others had generally been willing to consider the possibility, but Thóra could see in their eyes that they didn't think her investigation would lead anywhere. Linda appeared to feel otherwise. 'One of the things I've discovered is that a girl who lived there was expecting a baby. Lísa. Were you aware of that?'

The woman blushed suddenly. 'Yes. But not until afterwards. It was revealed by the autopsy, and because of my position I was summoned to a meeting at the Regional Office, where we went over it. It took me completely by surprise.' She rubbed her forehead. 'It didn't occur to me that the disaster might be connected to it, at that point. Everything was focused on trying to discover who the arsonist was and stopping them from doing it again. A lot of emphasis was also placed on keeping it from the media.'

'Did you suspect anyone in particular?'

'God, no. It's such a terrible thing to do that you don't want to point the finger at anyone. I'm still convinced that there's no way an employee could have done it.' Linda's blush deepened. 'The only possible person I could think of turned out to be innocent when they compared his DNA to the foetus.'

'Who was that?'

'A young man who worked mainly on the night shift. The one who died in the fire. Friðleifur.'

'Oh, really? It's my understanding that he was an all-round good guy. Is that not right?'

The woman placed her palms flat on the table. 'He was all right, but he was far from a model employee. I never particularly liked him, or the other guy who worked the shift with him; I had my doubts that they were doing their job properly. I don't like to speak ill of the dead, but that's just how it was.'

'Did you catch them doing something wrong?'

'No, I can't say I did; if I had caught them, they would have been fired. I worked at the weekend on occasion, and more than once I found the place in a suspicious condition — beer cans lying about, that kind of thing, which suggested that one or both of them had been drinking at work. They turned out to be completely sober, both times, and had excuses that the director accepted, though I disagreed with her. Who'd be gullible enough to believe that they kept finding the cans littered around the garden and decided to clear them up? Not me, that's for sure. Then there were huge supplies of intralipid, an IV medicine that's given when oral nutrition is insufficient, which went missing, along with the butterfly needles and tubes used to administer it. On two occasions I found empty bags in the wastepaper basket in the duty room, which they couldn't explain; they said they must have already been there when they came to work, but I simply didn't believe it. No more empty bags or needles were ever found, but the supplies continued to dwindle mysteriously. I felt Glódís didn't deal with the problem effectively; she wanted to give herself more time to get to the bottom of it, which of course never happened. And people were hardly queuing up to replace them if they had to let them go, which was no doubt a factor in her deciding to turn a blind eye.'

'Do you think they were into drugs, or were selling them there at night?'

'Well, I'm no expert in recreational drug use, but I can't see how IV drips would be involved. But they clearly shouldn't have been anywhere near the stuff, much less setting up needles, preparing mixtures or anything like that.'

'Wasn't it stored in a locked cabinet?'

'No; that was one of the things that needed sorting out. We were still waiting for a refrigerator that was specially designed for storing that type of drug. The drug could be stored at room temperature, but it was better to keep it in cold storage. While we were waiting for lockable storage it was kept in a little fridge in a room next to Glódís's office. We kept a stock of needles and other medical supplies there, stuff we had to have quick access to. The room was locked, of course, but the night watchmen had master keys to all the doors.'

'I understand Friðleifur's sister and a friend paid him a visit very early one morning. Was this a frequent occurrence?'

Linda scowled. 'No, I don't think so. That sounds typical of him, though.'

It was clear that Thóra would have to contact Friðleifur's sister and the other night watchman, who hadn't answered any of her calls. 'There's something else I'm extremely keen to find out: the name of the girl who lived in Apartment 06. She'd been admitted to hospital shortly before the fire. I'd like to be able to speak to her, in case she has any information.'

'Oh, God.' The woman sighed. 'I might have to disappoint you there. You may not know enough about her condition; she's got what's called 'locked-in syndrome' and her communication is extremely limited.'

'It's my understanding that she can convey messages with her eyes. Isn't that right?'

'Not everyone is capable of communicating that way. I hope I'm not insulting you.'

Thóra shook her head. 'Could you explain this 'locked-in syndrome'?'

'It's one of the worst afflictions imaginable, to my mind. It's a brain-stem injury that severs contact with all the muscles controlling voluntary movements, except those that move the eyes. There's actually an even worse version, in which you lose control of your eyes as well. It's sometimes likened to being buried alive and it's very different from a coma, because the person affected is still conscious. In other words, the lower part of the brain is damaged, while the upper part is fine.'

'What about the nerve endings? Can these people feel anything?'

'Yes, often, as in this case. The girl's name is Ragna Sölvadóttir; she ended up like this after falling from a great height several years ago, and she has no hope of recovering. Usually the syndrome is the result of a stroke or accident, sometimes other causes, but luckily it's rare. I don't know what's happened to her, but I imagine she's been moved to another residence or a similar institution. She can't just go home while she waits for a place to open up, and her parents have moved out of Iceland. In search of work, I believe.'

Thóra couldn't think of much to say. The thought of this syndrome sent chills up her spine, but she pushed it out of her mind. Was there any possibility that the person who had impregnated Lísa had also made a move on this girl, who was in a similar condition? Perhaps she could get a description of the man, which might allow them to track him down. 'You don't know whether something in Apartment 02 was connected to a hose, a hose that could be described as short, specifically? That was Natan's apartment. Forgive the odd nature of the question, but I can't really explain it any better since I received the information in a rather cryptic message.'

Linda shook her head. 'I can't remember anything like that. If this is related to the fire in any way, then I would doubt the information, because Natan couldn't have been involved. If he was, I'd be flabbergasted.'

'What about the others who lived there? Is it possible that one of them, or one of their relatives, could have done it? I mean, both the fire and this situation with Lísa.'

The woman pondered the question for several moments. 'I can't think of anyone, to tell you the honest truth. Although the centre had only been up and running for a short time, I managed to get to know everyone there pretty well, and no one comes to mind. Naturally, I didn't know their relatives as well, but I seriously doubt any of them would be capable of such a terrible thing. Most parents of disabled children that I've known, which is quite a few down the years, only want the best for their child and would fight tooth and nail for them. These people would be the very last to commit murder; I simply can't see it.'

Few people could imagine someone killing another person, but nevertheless, it happened again and again. 'I've watched some footage from the residence, taken by the filmmaker who spent a bit of time there.'

Linda nodded, clearly remembering the man.

'In the background I heard some words that have come up in my conversations with Jakob, but I can't find an explanation for them and I was hoping that you could tell me what they mean.'

'What were the words?' The woman seemed surprised.

'*Look at me* . . . Repeated by a man, I think, quite angrily.'

Linda gave Thóra an indecipherable look. 'Yes. I'm familiar with that phrase. Tryggvi had a therapist who used rather unorthodox methods to stimulate the boy. He would repeat the phrase over and over in his attempts to reach him. He actually forced the boy to look into his eyes in order to get a response. It made Tryggvi howl; he found the therapy enormously stressful, and the man would react by howling back at him. It was quite distressing to hear.'

'A therapist? Was he a developmental therapist like you?'

'No.' The woman's expression hardened. 'Tryggvi's parents, especially his mother, wanted him to undergo unconventional treatment in the hope of achieving a better result than they were seeing with us. The couple hired this man, Ægir Rannversson, but I never could work out what his qualifications or his educational background were. He'd recently come back from some time abroad, where he'd worked on or studied autism, but it wasn't at any respected educational institution, that much is certain.'

'And did his method produce any results?' The silence was even longer this time, but finally the woman spoke up again. 'Yes, it did. Whether they would have been permanent, I can't say, but he did get the boy to express himself more than anyone had dared hope, though he wasn't about to start speaking or anything like that. He articulated himself more through these incredible drawings he did. I mean, I couldn't have interpreted them, but the main change was in how much more alert he was to his surroundings. He was highly autistic, and he found lots of everyday things intolerable. He was captivated by strings of lights and candles — he could stare at them for hours at a time. But he hated the sound of the toilet being flushed, for example, or the phone ringing. These things became significantly better after his treatment, however, and who knows how much more he might have improved if the treatment had been able to continue. Mind you, he could just as easily have regressed over time; it had happened before. His mother told me that he couldn't bear being near a TV that was turned on, and later radios, too, for no obvious reason. But of course no one knows what might have happened. Following complaints from the residents and their families about the noise from his sessions, Tryggvi's parents put a stop to them and chose not to move his therapy elsewhere, since it was out of the question to try to get the boy into a car. Luckily, the progress he'd made seemed to stick, even after the treatment stopped.'

Now it was Thóra's turn to be silent. Neither Einvarður nor Fanndís had mentioned this; if anything, they'd implied that Tryggvi had made no progress. Sometimes what was left unsaid had the most significance. Given how concerned they'd been about their son's development, it was extremely odd — and even odder to hear that they had actually paid attention to the complaints to such an extent. Might it not have been possible to tone down the screaming and conduct the therapy in a quieter manner? 'So if he'd started to open up, would he have been a lot more likely than before to leave his own apartment? Was he perhaps even capable of roaming around at night?'

'Maybe, yes.'

21

Saturday, 16 January 2010

For once, the weather was glorious. Nevertheless, Thóra was thankful to be wearing a coat long enough to protect her bottom from the cold plastic benches in the stands. Out on the Astro Turf, Sóley ran around with the rest of the team, none of them showing any sign of following either the rules or the ball, which as a result was nearly always on their half of the pitch. This practice match had been set up at short notice and Thóra thought the coach had probably decided the cold conditions might benefit his team, allowing them to lose by fewer points than usual or even to manage a draw. This was rather optimistic, particularly in light of the fact that there was no risk of the team's opponents mixing up the goals or losing sight of the ball in a flurry of snow.

'Turn around, Sóley! Wrong way!' called Matthew, cupping his hands around his mouth. Sóley stopped, turned to them and waved, smiling. As she did so, a group of girls ran past her after the ball. 'She's getting better,' he said to Thóra, somewhat unconvincingly.

'Isn't it bad for the pitch to let them play in winter?' Thóra knew less about football than Sóley, but she did know the pitch was new and she didn't want the 6th Girls' Division damaging it if they were only going to lose.

'They're so light it hardly makes any difference,' Matthew replied. To further emphasize their minuscule stature, they were playing against a backdrop of the magnificent sparkling sea on the other side of the pitch and the Reykjanes mountain range. 'Go on, Sóley! Go on!' Again Thóra's daughter stopped to wave; the game was forgotten, and had been lost long ago.

'It might not be a good idea to encourage her.' Thóra glanced at the clock. Fifteen minutes left. 'It looks to me like her concentration can't handle it.' Her phone rang in her coat pocket and Thóra took it out. She didn't recognize the number but the voice was familiar. It was Grímheiður, Jakob's mother. At first Thóra seriously regretted answering, preferring not to let work interrupt her on the weekends, but after she'd spoken to the woman, she felt differently. She thanked Grímheiður and said goodbye.

'What is it?' Matthew was startled when he saw Thóra's expression.

'Jakob is being moved from Sogn. He was taken to the National Hospital with serious injuries last night, and underwent surgery on his eye.'

Matthew turned back to the match. 'What happened?'

'Jósteinn attacked him. With a knife and fork in the middle of their meal. He'll be lucky to keep his eye, and he has multiple other wounds, so I'm told.'

This was enough to draw Matthew's attention away from the ball. 'What? I thought Jósteinn was his benefactor or something? Isn't he paying for the investigation because he likes Jakob so much? Were they fighting about something?'

'No, not as far as I understand. The attack was completely unprovoked, according to Jakob's mother.' Thóra put the phone back in her pocket. It was clear that this attack would have a decisive effect on the issue of reopening the case; surely Jósteinn was unlikely to continue paying for the investigation after what had just happened. 'I really don't know why I'm surprised. The man is ill, capable of anything, and I should probably be grateful that I didn't leave my meeting with him with a fork in my temple or something.'

Matthew wasn't amused. 'That's enough of that kind of talk.'

Thóra ignored him. She had no desire for any further communication with Jósteinn, but it was an interesting development nonetheless, and her desire to get Jakob out of Sogn was now quite strong. She knew it was dangerous to think this way; she mustn't become emotionally attached to the case. That would increase the risk of her missing something, or simply ignoring anything that didn't suit her. But unfortunately it wasn't always possible to control one's emotions, and it was simply impossible not to care at all about Jakob. 'I don't know, maybe I should go and see him in hospital. Take him some flowers or chocolates.'

Matthew shrugged and turned back to the match again. 'Would you be allowed? Won't he be under police supervision?'

'I think I would, given my involvement in his case.'

'Then you'd better hurry up, because you won't be in that position for much longer. Surely Jósteinn will stop paying for the investigation, now that their friendship has soured.' Matthew suddenly sounded rather angry. 'I don't understand why you're taking on cases like this, anyway. There's loads of work around for lawyers; masses of it, dealing with money — nice, harmless paper-based transactions, even if their origins might be ugly.'

'That kind of work is all allocated through nepotism; and in any case, we can barely compete with the big firms, who have loads of specialized lawyers on their payrolls.' She neglected to add the most important reason: that she found financial claims and business law indescribably boring, and even Bragi, who generally managed to find something interesting in all his cases, was unlikely to be persuaded away from the divorce cases he loved so much. 'I'm continuing with this case, unless Jósteinn stops paying. It's caught my attention, and it's not as though we're suddenly drowning in work. We could use the income, even though the case might turn out to be less weighty than it seems.'

'The bank got in touch and offered me my job back.' Matthew didn't look away from the pitch as he said this. 'Albeit at lower wages, since the scope of the role is only a fraction of what it used to be.'

'That's great!' Thóra leaned into him. 'Aren't you happy?'

'I don't know.'

'When did they ask you?'

'The day before yesterday.'

'And you waited to tell me because . . . ?' Thóra moved away from him again, glad she hadn't yet made an appointment for that wax.

'I don't know exactly. I needed time to think about it and I had to do that alone. On the surface it might look like a good offer, but I need to think it over carefully.' He turned and looked her in the eye. 'It would have confused me to discuss it with you. It's nothing to do with you personally, it's me. I've never found these sorts of things easy. I feel better when the answers are clear in my mind — yes or no — and when I don't need to think about it any further.'

Thóra nodded slowly. 'I understand.' She felt bad about how put out she sounded; it wasn't as if he were confessing to an affair or telling her he'd squandered their money on slot machines or Icelandic stocks. 'So what have you decided, since you've now told me about it?'

'Nothing. I'm still thinking.' Sóley and her team were still running around on the pitch, apparently entirely unconcerned that their opponents' score made it look more like a volleyball match. They celebrated enthusiastically when they managed, coincidentally, to kick the ball in the direction of their opponents' goal. The ball rolled slowly into the penalty area and the other team watched this unexpected development in amazement until the goalkeeper strolled out onto the pitch and grabbed it. The few spectators applauded as if a goal had actually been scored. Matthew clapped along loudly, and when the applause died out he added: 'I probably will take the job, even though I really don't want to go back to that office.'

'That sounds sensible.' Thóra smiled. Another salary wouldn't hurt. 'You can always change jobs later. It's not like they're hiring you for life.'

'No, that's true.' He was obviously making an effort to be upbeat. 'Which of course is all this job has going for it, apart from the fact that I'm finding it incredibly difficult just sitting about doing nothing.'

'And it hasn't exactly made things easier having Mum and Dad hanging around . . . ' There was no need for Matthew to respond to this. 'Well, anyway, you'll figure something out. It's not as if we're broke.'

Matthew smiled at her. 'Don't you need an assistant?'

She smiled back. 'Get rid of Bella for me and you can apply to be our receptionist.'

The match ended with Sóley's team being thrashed as usual; in fact the winners even seemed a bit shamefaced, as if they'd been playing against a team of younger girls and had got too carried away by the game to keep their victory to a modest level. But Sóley and her teammates didn't take the loss to heart and came off the pitch with their heads held high, in the true spirit of sportsmanship.

★   ★   ★

Jakob wasn't handcuffed to the bed or restrained in any other way. Nor were there any guards posted at his door. The hospital room was

320

securely locked, though, so he couldn't have got far if he had made a run for it — which seemed unlikely in any case, considering his injuries. The nurse who had opened the door for Thóra had called for authorisation to let her in, which didn't appear to be a problem. Not knowing the full story behind the attack, Thóra had brought Matthew with her just to be safe; it was entirely possible that Jakob had started the fight and she knew she might be in for a thrashing similar to the one that Sóley's team had suffered if he felt like turning his anger on her. Matthew's presence didn't seem to bother anyone, which reinforced the impression that people weren't particularly worried about Jakob. Thóra didn't quite know how to interpret this, but in the end she decided it probably wasn't a good thing: they weren't even considering that they might need to keep an eye on him. Of course there could be an entirely different, quite practical explanation; perhaps it was simply yet another manifestation of savings and cutbacks.

Jakob was lying in a hospital bed with the blanket pulled up to his chin. His right eye was covered with thick white bandages and he had made an attempt to put his glasses neatly over them. The large, clumsy frames were crooked, since one arm did not reach his ear, which had also been damaged — it too was covered with bandages, and taped to his head. The result was rather comical; even more so as Jakob turned his head quickly away from the television to see who had come, which meant the glasses dropped and ended up so crooked that they lay almost at right angles to his face. He hurried to straighten them with his chubby fingers. 'Hello, Jakob,' said Thóra. She held out the box she'd bought on the way. 'We've brought you some chocolates. You remember Matthew, don't you?'

'Yes.' Jakob stared at the colourful box. 'Can I have some now?'

'Of course.' Thóra immediately regretted saying this. He might well be nil by mouth. 'Are you allowed to eat? Has anyone told you you shouldn't?'

'No. No one.' Jakob shook his head to emphasize his words. 'But I'm still hungry. I couldn't finish my supper last night.' He didn't need to explain any further what had disturbed his supper. 'I got food before but I should have had two meals because I'm owed one from yesterday.'

'Of course.' Thóra smiled. She opened the box and placed it on the table next to him as Matthew pulled two chairs up to the bed. 'Watch out for the cracknel.'

Jakob took Thóra at her word and chose carefully. With his mouth full of chocolate he muttered politely, 'Thank you very much.'

'You're welcome.' Matthew took the empty wrappers from him and threw them in a rubbish bin by the sink, then sat back down. 'How are you feeling, apart from hungry?'

'Bad. I'm itchy but I can't scratch because there are bandages in the way.'

Thóra pointed to the television remote. 'Would you mind turning down the volume or turning it off, just while we're here? Then we can

hear you better.' The actors in the film had suddenly burst into song.

Jakob looked at the screen and spent a few moments making up his mind. In the end he reached for the remote and turned off the TV. 'I've seen this movie anyway.'

'Thanks, that's much better.' Thóra smiled at him again. 'Has your mother been able to visit you?'

'Yes. She was here before.' Jakob selected another chocolate. 'She's going to come back later. I can see our house from here, so she can see me too. We live on the third floor and if I'm not home, Mummy needs to carry the food all the way up the stairs on her own.' He pointed towards the window with his right hand, which was also wrapped in bandages.

'I'm sure you've been a great help to her.' Thóra looked out of the window but couldn't see the house he meant. 'Hopefully you'll be able to go and help her again. But first you've got to get better, and then a few other things have to happen. But let's not worry about those things now.'

'No.' Jakob closed the box. 'We can talk about all sorts of other things. Like my eye.' He placed his hand on the part of his glasses that lay over the bandages.

'How did this happen? Do you think you're up to telling us about the attack?' said Matthew.

'It was bad. I was eating and then all of a sudden . . . just really bad.'

Matthew nodded sympathetically. 'Was he sitting next to you?'

'Yeah. He was having some fish and then he suddenly stood up and just . . . just really bad.'

'So you didn't punch him, even as a joke, or anything like that?' asked Thóra.

'Nah. I was eating my fish. We were supposed to get rice pudding if we finished it all.' His expression turned sad. 'I never got any.'

'I'm sure they'll give you some.' Thóra resolved to remember to ask the nurse in reception whether it would be possible to bring Jakob a bowl of rice pudding. 'Has he ever tried to hurt you before? Maybe he was stopped by the staff?'

'No, never. He's always good. Except now. Maybe he didn't like the fish.'

'Maybe. Did he say anything when he attacked you, or just before?'

Jakob stared at Matthew thoughtfully, his mouth wide open. 'Yes, he did. It was really strange.'

'Do you remember what it was?' Thóra leaned closer.

'He said that it would be better for me to be in Reykjavík. I remember because I was so happy and I was going to say that I thought that too but I couldn't say anything because . . . all of a sudden everything hurt so much and I couldn't see anything.'

Thóra's stomach lurched at the thought of someone with a fork in their eye, and she felt like she had to interrupt Jakob in order to block out the image. 'Maybe we should talk about something else, something more fun. I'm sure you'll have to discuss this with the police and various other people, which is why it's probably not a good idea to be talking about it too much

324

now.' Suddenly her recent conversation with Jósteinn popped into her mind. Again she interrupted Jakob, who looked as if he were about to say something. 'Did he say better? That it would be better if you were in Reykjavík?'

'Yes.' Jakob nodded so eagerly that his glasses slipped again. 'That's what he said.'

Thóra tried not to seem surprised. 'He didn't say anything else?'

'He did, he said one more thing. He said that I should be good and talk to you. But then he started to cut my ear and jab my eye so I screamed and I didn't hear him after that. Maybe he said something else.'

Thóra doubted it. What Jósteinn had said completely explained the attack. He believed Thóra's investigation would make better progress if she had easier access to Jakob.

★   ★   ★

Thóra didn't tell Matthew about her suspicions until they'd left the hospital. 'Are you serious?' Matthew stopped, seeming upset. He was always direct and to the point about everything, and for him not to have told her about the bank's offer was the closest he'd ever come to scheming. To manipulate events in the way Thóra believed Jósteinn had done was so alien to him that all he could do was gawp at her.

'I can't prove anything, or confirm it without asking him directly, but it completely fits with what we discussed.'

Matthew shook his head irritably. 'I don't

325

know which is crazier — to attack someone like that unprovoked, or to injure them for a specific purpose.'

'No question — it's crazier to do it for a purpose.' Thóra breathed in the cool air. 'He's not a normal man, remember. He's capable of anything.' She looked up along the building and saw Jakob's face in the window. He wasn't watching them leave, he was just peering out over the hospital grounds, in the direction of his mother's house. She turned back to Matthew. 'If I'm right, there's no question that Jósteinn wants to keep the case going.' She pointed at the sad sight framed in the window. 'If so, then I'll keep investigating. That's all there is to it.'

Matthew said nothing.

22

Sunday, 17 January 2010

The jogger was flagging, but he focused on his goal. He chose a car parked up ahead in the distance and thought only of getting that far. Then and only then would he slow down. This way he hoped to be able to resist the temptation to stop, put his hands on his knees and breathe as deeply as his lungs could tolerate. Last autumn he had run this same circuit without breathing through his nose, but after being largely sedentary during the winter he had expected too much of himself on this first warm, ice-free day of the new year. He was alone, which would no longer be the case as spring approached, when he would hardly be able to go ten yards without meeting other joggers. Then they would feel exactly like he did now, whereas he would be one of the few in shape. For a moment he managed to forget his fatigue as he imagined himself in the spring sunshine, straight-backed, going at an even pace, passing one red-faced, sweaty runner after another.

At the moment when he was feeling best about himself, his body decided that it had had enough. Suddenly he couldn't take another step; the burning in his lungs became unbearable, his heart pounded, he tasted blood and his legs were on fire. He stood panting on the pavement and it crossed his mind to take a taxi home. It was a long trip back and there were few things more embarrassing than staggering along in your running gear. However, his taxi plan fell apart because he had neither a phone nor money on him; there was no one out and about in the area, even though he was only a short distance from the popular Nauthólsvík Beach. He sighed heavily. It was then that he spotted the bench. He could rest there and massage the worst of the pain from his legs. Then he would have some hope of making it home free of shame — albeit not very quickly.

The surface of the bench was cold but he got used to it immediately, as if his body had reached its maximum level of pain. The bench was neither warm nor comfortable, but he couldn't recall ever having been so glad to sit down. Slowly but surely the pain receded, but now he was aware that his body temperature was dropping rapidly; he was dressed lightly, since he hadn't been planning to sit outside, not moving, in these tight, thin clothes. The wind that had felt so agreeable such a short time ago was now cold and biting, and his sweaty body quickly became chilled. He really ought to keep moving, but he couldn't get himself to stand up immediately. He hammered his folded arms against his chest, as his grandfather had taught him when he was a small boy. It helped.

When he'd stopped punching heat into himself, the lapping of the waves caught his attention and he held his breath to enjoy it to the utmost. He turned to look across the bay and stare at the ocean. A loud electronic jingle suddenly tore through the peace and quiet, giving him a massive shock; he had thought that he was there alone and felt uncomfortable at the thought that someone had snuck up on him unawares. He turned around to look but saw no one. The ringing continued, however, now higher and more intense. The jogger quickly worked out where it was coming from; he noticed a blue gleam beneath the bench and reached down to pick up a rather cheap-looking mobile phone. On the blinking screen he saw the word *Mum* and for a second he considered answering, but he was still so exhausted that he didn't trust himself to explain to this person who he was and how he had come to be answering a stranger's phone. Instead he stared at the screen until the ringing stopped, at which point a message appeared: *7 missed calls.* Some drunk idiot must have lost his phone last night and was probably still asleep at home. The jogger turned back to the sea; the phone could wait, he would take it home with him and then call the mother to let her know where she could come and get it. He decided to check whether the guy's wallet might also be around somewhere, so that he could return it along with the phone.

It was then that he spotted the feet in the brown scrub where the land sloped steeply down to the sea. He actually had to think about it for a minute before he realized what they were; at first he thought they were funny-looking rocks, but then saw that they were black shoes, and that in the shoes were feet, which also looked oddly blackened. The realization shocked him out of his fatigue, and he forced his stiff legs to walk over towards the dip. He was afraid of what he might see when the rest of the body became visible; hopefully it was just the drunk owner of the phone who'd had too much fun the night before, but the completely motionless feet and the rather uncomfortable position of the body suggested otherwise. He noticed an odd burnt smell coming off the brown scrub as he approached, and thought to himself how strange it was that someone had decided to lie down in the one place where the scrub had been burned and the smell was so bad; although this was a trivial point when you also considered that he was partly lying in the grass and partly hanging down a rocky slope. Just before the entire body came into view, the jogger realized that no one, either living or half-dead, would choose this as a place to rest.

As he ran off in search of help, having forgotten all about the phone that he was clutching in one hand, the jogger felt neither pain nor fatigue. The only feeling left was nausea.

★　★　★

'I just thought you should know.' Thóra took the old woman's hand, which was rough and cold, and felt it jerk at her touch. Thóra had called Grímheiður after her visit to the hospital to tell her what she thought she'd understood about the reason for Jósteinn's attack. The panic this

330

seemed to have provoked in Jakob's mother had prompted Thóra to drop by and see her on her way home. Now she and Matthew sat with her in the narrow kitchen that Jakob missed so much. The apartment was small but welcoming and reminded Thóra of her grandparents' home when she was a child, which had had ornaments along all the walls whose sentimental value far outweighed their actual price. Here, framed photographs took pride of place, most of them of Jakob at various ages, but also some of his deceased father. 'I completely understand if you want to think about this a bit; even if as a result you might prefer me to resign from the case.'

'What's your hourly rate?' The woman bit her thin upper lip, which was almost the same colour as her face. When she released it again all the blood rushed back and it reddened as if she'd put lipstick on it but forgotten the lower one. Thóra named the lowest possible rate, the one she offered her closest friends. The woman's face revealed that she'd been expecting something lower. 'Can't I have a discount?'

Thóra was in a quandary; there was no way the woman could afford to pursue the case unless the firm simply did the work for free. 'The rate doesn't tell the whole story. The number of hours worked does tend to pile up in these kinds of assignments, but if everything goes to plan the majority of those hours would hopefully be reimbursed. In the part of the law that covers the reopening of cases, it's stated that the cost of the petition — and of the new trial, if the petition is approved — will be paid by the State Treasury.

On the other hand, we don't know whether Jakob's case will be reopened and even if it is, there's no guarantee that the courts will consider the entire portion of the expenditure recoverable.'

'But . . . ' Grímheiður stared open-mouthed, the colour now drained from her upper lip.

'On the other hand, if I'm right, and Jósteinn still wants Jakob's case to be reopened, then he'll hopefully stick to his word about paying the cost. If that's totally unacceptable to you after what's happened, I will of course stop working for him, and then we can take the chance that the case will go well and the costs will be paid by the Treasury.' Thóra felt sorry for Jakob's mother; it didn't take a psychologist to see that the woman had two choices, both of them bad. She could give the green light and indirectly receive money from a man who had maimed her son, or she could refuse any further assistance from this odious benefactor and effectively prevent Jakob from having any chance of returning home.

'What would you do?' Grímheiður directed her question to Matthew. She was of the old school; his words had more weight than Thóra's, since he was more likely to come to a rational conclusion, being a man. Thóra didn't let this bother her and smiled wryly to herself.

'Me?' Matthew had been following the conversation but clearly hadn't expected to be directly involved. He carefully put down the doughnut that he'd been intending to enjoy, after Grímheiður placed a box full of them on the table in front of him, along with some coffee that she'd brewed the old-fashioned way. 'Well, I guess I would let the investigation proceed. Look at Jósteinn's payments as compensation for the injury. The damage has already been done and although it goes completely against your instincts to accept anything from this man, it's the most sensible decision when you put aside your feelings and look at the bigger picture.'

'In other words, it doesn't matter where the assistance comes from.' The woman appeared satisfied with Matthew's answer and she filled his cup. 'But what will people think?'

'Does it matter?' Matthew meant this sincerely; he cared little about others' opinions. 'The case is about Jakob, not some strangers in town.'

Grímheiður put the coffeepot down carefully on a tray that Thóra would have bet everything she owned Jakob had made. Her pale eyes suddenly filled with tears, which she self-consciously wiped away with her hands. 'Sorry. I really don't know what's wrong with me.'

'You don't need to apologize for anything. I have a son; a daughter, too, and I understand how you feel. What Jakob's been through, both last night and over the years, is more than most mothers have to deal with. You deserve credit for your endurance.'

'Thanks,' muttered Grímheiður, so softly that she could barely be heard. 'He's got to be allowed to come home. I'm so worried about him. What if he's sent back to Sogn? What will this Jósteinn do then? Stab him again to send him back here? The hospital's had its own cutbacks and they can't keep readmitting him.'

'I'd advise you to speak to the Icelandic Prison Service and even try to get the hospital on your side. Sogn is categorized as a hospital, not a jail, so these institutions could act jointly to get Jakob placed elsewhere, in consultation with the court — which would also have to get involved, since he was pronounced not criminally liable. It must be possible to find some sort of interim solution to his predicament. Unfortunately, Ari will probably have to be involved as well, as Jakob's supervisor, but I can speak to him if you'd prefer not to.' Thóra was afraid that no matter what solution the authorities chose, it would be one that neither Jakob nor his mother would be happy with — although at least he would be safe.

'I've never been good at talking to government agencies, and certainly not to that lawyer.' Grímheiður glanced quickly at Thóra. 'I've never been able to speak plainly to those people about what's on my mind.'

Thóra assumed the woman meant government officials. 'Maybe I can help you.' You never knew, perhaps Einvarður would be willing to use his contacts within the Ministry of Justice. The Prison Service answered to the Ministry and it was the least Thóra could do for Grímheiður and her son.

'I would be very grateful.' Two more tears appeared, but Grímheiður wiped them away immediately, sniffed and pulled herself together. 'How's it going with the case otherwise? Have you found anything that might help Jakob?'

Thóra told her the main details of what she

was working on, without actually giving anything away. There was no way of knowing whether it would bear fruit, and she was keen not to give the woman some scrap of information that she might obsess over for a lifetime if Thóra didn't make any progress. 'Hopefully I'll be able to complete this over the next few days and then I can assess whether there's reason enough to request a reopening of the case.'

'Do you want to see his room?' The question came out of nowhere. Perhaps the woman wanted to elicit even more sympathy from Thóra, in order to increase the likelihood that her assessment of the evidence would be favourable to Jakob.

'Certainly.' Matthew got up off the kitchen chair with lightning speed. A fear of being confined in a small kitchen with an unfamiliar, weeping woman had overcome him.

They followed Grímheiður into a small carpeted hallway where the door to Jakob's room was located. 'Here it is. Just waiting for him to come home.' She opened the door and waved them in ahead of her.

'Very nice,' said Thóra, just to have something to say. It was difficult to comment much on the room; it was like every other room in the apartment, packed with things and three sizes too small for its contents. Still, there was not a speck of dust to be seen. There was even a radio playing softly, as if Jakob had just stepped out. Thóra looked around. 'You certainly have kept it looking tidy. I wish it were this clean at my place.'

'I don't have much to occupy me these days. Jakob was never much for cleaning up his room, and I was used to helping him. Now what I'd like most of all is for some naughty little boy to make a mess of everything so I can remember how things used to be, but I wouldn't dare.' She looked at some of her son's things that had been set up on a shelving unit. 'Something might break, and Jakob is so careful with his belongings.'

Matthew gently lifted a pair of binoculars that stood on end on the bedside table. 'These are fantastic.' He held the binoculars up to his eyes.

'They were a Christmas present from me and his father. The year before he died.'

Matthew put the binoculars down hastily. He left the other things alone and started examining the posters hanging on the wall above the bed, which was neatly made. There were loads of them, some overlapping; for example, the bumper of a Formula One car peeked out from beneath a poster of the Manchester United football team. 'What's this?' Matthew pointed at a rather faded picture of a figure on a white background, on which were written the words: *Even angels have bad days*. 'Isn't this an angel?' He looked at Thóra and then at Grímheiður.

'Funny that you should ask about this poster in particular.' Grímheiður smiled. 'It's been a favourite of Jakob's for almost ten years. He got it at the summer camp he went to run by the State Church. It was an experimental project, but I don't know if they carried it on because Jakob was too old by the following year to be eligible to go. Perhaps the course wasn't run again.'

Thóra went over and stood next to Matthew to look at the poster. Perhaps the picture could explain Jakob's reference to the angel when he was trying not very successfully to describe the fire. The mind sometimes sought out the familiar when it was under great strain. As the caption indicated, the angel's existence had once been brighter; its golden halo had fallen from its head and the little harp in its arms had a broken string. It was missing one sandal and a feather drifted to the ground from one of its small wings. Thóra sensed that their interest in the poster surprised Grímheiður, and she asked the first thing that crossed her mind. 'What made you say the course might not have happened again?'

'Oh, it was a bit of a disaster. Although Jakob loved it and the organizers did what they could to make the experience memorable, some of the participants had far too many problems to fit in there.'

'Oh?' Thóra turned away from the wall.

'Yes, all sorts of things happened that I can't imagine the staff would have wanted to encounter again.' Grímheiður shook her head, her expression sad. 'No one had properly considered how the participants might cope — just like at that damn residence.' She took two steps over to Jakob's desk, lifted a blue stapler and blew invisible dust off it. 'One girl nearly drowned when she fell into a river near the camp that she was constantly visiting, another ate poisonous mushrooms, and then there was one who tried to set his sleeping bag on fire. That was a close call; things could have turned out far worse.' Grímheiður put the stapler back down on the table, positioning it in precisely the same spot. 'That boy didn't enjoy being at the summer camp at all, and I can't understand who could have thought that he would. He was very autistic and couldn't tolerate new circumstances. The poor thing.' Lowering her voice, she added: 'He died when the centre burned down. Tryggvi.'

'Tryggvi? Einvarðsson?' Thóra was careful not to appear too interested, but this could be pretty significant, even though burning one's sleeping bag wasn't quite the same as using petrol to set a house on fire.

'Yes, him.' A light suddenly came on for Grímheiður. 'Do you think he started the fire?' Then she shook her head violently. 'It's impossible; he wasn't any more capable of it than Jakob. Tryggvi never left his apartment voluntarily. He would never have gone swanning around the residence on his own initiative.'

'No, no. Of course not.' Thóra acted as if she were dismissing this idea. Clearly not everyone was aware of Tryggvi's progress with the therapist. 'Did you say it was a summer camp organized by the Church?' It couldn't hurt to get some more information about the incident with the sleeping bag.

From the small radio on the table came the tinny, irritated voice of the DJ complaining that the person who was supposed to take over from him hadn't turned up.

23

Sunday, 17 January 2010

Lena was lying on a nice soft sofa, but she couldn't get into a good position, due to the weight of the book she was holding. She put it down on the glass table; she wasn't reading it anyway, and there was no point making herself uncomfortable. She had been finding it difficult to focus and the simple act of her mother walking into the room in the middle of a phone conversation, indifferent to her daughter, had made her lose the thread. Instead of peering at the small print, Lena watched her mother. She crossed the room, making sweeping hand gestures. The person she was speaking to was probably making the same gestures, because Lena's mother's friends all acted more or less the same. If Lena squinted in their vicinity she had trouble telling them apart. It was mainly her mother who stood out; more often than not she was the centrepiece, but in a completely different way to how Lena was with her friends. Her mother was always the most miserable; she could complain the most and wallow in the others' sympathy and empty words of encouragement. *'My dear Fanndís, I don't understand how you cope, can't you take a break and try to forget all of this for a while? God knows you deserve it.'* Lena wished she could peek into the past and see what things had been like before Tryggvi was born and her mother became an embodiment of sacrifices for her child. Perhaps the women had been more like Lena and her friends, giggling and chatting together easily.

After Tryggvi's death, Lena hadn't expected significant changes, and she'd been proved right. Her mother, of course, no longer played the role of the steadfast and dedicated parent who gave her all for her disabled son; now she smiled bravely through her tears, unable to come to terms with her loss. Both roles were characterized by how her mother said one thing but implied the opposite. Once it had been: *Isn't this terribly difficult for you, my poor Fanndís? No, no. You've just got to tough it out, even when everything seems hopeless.* Now it was: *But what do I really have to complain about? In the Third World there are people who have lost their children and can't even feed the ones who are still alive.*

Lena was suddenly overwhelmed by irritation. As if her mother had some sort of exclusive right to feel bad about Tryggvi. When all was said and done, Lena and her father had loved him just as much, even if they weren't constantly seeking attention after his death. Lena had never discussed the subject with her friends; her grief, like all the other feelings churning inside her, was private. Other people couldn't possibly understand. She doubted her father did, even though he'd had a very difficult time with it all too and hadn't been able to hide it either from her or from others who knew him well. It was as if he'd shut off part of himself; he was never properly happy, even though he tried to pretend to be for his wife and daughter's sake. Although it had often been difficult at home, Lena couldn't remember having seen him as miserable as he was now. If she were forced to choose which of the three of them had been most affected by Tryggvi's death, she would pick him.

'Oh, thank you, my dear. I'm thinking of you too.' Her mother hung up. She stared for a moment out of the living room window before turning to Lena on the sofa. 'Don't you have any classes today?'

'It's Sunday.' Lena looked at her mother, having long since become accustomed to this kind of thing.

'What's wrong with me? Of course!' Her mother was embarrassed. 'Where did your father go?'

Lena shrugged. 'He went out somewhere. He didn't say where.'

'Oh?' Her mother seemed almost insulted. 'Not to work, surely?'

'He didn't want to interrupt you while you were on the phone; he can't have gone far. Maybe he's just washing the car, now that the weather's good enough.' If she had to name one hobby of her father's, it would be washing the car. He would probably be happier if he'd gone to work at a carwash instead of going into law and taking a job at the ministry. 'Have you heard anything more from the lawyers who came to see you? About that Jakob, and the fire?'

A flash of anger crossed her mother's face but

she managed to suppress it and return to her usual persona: the noble, elegant woman enduring great hardship. 'No. Nor do I expect to. It's utter nonsense and I don't understand why they're opening old wounds for all the victims' relatives.'

Lena just restrained herself from shrieking at her mother. 'It's hardly fair to let the wrong man rot in prison just to protect a few people's feelings, is it?' How could her mother, who pretended to be so good, not let such a thing bother her? Lena felt bad enough herself.

'Oh, darling, come on — that's enough.' Her mother walked to the window and pushed the net curtain aside. 'He's not in the driveway. But the car's there, so he hasn't gone far.'

'Maybe he went out for a run, Mum. Jesus. If you're so worried about him, spend more time with him and less on the phone.'

'You're one to talk.' Her mother's mask had slipped now and she made no attempt to hide her anger. 'Where did you go last night?'

'Out with my friends.' Lena looked at her curiously. 'You already knew that.'

Her mother grabbed her earlobe and rubbed it energetically. 'Yes, that's right.' She plonked herself into a chair opposite Lena. 'I'm really not myself. Your father's acting a bit oddly these days and I don't know whether it's because of work or the reopening of the case.' She feigned interest in the book between them. 'He went to work last night after you left. He hasn't worked in the evening in years, let alone at the weekend.'

'He's super-busy right now. You know that.'

'Yes, yes. But I'm still concerned. He's reached the age when his heart could give out and he should think about slowing down, even if things are frantic.'

'If he had a study here at home he wouldn't need to go to work at the weekend or in the evenings.' Lena spoke carefully, knowing this was a sensitive issue. Although the house was large, there was only one spare room — Tryggvi's old room. Everything in it had been left undisturbed, as if they were still expecting him to come home on weekends, as had been the idea when he moved to the unit. After he died, the door to his room had been shut and Lena never went inside; nor did her dad. She didn't know how many times her mother had looked in there but twice she'd found the door open and seen her mother crying on the bed. Both times Lena had crept away unseen. She knew very well her mother's tendency to dramatize every little thing and had quickly suggested to her dad that they clean out Tryggvi's room and turn it into the study her father had long dreamed of. She didn't attempt to gloss over the reason for her suggestion, and together they'd been trying slowly but surely to make it happen, while her mother always deftly avoided taking the final decision.

'Yes, we need to think about that.' In other words, discuss it endlessly.

'Why can't we just do it now? Nothing's going to change in the near future. I know it'd make Dad very happy.'

'Yes, I'll speak to him about it tonight.' Another delaying tactic.

Lena sat up. 'How about we just take a look at the room now? Go over what you want to do with his things? I'm not saying we have to start boxing them up tonight.'

Her mother opened her mouth and closed it again. Her slender fingers stopped rubbing her ear. 'Well, I'm not feeling well enough to do it now, Lena. You have to understand that I simply haven't recovered yet.'

'Maybe because you still have to work through it properly. I think sorting out Tryggvi's room would actually do you good. There are so many people having a difficult time at the moment, who could make good use of a lot of what's in there.' Lena prepared to stand up. 'Come on — Dad will be so pleased, and if you really are worried about him having a heart attack or whatever then surely you can see that this will help.' She wriggled to her feet. 'Come on, it'll take fifteen minutes, max.'

'We're not going to start packing anything? Just have a look?' Lena nodded and her mother sighed deeply. 'I really can't be doing this. I still need to do the shopping, and that's just the tip of the iceberg.' It would be difficult to squeeze as much as a child-sized carton of chocolate milk into the jam-packed fridge, but Lena let it go; it was a major victory to get her mother to consider this at all.

The air in the room was heavy; it was much hotter in there than in the rest of the house and the smell was different. It was as if they were entering someone else's home, where the heating was turned up to tropical levels. 'Shall I open the window?' Lena didn't wait for an answer. However, the fresh air didn't seem to have much effect. 'Well, where do we start?'

Her mother was still standing in the doorway. 'We'll never manage to finish this in such a short time. Shouldn't we start on it after I've done the shopping and the cooking?'

'No, Mum. Let's start now.' Lena opened the wardrobe. In it were countless hangers, one suit and a pile of old jumpers and T-shirts that had been left behind when Tryggvi went to the residence. 'This, for example, could go to the Red Cross. The suit is almost new and I'm sure there's someone who could use it.'

'It's brand new. He was supposed to wear it at Christmas.' Her mother's voice was devoid of all emotion. 'I'm not sure I want to give it away. Or the jumpers. Your late grandmother knitted one of them.'

Lena shut the wardrobe slowly, though what she really wanted was to slam the door as hard as she could. 'Okay. What about the books?' High shelves full of illustrated books about animals, cars and astronomy stood at the opposite end of the room. 'I doubt any of us will read them.'

'I was taught never to throw books out. Don't you remember how he used to look at them for hours? There's something horrible about the idea of getting rid of them.'

'Yes, Mum, of course I remember.' This was going to be more difficult than Lena had expected. 'We don't need to throw them out or give them away; we can box them up and store them.'

'It's all the same in the end.'

Lena wasn't going to give up that easily. 'We can put the ones on the shelves into storage, at least. They haven't been opened since I don't know when.' Lena pulled out the smallest drawer in her brother's sturdy desk, yanking it so forcefully that she was lucky not to pull it completely off its runners. In it were all sorts of things: crayons and other stationery, a deck of cards Tryggvi had used to build cardhouses and dice he'd loved playing with. At the back of the drawer was a bright red cigarette lighter she wouldn't have noticed if she'd opened the drawer normally. She decided not to say anything and shut the drawer again without mentioning its contents. 'We can probably give most of this away.'

'It depends what's in there, of course.' Lena's mother leaned against the doorframe, clearly not intending to actually enter the room. 'Even if things aren't in constant use, that doesn't necessarily mean they should be recycled.'

'Who said anything about recycling?' Lena opened the next drawer. It was larger and heavier than the previous one, and she had to use some force. 'Although we shouldn't rule it out.' The drawer was full of stones and pebbles, but not the kind of stones she'd imagine someone wanting to keep. She remembered a trip to a mineralogical museum where the stones had been beautiful and eye-catching, in every colour imaginable, many of them sparkly. These ones were all grey, irregularly shaped and uninteresting — just rocks. 'Where did he get these stones?'

'From outside. I let him keep them in there.'

'Did he used to just pick them up off the ground? I never noticed him doing that.' She'd taken countless walks around the neighbourhood with her brother, and he'd never shown any interest in stones — insofar as he'd shown an interest in anything.

'It was a new thing for him. He began doing it just before he moved; you'd just started university and you didn't have time to go out walking with him any more.' Her words weren't accusatory at all; the family had perfectly understood the change in Lena's situation after she'd started classes. Lena picked one up and rolled it in the palm of her hand. 'Still, shouldn't we get rid of them? They're just rocks; they can't have any sentimental value.'

'For me they do.'

This was a huge step forward and Lena was so happy she had to turn her back to hide from her mother how triumphant she felt. It gave her hope that their home life would return to normal over time — or as normal as it could be, at least. She let the stone drop back into the drawer, where it landed on top of the pile and rolled down until it hit the back of the drawer with a thunk. The drawer was hard to shut again but after she'd managed it Lena pulled out the next one, prepared to find more rocks. Instead, the drawer held a stack of loose papers. The top sheets were blank and Lena picked up a few of them to check whether they were all like that.

'What are you two up to?' Her dad's voice came from the hallway, sounding strange.

'Nothing special.' Her mother finally entered

the room. 'Lena suggested we go through Tryggvi's things if we want to set up the study that you've been talking about.'

'Really?' Her father walked in and looked around. To Lena's knowledge he hadn't set foot in the room since Tryggvi had died. 'Oof, the air is bad in here.' He went over to his wife and put his hand on her shoulder. 'Thanks, you two.'

'Where did you go?' asked Lena's mother, adding a tiny white lie: 'Lena and I were worried about you.'

'I was out in the garden. The snow's melted and I wanted to pick up the rubbish from the New Year.' He turned to Lena. 'How's it going?'

She didn't reply straight away, as she was too absorbed in browsing through the drawings on the back of all the sheets of paper. They were all alike, showing a figure which could either be standing or lying down, depending on how you turned the paper. It was rather grotesque, with no eyes and no nose, just a big open mouth, which Lena interpreted as a symbol of despair. Tryggvi had added something new to this figure, that she hadn't seen in other drawings of his: some sort of dark sheet coming from its black, gaping mouth cavity. Lena suspected what the picture was meant to show, but when her father asked what was on all these sheets of paper she just turned one of the drawings towards him in silence.

'Where did you find this?' Her father ripped the drawing from her hand abruptly. He examined it for a few moments, his face grim, then took the rest of the pictures from Lena.

348

'In the drawer.' She pointed to the stack. Her father immediately started to gather up the sheets.

'I don't like this at all.' He put the papers on the desk when he couldn't fit any more in his hands. 'I'll deal with this room. There are lots of things in here that people don't need to see.'

Fanndís and Lena watched in surprise. Her mother, who hadn't seen the drawings, rubbed her ear feverishly.

As her father tore the sheets of paper to shreds in front of Lena, she felt dreadful. She was starting to suspect that the calm, normal family life she longed for was just a crazy dream that would never come true. Could this violent reaction be connected to the lawyer's investigation? He must have known about the pictures but not been disturbed by them until now, when the fire was being reinvestigated. She still had the lawyer's German friend's phone number somewhere; maybe he could tell her how the investigation was going. Clearly her parents weren't about to. A white scrap of paper fell off the desk and drifted to the floor.

24

Monday, 18 January 2010

'I need a pay rise.' Bella's tone made it clear that this was more of an order than a request, and Thóra felt like laughing out loud. If she hadn't been late for a meeting with Glódís at the Regional Office for the Disabled, she would have enjoyed continuing this discussion with her secretary.

'There's a recession, Bella, and pay rises aren't on the agenda, not in this office or anywhere else in Iceland. Did you mean a pay *cut*, maybe? Then we can talk.'

'Cigarettes have gone up, petrol has gone up, everything's gone up, so now wages should go up.' Her order of priorities was clear.

'Sorry, Bella. I really am.' Although there was little love lost between Thóra and her secretary, Bella's feelings were understandable in light of the recent price increases, and when you added increased taxes into the equation her wages must have been stretched even further. 'We've been hit by inflation too, so there's no room to improve the terms of anyone's contract — yours *or* ours.'

'Then pay me cash in hand.'

Thóra was in no doubt that Bella was entirely serious. 'I can't; you know that.'

'Why not? Then I can claim unemployment benefit and still work, which is like a pay rise, but you don't have to pay it.'

'It's illegal, Bella, and the state needs the money to pay those who are actually unemployed. Think for once before you speak.'

'All the state's money goes to fuck knows where, so I don't see why I can't have some of it. It's up to the people in this country to make a stand,' Bella exploded in misplaced indignation. 'So I'm going to leave early today. I'm going to protest, and I promise they'll regret having made me angry. Arsehole politicians.'

Thóra frowned. She was quite sure that Bella would carry out her threat, and she hoped the riot police shields were sturdy enough. To her knowledge there were no demonstrations planned, but her secretary alone would doubtless be a match for pretty much anyone in that department. Especially now that there was nothing but instant coffee in the office. 'You're not going in your fleece with the company name on it.' That would be a great photo on the front page of *Morgunblaðið*: Bella foaming at the mouth with their logo on her chest.

'I will if I don't get a pay rise.'

Thóra mentally kicked herself for having mentioned the fleece. Now Bella would definitely wear it. 'I'll discuss it with Bragi next week. This week's bad for both of us. I can't promise anything but it might be possible to compensate you in some other way. Maybe with a free quit-smoking course, or something that works out as the equivalent of a pay rise.' She hurried out and closed the door behind her quickly, just in case something came flying at her from behind.

The weather was still fine even though it looked as if it wouldn't hold for the rest of the day. It was a touch cooler than when Thóra had arrived that morning, and the dark clouds over Faxaflói Bay appeared to have edged nearer to land. Skólavörðustígur Street was still half asleep even though the shops had already opened and, surprisingly, there were some vacant parking spaces. At the end of the street Leifur Eiríksson continued his dispassionate observation of human life from high up on his plinth, and behind him towered the steeple of Hallgrím-skirkja Cathedral. She had parked the car in a car park a short distance from the office when she'd arrived at work that morning, since it was unclear whether she'd have any more luck than before getting in touch with anyone. If she'd known she'd be leaving again so soon she would have parked in a space right outside, at a meter that the parking attendants monitored a bit too diligently for her to park there for very long. She enjoyed the short walk and in her mind she went over what she wanted to discuss with Glódís. She could have just spoken to her over the phone, but Glódís hadn't wanted to do that, saying she was busy when Thóra reached her and suggesting that they meet. Since it was hit and miss whether the woman answered her phone calls, Thóra agreed to meet her. Glódís hadn't mentioned the e-mails she hadn't deigned to answer, and Thóra suspected that she'd only picked up the phone by mistake, without checking who it was. In any case, Thóra now had answers to both her questions courtesy of the developmental therapist, Linda: the name of Tryggvi's therapist and the name of the surviving resident, Ragna Sölvadóttir. But Linda hadn't known where Ragna was now, so it was important that Thóra extracted that information from Glódís.

Earlier that morning Thóra had called Sogn and spoken to the director about Jósteinn's attack on Jakob. According to him, the matter was under internal review and decisions were still to be made concerning what measures should be taken. She got the sense that although the attack was serious, Jósteinn was a sick man; after all, he wasn't at Sogn for nothing. Since the court had found him not criminally liable, the staff had few available options for correction; most likely they would increase the dosage of his medication and place him under stricter supervision, as well as temporarily depriving him of his privileges. The director admitted that these 'privileges' were pretty negligible, mainly consisting of allowing him a radio in his room. In other words, there was no axe hanging over Jósteinn's head, and with his distorted sense of morality you could hardly expect him to repent, or even realize the consequences of his actions.

When Thóra mentioned her own theory about the reasons behind the attack, the man didn't seem that surprised. Quite the opposite, in fact: he thought it was more than likely. The incident had confounded his staff, given Jósteinn's supposed friendship with Jakob; none of them had been aware of the two men falling out. Jósteinn himself had revealed nothing, claiming memory loss, which was clearly a lie. The director had asked Thóra whether this meant the petition to reopen Jakob's case would now be shelved, but she told him that was why she was calling, to determine whether Jósteinn still wished to pursue it. She also told him Jakob's mother had yet to give a definitive answer about whether she and Jakob still wanted Jósteinn's backing for the investigation — although Thóra was taking Grímheiður's lack of response as a 'yes'. The director offered to ask Jósteinn, since he couldn't allow Thóra to speak to him on the phone; he was still being held in semi-isolation. He was anxious to explain to Thóra that this isolation was not like segregation in prison: Jósteinn's daily life was completely unchanged, with the exception that he wasn't allowed to interact with the other residents or to receive visitors. Thóra accepted his offer with thanks and half an hour later the man called back and reported that Jósteinn definitely wanted to continue the investigation. He had actually seemed alarmed, for the first time since the attack, at the idea that the investigation might be brought to a close.

Afterwards Thóra had contacted Grímheiður and spoken to her for far longer than necessary. This wasn't Thóra's choice, but the older woman seemed desperate to share the rationale behind every aspect of her decision; and as she admitted to Thóra, she tended to get confused by her own thoughts, which seemed to move in endless circles instead of lining up neatly. It was different when she talked; speaking required her thoughts

354

to be channelled in a particular direction, making it more likely that they would lead to a specific conclusion. Thóra let her ramble, as clearly this was what she needed to do to get things straight. She had long since lost count of the 'yes'es and 'no's that she'd added to the conversation by the time the woman finally came to a conclusion: it would be best for Jakob if they kept the investigation going, even though accepting Jósteinn's help went against all her instincts. When the call ended, it turned out to have been worth every minute; a conclusion had been reached — the right one, in Thóra's opinion. Her other calls were unsuccessful; Ari wasn't answering the phone, and her random calls to some of the former employees on Glódís's list had been fruitless. People's phones were either turned off or they didn't answer.

The trip to the Regional Office went smoothly, except when Thóra nearly drove onto the pavement in her irritated attempts to turn off the radio. A newsflash had been announced and this had annoyed her for some reason; she couldn't take any more agitation. She was only one piece of bad news away from having some kind of minor breakdown, and she didn't want to behave like a madwoman in front of Glódís. Admittedly, it looked as though Glódís was the one heading for a breakdown; she looked a lot worse than when Thóra had last seen her. The black roots of her two-tone hair had inched out even further, and the bags under her eyes didn't help.

'Let's have a seat in my office.' Glódís didn't wait for a reply, but turned on her heel mid-sentence and walked away from reception. The secretary who had announced Thóra's arrival raised an eyebrow and shot Thóra a look that spoke volumes about Glódís's reputation at the office.

'I have a lot to do, so let's get straight to the point.' Glódís sat behind her desk, adopting an expression not dissimilar to Christ's on the cross. Her workload seemed not to have diminished at all, even though Thóra would have imagined her position at the Regional Office might have been downscaled. 'You probably want answers to the questions you sent in your e-mails, which I haven't had time to respond to, but — '

Thóra interrupted her. 'I already have them. However, I need to find out where Ragna Sölvadóttir is now. I understand that she's the girl with 'locked-in syndrome' who lived at the residence but escaped the fire.'

Glódís lifted a pencil from the table and tapped it against her palm rhythmically. 'You can't know much about the syndrome if you think you'll get anything out of her in person.'

'I completely understand her situation and I'm not planning to speak with her in private — I'll have the assistance of a therapist or someone who's capable of communicating with her effectively.'

'It's not a good idea to upset her, and I see no reason for you to do so. As I've said, I'll answer all your questions — which I'm much more capable of doing than Ragna, since she generally just stares into the middle distance. It's not like she has anything to add to what's already come out, so you don't need to disturb her.'

Thóra didn't recall Glódís saying that she was going to answer all her questions; in fact her response had been entirely to the contrary. 'I must insist on meeting her, though I'm certainly very grateful for your willingness to give me more of your valuable time. But as they say, 'two heads are better than one', and your answers have sometimes been a little inconsistent.'

'What do you mean?' Glódís was now tapping her palm more forcefully, but more slowly. 'I've been completely open with you — *too* open, in fact.'

Thóra smiled politely. 'You didn't tell me about Ragna, or that Tryggvi Einvarðsson had undergone special treatment that seemed to be having some positive results. I understood from you that Jakob was the only male there capable of moving about freely. Nor did you mention that the night watchman Friðleifur and his friend had been suspected of drinking at work and possibly stealing drugs. Perhaps there are other things you forgot to mention.'

'None of this is relevant to the fire.'

'I'll be the judge of what's relevant to my investigation.' If they were to avoid just sitting there bickering, Thóra needed to change her tactics. She had deliberately spoken brusquely, because she wasn't going to make any progress by listening to half-truths and outright lies. 'But I must emphasize that I am very grateful for what you've told me. I do realize that you're concerned about those who died, but it simply isn't fair that their rights should outweigh those of Jakob, who's still alive.' She was trying to give Glódís a way out that would encourage her to continue the conversation. Still, Thóra decided to drive the point home a bit further: 'I could probably get this information from Einvarður, Tryggvi's father. He has made it clear several times that he wants to be of help to me.' She didn't mention that he too appeared to have carefully selected the information that he'd chosen to share with Thóra.

'There's no need to trouble him with this.' Glódís's arrogance seemed to have diminished. 'I'll find out where Ragna is and let you know, as long as she has no objection to meeting you.'

'I'd really appreciate it.'

'I doubt it'll do any good, though,' said Glódís, putting down the pencil and rubbing her hands together. 'I think I should also mention that Tryggvi did indeed display a certain amount of progress — not inconsiderable, in fact — but you need to keep in mind that it was all relative. He was severely autistic, so even major advances still left him seriously disabled.'

'So do you think it's possible that he could have roamed about the unit at night?'

'I very much doubt it. The progress he made was mainly to do with expressing himself. All of a sudden he started interacting a little with people around him, though not in the sense that he had conversations with them, more that he started to take in some of what was directed at him and attempted to respond.'

'Did he speak?'

'No, he had a long way to go before that was

likely to happen, if he ever would have achieved it at all. He expressed himself in another way; through drawings, clapping and gestures. It was all very primitive, but it was still a huge success if you consider that up until then, Tryggvi had gone through life without giving any indication that he was aware of those around him. Well, that may be a bit of an exaggeration; he *was* aware of people, but he made no attempt to communicate with them. He found their presence uncomfortable, especially if they were strangers or there were too many people at once.'

'So in your professional opinion, he couldn't have played any part in the fire?'

'Absolutely not.' Glódís sounded confident, even more so when she added: 'It's out of the question.'

'And what can you tell me about Friðleifur and the drinking at work? Is that an unjust allegation as well?'

'I won't deny that his shift was under suspicion. But the suspicion turned out to be unfounded; they were both tested for alcohol three times, if I remember correctly, and the result was always the same: they were absolutely sober. So it was never more than a suspicion, which means that there's no reason for me to discuss it with you. I don't feel it's right to spread rumours that have no basis in reality.'

'But what about the drugs? Could they have been on dope? You can't buy a drug test kit at the chemist for that.'

'They weren't on any drugs, unless caffeine counts. After the rumours started I made sure I was there when they finished their shifts at the weekends, and they weren't high at all; each time they only seemed tired after being up all night.' The phone on Glódís's desk rang and she asked Thóra to excuse her. She answered and listened to the person on the other end of the line. The dull echo of a man's voice came from the receiver, and he sounded annoyed about something. Glódís blushed slightly before interrupting to say: 'I have a visitor, can I call you back in a moment?' Then she hung up and turned to Thóra. 'Where were we?'

They continued speaking for a while longer, but Glódís's eyes wandered constantly to the phone and her replies were distracted. Thóra decided to call it a day and concluded the visit by making Glódís promise she'd try to arrange a meeting between Thóra and Ragna. She followed Thóra only as far as the door of her office, and after saying goodbye she closed it behind her. As Thóra walked down the corridor she heard the murmur of Glódís's voice.

★　★　★

'She was here in my office, so it was a bit difficult to talk to you.' Glódís realized that she was speaking too loudly, as she did when she was anxious. She'd felt as if Thóra was never going to leave, but she knew that Einvarður was waiting for her to call. She hadn't wanted to irritate him, but she couldn't tell him who was sitting in front of her. As a result, he'd probably thought that she was being difficult; he certainly sounded tetchy when he answered on the first ring.

'What did she want?'

'She wants to meet Ragna. And she was asking about the night watchman Friðleifur, as I explained; she'd heard about the alleged discipline violations at the residence and wanted an explanation. I told her the truth, that the rumour turned out to be nonsense.' Glódís didn't dare tell him what they'd said about his son. She was afraid he would want a word for word account of the conversation and would subsequently find fault with everything she'd told the lawyer.

Einvarður was silent. 'Did Tryggvi have anything to do with this Ragna? I don't really remember her.'

'No. I doubt he even knew she lived there.'

'How about the night watchman, did he know him?'

'Not well. Friðleifur and the other night watchman went into the apartments several times a night to make sure that everything was all right — in fact, no, they only went into the apartments whose residents were connected to machines. It's possible that they might have had to enter Tryggvi's apartment at some point, if they'd heard a noise, perhaps, but it would have been something completely incidental. They also interacted with the residents a bit in the mornings, since they helped get them out of bed and prepare a light breakfast.'

'I see.'

Glódís didn't like his tone of voice and was apprehensive about what he was going to ask her next. It would be better if they discussed her conversation with Thóra as little as possible. 'When you called before, you mentioned some files. What did you mean?'

'Oh yes.' It was clear from his tone that he was not at all keen on changing the subject. 'Yes, I wanted to be absolutely clear on whether files from the centre are in circulation or in storage somewhere.'

'What?' Glódís didn't know what he was on about. The files were scattered throughout the administrative system and beyond. There was a whole heap of them at the Regional Office; some at the Ministry of Welfare and copies of this and that had found their way to the police and the courts for the trial, and then from there to the lawyers who had been connected to the case. There were even quite a few at his own ministry.

'Are any files concerning my son still in circulation? I expect you to tell me the truth, and I would remind you that it's thanks to my intervention that you still have a job.'

She stuttered. It was unusual for him to mention what he'd done for her so directly. She couldn't deny that she would have been out on the street if he hadn't stepped in in the wake of the fire. She was grateful for that, of course. On the other hand, he shouldn't forget that she herself had done him a favour, so he was out of line speaking to her like this. But instead of pointing this out to him, she decided to swallow her pride and simply answer the question. 'Well . . . I . . . it . . . ' She pulled herself together. 'Yes, there are numerous files on all the residents and the home's operations, here in this office and elsewhere.'

'I'm not asking about reports and suchlike; I mean things that belonged to my son. His property. Did everything get burnt or was there anything of his that might have been kept elsewhere?'

'Everything got burnt.' Glódís wasn't sure exactly what he meant. 'None of the residents' belongings were removed from the home, except perhaps by their relatives. We had nothing to do with them.'

'I'm not talking about clothes or anything like that. What I want to be sure of is that we, Tryggvi's family, get everything that belonged to him that might be in your possession. Things that are important to us, but meaningless to anyone else. His drawings, for example.'

Glódís was relieved. He didn't want her to start deleting files. For a moment she'd thought he suspected his son of being involved in the fire and wanted to get rid of some piece of evidence, to keep it hidden from the lawyer's investigation. 'No, we don't have anything like that. Definitely not. It was all at the home and would have burned along with the building. I'm absolutely certain.'

Einvarður seemed relieved and his tone became more natural, even friendly, as it had always been before. He thanked her warmly and said goodbye, though only after a brief and stilted attempt at polite small talk, as if nothing out of the ordinary had been discussed. After hanging up she stared at the phone in surprise, as thoughts began to run through her mind. Could it be that he'd discovered something linking his son to the case, or was he doing the same thing he'd done when he and his wife had pulled Tryggvi out of treatment without warning? Then, he'd asked to be given all the pictures that his son had drawn, and had been very determined about it. Glódís had only taken him seriously when he called a second time, furious, after his wife had mentioned that pictures had been put up again on all the walls of their son's apartment. And what had she got for her trouble besides a terrible pain in her back, after Jakob attacked her for taking one of the drawings from him? Perhaps this Thóra woman was looking under stones that were better left unturned. But it wasn't this thought that was causing Glódís the most distress. In her agitation she'd misled Einvarður: she'd forgotten about Tryggvi's developmental therapist, Ægir. When his services were no longer required, he'd packed up all his things — including a whole heap of papers he'd used in the young man's therapy sessions. Not all of Tryggvi's drawings had been destroyed in the fire.

25

Monday, 18 January 2010

Ragna Sölvadóttir's condition turned out to be much worse than Thóra had imagined. She lay on her back, but the nurse had turned her head so that the young woman could look straight at the person speaking to her. A therapist sat close beside Thóra. A thin blanket was spread over Ragna's wasted body and her shoulders stuck out from beneath it like coat hangers, her collarbone jutting through her skin. Thóra was sure it must require the utmost care simply to handle the girl so that she didn't break. It wasn't her scrawny body that made Thóra most uncomfortable, though, but how still the girl was. The lack of movement was so absolute that Thóra felt as if she herself had to be completely still, as if the slightest twitch would be rubbing the girl's face in the difference between their lives. Considering how the therapist was moving around in her seat, however, Thóra was probably being unnecessarily sensitive. The therapist was an employee of the Regional Office who had been drafted in to assist her, although the speed at which everything had occurred after Glódís had called and given the green light for her to meet Ragna had made Thóra's head spin somewhat, and she would have liked to have been better prepared. She had expected it to take several days to organize this meeting, not a few hours. She had the sneaking suspicion that perhaps this had been precisely the aim — to surprise her in order to ensure that her conversation with Ragna would be as muddled as possible. Unless Glódís had finally realized that it was pointless being stubborn; Thóra's investigation would follow its course with or without her help.

The therapist placed her hands on the cards that she'd laid in her lap. She had a gentle voice and her enunciation was very precise. There was no risk of her words being misunderstood. 'So to be clear, you understand who this is, and are prepared to answer her questions?' The woman's whole demeanour was relaxed, and her brief introduction of Thóra and the purpose of her visit had been clear and reasonable, as if Thóra were meeting with a fully capable woman. There was no pity in her voice nor any trace of the childish tone that Thóra felt trying to emerge in her own questions. She would have to get a grip on herself and be careful about talking down to the young woman; although her body had almost entirely given up, her mind was clear.

The girl blinked once. *Yes.*

'That's good. We're not in a hurry, Ragna, so just take your time. I have the cards and you know them quite well by now, don't you?'

Again the girl blinked once. *Yes.* Her eyes were an unusual colour, so dark blue that Thóra thought at first they were brown. She felt as if they were expressing some terrible sorrow, even though she couldn't put her finger on what was making her feel this way. There were no tears in the girl's eyes, nor did she seem upset in any way; she just stared ahead, wide-eyed. Before they'd gone into the room the therapist had told Thóra that the few people who'd been injured in this way always started by spelling out the same thing from the cards: *Kill me*. After sitting at the girl's bedside for a few minutes, Thóra wasn't surprised. The woman had added that this death wish generally passed; humans had an extraordinary capacity to adapt and these people usually took comfort from the knowledge that their situation could be even worse. When Thóra had exclaimed in surprise and asked how that could possibly be, the therapist had replied that there was a slightly more severe version of this condition, where the brain couldn't make contact with any voluntary muscles at all, including the ones that controlled eye movements. In order to distinguish such a condition from a coma, they had to measure brainwaves; the only difference between the two was consciousness. Thóra's mouth went dry, all the way down into her throat, as her mind automatically started trying to fathom what such an existence could possibly be like.

'Then perhaps it's best if Thóra takes over now, and I'll just deal with the cards.' The therapist smiled at the girl and then looked at Thóra. 'Go ahead.'

Thóra was actually speechless. She'd become lost in her own thoughts and was quite unprepared to take over, but she recovered quickly. 'I don't know how well you knew Jakob,

367

who lived at the residence, but I'm working for him. I honestly think, as do several others, that he's not guilty of starting the fire.' The girl's eyes remained still. 'It would help me considerably to be able to ask you some questions about your time there, because you're the only surviving resident apart from Jakob; and he has a limited ability to describe or understand what happened.' Thóra was deliberately not beating about the bush; it was part of her policy of treating Ragna in the same way as she would a fully functioning individual. 'Some of what I want to ask is unpleasant and personal, and I understand and respect it if you don't want to answer some of the questions. It's your choice.' Ragna still gave no indication of whether they should proceed or not; naturally, she had blinked, but had been careful to do so in the middle of Thóra's statements so that her blinking would not be misunderstood as replies. Thóra inhaled sharply as she ran her eyes over the smattering of notes that she'd jotted down in the quarter of an hour she'd had to prepare. 'Actually, I need to know one thing before I start, and that's whether you knew all the residents by name?' If she hadn't, it would be difficult for Thóra to phrase her questions in such a way that Ragna would understand who she was referring to in each instance.

One blink. *Yes.* Saliva trickled from the girl's mouth and a little wet spot appeared on her pillow.

'I'm happy to hear it.' Thóra smiled at her. She looked at her paper and then again at the girl.

'Considering your acquaintance with Jakob, do you think that he could have had reason or the ability to set the residence on fire?'

The young girl's eyes sought out the therapist, who gripped Thóra's shoulder. 'Make sure you ask only one question at a time. That was two: whether he might have, and whether he could have, started the fire. It makes it much easier keeping it simple.'

Thóra nodded, embarrassed. 'I'm sorry,' she said, directing her statement at Ragna. 'I'll be more careful. What I want to know is whether you consider it possible for Jakob to have started the fire.'

Ragna looked again at the therapist, who raised one of the cards and started pointing at the symbols on it. Finally she looked at Thóra. 'She doesn't know, or has no opinion on it.' As the woman spoke she looked at Ragna, who blinked once in approval at what the woman had said.

'Very good.' Thóra saw no reason to ask Ragna the first part of the original question, about whether Jakob might have had a reason for starting the fire. She probably wasn't in any position to know. 'I expect you never went into Natan's apartment, but do you know of anything that might have been connected to a short hose there?' The girl's eyes flitted back and forth and she appeared to have been upset by the question, though perhaps Thóra wasn't sufficiently quali-fied to judge. The therapist used her cards and finally asked Thóra to ask a different question, since the girl's answers weren't sufficiently clear; she was spelling out *hose short in my room.*

These words told Thóra nothing, but she had no idea what she could ask that would help to clarify. In order not to waste time going down a dead end, she asked another question she felt more confident about. The therapist had warned her before they went in that they couldn't spend much time with Ragna as patients tired easily during this kind of communication. 'Was there much interaction between the residents?'

Again the two women communicated through the cards. 'Her answer to this is both yes and no, which I interpret to mean that it varied, presumably depending on who was involved.' Ragna blinked once, so the therapist's understanding was apparently correct.

'Did the other residents regularly come to visit you in your apartment?' One blink, which allowed Thóra to continue along the same lines. She read the names of the residents one by one and received either one blink or two in return. The result was that two of them visited her with any frequency: the deaf-blind girl, Sigríður Herdís, and the epileptic Natan. Ragna's reply concerning Tryggvi was difficult to understand and the therapist told Thóra she was indicating that she couldn't answer the question with a simple yes or no. There was a short exchange between them, and finally the therapist put the cards down carefully in her lap and informed Thóra that Tryggvi had come to see Ragna only once. It was a similar situation with Jakob: he had only visited twice, which fitted in with his saying he'd felt uncomfortable in her presence. However, it was Tryggvi's visit that interested

Thóra, because here she had a witness who could confirm that he'd moved voluntarily around the centre, even if such a thing was rare. His involvement in the fire was starting to look more likely than she had thought, and this possibility was enhanced by the way his parents and Glódís had remained silent about so much that concerned him. Why did they seem to want to keep his progress secret, even though it had been relatively minimal? Perhaps the therapy sessions had not only improved Tryggvi's social skills but also further opened up the horrified fascination with fire that his parents had also kept quiet about. Thóra had made contact with an employee of the summer camp, who had been only too happy to tell her about the incident when the sleeping bag had been set on fire. According to her, Tryggvi had got hold of some matches and lighter fluid that had been used to light a small bonfire the previous night, which had fascinated him. He had used them to set fire to a sleeping bag in one of the bunks, no doubt to relive the enjoyment he'd experienced during the bonfire the night before. Luckily he hadn't been all that stealthy and they'd managed to extinguish the fire before it did much damage. The woman went on to tell Thóra that Tryggvi's parents had been extremely upset and informed the camp organizers that the boy was obsessed with fire and that they should always be sure to lock away any firelighting materials so that he couldn't get his hands on them. His parents had omitted to mention this when enrolling him in the camp; it had been so long since anything like that had happened that they had simply forgotten to mention it. It somehow hadn't occurred to them that any fires would be lit at the camp. Tryggvi's father had then decided to visit him immediately, and everyone had considered the matter closed, especially as it had been just one of many trying incidents during that difficult week.

'Did Tryggvi visit you around the time that you left the residence for the hospital?'

One blink. Yes.

'Did he say anything?' Tryggvi had reportedly never spoken, but Thóra decided to ask nonetheless. It could be that he'd made more progress than people wanted to admit; similar things had been kept quiet.

Two blinks. No.

'Did he get into bed with you?' Thóra was looking straight at Ragna, but out of the corner of her eye she saw the therapist turn her head sharply in her direction.

Two blinks. No.

'Did anyone else ever get into bed with you?' The therapist gripped Thóra's arm firmly, but Thóra shook her hand off and focused on the young woman's reaction. For a long time nothing happened; they just stared into each other's eyes. Then the girl blinked.

One slow, heavy blink. Yes.

★　★　★

Thóra sat outside in her car in the National Hospital's crowded car park. The heater was trying to battle the hoarfrost on the window and

372

Thóra put her hands under her thighs to protect them from the cold seat. But it wasn't the frosty windscreen or her cold thighs that bothered her; her mind was in overdrive and it would be dangerous to launch herself out into the traffic before she'd tried to put her thoughts in order. This was serious stuff, and the conversation with Ragna had ended long before Thóra had received answers to all her questions. There had proved to be a limit to how long Ragna could keep up a conversation. Although it could have continued for some time after it emerged that someone had climbed into bed with the young woman, it came to a natural conclusion when she simply couldn't go any further. Thóra didn't know whether it was from agitation or fatigue, but it was difficult to understand how a person might feel who was only capable of expressing themselves one letter at a time. Ragna had made her feelings known very simply: she had shut her eyes and not opened them again until she was asked whether she wanted to conclude the conversation. Then she blinked once. Yes.

Thóra was startled by a brisk tapping on the window. Outside stood the therapist, insufficiently dressed for outdoors and shaking like a leaf. It took Thóra a moment to catch her breath and free her hands from beneath her thighs. 'Sorry, I didn't mean to frighten you,' said the woman after Thóra rolled down the window and wrapped her arms around herself to better preserve her body heat. 'I simply must ask you about what happened in there.' This came as no surprise to Thóra. Although the therapist had initially been totally opposed to discussing these sensitive matters, she had changed her mind almost immediately and quickly became just as eager as Thóra to know what had taken place. After leaving the girl in the care of the nurse, it was clear that the woman wanted Thóra to tell her everything about the investigation, but Thóra merely thanked her for her help and hurried away. 'I must point out that the topics of these conversations are usually of no concern to me; I sort of put myself in the role of stenographer, but in this case I find it very difficult.'

'Hopefully there isn't generally a need to ask the sorts of questions that I just did.'

'No. At least I've never been at that kind of interview before.' The woman smiled, but her smile disappeared quickly as her teeth began to chatter. 'Of course I'd heard of something similar happening at the National Hospital some decades ago, and then again recently at a community residence, but it was completely hushed up. A girl there became pregnant, but she died before further news of it got out. At least that's how I heard it.'

'I think the second story you're referring to relates to the same case we were discussing with Ragna.' Thóra was in a dilemma: she didn't really want to speak to this woman, but she might need her services in the near future. It seemed clear that news of Lísa's pregnancy had spread throughout the Regional Office, but had stopped there, since the woman had only heard secondhand rumours.

'I'm bound to confidentiality about what I

hear in these kinds of interviews. You needn't worry that it will go any further.' This sounded credible. The same applied to interpreting in court. Had Thóra been given time to prepare more thoroughly, this was one of the things she would have swotted up on, but now she had to decide whether the woman was telling the truth. 'I'm trying to find the man who forced himself on one of the inhabitants of the care home that burned down. The woman was pregnant when she died in the fire and I suspect attempts have been made to cover this up.'

'But what did she mean when she kept repeating the word oxygen?'

'I have no idea, more's the pity.' This was one detail that had perplexed Thóra. When the girl had first spelled out the word, they had both thought she was in respiratory distress, which turned out not to be the case. How oxygen was related to the horrible thing that had happened to her was difficult to understand, but in the girl's mind clearly the two were inextricably — if inexplicably — linked. 'Did the description of the man mean anything to you?' The likelihood that anyone would recognize the perpetrator from the description the girl had given was negligible: *dark hair, blue-grey eyes, slim, straight teeth.* Why couldn't the bastard have had a wart or a tattoo in the middle of his forehead?

'No, but I didn't know anyone there. I never set foot in the residence, I'm afraid.' The woman hopped from foot to foot. 'What about the police? Shouldn't you let them know?'

'Yes, absolutely — I'll contact them as soon as

I get back to my office. It's too cold to do it now.' Even though the police had honoured Lísa's parents' request to keep her case quiet, the rape had taken on a different aspect now that it was clear there had been two victims — especially since one of them was still alive.

'Sure, of course.' The woman stood up straight and prepared to leave, even though she was obviously itching to ask Thóra more. It was probably as difficult for her to formulate her questions as it was for Thóra to digest what had happened.

'One question before I go.' Thóra sat on her hands again, this time to heat up her fingers a little before driving off. The wind blew into the car and the heater couldn't compete. 'Do you think you might have misread any of the cards? Might she have been trying to say something else? Those symbols are pretty close to each other, and it must be difficult to read them with absolute precision.'

'No, that's highly unlikely. I asked her about all of the symbols, as you saw, and she specifically agreed to those I pointed at. Obviously it's harder to communicate through the cards than through standard spoken language; it's impossible to have icons for everything in the world and communication becomes stilted when we have to spell out each word. But what I told you was what she indicated. I've been doing this long enough to assure you of that.'

'I'm sorry. I was just hoping there would be some simple explanation for her bizarre responses. This thing about the oxygen is completely incomprehensible, and I have no idea what she was getting at when she mentioned the radio.' Just before the girl had given up she had spelled out *radio*. 'Of course she was probably trying to say something more about it, but I was hoping it might have been something else. Something clearer.'

'No, sadly.' The woman had turned blue from cold in the exposed car park. 'But if I think of something, I'll be in touch, of course.' She gathered herself to leave again, but before she sprinted in the direction of her car she added: 'You shouldn't delay in contacting the police. People with locked-in syndrome usually die young, and she may not have long left. Death can strike quickly if the patient gets ill, and I know investigations and hearings take time. The person who did this mustn't get away with it. She deserves to live to see him sentenced.' And with that she ran off into the wind.

With the woman's words ringing in her ears Thóra drove back up Skólavörðustígur Street, immensely relieved to have taken her car instead of walking the short distance, as she'd thought about doing. It wasn't the north wind that made her jog in from her parking space, however, but the overwhelming desire to report what she'd learned to the authorities. With the same haste she called the police, before even removing her coat. She introduced herself and asked to speak to the person who had led the inquest into the fire. It would be best to speak to him so that she wouldn't have to waste time explaining the facts of the case; he must have been aware of Lísa's condition and the results of the investigation. After something of a wait, which at least gave her time to take off her jacket, a man came on the line, introducing himself in a deep voice as Úlfar. Thóra gave him her full name and was just about to tell him why she was calling when he interrupted her.

'Did you say Thóra Guðmundsdóttir? Lawyer?'

Thóra was surprised. 'Yes, that's right.'

'Has someone been in touch with you?'

This didn't make things any clearer. 'Er . . . no.'

The man was silent, apparently thinking things over. 'Your name is on a list I have here in my office, in connection with a case that came up yesterday.'

'I'm extremely busy, I'm afraid — I don't have time to take on new cases at the moment. Could you take me off the list for the time being?' A while ago Thóra had asked for her name to be added to a list of lawyers whom police suspects could contact when they needed a defence solicitor. This had been part of a plan that her partner Bragi had cooked up in response to the recession, although it hadn't led to anything — until now, apparently.

'It's easier said than done to take you off the list that I'm talking about. No one here has requested legal assistance from you — this is to do with a very serious case that you seem to be linked to.'

Thóra was too taken aback to fully absorb the implications of what he was saying. 'I don't really understand. I actually called to report a serious crime. Perhaps we're talking about the same thing?' Had the therapist beaten her to it in reporting the rape?

'If the crime you were going to report involves a death, then it's possible. If not, then we're talking about two unrelated cases.'

'A death?' Thóra's heart skipped a beat; maybe Jakob had died of his wounds. He hadn't seemed to be anywhere near death's door the day before, but what did she know about medicine? 'What's the name of the person who died, may I ask?'

Rather than answering her, he changed the subject, or so it seemed. 'Do you know a young radio host named Margeir?'

26

Monday, 18 January 2010

'I'm not making this up, Halli. I would have thought you'd understand that.' Berglind clamped the phone between her shoulder and ear so that she could fold the washing. 'The clothes smelled disgusting; I washed them three times using more and more detergent but the smell won't go away.'

'Please, Begga, not now.' Halli sounded tired. 'Of course I believe you, but there has to be some explanation. Maybe a neighbour's cat just sprayed the clothes?'

'Didn't you hear what I said? This isn't the odour of cat urine. I don't know what it could be. Something spoiled or rotten.'

'Then maybe the cat just ran into the washing with a dead animal, I don't know.'

'The washing doesn't hang down to the ground, Halli. And even if it did, cats don't carry prey that's rotten.' Berglind immediately regretted having said this. She realized how unreasonable she must sound to her husband.

'Begga. I've got to go to work. I know nothing about this and it seems anything I say will just annoy you more. Throw the damn stuff in a bag and I'll take a look at it when I get home. If the stink is as bad as you say, then it'll still smell this evening.' He didn't heave a sigh as he said this, but he might as well have done.

'Fine.' Berglind put down a white T-shirt that was sparklingly clean but smelled as if it had recently been dug up from a damp grave. 'See you later. Sorry to disturb you.' This wasn't meant to sound bitter or sarcastic, but it did anyway.

'Okay,' said Halli. There was a brief silence, which she found herself unable to fill. 'Don't hang the clothes outside, Begga. Use the dryer.'

'I will.' There was such a lot that Berglind wanted to say to him, but she could neither put it into words nor expect him to appreciate the timing. 'Come home early.' He didn't acquiesce immediately, as she had hoped he would. 'Please.'

'I'll try.'

'*I'll try*' was the same as '*maybe*'. Both were polite ways of saying no. The smell seemed worse when the conversation finished; Berglind turned from the table, grabbed a plastic bag and hurriedly stuffed the washing into it. Then she tied a knot at the top and put the bag into a corner of the little utility room. She hurried out and shut the door behind her, determined not to think about the stench any more or to let it put her off her chores. There was plenty to do and it would soon be time to feed her son. 'Pési, darling? Are you hungry?' she called. No answer. The silence made the house seem empty, as though she wasn't even there herself. 'Pési? Where are you, sweetie?' Still no answer. Berglind rushed to the hallway on the ground floor where she could see into the kitchen and the living room, but Pési wasn't in either of them. Upstairs also appeared to be empty, but that didn't really mean anything: Pési was still so little that he didn't make much noise. He was probably doing a puzzle in his room or messing around with something. All the same, Berglind dashed up the stairs, two steps at a time. Her worries weren't assuaged when she found her son's room empty — as, it transpired, were all the other upstairs rooms.

On her way back down the stairs it crossed her mind that Pési might have wandered outside while she was on the phone; maybe he got bored in the house and missed preschool. Berglind's decision at the end of last week to let him stay at home for a while had, in retrospect, perhaps not been a good one, and every time he asked to be allowed to return she'd had to face the fact that Pési's absence from class wasn't just for his sake but for hers as well. She felt so much better having him at home and not being alone in the house while she was on this ludicrous so-called sick leave. It was an absurd thing to call it. Physically she was perfectly healthy, and mentally she was a little bruised at worst. No holiday from work was going to heal those particular wounds, and sometimes she thought her absence was mainly for her colleagues' benefit. She felt guilty at this thought; her boss's suggestion had been made out of concern. An unusual level of concern, come to think of it. It would have been nice if her closest relatives had been as understanding and had displayed as much genuine interest in her problems. Her disappointment at Halli's reaction on the phone still smarted. 'Pési?' Silence. He must have gone outside.

The front door was kept locked and Pési had never quite been able to open it by himself. Naturally, he grew bigger and stronger every day, so it could just be that this was the first time he'd managed it. Berglind opened the door and was hit by an ice-cold gust of wind. The weekend's fine weather was well and truly over. Her coat hung on a hook in the hall, with Pési's jacket next to it. If he had gone out, he was inadequately dressed, even ignoring the fact that he was too young to be wandering around alone. Instead of putting on her coat, Berglind ran back to check whether he'd been messing about in the garden. He could sometimes manage the sliding door if he pulled with all his might, and he was used to playing outside — though he'd rarely gone out there in the sleet of recent months. It was also possible that she'd left the door half open. She couldn't remember whether she'd shut it behind her when she took the clothes from the line, irritated at foolishly letting the fine weekend weather dupe her into hanging the washing outside. Mind you, it was cold out and there was no chance that the door had stood open all that time. When she entered the room she saw the curtains moving in the breeze.

'Pési?' Berglind drew them back and was relieved to see her son out in the garden. She pushed her way out through the half-open door. Her son had his back to her, and appeared not to hear her. Fortunately, he was wearing a long-sleeved T-shirt, but he still had far too few clothes on for the middle of winter. His blond hair fluttered in the wind, reminding Berglind that he was well overdue for a haircut. 'Pési? You can't go out like this without letting Mummy know.' He remained absolutely motionless, giving no indication that he was aware of her. He stood directly underneath the line where the white washing had been hanging that morning. It could be that he'd found the dead animal Halli had been talking about, which would explain the stench. That would definitely scare him; she didn't know whether Pési had ever seen anything dead. 'Come on, Pési, darling. You'll catch cold if you stay out for long dressed like this.' She went over to him and spoke calmly, so as not to startle him when she took his shoulder. It was rare for him to be so distracted; it did happen from time to time, of course, but always in the evenings when he was very tired.

'Bad smell here, Mummy.' He didn't turn around.

Berglind felt a stabbing pain in her heart; he was the only one who knew that it wasn't her imagination. 'I know, darling. Let's go inside.' She had nearly reached him when he moved slightly, pawing at the grass with his bare feet. 'Your feet must be like blocks of ice, Pési, sweetheart. I think I'll need to make you some hot chocolate if we want to get them warm again.'

'I don't want hot chocolate. I want to be outside.' He finally turned around and looked at his mother with sad eyes. His hair still blew in the wind a little, but suddenly it looked almost as if it was being smoothed down somehow; protected from the gusts by invisible means.

'Come on, Pési.' Berglind gave up trying to seem bright and cheerful; instead her voice was full of urgency and unease. 'Let's go inside.' The air was tinged with a familiar metallic tang. 'It's too cold to be outside.'

He didn't reply, but stared at her as if he didn't recognize his own mother. Berglind wasn't even sure if he could see her. But he couldn't be looking at something in between them, since there was nothing there. 'What are you looking at? My jumper?' At moments like these it was better to talk, even though no one might be listening except you.

'I want to go in now.' Pési continued to stare straight ahead, hypnotized, his expression unaltered. He was even paler than usual; the only colour in his face was two red spots high on his cheekbones. The ghostly white hands sticking out from his thin sleeves looked as if they belonged to an overgrown porcelain doll.

'Come on, then.' She held out her hand, but it failed to draw him out of his hypnotized state. 'Let's go in, Pési.' She went up to him, bent down and took his little, ice-cold palm. Then she felt her shoulder-length hair electrify and rise slightly. Brittle, fragile leaves were lifted into the air and blew across the grass.

'Who was driving, Mummy?'

Berglind squeezed his small hand. She was desperate to pull him inside with her, get away from the oppressive stench that lingered under the washing line and stand with him in the

385

kitchen, surrounded by the fragrance of hot cocoa. There they could chat together comfortably about everything but the terrible event that had destroyed their lives. She would do anything to free herself from this burden, but didn't know what this 'anything' might be. She and Halli hadn't realized until too late what a good life they'd had before. They were broke, their journey to work was too long, Pési was ill too often, she was always getting split ends, the weather was awful . . . these complaints sounded ridiculous now, compared to what was to come after. A year ago she would have been at work, not standing half dressed out in her garden like an idiot, trying to coax her son back inside. Once again she wondered why things had escalated so slowly before becoming unbearable; although the spirit had manifested itself immediately after the accident, it wasn't until around the time of the financial crash that they had begun to feel as if they couldn't stand it any more and had turned to the church for help. In other words, nearly a year after the actual accident. Berglind had the feeling that something had pushed the haunting to another level, but it was difficult to say what that might have been. Nothing had changed in her and Halli's behaviour during that time, and Pési had continued to be the same little angel, following a routine that developed gradually with his increasing maturity. Whatever had caused it, it must have been something external. The best Berglind could come up with was that the changes were connected to Magga's family, but when she had spoken to their neighbour, who knew their circumstances, the woman hadn't known anything useful. Magga's family were still overwhelmed by grief and trying to come to terms with what had happened.

Suddenly Pési appeared to jump start. All at once he seemed to feel the cold, because when he started speaking his teeth chattered. 'There was someone in the garden, Mummy. I saw them earlier.'

'Come on. You're going to get ill if you stay out a minute longer in this cold.' Berglind herself was feeling the cold even more now, and she stamped her feet in an attempt to get rid of the chill. It had no effect.

'There's a bad smell when someone dies, Mummy.' He looked at her but instead of staring into her eyes, he looked at her open mouth. 'Not straight away, though.'

Forgetting her earlier idea of taking him carefully by the arm, Berglind grabbed her son by the shoulders, picked him up and ran inside with him.

★　★　★

The priest couldn't hide the fact that he was keen to get going. He kept starting his sentences with the phrase *Well, then*, but then he lost his bottle, repeatedly missing his chance to make an exit. Had he done a better job of concealing his desire to be elsewhere, Jósteinn probably wouldn't have done anything to delay his departure; but his opportunities to make other people suffer were decreasing, and he fully exploited every single one he came across. 'I'm just not sure that God exists. And if he does, then I can't understand the hand I've been dealt.'

'You shouldn't worry about it. God loves you just as much as those who have done no harm. You simply need to work at realizing that and thinking about what you've done. When you recognize how wrong it was, you will repent, and repentance is the first step to letting God into your life.' It was far too hot in the room, just the way Jósteinn liked it, and small beads of sweat had formed on the priest's forehead.

'You misunderstand me. I'm not searching for God. I asked how he came up with the idea of creating a man like me if he's as perfect as you're making out.'

'No one is entirely evil, Jósteinn. We've discussed this before.' The priest glanced sideways at the window and the freedom waiting outside. 'But we don't need to go over it again. You're a smart man, and I know you remember everything I tell you.'

'So you're suggesting that your God created me?' Jósteinn stared down at his lap, at the legs of his ripped velour trousers that had once been dark wine-red but were now almost pink.

'Yes, I am.' The priest laid his hands on his knees and prepared to lever himself up from the low couch. 'Well, then . . . '

'But if he *has* created me and I am the way I am, I don't understand it.' Jósteinn shut his eyes and listened carefully. He had read that if one of your senses didn't work, the others made up for it. He couldn't hear anything more clearly, just the faint sound of the cook's radio from out in the corridor, water running in a bathtub further back in the house and the priest's shallow panting as he suffocated from the heat. Nothing he hadn't heard while his eyes had been open. 'Your God is either kind of incompetent, or exceptionally unkind.'

'We can discuss this when we next meet, Jósteinn. I wasn't born yesterday and I'm fully aware that you're trying to provoke me. But it's completely normal for you to be pondering this and the fact that you are is a good sign, in my view. It shows me that you're on the right track. Salvation harms no one, believe me, and your heavy burden will be lifted if you seek salvation wholeheartedly.'

'Oh, I thought you knew. I don't have a soul to save.' Jósteinn opened his eyes again and tried pinching his nose. He neither saw nor heard more clearly as a result. 'Either I never had one, or I lost it somewhere along the way,' he said nasally. Maybe he would have to do this for longer to experience heightened perception.

'What nonsense, Jósteinn. Of course you have a soul. Everyone has a soul.' When there was no answer, the priest's face lit up like someone who's glimpsed his opportunity. 'Well, I think I should visit you more often, Jósteinn. Pay more attention to you. And your soul.' He stood up.

'How do you know I have a soul?' Jósteinn let go of his nose, but continued staring at his knees.

'Because, Jósteinn, although you attacked your friend Jakob, I understand that you're helping him, spending your own money to help him and

389

his mother. That's not the action of a soulless man.'

Jósteinn smiled but didn't look up. 'What *that* is, is a huge misunderstanding.'

'How so?' The priest was still standing by the sofa.

'I'm not doing it to be kind to Jakob. It's not compassion that motivates me. Far from it.' He smiled again before trying to cover both his eyes and his ears simultaneously. 'I'm only doing it in order to inflict pain. To . . . harm.' The smile vanished. 'It's quite possible to do that without having a knife.'

The priest said nothing. Jósteinn wouldn't have heard him anyway, now that he had his hands over his ears. He had seen a great deal in his work at Sogn, so Jósteinn's peculiar behaviour didn't surprise him, but he did find his declarations more difficult than normal.

'Sometimes good is bad and bad is good.' Jósteinn dropped his hands and glanced briefly into the priest's eyes, for the first time since he'd arrived. 'But there are also examples of bad being bad, and that's how it is in this instance. I can promise you that I have only bad intentions.'

★ ★ ★

Thóra swore quietly as she waited for the man, not because of the location, which was far from ideal, but because of how upset she was by what had happened. The bustle in the packed café in the Skeifan shopping area wasn't enough to distract her. It wasn't until Ægir appeared fifteen

390

minutes late that she managed to direct her thoughts elsewhere. He stood in the entrance, looking around for her, and when she stood up and waved at him, he smiled amiably and threaded his way between the densely arranged tables. Nothing in his bearing suggested a tyrant who might apply severe methods in his therapeutic treatment of autistic patients. On the contrary: he seemed rather gentle, apologizing for the inconvenience to everyone he slid past. His appearance, however, might inspire fear in particularly sensitive individuals, with his pitch-black hair and snow-white face. His eyes, also black, stared out from beneath his floppy fringe, and Thóra even caught the glint of a gold ring in one of his eyebrows.

'Hi.' He extended his hand. 'I assume you're Thóra.' She nodded and he sat down at the tiny table that barely accommodated the two cups of coffee Thóra had ordered, assuming the man would turn up on time. Now her cup was empty and the other one had stopped steaming.

'Sorry I'm late.'

'No problem.' Thóra gestured towards the cup. 'I don't know whether it's still drinkable.'

'Not to worry. I drink tea, but thanks anyway.' Thóra seriously regretted not having drunk his coffee as well. 'I understand you want to talk about Tryggvi? I've mainly come out of curiosity — it's been more than a year and a half since he stopped having treatment with me, so I have to admit it's been a long time since I gave him any thought. Of course I couldn't stop thinking about him after the fire; that was horrendous.

But why do you want to talk about him? Didn't you say you're a lawyer?'

Once again Thóra explained her connection to the fire at the residence. She had repeated the story so many times now that she could have done it in her sleep. 'I particularly wanted to discuss the progress he was making. I can't imagine anyone knows better than you what this consisted of and how significant it was. I've been hearing some quite contradictory stories about his condition.'

'Okay, that shouldn't be a problem.' Ægir leaned back and folded his arms. 'Though I do need to point out that in my opinion, he was only in the very early stages of improvement; he could have advanced much further if I hadn't been asked to stop treating him. I don't think I've ever been as disappointed, professionally.'

'Can you describe the nature of the improvements?'

'Oof, where do I begin?' Ægir exhaled gently. 'I don't know how much you know about this level of autism, but broadly speaking, Tryggvi was suffering from a severe developmental disability that hampered his communication to such an extent that he was barely able to express himself to others. He had no social skills, so he played no part in what went on around him beyond that of an indifferent spectator. Few people are autistic to such an extreme degree; many can make themselves understood, even though their ability to communicate is always impaired in some way, as is their social behaviour. Tryggvi could stare at a fan, or anything mechanically repetitive, for hours at a time. He could also sometimes fall into patterns of movement for long periods, rocking back and forth or wringing his hands incessantly, for example.'

'So were you able to overcome all this?'

'Not to any miraculous degree, but I was able to significantly reduce his repetitive behaviour, and I got him to look people in the eye and accept their presence. As I said, he still had a long way to go.'

'Tryggvi must have undergone some other forms of treatment before you came along; how did you manage to succeed where others had failed?'

'It's not as if his previous teachers or developmental therapists didn't do anything for him — far from it. For example, he spent endless amounts of time browsing illustrated textbooks, though he didn't read the words. His tendency to inflict harm on himself had also already been suppressed. As a toddler he would bang his head against things whenever he could, even to the point of cracking his skull. So a lot of progress had been made. For any improvement to be possible in people as autistic as Tryggvi, it's essential that their behavioural therapy begins very early. His parents, particularly his mother, were very concerned that he receive the best treatment available. She watched his diet very closely and followed the newest developments in that area, since in some cases the effects of autism can be reduced by changing a patient's nutritional intake. For instance, Tryggvi stopped eating both gluten and sugar, and according to his mother it reduced his symptoms. Not that I was able to judge — I didn't meet him until after they had been removed from his diet. Also, both his parents were very much alert to any developments in autism medication. They were kind of unique, actually, because the parents of autistic children sometimes focus on one particular factor: food, drugs or specific treatments, but few have been so aware of all the different aspects. They were terribly fond of him, but of course the same goes for all the parents of autistic children that I've encountered.'

'So why did they stop the treatment, just when things were starting to look up?'

Ægir shrugged. 'God knows. All I can think of is that the methods I was using weren't to his mother's liking; I didn't exactly take the 'softly softly' approach. I had to use a great deal of discipline to get results, and you've got to bear in mind that in this instance what we had was an individual who shunned human communication and attempted to avoid it by any possible means. So I had no other choice but to force him into acknowledging I was there. It was noisy, and must have been hard to watch. Still, I thought she realized that the end justified the means, but that was clearly a big misunderstanding on my part. It probably didn't help either that other residents and visitors complained about it. It was a real shame, that's for sure.'

'How much progress did Tryggvi make under your guidance?' The man had yet to answer the question that was really plaguing Thóra.

'Quite a lot, but again you have to consider

that we were starting from zero. He had started to draw more, pictures that seemed to better reflect what was on his mind, and he wasn't as afraid of everything. I got him to look me in the eye and accept my presence, as well as his mother's.'

'But did he move around the building voluntarily? In search of company or food, for example?'

'No, I very much doubt it.' Ægir shrugged. 'I suppose he *might* have left his apartment on his own, but not in search of either company or food. That would really surprise me.'

'I know of one instance when he paid a visit to a bedridden girl who lived there. I don't know why he went to see her, but he walked in and looked at her, in any case.'

'You see? Progress.' He rubbed his chin and stared around at the chattering crowd. 'If it was one of the girls who couldn't move, I'm not surprised he visited her rather than any of the other residents. A person who couldn't speak would have suited him well, and maybe he was drawn by the silence in her apartment. I went with him a few times to see the girl in the coma, in order to get him used to the unknown. Obviously she was the most harmless person in the place and I didn't want to bother those who were conscious, but she couldn't move a muscle. A couple of times we stopped in her doorway. We had the director's permission, of course, she was extremely cooperative, and Tryggvi didn't do anything to the poor girl, just stared at her in fascination, probably because she was so still.

Naturally, she didn't know we were there, since she wasn't conscious. I wasn't aware of him ever having visited her without me.'

Thóra didn't feel like correcting this misunderstanding; it didn't matter whether Ægir thought it was Lísa or Ragna Tryggvi had visited. 'How did he express himself with the pictures, anyway? I've seen a few of them — on a video recording, admittedly — but I couldn't work them out at all. In them was a person lying down, and then another person holding onto a large circle which was divided into three. There were also flames in some of them.'

'Of course the pictures weren't the same every time, but both figures you describe were frequently involved. The person lying down was probably the girl in the coma, who he was really fascinated with, as I mentioned. She turned up in his drawings when I started my treatment, but she began to appear more and more frequently and by the time I stopped working with him she was in every picture. No matter what the subject of the picture was. As far as the other figure is concerned, it came and went and I think it symbolized his mother; I couldn't give you a better guess than that. The ring she usually held was a peace symbol, in my opinion, but I couldn't confirm that for certain any more than anything else in his imaginary world.'

'And the flames?'

'They were another thing that fascinated him, but I suspect you're reading more into them than you should. They're not related in any way to the fire at the residence. It's one thing to draw fire, quite another to start one.'

'But that did actually happen: he was caught doing exactly that some years ago. That's not to say that he was responsible for the fire, but it certainly raises some questions.'

'The flames in his drawings symbolized distress and fear. It wasn't any more complicated than that. He drew fish when he was hungry and a sink when he was thirsty. Why he chose these things and not others, I don't know. He drew every picture in one go, with one unbroken line, so to speak. And if you examine the drawings very closely, you can see all kinds of things in them that are more important sometimes than the main subject.'

'What did *o8INN* or *OBINN* mean? It was in all the pictures and I wondered whether it was his signature or something like that. Would that fit?'

'No, I never understood what that meant. He was angry at the letters so he connected them to something bad; he always drew them last, but I'm not sure that they stood for something that we can understand. Maybe it's something he saw during his life that burned itself into his consciousness. He couldn't read or write, so he saw it and copied it, in precisely the same way that he drew a house or some equipment that he came across, say. Since the text was in all likelihood a mirror image, like everything else that he put on paper, it's hard to say what it was supposed to represent; no words begin with NN, for example. It didn't ring any bells with his parents, either, but you never know, maybe he might have added more letters to the others over time, and the text would have become clearer. Unfortunately, this never happened, because shortly after these letters started appearing in every drawing, his parents decided to terminate the treatment.'

'Do you still have any of the drawings?'

'Funny you should ask. I did have a bunch of them, until today. The former director contacted me and asked whether she could have them. She always seemed a decent sort, I said yes. So I don't have any; I took them to her on my way here and that's why I was late.'

'So Glódís has all of the drawings?'

The man nodded. 'Yes, at least the ones that I had.'

27

Monday, 18 January 2010

The advertisement hoardings on the outside of the Kringlan Shopping Centre were trying their best to make everything appear normal; here everyone was wallowing in cash and everything was as affordable as before. The few cars that were parked outside told a different story, and although Matthew had been watching for nearly ten minutes, no one had gone in or out of the shopping centre. He clearly remembered how the place had been buzzing with life nearly eighteen months ago, when he'd gone with Thóra and Sóley to buy Sóley some trainers a week before everything collapsed. He'd felt his heart nearly stop when he saw the price on the plain pair that she chose. The trip had been torture for him from beginning to end, and he could never be persuaded to go in there again; they'd trekked through the shopping centre, where people kept bumping into each other and no one apologized. Thóra's mood hadn't been much better when Sóley finally chose her shoes, which of course turned out to be the first ones they'd looked at, and she paid for them without a murmur of protest, probably considering it an acceptable ransom to be able to get out of the building. Sóley had subsequently worn the shoes only twice; in the end she'd said they were uncomfortable. Maybe they should repeat the fun and see whether Sóley would make a better choice. Who knew, maybe this time they would leave the place with comfortable trainers at a reasonable price.

Matthew looked at his watch. He had arrived too early, because he'd been afraid he wouldn't be able to find the place where he was supposed to meet the girl. He was standing across the road from Kringlan, outside Reykjavík University, where Tryggvi's sister Lena had asked him to meet her. She'd called him out of the blue, saying that she needed to speak to him briefly — in private. Since the offer was much more exciting than watching Thóra's parents bicker over whether to have tea or coffee, he had immediately agreed. He'd then tried to reach Thóra, but she didn't answer either her mobile or her office phone — and Bella didn't answer the main number, obviously. Therefore, he could only hope that he was doing the right thing in accepting, and he now waited rather self-consciously at the main entrance, a middle-aged man staring at the young people going in and out. This is why he'd been focusing his attention on the shopping centre instead; it made him feel better than being caught staring at the students.

Suddenly the flow of people out of the main door of the university increased. Several students milled around near him, happy to be out of class and trying to light their cigarettes before huddling together to generate some shelter. It wasn't the secondhand smoke that irritated Matthew, but the fact that the gaggle of kids were now making it difficult to see the entrance. He wasn't so good at recognizing people that he felt he could recognize Lena from the back, and he wasn't certain she would wait around long if she didn't immediately see him outside. So he moved away from the group, but then ended up among the crowd of people streaming out. Half the young women could have been Lena, judging by their height, weight and hair colour, but a light tap on his shoulder freed him from having to try and look into every face.

'Hi. Have you been waiting long?' Lena smiled, briefly revealing her beautiful white teeth. Smoke from the cigarette of a young man standing near her in the crowd drifted into her face and she frowned and waved it away. 'Ugh, ever since I gave up I find smoking so disgusting.' Her clothes were dictated more by fashion than the weather, which meant no hat. The wind whipped her long hair around her head but it appeared not to bother her, and she made no effort to control it. A heavy bag hung from her shoulder, making her stand slightly crooked.

'Who's this?' A young woman the same age as Lena, though not quite as stylish-looking, stared curiously at Matthew.

'Nobody you know. Call me later, maybe we can do some coursework together tonight.' As soon as the last word was out of Lena's mouth she made it clear that she was done with her friend and it was as if the girl was no longer standing there next to them. Yet still she remained, with a face like thunder, then turned on her heel and disappeared into the throng of students. 'Sorry. She's okay, but she can be a bit intense.' A young man bumped forcefully into Lena's shoulder, but she didn't wince. Her bookbag swung and bumped into her thigh with a soft thud. 'Shall we go over to Kringla so we can talk in peace? There's a café here in the university but it's packed at this time of day.'

'Fine.' They waited to cross the street while a fleet of students' cars passed by. Matthew had never been good at making small talk, but was grateful that Lena seemed to be an expert at it. She talked constantly, not about her brother or the fire, but about everything and nothing. All he had to do was interject with a couple of banalities every now and then, depending on what the cadence of her voice suggested was required.

He was relieved when they finally found some seats in Kringla Bar. He asked for a coffee and she ordered a Diet Coke, throwing her mobile phone unceremoniously onto the table and hanging her heavy bag on the back of the chair. As soon as the waiter was gone she started talking again, now chattering away about the price of textbooks and how her friend had had to postpone his studies because of it. 'I'm sorry to hear that, but shouldn't we talk about the fire and Tryggvi?' Matthew interjected. 'Unfortunately I've only got about half an hour.' This wasn't exactly true, but it increased the likelihood that the girl would stick to the matter at hand. He was too old to be sitting in a bar, discussing young people's problems.

'Yes, of course.' She smiled sheepishly and swept back her hair. 'Of course I didn't want to meet you to discuss the price of books. You'll have to excuse me — I'm just a little bit nervous about this case and I find it difficult to talk about it.'

'No problem.' Matthew was silent. He preferred not to have to lead the conversation, because it could take him an eternity to get out of her what she really needed to say. He'd pinned his hopes on her having some specific piece of information up her sleeve that she wanted to share. When Lena continued to look at him awkwardly, he felt he had to say something. 'Is it the investigation that's making you anxious, or something else? There's nothing about it that you need to fear. We're just exploring whether any elements of the case were misconstrued.'

'No, I'm not afraid of the outcome.' Lena then seemed to realize that she sounded rather unconvincing and hastily added: 'Well, not exactly *afraid*, but . . . It's just, you never know what's going to come up and that's kind of unnerving.'

'Are you referring to your brother? Are you worried that he's connected to this somehow?'

'Yes, actually. I know it's really unlikely, but I'm still worried. I don't know what effect it would have on my mum and dad. Can you imagine how they'd feel if they had to face up to the idea that the son they've been mourning was actually involved in starting the fire? Responsible for his own death, and all those other people's? Even I can hardly get my head around it, and

I'm nowhere near as close to the situation as they are.' She said nothing as the waiter brought them their drinks, but then continued once he'd gone behind the pretentiously designed bar at the back of the room. 'But in any case, you mustn't think that I've decided he's connected to this or anything. I'm just a bit worried.'

'No, I don't think that.' Matthew sipped his coffee then wiped the foam from his upper lip. 'I can't tell you anything about your brother's possible role in this, simply because I don't know if he actually did anything.'

'Are you a lawyer?' Lena hadn't yet touched her drink; instead she drew stripes in the condensation on the glass.

'No, I'm not. I'm just helping Thóra. She's a lawyer, conducting the investigation.'

'I see.' Lena stopped fiddling with the glass and placed her hands on the table. 'So if I tell you something, you're not bound to confidentiality.' Matthew decided not to explain that lawyer-client privilege was intended for clients, not potential witnesses or other parties to a case. That would just complicate things, and besides, he wasn't entirely clear on all the details.

'Not professionally, no. But I'll treat whatever information passes between us as confidential — though I would have to tell Thóra, who'd treat the information with the same discretion. However, if something emerges in our conversation that could prove Jakob's innocence, she would almost certainly use it in one way or another. The most important thing is that an innocent person doesn't shoulder the blame for someone else.'

'Okay. Of course that's fair.' She took a slow, calm sip. 'But you're not sure that Jakob *is* innocent, are you?'

'No, but the investigation is still ongoing, so that doesn't mean much.'

'But has something come out suggesting that Tryggvi had something to do with the fire?' She blushed slightly and looked away from Matthew. 'It would just be good if I had a little bit of advance warning. That's why I called you. I'm worried about Mum and Dad and maybe I could start preparing them if there's a chance of bad news.'

Matthew felt for her; her pain was obvious and he was convinced that she felt she had reason to be concerned, rightly or wrongly. 'This must be hard for your parents. Do they have the same concerns as you; do they think Tryggvi might have been involved?'

'No . . . yes . . . I don't know. It's impossible to talk to them. It always has been, actually, but now the situation is a hundred times worse. After Tryggvi died, they wouldn't let me out of their sight and wanted to know everything I was doing, and they're still really grumpy. It's like they think something just as bad will happen to me and they want to prevent it but don't think they could, and because of that they're pushing me away, almost. As a result, I feel a bit neurotic too. I just want them to let me run my own life and have some time to myself — when I can.'

This was typical of young people who still lived with their parents and Matthew was fairly certain that he would have said precisely the same thing in his day, without needing to have experienced a family tragedy. 'They just want the best for you.' This was the answer that he absolutely would not have wanted to hear himself. 'It's our understanding that Tryggvi made significant progress at the centre, after undergoing special therapy that helped him to start expressing himself, or at least to modify his behaviour. Is that right?'

Lena shrugged her slender shoulders. 'I wouldn't say he started expressing himself openly, but he'd grown more aware of his surroundings, that's for sure. Maybe he'd finally have started talking to us, who knows? It's not like he was making conversation or anything like that, though. Far from it.'

'But he was starting to express himself in new ways, which was a huge improvement, wasn't it?'

'Yes, compared to how he'd been before. He drew more, and his pictures were more focused.'

'Is that how he conveyed messages? Through his drawings?'

'No, not directly. I'm not sure he really thought of the drawings as messages to us. His mind didn't work like ours and it wasn't easy to understand what he was on about.' Lena took another sip of her drink and was careful to place the glass precisely on the wet ring that it had left behind on the table. 'There was nothing in them that suggested Tryggvi wanted to burn down the residence, if that's what you were thinking. Tryggvi would never have planned anything; even if he *was* involved, it would just have been something that happened. He wouldn't have

406

thought about it beforehand. I'm quite certain of that.'

'Do any of his pictures still exist? Besides the one in your living room?' Matthew found the way Lena was talking about her brother's pictures rather peculiar. It was as if she were trying to get him and Thóra to stop nosing around after them. If that was the case, her plan had completely misfired.

'Uh . . . ' Lena hesitated. 'No. Not any more, anyway.' She paused before continuing. 'We had some from the time when Tryggvi still lived at home but we threw them out when we were going through his room; they only rubbed salt in the wound. I can assure you they weren't connected to the fire at all. At least as far as I could see.'

'Were you ever present when Tryggvi was in therapy? I'm trying to find out whether he might have expressed himself in a different, clearer way to the person treating him. Perhaps even without pictures.'

Lena scowled. 'It was a horrible thing to have to watch, and Tryggvi hated it. It might have worked, but for fuck's sake, what was the point, really? It's not like Tryggvi could enjoy the results, and it's awful to think he suffered like that for nothing before he died.'

'So you witnessed it?'

'Once, twice. That was enough.' Her beautiful face became severe. 'The man repeated the same thing over and over: *Look at me, look at me* . . . He held Tryggvi's chin and forced him to look into his eyes. He said he was getting Tryggvi

407

to form a relationship or a connection with him, something like that. I don't remember which, and anyway it doesn't matter. My brother would writhe and twist his head trying to escape, but he couldn't.' The anger in her voice was gone when she continued. 'Tryggvi couldn't look people in the eye. He found it uncomfortable. I don't understand how Mum could bear to be there.'

'Was she always present during the sessions?' Matthew knew that Fanndís had often hung around at the care home, but he was surprised to hear that she'd been involved in the therapy.

'No, not always, but often. She didn't pre-arrange it or anything, but if the man was there when we arrived, she used to go in and watch. I don't know what she did when she went alone or with my dad, but presumably the same.'

'And what did you do while the therapy was going on? Did the residence even have a waiting room?' Matthew couldn't remember seeing such a thing during his and Thóra's visit to the burned-out building.

'I just hung around in the lobby. That was all right, because I got to know some of the staff members and could chat with them. Several of them were my age.'

'Did you know the night watchman who died in the fire?' Matthew couldn't remember what the man was called and cursed himself for not having memorized the names of the main people involved before coming to this meeting. It would have been better if Thóra had accompanied him, but he hadn't had much choice.

'Friðleifur? Yes, I knew him.'

'It's our understanding that he was suspected of having been drunk at work. Were you aware of anything like that?'

'No.' Lena frowned. 'He was certainly never drunk when I was there, but he actually worked mainly at night, so I don't know what he got up to then. I met him mostly on weekend mornings before he went home from his shift. I'm no expert but I'm pretty sure he wasn't drunk on those occasions.' She stared at the melting ice cube floating in her glass and corrected herself. 'No, I'm absolutely sure.'

'It's also our understanding that he received visitors, in the mornings on the weekends and maybe during the night. Do you know anything about that?'

Lena continued to stare at the ice for a moment but then shrugged apathetically. 'I only know that he was told off about some beer cans; maybe he had visitors who were drinking beer or something. It wasn't long before the fire, but I have no idea whether it was him, the other night watchman, someone they let in, or what.' She looked up briefly from her glass at Matthew. 'Do you think maybe they let in some visitors who started the fire?'

'There's really no evidence yet. But do you know which of their friends or acquaintances might possibly have come to visit? We need to speak to those people, if possible.'

Lena shook her head. 'No. It was just some people. I didn't know the night watchmen that well. Friðleifur maybe a bit more, but I didn't really know anything about him.'

'What was the name of the other night watchman again?'

Lena was silent and appeared to be engaged in a psychological tug-of-war. 'You'll find it out anyway, won't you? Whether I give you his name or not?'

'Yes, we already have it. He just hasn't answered Thóra's phone calls and I can't remember it at the moment. Obviously he would know better than anyone what went on there at night-time even if he was sick at home on that particular night. Apparently.'

'Okay.' She took a sip of her drink and looked at her phone, as if she were hoping it would ring and save her. The grey screen stared back at her without blinking. 'You won't say where you got the name, will you? I don't want to get anyone into trouble.'

'No, no. I won't say a thing, since there's no reason to. As I said, we already have it — I just can't remember it.'

Lena nodded so slightly that it was barely noticeable. 'Look, there were two different teams who worked on the night shift, one week on, one week off, and it was generally always the same guy working with Friðleifur. Occasionally it was someone else, but your best bet by far would be to talk to the man who usually worked with him. The others are probably less important, because they were only with him for the odd night now and then.'

'And what's his name?'

'Margeir. I don't know his surname.'

28

Monday, 18 January 2010

The hot tub was warmer than usual and dense steam rose in the cold. From the dark sky snowflakes drifted down onto Thóra and Matthew's heads as they sat there soaking, with wrinkled fingers and just as wrinkled toes. Sóley was in the children's pool with her arm round Orri, but Thóra didn't take her eyes off them in case she lost sight of Sóley's brightly coloured swimsuit and Orri's chubby form in the steam that surrounded the group of kids in the shallow water. She and Matthew had given in to their repeated pestering and gone to the pool while Thóra's mother prepared dinner. There weren't many adults there and they sat alone in the hot tub; this was the life. This was actually the only sport that Thóra liked doing; unlike Matthew's running, you could stop whenever you wanted. When you went out for a run, once you got exhausted you still always had to get back home.

'I don't really know what to think.' Thóra slipped further down into the water to warm up her shoulders a bit. 'The police were keeping their cards close to their chests but I'm convinced it's Margeir they found dead at Nauthólsvík Beach yesterday. Why would they be concerning themselves with calls to and from his phone, unless it's because they can't ask him

411

personally?' Although she'd resolved to avoid watching the news, she'd scanned the Internet after her conversation with the policeman in the hope of finding out what the case was about. The reason the police were interested in speaking to her was that she'd called Margeir's mobile phone the day before, and the day before that, too. At first Thóra didn't understand what the problem was, but she soon worked it out and explained why she'd been trying to contact him. Once that was out of the way, she managed to get to the real reason she'd phoned them, which was to report that Ragna Sölvadóttir had also been abused at the residence. She'd also tried to find out — unsuccessfully — why the police were investigating Margeir's phone. Because she'd made so little progress on that front, she'd taken a chance on the news, which reported that the body of a young man had been found at Nauthólsvík, apparently the victim of a crime. The name of the deceased could not yet be disclosed. But it seemed clear to Thóra from talking to the police — the mention of a death, then the questions about her calls to Margeir — that the mobile she had called must have been found on or near this body, in which case it was likely to be Margeir.

'Maybe he's avoiding the police for some other reason; maybe he's suspected of something and doesn't want to talk?' Matthew wiped the melting snowflakes from his forehead before the water ran into his eyes. 'This could just be coincidence.'

'I doubt it.' Thóra watched Sóley splash water

playfully at Orri, who shrieked with delight. 'From the way the policeman sounded, it seemed serious.'

'Well, there aren't many things more serious than cold-blooded murder.'

'Sure, sure, but the police mentioned a death and there was nothing in the news about any accidental deaths. So it must be related to the fire. Anything else would be too much of a coincidence. On the other hand, Margeir was ruled out as being the father of Lísa's child, so it can't be anything to do with that aspect of the case. Not unless the tests were never actually carried out and Glódís was lying to me when she said she'd seen the results of the tests on the night watchmen.'

'Surely the tests were done? The night watchmen must have been the prime suspects.'

'Yes, it would have been ridiculous to seriously suspect anyone else. I'm just a bit paranoid. However much the paternity tests cost, the night watchmen must have been included. Unless a decision was made not to investigate the rape; if they'd been planning to bury the matter anyway, it would have been pointless to waste time and money trying to find the guilty party.' The steam in the children's pool had thickened and Thóra sat up to get a better view. 'I've also been thinking a lot about what Ægir said about Tryggvi's therapy and the way it ended. And after what he said about the drawings, I'm extremely keen to find them — especially given what you sensed from Lena. The fact that Glódís won't let me see the pictures makes me even

more bothered about not having access to them.'
Thóra had got in touch with Glódís straight after
her meeting with Ægir and been told that
Thóra's visit had reminded her that there were
still files around that should have been handed
over long ago. It wasn't appropriate, as far as the
relatives were concerned, for an unrelated party
to have access to such files and thus it was out of
the question to give them to Thóra when they
were finally returned. The pictures would go
straight to Tryggvi's parents.

'But are you sure they won't let you look at the
pictures once they've got them back?'

'I don't think so, and if that's the case, how
can I be sure they won't just remove any pictures
that depict precisely what I'm looking for — a
connection to the fire or to Lísa? Maybe there
are pictures of her naked, who knows?' Thóra
pulled herself up even higher in the water as she
noticed Sóley and Orri looking like they wanted
to get out of the pool. 'Given his paternity test
was negative, it's highly unlikely, of course;
but he could have drawn a picture of the man
who impregnated her, seen the deed through
the doorway.' She stood up and waved to the
children in order to ensure that they could make
their way the short distance over to her. 'But
considering the primitive appearance of the
figures he drew, I don't know how useful they'd
be in finding the person who forced himself on
Lísa.'

Sóley led Orri to the hot tub; steam drifted up
from the children's bodies but by the time they
reached the tub they were starting to shiver. 'Is

this tub horribly hot?' Sóley stuck one foot just slightly into the water and pulled it straight back out.

'It feels like it at first. Jump in before you get covered in icicles.' They did as Thóra said but it wasn't long before Orri's eyelids started to droop. His blond head sunk to his chest and there was nothing for it but to go home.

In the changing room Thóra and Sóley had to take turns keeping Orri awake while the other one got dressed. He sat on the bench wrapped in a towel, struggling to keep his eyes open. Thóra checked her phone to see if her mother had tried to call; she had said she'd let Thóra know if she needed anything from the shops. When she saw on the screen that she had indeed received a message, her heart sank a little; she would have preferred to go straight home. The message wasn't from her mother, however, or from ja.is, and since her mother wasn't particularly familiar with the Internet, Thóra suspected Gylfi had sent the message on his grandmother's behalf. He was careful with his minutes and wouldn't have wasted any krónur talking about something as boring as food shopping. She opened the message on the way out of the changing room: *Facebook.com final goodbye Friðleifur*

* * *

Although Thóra had registered on Facebook when her old law school class had created a page for their graduation anniversary party, she hardly ever logged on to it. She had terrible trouble

415

with this form of social media, which seemed purely designed to fill her inbox with endless announcements. Matthew was worse than she was, having refused to even register on the site back before the novelty wore off for Thóra. As usual, after dinner she'd asked Gylfi to help her investigate this strange message, rather than spend hours in front of the computer in the hope that Facebook would finally let her in.

'Why didn't you just choose a password you knew you could remember?' Gylfi pushed the keyboard towards his mother, frustrated and amazed.

'Calm down, I've got it here.' Thóra opened a file where she kept usernames and passwords. She was very happy with this system, which had often proved useful. 'Here you go.' She pushed the keyboard back to Gylfi and pointed at the password.

'That's the worst password you could choose,' he muttered, typing in Thóra123. 'And you'd have to be pretty stupid not to remember it.' He shook his head in amazement. 'Not to mention keeping this kind of file in the first place.'

'Yes, okay. Let's get on with it.' Thóra moved her chair sideways slightly so that Matthew, who was standing behind them, could see better.

'Oh, what fun! Are you playing a computer game?' Thóra's mother stood in the doorway to the study. All three of them turned and nodded. It was easier than explaining what they were actually doing. 'Not some war game, I hope.' She left before they had an opportunity to respond.

'It's a shame Grandpa and Grandma aren't

416

staying here permanently,' said Gylfi, turning to Thóra's Facebook page, which was now open. 'It would be fun if they lived with us all the time.' The cursor arrow swept across the screen. 'You have six friend requests, one event invitation, and seven friend recommendations. And you've got a hundred and thirty-two other requests. You're obviously on here a lot.'

'Very funny.' It had probably been more than a month since Thóra had logged on. 'Check whether any of it's related to Friðleifur. Maybe I have a friend request from him.'

'But he's dead.' Matthew was watching with interest, since he'd never seen this kind of webpage. 'Is that possible?'

'Yes, if someone keeps his page going and knows his user-name and password. I don't know whether a member's death would necessarily be reported to Facebook. You could of course send them an e-mail and ask that the page be closed if you notice anything unusual, but I don't know how you go about that. Still, I'm sure his friends would have reported it if his page were kept going after his death.' Gylfi checked Thóra's friend requests, but none of them was from Friðleifur. 'He isn't here, or under friend recommendations. Maybe there's something in events.' He opened the notifications page and started scrolling down the extremely long list. 'No, nothing here either.'

'Isn't it possible to search for him?' Thóra tried unsuccessfully to spot something on the screen that fell under the category 'search engine'.

'Yeah, sure.' Gylfi clicked on a box marked 'Search' and entered 'Friðleifur'. In a second the results of the search appeared, twelve in all. None of them turned out to have his surname. On this page it was also possible to choose to view the results for groups that were connected to this name in one way or another. There turned out to be five, one of which was called *Final Goodbye — Friðleifur*. It had three hundred and thirty-eight members. 'Bingo.'

'Go into that page.' Thóra wanted to grab the mouse from her son but stopped herself in case she messed up what they'd already found.

'You're lucky — it's an open group, so you don't need to get someone's permission to become a member,' Gylfi told her. 'You do have to become a member to see it, though. Do you want to?' The arrow rested above the tab for that choice.

'Absolutely. Is it really not possible to see it otherwise?'

'No. Not as far as I can tell, anyway.'

'Are you sure this is wise?' Matthew's expression made it clear that he wasn't exactly happy with the idea.

'Yes, of course. What's there to worry about? Click on it, Gylfi.' Once again the screen changed and they found themselves viewing a page dedicated to preserving the memory of Friðleifur. Thóra asked Gylfi to enlarge the man's photo. She didn't recognize him, having only seen a picture of him dead, after the fire had completely ravaged his features. He'd been dark-haired, with rather pockmarked skin around his jaw, probably

418

due to adolescent acne. It was a sad picture, somehow; his smile looked rather mournful, as if he knew what was in store for him. His straight teeth were visible behind his dark lips and he appeared likeable, even handsome in his own way. His hair was curly and unkempt, falling over his forehead and down into his eyes. The photo was grainy, as if it had been enlarged several times; this made it seem unlikely that it was his relatives who had set up the page.

'Do you want to swap seats?' Gylfi stood up. 'You should be all right now — it's hard to mess it up once you're in.' Matthew took his seat and Gylfi left them with a yawn. 'Just call me if you get in any trouble.'

According to its opening text, the page had been set up to allow the friends of Friðleifur, who had died far too young, to say their final goodbyes. It gave the date of his death and people were encouraged to convey their sympathies and to share photos of Friðleifur. Members were asked to make sure their photos were tasteful and it was made clear that any photos that were considered inappropriate would be removed. Nowhere did it state who was responsible for creating the page or who managed it.

'You can find anything on the web,' said Matthew. 'I guess it's not quite life after death, but Internet after death?'

'Hey, I think this is a pretty good idea — and probably a useful part of the grieving process. I guess it's just a modern version of the obituary. Maybe this is how we'll be remembered one day.'

She scrolled through some comments from those who had visited the page. The most recent post was four months old, but there were numerous other entries.

'Ugh.' Matthew was far from impressed by Thóra's vision of the future. 'Am I crazy, or are these comments a bit weird?'

Thóra nodded. 'I've often thought of you as crazy, but you're right, this isn't really what you'd expect to see on this kind of page.' Most of the posts were about drinking and hangovers. She read them aloud: ' "Thinking about you after a mad session — my head's killing me. Wish you were here!'; 'Got wasted on Friday, thought of you often'; 'Friðleifur, mate, where were you at the weekend? I puked my guts out, it's not the same without you'. Of course I don't know how young people remember their dead friends, but this is pretty weird.' She continued to browse through the posts, which went on for several pages. 'There must be something here that my mysterious texter wants me to see . . . 'Miss you loads, am really hungover'; 'Cheers, mate! I'm raising a glass to you'; 'You don't know what you've got 'til it's gone, got ducking frunk, life without you sucks big time'; 'Miss you, our hero — we're lost without you'.'

'What do they mean?' Matthew watched as Thóra continued to skim through the posts. They were all along the same lines. 'Was he a drug dealer?'

'What makes you think that?' Thóra ran her eyes down the screen without seeing anything that might help her; there were just endless messages about partying. 'I'm wondering whether Friðleifur and the other night watchman were selling access to the bodies of the two girls, Lísa and Ragna. To the other residents, even.'

'Now hang on a minute, there are far too many people posting messages here for them all to have come to the residence for something like that, surely? It can't be something many people are into and besides, there are lots of posts from women, too. I don't think you can read anything into this other than that he prevented his friends from drinking themselves to death, since everybody on here seems to have got really drunk after he died and wished he was there to stop them.'

'My interpretation is that his friends simply got really drunk in his memory. Maybe he was a huge party animal and mostly hung around with people who spent their whole lives getting wasted.'

'That doesn't make much sense — why would a party animal get a job working night shifts at the weekend?'

'Unless he drank at work, as he was suspected of doing. Maybe he did hold parties there after all. And he only worked every other weekend.' She read the final posts, which were also the oldest, dated about a month after Friðleifur's death. ''Have an awesome time with God, I'm sure he'll be happy to see you — party in heaven!'; 'Bye Friðleifur, trouble-shooter deluxe, I miss you, man'; 'Friðleifur, my friend, have a good trip to heaven, when we meet there one day it's gonna be mega'.' Every comment was in the same vein.

'Did you notice whether any of the people who've posted are connected with the case?'

Thóra shook her head. 'If they are, I've missed it. I can't actually remember all the names, but from the little pictures they all look on the young side, so I doubt any of them worked at the centre. Apart from Friðleifur and Margeir, who were both around twenty, all the employees were much older than the writers of these comments. Also, it looks to me as if these are just his friends. There are no comments from any relatives as far as I can tell.'

'Yes, I'm sure you're right. Do you think Gylfi or Sigga might know anyone from this group? It might be worth showing them the pictures and comments — maybe they could work out why the messages are so weird.'

'Maybe, although these people don't really look like secondary schoolers to me. They also seem a lot more involved in the party scene than Gylfi and Sigga. But you never know.' Thóra was beginning to feel more confident about navigating the site and managed quite easily to arrange the group's members into alphabetical order, with their profile picture and country of origin also showing. As it turned out, this didn't help much, because all the members seemed to have chosen not to share their personal information or profile pages with strangers. Nevertheless, she went through the list in its entirety and noticed two familiar names: Margeir and Lena. Neither of them had posted a comment. It wasn't that odd that they'd joined the group; Margeir was Friðleifur's main colleague and Lena had told

Matthew that she'd met Friðleifur during her visits to the residence.

'Maybe you could call her and ask her about it?' Thóra looked at Matthew. 'Maybe she knows what it all means, even if she didn't know him that well and has no idea what happened there at night.' She peered at the image next to Margeir's name but didn't recognize the face. Unlike Friðleifur, Margeir was fair and freckled, and he had a serious expression that didn't fit at all with his appearance.

Matthew frowned. 'I can't say I'm wild about the idea. Can't you call her?'

'I could, but she seems to trust you. Why don't you want to talk to her? I thought you thought she was okay?'

'She is okay, sure, but she's just so young, and I find it uncomfortable dealing with her. I'm not formally involved in the case and it might be misinterpreted. What do you think her father would say, for example, about a middle-aged man constantly bothering his twenty-year-old daughter?'

'It's hardly harassment to meet her once at a café and call her once. But I take your point. I'll call her.' Thóra said this last sentence slightly distractedly, since her attention was now directed at a photo album on the page. 'Look.' She pointed at a photo of three young people. Thóra enlarged it and saw that it was Friðleifur and Margeir, and between them an unfamiliar girl who hadn't been tagged. She had her arms around their shoulders, almost hanging on them. The girl was in a short dress and high heels, making her look as tall as the two men.

Matthew pointed at the photo. 'Wasn't this taken at the residence? I think I recognize the background from the video recordings.'

Thóra shifted her attention from the people to their surroundings. 'I'll be damned.' Behind the trio she saw a whiteboard and a key cabinet like those on the wall of the night watchmen's office. 'Well, well. So they *were* having a party on work time after all. At least, this girl seems to be enjoying herself.'

They looked through more photos and even though most of them showed Friðleifur in other environments, there were several of him at the care home, either with Margeir or with other unfamiliar young people of a similar age. The guests were generally dressed up to the nines. One or two were holding beers. There was no sign that they were roaming freely through the building; most of the photos appeared to have been taken in the same room, and none of them showed any of the residents or visitors in costume — neither an angel nor anything else.

'This is one of the strangest things I've seen.' Matthew leaned back in his chair.

'Yes, I agree. Still, this explains why Friðleifur's sister hasn't called me. Sveinn mentioned how she'd smelled of alcohol, so she'd been partying like these people, no doubt — but pretending to come and visit with her friends in order to help.' Thóra continued to examine the photos. 'Now I understand why that woman who lived in the neighbourhood spoke of the street being noisy at night on weekends. It also explains why the residents at the centre weren't always very happy; they could hardly have slept well through all that mayhem, even if it didn't happen every night.' Thóra leaned back thoughtfully. 'There must have been something to attract these people into coming all that way; the place wasn't exactly easy to get to. Either Friðleifur and Margeir were really popular, or they had something that people wanted when they were out partying. One thing's for sure, though — the number of people eligible to be the father of Lísa's child is rather higher than I first thought.'

29

Tuesday, 19 January 2010

Thóra felt as if her thoughts were bouncing back and forth inside her brain. It didn't matter how much she tried to organize them and think logically; one thought was always stronger than the others: who had sent her the message? She scrutinized the photos on Friðleifur's Facebook memorial page and pored over every face, as if one might hold the answer to her question. *Yes, it was me!* Whoever it was had to be connected to the case; given what she had seen in the photos, there was no other possible explanation. But she couldn't for the life of her understand why this mysterious person couldn't simply call her or send her a detailed explanation of what he knew. He either had to be guilty of something in connection with the case, or else he was some oddball who got his kicks out of teasing her with scraps of information.

In front of her was a sheet of paper on which she'd scribbled all the leads she had uncovered, but there was disappointingly little of any use in it. Of course there had to be some simple explanation of events; things didn't happen by themselves or through a series of coincidences, but the problem was, as so often, in distinguishing the wheat from the chaff. Until that happened, all the names, places and things she had been told would remain one great big jumble of information in which everything appeared equally important. She was reminded of what the IT technician had said when he came to repair the office Internet server. He'd spent most of the day on his repairs and said that it would take no time at all to fix the fault once he found it; the problem lay in identifying it. And that was indeed how it went — as soon as he found the problem, his job was pretty much done. Maybe she should call him. Getting the opinion of a stranger was surely no crazier a strategy than any other, even though an IT guy might not be the most appropriate stranger to pick. She dialled the extension of her partner, Bragi, but he must have been out of the office as Bella picked up the phone after several rings. Thóra asked if she knew when Bragi was due in and received the answer she'd expected; Bella had no idea, and she didn't care one bit. After hanging up on the employee of the month, Thóra decided to try once more to reach Ari. Again, he didn't answer the phone, which got on Thóra's nerves even more.

She realized it was pointless spending any more time mulling over her scribbles, so she went online in the hope of finding further news of the man who'd been found dead in Nauthólsvík. Information turned out to be rather scarce, but it had been confirmed that he was a male in his twenties, and that he was not considered to have died of natural causes.

The police clearly wanted to say as little as possible about the case, but the news report concluded that they were still trying to identify the deceased. Thóra found this puzzling; it didn't usually take long to find these things out. Maybe the dead man was a foreigner, after all, and it was pure coincidence that Margeir's phone had been found in the same place — if she was right about that. It would be absurd, yes, but not impossible. The fact that the police hadn't called her in for questioning even though she had recently called Margeir might simply indicate that he and his phone weren't associated with the death of the man reported in the news — or that the police were just busy with other things. Disappointed that there was no more to learn on the subject, she went back to the main page of the website and saw that a new story had been added while she'd been reading.

The headline read SERIOUS ASSAULT AT SOGN. Thóra was actually rather surprised that Jósteinn and Jakob's conflict hadn't been leaked sooner. The story was neither long nor detailed and consisted of a brief description of the incident and Jakob's injuries. An employee of Prison Services was quoted as saying that he didn't want to comment on the matter, and the same went for the doctor on duty at Sogn. Brief mention was made of Jakob and Jósteinn's previous crimes; neither of them was identified by name, but it was specified that one of them suffered a mental disability. It was, by and large, a factual and neutral account — except for the line describing the attack as gratuitous and unusually vicious. Still, Thóra doubted that Jósteinn would lose much sleep over that. Her attention was drawn by the statement that the two men's continued custody at Sogn was in doubt due to the risk of subsequent attacks, and she was particularly interested to read that the decision concerning their institutionalization was being finalized. This must mean Jakob might soon be released from hospital.

She looked at the clock. It was still two hours before her scheduled meeting with the sheriff regarding the divorce of a couple who had finally agreed to share their debt burden equally. As so often in these cases, they had managed to re-establish a civil relationship and might even end up as friends. She had plenty of time to drop in on Jakob. There was a fair chance of him being sent to Akureyri, almost 400 kilometres from Reykjavík, and with the weather the way it was she was very keen to avoid having to drive cross-country to speak to him. She really ought to visit him while they were still only a few minutes away from each other.

★ ★ ★

The sterile smell from Jakob's bandages was not immediately noticeable, but after nearly an hour it had managed to work its way so thoroughly into Thóra's senses that she felt she was suffocating. 'Don't you find the air a bit close in here, Jakob? Should I open the window a bit?' She looked hopefully at him and pointed at the curtains, which had been drawn so that they could see the laptop screen better. Thóra had taken it with her in the hope that Jakob might know someone on the memorial page for Friðleifur.

'No, no. I'm cold.' Jakob pushed his thick glasses back into place. They seemed incapable of sitting properly on his nose and kept slipping down. Every time she looked at them she wondered who had chosen the frames and when the glasses had actually been bought. If she'd had to guess, she'd have said they were originally bought by Tootsie in the early 80s. 'OK, never mind. Shall we look at the next photos?' Thóra smiled at Jakob, who seemed relieved that she wasn't going to press the issue with the window. It was fair enough; her wool sweater was light but warm, and he was in a short-sleeved T-shirt marked National Hospital Laundry Room. His bedcover was thin, as well — it looked like a blanket enclosed in a duvet cover.

'Good. I don't want to get a cold. Mummy says that's bad when you're injured like I am.'

'She's quite right.' Thóra couldn't help but smile again. The impassioned way in which he communicated was infectious and it made a refreshing change to speak to someone who was genuinely interested in whatever she said to him. 'Well, do you recognize anyone in these pictures?'

'Umm, yes.' Jakob moved nearer the screen. 'No. That one looks just like that actor.'

'Yes, he does a bit.' Until now Jakob had recognized no one except the two night watchmen, Margeir and Friðleifur. That didn't prevent him from scrutinizing every photo with the same concentration as he had the first. 'How about in this one?' Thóra chose the next photo,

430

which had been taken at the residence.

'Yes!' Jakob poked the screen repeatedly, so hard that the fabric of it rippled slightly. Thóra didn't dare do anything but inch the computer away from him. 'Friðleifur! Again!'

'Yes, that's him. We don't actually need to think about him, remember? Or about Margeir. If you recognize someone besides those two, let me know.'

'Yes, I know.' He looked at Thóra and seemed pleased with her expression, perhaps fearing that she would be frustrated with him. 'Can I still ask you one thing?'

'Of course.'

'Do I get to go home now? I've been hurt and I don't want to go back to Sogn. I should get to go home, I think.'

'I think so too, Jakob.' It didn't surprise Thóra that he should mention this. 'I'm hopeful that you'll be able to, but I don't think it's going to happen very soon, unfortunately.'

Jakob looked sadly into her eyes. 'What does hopeful mean? Good hope?' Suddenly his face broke into a smile.

'Yes. It means exactly that. I have a good hope that you'll get to go home, which means that I think it will happen one day. Then someone will call you and say: 'Hey, Jakob! You know what? You can go home today!'' Thóra placed her palm on the rough back of his hand. 'But it won't be today and not tomorrow. Later. Hopefully.'

Jakob nodded and his glasses slipped down to the tip of his nose again. He pushed them into place, looking tired. His wounds were still

431

healing and in order to see the screen he needed to raise himself up onto his elbow in bed. 'Can I see more photos, maybe?'

'Certainly.' Thóra selected the next photo. In it were Friðleifur, Margeir and an unfamiliar man, making faces at the camera, sticking out their tongues through their upright index fingers and little fingers. She had seen numerous photos of her own children doing this. She still had no idea what was so clever about it, but supposed she ought to be grateful that such a ridiculous pose hadn't been popular in her youth.

Jakob laughed briefly when he saw what was in the picture. 'Silly!' He tried to imitate the pose, not very successfully.

'I agree.'

Jakob dried his wet fingers and turned back to the screen. 'Hey, I know this girl.'

Thóra leaned in for a closer look. She had thought that the photo was of three men, but it could be that she'd misinterpreted it and that the night watchmen's guest was a young woman. However, this wasn't the case — the goatee on the unknown man standing between Friðleifur and Margeir made that much clear. 'Do you mean this man? Friðleifur?'

'No. We'd stopped counting him, remember? I'm talking about this one.' He wasn't pointing at one of the trio, but rather at a person in the background who Thóra hadn't noticed.

She bent even closer to the screen and saw from the profile that it was a young woman. 'Who is this, Jakob?'

'It's Friðleifur's friend.' He smiled broadly,

extremely pleased with himself.

'Do you know her name?'

The smile disappeared. 'Don't remember.' He became agitated and squirmed in the bed.

'But you met her at the residence? When she visited Friðleifur, maybe?'

'No, no.' Jakob pushed his glasses so close to his face that the top part of his nose whitened.

'So you didn't see her at the residence?' Thóra thought he must be mistaking her for someone else.

'Yes, she was there. But not visiting Friðleifur. She was just his friend. She was visiting her brother. Tryggvi.'

Suddenly the disinfectant smell seemed to vanish and Thóra instinctively sat up straight. 'Lena?'

Jakob slammed his hand down hard on the bedframe. 'That's right!'

★ ★ ★

Thóra buried her face in her hands over the same scrawled-on piece of paper that she'd left behind on the table when she'd gone to visit Jakob. Matthew was lying on the sofa that he'd claimed for himself in her office. 'What's wrong?' He shifted the embroidered cushion that he'd placed under his head. 'Isn't this a good thing? Now you've got a witness who can testify to what went on there — though there's no way I'm speaking to her again.'

Thóra sighed. 'I'm glad someone's happy.' She looked up. 'I'll talk to her, that's not a problem.

433

I'm just trying to understand what this means. Was she just there on a normal visit as a friend of Friðleifur, or was she there to get — or do — whatever made the care home as desirable an after-hours nightspot as the photos suggest?'

'She'll be able to give you an answer to that, surely.'

'Probably. But there's something else bothering me.'

'Oh?' Matthew had closed his eyes. He had stopped at Thóra's office on his way back from the gym because he knew that Thóra's meeting with the sheriff would be over. It had actually taken less time than anticipated; the former couple had been too depressed to bother committing themselves much, since their debt was huge, even though they were planning to share the burden.

'I don't know, maybe I should have contacted the police.'

'Because of the photo of Lena?' Matthew asked, surprised.

'No, not that. I'm going to talk to her about that first. If something comes of it, then hopefully it won't be long before I can formally request a reopening of the case. I'm keeping my fingers crossed that she also knows, or at least suspects, something about who abused Lísa. That way I could start putting together a complete theory of what happened there.'

'Then why are you wondering about the police?'

'Precisely because of Lísa.' Thóra turned the computer screen towards Matthew. 'What if there's a picture of the man on this site? They could make use of it in their investigation of the abuse.' She saw that he didn't quite get it. 'We let Ragna look at the photos, do you get it? Show them to her one by one.'

'Aren't you obliged to tell the police? Is there even any question about that?'

'Yes I am, but I'm worried they wouldn't tell me the outcome and then the opportunity to help Jakob by discovering who really started the fire will slip out of my grasp.'

'If they find out that way, they wouldn't hide it from you, would they? You'd be given the information.'

'Not necessarily. They've already looked into it once, with Lísa, so there's bound to be some reluctance to rekindle the investigation. Ragna isn't exactly an ordinary victim and it's not at all clear whether she'd want to press charges or communicate with the police.'

'Call the police. Then visit Ragna afterwards and ask her what she told them. She knows you're trying to help Jakob, so she shouldn't be trying to hide anything from you.'

Thóra picked up the phone. Sometimes it was best just to go for it. She dialled the number of the police station and asked to speak to the same man she'd spoken to before. Some time passed before his voice came on the line. He didn't seem particularly enthralled to hear from her and clearly expected her to try to get something from him regarding the investigation of the case concerning Margeir's phone. However, she knew that would be a waste of time and instead got straight to the point, as much as she could with a case so hard to explain. It was easier said than done to explain to him that a burnt-down community residence for the disabled out in the middle of nowhere had once been a party den, and that on a Facebook page set up in memory of one of the people who'd died there, they would probably find some photos of a man who made a habit of sexually abusing paralysed girls.

The response she got was probably a reflection of how bizarre the whole thing sounded. 'You know, I'm really busy with something else at the moment so I can't promise anything. If I've understood you correctly, this girl's not going anywhere any time soon, so there's probably no great rush. But I've made a note of what you've said and we'll look into it when things slow down. I doubt it'll be this week, but next week, hopefully.'

Thóra hung up and turned to Matthew. 'Come on, we need to stop off at a florist's. Let's go to the hospital. Jakob can't hang around waiting for the police to find time for this.'

On the sofa, Matthew sighed deeply.

30

Tuesday, 19 January 2010

Jósteinn removed the processor from a computer that he'd taken apart and placed it on a plastic tray. His plastic gloves were making his hands sweaty and he desperately wanted to remove them and scratch until the top layer of skin dissolved into little particles that he could sweep off the table top into the bin. That bin, a poisonous green colour, had got on his nerves ever since he'd gained access to this room several years earlier. He had long ago stopped keeping track of how much time he'd done at Sogn; the number of years might as well be the number of stars in the sky. If he were to count them down, things might look different, but here he would remain until he either kicked the bucket or got so decrepit that the authorities no longer believed him capable of perpetrating a crime. Neither of these visions of the future was to his liking, but this didn't keep him awake at night; here he had his computers, and he understood them much better than the people who would otherwise be getting in his way in the world outside.

His Achilles heel had always been the fact that he didn't understand other people. The psychiatrist who had evaluated his mental state for the court said that Jósteinn had all the symptoms of a sociopath — a person who lacks morals because he isn't able to learn from past mistakes or experience and is therefore governed almost exclusively by antisocial urges. Regret, said the same doctor, doesn't exist for him. This diagnosis was entirely correct; Jósteinn wouldn't have wanted to change anything he'd done in the past, except perhaps to hide it better from the police so that he could have had longer before getting caught. Then he could have created more memories to comfort himself with. It wouldn't have changed anything if he had harmed or abused more people — either way, he could never serve more than this one life sentence.

It would undoubtedly have been easy to trick the doctor; he knew how to appear perfectly normal even though emotions were completely foreign to him — well, all except for anger, which he knew intimately. As a child he had learned from experience and trained himself to smile when people tried to be funny, or to put on a sad face when they complained. The problem was that he'd had a tendency to overdo the emotions, which had always made others uneasy. He could have tried to dodge a correct diagnosis in order to receive a conventional sentence, which would have been shorter, but he had become as indifferent to his own suffering as he was to that of others. Maybe it was all the faces he'd been forced to confront as he played the part of a normal man who went to work every weekday morning, all year round. Every moment of eye contact with a colleague at the computer workshop had been agony, but he'd had to grin and bear it in order not to raise suspicion. The job had suited him perfectly; he had lived and breathed computers since his teenage years and it hadn't required much human interaction. He would surely have given up and been arrested much sooner if his workplace had been busier. The torment of other people had slowly but surely weakened the self-preservation instinct that had kept him beneath the radar of the authorities, and caused him to blurt out things about the pictures. He couldn't remember when this aversion to meeting people's gaze had first manifested itself; it had simply grown, calmly but quietly without his awareness, until finally it took all the strength he could muster to make even the briefest eye contact.

'Dinner's ready.' The door behind him had opened and in the doorway stood a guard whose name Jósteinn could never remember. 'Pack up your things; you might not be allowed to continue after dinner.'

'Why not?' Jósteinn lifted the processor and held it up to the light. He could often salvage parts from a machine that had been dismissed as useless, but this time, unfortunately, he suspected that this wasn't the case. He needed a processor for the computer he was building. Oh well — the nobodies who got his renovated computers would have to wait a little bit longer this time.

'We're expecting a man from Prison Services who needs to discuss something with you. Probably the incident with Jakob.' The man leaned against the doorpost, his arms crossed over his chest. 'Hurry up.'

'Have you heard whether we might be getting more computers? It's funny how things don't seem to get thrown away so much now that we're in recession. Do you think they've been saving much money that way?'

'Get a move on, Jósteinn, or I'll write you up. You're a whisker away from losing this job.'

'Fine.' This was the advantage of being diagnosed as a sociopath; it was clear to those who looked after him that he didn't care about being punished. So just as he'd suspected, his circumstances hadn't changed after he'd attacked Jakob. He had carried on rebuilding computers and every day was like the previous one, which was like the one before, and so on. No doubt there would be consequences, but they would be meaningless and only imposed as a formality. He put down the processor and stood up. The smell of food from the kitchen had followed the guard into the room. Hunger was a physical sensation and not connected to his state of mind, which meant he felt it like everyone else. Not all aspects of his humanity had been left out when he was created. 'What's for dinner?'

'Lamb stew. Just right in this weather. If you don't hurry up, all the meat will be finished. Everyone's famished from lunch today.' Lunch had been a vegetarian dish that was the Sogn cook's first attempt to nudge the menu in a healthier direction. The tasteless stodge had been left almost untouched on people's plates as they left the dining room, bitterly disappointed. Everyone except for Jósteinn, who'd left as hungry as the rest of them, but also very satisfied. His hunger was a diversion. Now, however, he'd got bored of it and would pounce eagerly on his supper. Since he'd attacked Jakob, he had to sit alone at a table far from the other inmates, which suited him just fine. He stood up, pleased at the thought of eating undisturbed by the meaningless chatter of those idiots. 'Why haven't you turned off the lamp? You know you're supposed to do that before you leave the room.' The guard nodded his broad chin towards the Luxo lamp screwed to the work table.

'I suspect I may be coming back.' Jósteinn grinned at the floor. 'It's unlikely anyone would be coming on official business at this hour. It's far too late and you don't want me sitting with the others in the living room tonight. Do you?' The guard's silence spoke volumes and Jósteinn smiled wryly. 'No, I think we both know I'll be back later.'

The guard didn't bother protesting. They were both intelligent men and there was no point arguing a lost cause; everyone knew that Jósteinn was allowed to be there whenever he wanted — even at night. Anyone trying to keep Jósteinn from what he called his work was fighting a losing battle; the fork buried in Jakob's head was still too fresh in the staff's minds for them to leave him unsupervised in the company of others. It was easier to let him spend his time messing about in the little workroom. This suited him just fine, and he wished that he'd thought of doing something similar before. He resolved to repeat this tactic every time the staff relaxed

441

their grip. Now all was as it should be; he had everything his own way again, and he could use this lawyer woman to stir up that idiot Ari. It delighted him to think how many others were tangled in his web. Everything was proceeding as planned, and that simpleton Jakob would get what he wanted in the process. That was fine for him, and meant nothing to Jósteinn. 'It'll be really great to get my teeth into some meat,' he said to the guard as he walked past him out into the corridor. His voice was devoid of joy or hope, yet he hadn't felt this good in years. Wasn't life wonderful?

★ ★ ★

Ari sat in his office and stared at the answering machine, which blinked to indicate the messages awaiting him. The small screen next to the light displayed the figure seventeen. This was certainly a fair number of unanswered calls, but it was far from being the highest figure the device had displayed. He'd already run through the numbers, most of which had also shown up on his mobile phone. In fact, friends and acquaintances had given up calling once he hadn't answered twice in a row. They knew which way the wind blew. Others who knew him less well were more optimistic. The lawyer, that Thóra who was working on reopening Jakob's case, had called the office five times, for example, and the same number of calls to his mobile. He would have to come up with some story to feed her, something that would explain why he hadn't answered his phone for days. He could hardly tell her the truth, but it was rather nice that there were still lawyers out there who didn't know what he was like.

But it was still all her fault. Her investigation of Jakob's case had caused him worries that had eaten away at his self-control little by little, like acid, until he'd headed straight for the cards. He had resolved to stay away from them some time ago, *not* because he'd been diagnosed as a gambling addict — that had been a huge exaggeration, he had simply enjoyed taking risks — but because he was unlucky by nature. He lost more often than was healthy — always, in fact — and for some incomprehensible reason this lack of luck had been interpreted as addiction. Of course his day would come. It didn't take much knowledge of probability to see that a huge win was on the horizon. He deserved it. Even though he didn't remember much beyond the first few hours of this most recent spree, he imagined that it had progressed in the same way as usual: he had gone online to play for a little while in the evening, and before he knew it the night was over and all the winnings that he'd initially accrued had been lost, and far more besides. Now he would sleep for most of the day. When he finally dragged himself out of bed he would try to compensate for the previous night's loss. And then it would be morning again, and he would have to give in to his fatigue as the jackpot moved a little further into the distance once more. And then the cards would stop working. With tiny gains that only very slightly offset the huge losses, it took him four nights to bankrupt himself.

Ari didn't want to contemplate how high his next credit card bills would be; he had never dared to add up all the spending limits on all of his cards. He found the best approach was to throw out his bills unopened, then call the card companies and have his accounts frozen one by one, while negotiating permission to pay the bills monthly until the debt was erased. This payment plan took a long time, and after the krona crashed he had maxed out his cards even more quickly than before. The wretched exchange rate was precisely what made the Internet casinos so exciting now: the stakes felt so much higher than they were before the króna fell.

He had used up his toothpaste at home some time ago and had to resort to brushing his teeth with water, which clearly wasn't very effective. He blew vigorously in the hope that his bad breath had gone, but it remained just as foul. The few krónur he had in the firm's account would be enough for some food and a tube of toothpaste until he was able to pay some of his outstanding bills. He'd better do that shortly; he would log in to his bank account on the Internet to check on its status, but he had accidentally left his ID-code key at home after trying to move some funds across to one of his credit card accounts in the hope that it might be authorized again. It turned out that he had very little to transfer and in any case, a woman at the credit card company had said it would take twenty-four hours to clear. That was too long to wait where

Lady Luck was concerned — she seldom visited him, and then always only for a brief period. So the jackpot slipped from his grasp once again. Although he was frustrated about this, neither that nor the losses of the past few days was his chief concern. Should he call this Thóra or leave it alone? The depression that always overwhelmed him at this point was at its peak, and he couldn't cope with any bad news.

What did she want from him? Surely not more files, and probably not advice. No, she must want to ask about something that he would find it difficult to answer; for example, why he hadn't put up a proper defence in Jakob's case. It didn't take a close analysis of the files to see that he hadn't argued the case with much diligence. He didn't want to go over it word for word with that self-righteous cow. She would hardly have done much better in his shoes; it wasn't that easy to stay focused when your life was falling apart. Admittedly, he had the tendency to make mistakes in the courtroom, but this could be attributed to *force majeure*: circumstances beyond his control that prevented him fulfilling his obligations to his client. In this case it hadn't been about any natural disaster but a war, a battle royale being waged in his private life. His wife had left him. She'd grown tired of the little apartment that had replaced the elegant family home he'd gambled away, and all his attempts to persuade her to return had come to nothing. He'd needed all his mental energy to deal with her, and when it had come to Jakob's case, he'd had nothing left. Of course he should have turned down the case, but he had really needed the money — and he'd also found it difficult to refuse the favour. He'd been confident that it would be a quick buck because the case would progress through the judicial system speedily; firstly because the authorities wanted to tie up the case as soon as possible to avoid prolonging the media circus, and secondly because of the accused's disability — no one had seemed to know what to do with him when the case was in court.

So why shouldn't he have taken the case and tried to argue it as best he could under the circumstances? It wasn't as if his client had had the brains to complain. Nor had he been of any help, spouting nonsense about angels and suitcases and all sorts of other rubbish that was of no use when it came to constructing a defence. In any case, everyone knew what the verdict would be: guilty, but not criminally liable. The judges didn't need it spoon-fed to them; they only had to look at the defendant. He had confessed, then of course withdrawn his confession in his own peculiar way, then confessed once more. There had been no point in dragging things out, and it was unfair to look only at the court documents when considering the case as a whole. It wasn't as though the prosecutor's performance had been any better. Everyone had sped through the hearing, since there had been no reason to extend the suffering of the poor man, who had stared wide-eyed and fearful throughout the proceedings.

Remembering this made him pluck up his

courage and he picked up the phone. It was better to face your demons head on. He dialled Thóra's number without hesitating, but at the second ring he also considered the idea that it was better to run away from your demons at top speed. At that moment Thóra answered and he stammered, 'Yes, hi, this is Ari. I see you've been trying to reach me.'

'Yes, hello.' Thóra sounded surprised and it sounded like she was in a car.

'Are you driving? Maybe I should call back later.'

'No, it's fine. I've been trying to reach you, and I'm only the passenger.'

'Was there something in particular you wanted?'

'Yes there was. I came across something that surprised me and I wanted to discuss it with you, to see if by any chance you might be able to explain it.'

'Oh?' Ari felt his palms sweating.

'Well, actually there are two things. One of them is the fact that you're related to the father of one of the people who died in the fire: Einvarður Tryggvason.'

Ari said nothing, but squeezed his eyes shut and licked his dry lips. 'Yes, we're distantly related. That had no bearing on anything.'

'Did you notify the judge of this? Or Jakob? I didn't see a note of it anywhere.'

'Uh, probably.' Ari swallowed; suddenly his mouth went dry. 'Yes, I think I probably did.'

'Right.' Now it was Thóra's turn to remain silent for a bit. 'Then I'll probably find it down at the District Court. I'm sure you recall that according to the 9th Article of the Codex Ethicus of the Icelandic Bar Association, you're obliged to make your client aware of anything that might have a bearing on your relationship with the opposing party. The article specifically stipulates kinship. It's also the subject of Article 33 of the Acts on the Treatment of Criminal Cases — fourth paragraph, if you'd like to look it up.'

'Yes, yes. I'll let you know. I'm sure I did, I think.' Ari cleared his throat. 'What was the other thing you wanted to ask about?'

Thóra didn't believe for a second that the man was telling the truth, but there was no need to force a confession out of him — it would be easy to prove he was lying by checking up. 'Well, the person who's paying for my investigation also appears to be an old client of yours. I'm a bit surprised that you didn't mention it when we spoke the other day. Jósteinn Karlsson, just in case you've forgotten. I understand that you're also his supervisor, so you must have at least some recollection of the man.'

Too fucking right I remember him. He interrupted her. 'I didn't think it mattered. What gives you the idea that there's something suspicious about it? Iceland is a small country, as you know, and its legal profession is even smaller.' Could his luck get any worse? Of all the cases in his long career, this was the one he least wanted to be dragged up again.

'I've met Karlsson, of course, and feel I should mention that he insinuated that the reason he

448

initiated this investigation was to stir up trouble for you.'

'That's strange. No one would be happier than I would if there was new evidence demonstrating Jakob's innocence. But it comes as no surprise that Jósteinn should be upset with me. People who are dissatisfied with the way their cases turn out usually blame their lawyers for it, as I'm sure you know. It doesn't seem to occur to any of them that they may be at least partly responsible for how things end up.'

'Maybe.' Thóra wasn't convinced. 'So he has no score to settle with you?'

'No.' Ari didn't think he sounded very convincing, so he repeated himself. 'No.' It came out just as hollow the second time.

'If I needed to reach you again, when would be the best time to contact you?'

'Uh, in the afternoons.'

'Fine. Thank you for this; I'll probably be back in touch before too long.'

'Sure.' Ari did his best to sound nonchalant, but he couldn't achieve the right tone. When he said goodbye, his palms were just as sweaty as they had been when they'd first started talking. Why had he ever considered calling the woman in the first place?

⋆　⋆　⋆

Thóra put her phone in her bag and looked at Matthew, who was driving down the street to their house. 'That was Ari, the lawyer. I'd be willing to bet that he messed up pretty badly in

449

Jósteinn's case.' She shut her bag. 'I'm itching to read through the court documents again.'

'Okay.' Matthew parked next to Thóra's parents' car. 'And there was I thinking we were going to play a computer game.'

31

Wednesday, 20 January 2010

The monitor was starting to flicker. It really was time to replace it, though Thóra was not at all keen on the idea, given how expensive everything had become. Ideally the useless hunk of junk would survive for however many months or years it took the króna to recover, but she couldn't really rely on that happening. She could of course try to buy a used monitor, but she didn't even know whether that kind of shop existed in Reykjavík. Unless she bought one from Jósteinn . . . No chance, she thought, shuddering; she would rather pay full price than negotiate a deal with someone who disgusted her. Her tolerance of him had diminished even further after she'd acquainted herself with the details of his crimes.

Thóra switched off the monitor and went to reception for a cup of coffee. She didn't hurry, since it was only instant. Her eyes were dry after poring over the court documents and other files from Jósteinn's case for far too long the night before. Eventually she'd stopped reading and gone to spend time with her family, including helping Sóley with an essay in English, which was supposed to be light-hearted and autobiographical. Her daughter was obviously extremely happy that they were currently all living together, because her list of family members and her descriptions of them filled several lines. Thóra also noted with interest that the cat had been named first. Sóley had then added that she had a dad every other weekend, but he now had a new wife, who was younger than her mum. Thóra decided to allow Sóley to write what she wanted, even though she was desperately tempted to convince her that the word 'uglier' meant younger in English. The essay continued in the same vein until the requisite two pages were filled. By that time, any interest Thóra might have had in perusing the verdict in Jósteinn's case had dissolved, and for the remainder of the evening she allowed herself the luxury of not thinking for a single moment about either him or Jakob.

'Isn't there any coffee?' Thóra stood by the kettle, with an empty cup and an equally empty Nescafé jar. 'What am I supposed to do, drink tea? You could have let one of us know; I could have dropped into the shop this morning or last night.'

'The coffee didn't run out yesterday evening. I finished it this morning.' Bella continued to stare at her monitor and the sound coming from the computer suggested that she was watching a video on YouTube. It was the monitor itself that made Thóra stop for a moment and bite her tongue. It was exactly like her old one, and the same age. Pleased with herself, she walked silently down the office hallway with her cup still in her hand, determined to replace her screen with her secretary's after Bella had gone home. She was still smiling when she walked past the open door to Bragi's office.

'Plenty to do, I see.' She nodded at the stacks of papers lying on either side of him. He was incredibly thorough about making copies and collecting files and could never be persuaded to throw anything away. Thóra's suggestions about getting Bella to scan old documents and store them electronically so they wouldn't need to worry about limited storage space always received the same response: he would consider it — but Thóra never found out what conclusion he'd come to. She never pestered him about it; the overwhelming likelihood that Bella would mess up the scanning made it difficult to insist on the idea.

'It's crazy busy in the divorce business. The crash has shaken more than the financial sector.' He finished writing something before looking up. 'But how's your case going? I peeked into your office yesterday and found it empty.'

'Oh.' Thóra walked in and took a seat. 'I was probably at the National Hospital. I had a very useful conversation there with both Jakob and a girl who lived at the residence for a while. I've even started a bit on the petition to reopen the case. It's all coming together, slowly.'

'How do you think it will go?'

'Well, hopefully I only need one last push to be able to demonstrate unequivocally that the evidence wasn't dealt with correctly. I'm uncovering more and more information that was never taken into account. I really don't understand why the case was rushed through court so fast. The defence was beyond pitiful — and not just because of the lawyer's poor performance. But it's all mounting up and it's important that I don't ruin things by putting too much in the report.' She put her cup down on the desk. 'I'd actually be much further along if I hadn't started examining the case of the man who's funding the bid for the petition. It turns out that the idiot who defended Jakob was also Jósteinn's lawyer, and I suspect Jósteinn has a score to settle. And there's more. It transpires that this lawyer is also related to one of the men who was killed in the fire. I'm sure he didn't let Jakob know about that, much less the judge, although he claims he did. I sent an enquiry to the Supreme Court and they've assured me it never came up, either there or in the District Court. Jakob's mother doesn't recall it having been discussed with her either, as it should have been with his legal guardian.'

'What luck.' Then Bragi reached for Thóra's cup and peered into it. 'I was hoping you'd conjured up some coffee.'

Thóra shook her head. 'Sorry. I'll pick some up later; I've got to stop at the shops on the way home anyway.' She got up to leave. 'I was wondering whether you could do me one small favour.'

'Certainly.' Bragi spread out his arms to indicate that she should fire away. 'What is it?'

'I was wondering whether you know the person who prosecuted Jósteinn's case; I remember he was about your age.' She told Bragi his name and he said he knew the man well. 'I wonder whether you'd be willing to call him and have a chat about it.'

'That should be fine. About what aspects, specifically?'

454

'The files don't state clearly enough how the police got hold of the photographs that Jósteinn's conviction seems largely to be based on. As I understand it, the police received an anonymous tip-off about where to find them while Jósteinn was in custody. His apartment had been searched before that but no photos had been found. I think it's likely that the police or prosecutor knew or suspected who the source was, although nothing was said about it during the trial or the verdict. Jósteinn's a real loner, which makes it unlikely that he had an accomplice or a friend who knew about them.'

'So who do you think tipped them off?'

'I have no idea, but I'm curious about how little attention Ari, Jósteinn's lawyer, paid to this detail of the case; he could at least have mentioned the doubt that must have existed about whether the photographs were actually Jósteinn's. Jósteinn isn't in any of the pictures, although his fingerprints were found on several of them. Don't get me wrong, I'm not saying he's not guilty, I'm simply wondering whether this flaw in the defence is the reason Jósteinn's got it in for his former lawyer — who also ended up as his supervisor, in fact.' She started towards the door. 'It's not a crucial detail; I'd just feel happier knowing what the man's up to.'

'No problem. I'll see whether I can find anything out.' Bragi pulled a telephone book from one of his desk drawers, but it was stuffed in so tightly that he had huge difficulty getting it out.

'Have you never thought of using ja.is?' asked

Thóra from the doorway. He shook his head and opened the thick, battered book.

* * *

The report was now four pages long and although Thóra could easily have added more information, it would be counterproductive to make it too comprehensive or include too many minor details. That would draw attention away from the main points of the case, which were that the defence lawyer had omitted to mention that he was related to one of the victims, and that a sex crime had been committed at the residence, which the perpetrator had had every reason to hide. It was also important to clearly convey how many people had regularly visited the place, most of them in the middle of the night — the same time of day the fire had been started — and some of them in an intoxicated state. These facts were relevant to the original investigation and therefore should have been taken into consideration; if they had been, they might very well have persuaded the judge to reach a different conclusion concerning who started the fire, or even to send the case back for further investigation. The only thing Thóra needed before submitting the petition was the full name of the person who had raped Lísa.

Thóra wondered whether she should call the police to check whether they'd got the name yet. It would hardly be much of a surprise, given that Thóra had all but handed them a description of the man, along with a photo, on a silver platter.

Her visit to Ragna the previous evening had gone very well. After explaining to the girl what she was looking for, she'd sat down at her bedside and gone through the photos on the Facebook page. Matthew watched the girl's eye movements and interpreted her reactions. She said *no* to one face after another until Thóra clicked on a photo of Margeir, Friðleifur and a young man who appeared to be absolutely paralytic — like most of the visitors, in fact. Ragna blinked again and again, which made it hard for Matthew to work out whether she meant yes or no, but she appeared to be very affected by the image. She then shut her eyes tightly and Thóra had to ask her three times whether this third man was the person who'd raped her, each time in a more gentle voice. Eventually the girl opened her eyes, stared at the screen and blinked once. *Yes.* Then she'd closed them and kept them closed until Thóra and Matthew said goodbye. Before they did, Thóra had told her slowly that she was going to go straight to the police station, and promised her that this man would get what was coming to him. It wouldn't matter if he denied it, since a DNA sample existed that could confirm his guilt regarding Lísa. Ragna would doubtless need to answer some questions from the police, but the burden of her secret abuse would finally be lifted from her shoulders. Before they left the hospital Thóra had let the duty nurse know what had happened and asked her to keep an eye on Ragna in view of the agitated state that she must now be in.

They'd gone straight from the National

457

Hospital to the police station, and for the third time that day Thóra opened her laptop and logged onto the Facebook page. Unfortunately the officer with whom she'd been in contact regarding the case was otherwise engaged. They either had to come back later or speak to his assistant. She chose the latter option. She felt that she had to report her discovery immediately; the crimes that the bastard in the photo had committed had been hushed up for far too long. As a result she had to tell the story from beginning to end, though she got the impression that the man had already heard some of the details. She was slightly relieved by this, since it meant that the case was at least on the police's agenda, even though Ragna had responded negatively when Thóra asked whether the police had spoken to her. Nevertheless, the officer did his best not to give anything away, having no doubt studied and practised the technique of letting an interviewee speak uninterrupted in the hope that he or she would say more than he intended. Of course in this case, it was a pointless tactic; Thóra had no desire whatsoever to hide anything from the police. It wasn't until they came to Thóra's second visit to Ragna that the police officer's poker face slipped, in the moment when she showed him the photo of the man Ragna had indicated was guilty. Luckily, the photo had a caption: *Good times — Margeir, Friðleifur and Bjarki*. Bjarki's appearance gave no indication that he was a pervert; he looked like a perfectly normal young man, albeit a drunk one. Often the worst of human nature can

458

hide behind the mask of ordinariness.

But now it was the police's job to find out who this Bjarki was; the name was too common for Thóra to be able to locate him herself. She'd checked to see whether he belonged to the Facebook group; he didn't, but it was possible to see who had uploaded the photo — a woman who was listed under her full name. Although Thóra had this information, she decided to leave it to the police to contact the woman; there was no point Thóra calling her if it meant that she might ruin the investigation, which would now surely shift into top gear.

Bragi appeared in the doorway. 'I spoke to the prosecutor but I didn't get much out of him. The police were given the photos during the last stages of the investigation and there was no clue to the sender's identity on the envelope. It was covered in fingerprints, since it had gone through the postal system, but none of the prints were in the police database. So no one knows who sent the pictures, although it's clear that it wasn't Jósteinn, both because he had no reason to strengthen the case against himself and because he was in custody when they were posted. His mother knew nothing about it. Apparently she came across as extremely unsympathetic in court. In fact the prosecutor thought she'd have had no hesitation in sending the photos herself, since she scarcely seemed to care about her son at all — and probably would have admitted as much. When she testified, it left most people feeling distinctly uneasy. Jósteinn is clearly the product of an abnormal upbringing — if you can call complete indifference an upbringing.'

'But did this guy know anything about Jósteinn's relationship with his lawyer; whether they had any conflicts or disputes while the case was being prosecuted?'

'He said it was impossible to tell. Jósteinn showed no reaction in court; he always stared at his lap and said little or nothing. In fact, he said that he noticed that they never appeared to communicate.'

Thóra thanked him, but sat there thinking for some time after he left, announcing that he could no longer bear the lack of caffeine and had to pop out for a coffee. Maybe Jósteinn's support of Jakob was nothing more than an act of decency. Nonetheless, she couldn't shake her conviction that all was not as it seemed when it came to his role in this whole affair. She stood up and walked over to the window in the hope that some fresh air would revive her. The traffic below the window passed by slowly. There seemed to have been an accident; two cars had stopped in one lane and the drivers were bent over their bumpers, apparently in search of dents. One of the drivers looked like he was at the end of his tether. The incessant honking of horns reminded Thóra of modern music: first there was some kind of melody, but then it became increasingly discordant until the noise became the continuous rumble of a cacophonous symphony. Thóra almost didn't hear her phone ring over the noise coming from the street.

'Hello,' she said, after reaching across the table in her haste to answer it before it stopped.

'Hi,' said Matthew, sounding unusually tense.

460

'Have you looked at the news online?'

'No, not since this morning. What's up?'

'They've identified the man found in Nauthólsvík. The one with Margeir's phone.'

Thóra pressed the receiver closer to her ear. 'And it's definitely Margeir?' She inched round the desk to her chair with some difficulty as the short phone cord inhibited her movement.

'No.' Matthew hesitated slightly, probably looking for the name on the screen. 'He was called Bjarki — Bjarki Emil Jónasson.'

'Bjarki?' Thóra sat down and logged onto the Internet. 'Are you kidding?'

'No. Of course not. What kind of a joke would that be?'

Thóra didn't reply, but continued to search for the news. Then she said, 'It must be the same Bjarki that Ragna identified. It can't be a coincidence.'

'That's why I called.'

Thóra thanked him somewhat distractedly as she read the article. There was little more to learn from it; it stated only that the deceased had been identified and along with his name it gave his age, and the information that he had been unmarried and childless.

The phone rang again and Thóra lifted the receiver without taking her eyes off the screen. 'What?' She thought it was Matthew, calling to add something.

'Er . . . hello, my name is Lárus and I'm calling from Telecom. Is this Thóra Guðmundsdóttir?'

'I'm sorry, I was expecting someone else. Yes, this is Thóra.'

'I'm calling about a request to find the IP address for some text messages sent through our network.'

'Of course, I'd forgotten about that. Did you find it?' She looked at the screen and focused on the call. Was she really about to learn who had been sending all the messages? She didn't expect the information to tell her much; the sender had probably used an Internet café, or the library, or somewhere like that.

'Yes, we found it, and I was wondering whether I could send you the number by e-mail. It's easier that way.'

'Absolutely.' Thóra gave him her address. 'Then how do I find out where this IP address is located?'

'I was going to put that in my message, but in fact the computer's registered in the public sector.'

'What?' The first thing that crossed Thóra's mind was the same thought she'd had initially — that someone in the police department or the prosecutor's office was behind all this. 'Can you be a little more specific?'

'Yes, sorry — the computer is registered with the Ministry of Justice.'

32

Wednesday, 20 January 2010

Thóra jumped into the car and shut the door behind her. Matthew had had to stop in the middle of the street to pick her up and she definitely didn't want to cause another traffic jam on Skólavörðustígur Street. 'Where am I going?' Matthew continued driving up the road.

'The Ministry of Justice.' She told him how to get there, then said, 'I'm going to speak to Einvarður, Tryggvi's father. I don't know what he's up to, but he must be responsible for those weird text messages. There can't be any other employees of the ministry connected to the case, and it's highly unlikely that a stranger's behind them, even if they did possess the information.'

'How do you think he'll react?'

'I don't know but I'm sure it'll be interesting. I'm beginning to wonder whether he just lost it when his son died. It's pretty hard to figure out what he's up to; if he was anxious to point me in a certain direction with regard to the investigation then it would have been much easier to just speak to me directly.' She gestured at Matthew to turn. The traffic was getting denser and they were making slow progress. 'But as I say, it's unlikely that anyone else within the ministry is connected to the case, unless one of his colleagues is trying to land him in the shit for some entirely unrelated reason. And where that person would have got hold of this information is a whole other mystery — to add to all the others . . . '

They sat in silence for the remainder of the journey, with Matthew focusing on navigating the area's one-way streets, which were becoming increasingly difficult to negotiate in the heavy snow. Pedestrians picked up speed and no one seemed to want to waste time looking in the shop windows, except for a woman of indeterminate age in a lambskin coat with her hair hanging loose, who had stopped to scrutinize some winter boots in a shoe shop while her dog sniffed eagerly at the corner of the building. On Skuggasund Street it was as if the nation had united in protest against the weather and gone inside out of the storm. It was absolutely deserted, and there were even plenty of parking spaces at the ministry. The empty streets filled Thóra with a sudden melancholy; it didn't take much, these days. When you've always believed that society is built on trustworthy foundations, it's very hard to accept the fact that this isn't actually the case. To make matters worse, it seemed that the country hadn't just stumbled on level ground, but had actually fallen off a cliff. The dark National Theatre building only magnified this impression. 'Why don't we ever go to the theatre?'

'What?' Matthew looked at her in surprise as he turned off the engine. 'I didn't know you wanted to. I'd be up for that.'

Thóra immediately regretted saying this. She

didn't want to go to the theatre at all, any more than she wanted the raisin doughnuts that often found their way into her shopping basket. They ended up there simply because she was upset about the bank crash, and everything Icelandic seemed so pitiable that she felt compelled to buy them. 'I guess I should have a look at the programme, then.' There were lots of things that were impossible to explain to Matthew; for instance, the other morning he had tried to pour out precisely ten drops of coffee for her mother, as she had asked. Ten drops simply meant a small cupful. He understood most Icelandic words, but combining them often modified the meaning. Daily life was yet another aspect of this endless transition; plenty of things that she thought were obvious escaped him completely. She scraped the snow off part of the windscreen at eye level, but Matthew dutifully removed it from the windows, the roof, the bonnet, the lights, the boot — even the tyres — before he so much as reversed out of the driveway. When he'd been employed at the bank and they'd gone to work at the same time, he had scoffed at her methods and asked whether she didn't just want to make two little holes in the frost on the windscreen, one for each eye.

The lobby was empty but there was a great deal of activity in the ministry's office wing. Sober-looking employees hurried down the long corridor, appeared in doorways and disappeared into others, their arms full of papers. The reception desk was empty. 'Should we call Einvarður and let him know we're waiting in

465

reception?' Matthew looked around for the receptionist but saw no one likely, or at least no one who paid them any attention.

'No, no. Let's just go in. I know where his office is.' This was yet another example of their difference in attitudes — he said nothing, but his expression made clear that in his opinion you should respect protocol in a government ministry, even if it might prevent you from reaching your goal. She smiled at him. 'Come on, otherwise we'll stand here until we're swept out with the rubbish at the end of the day.' He opened his mouth to say something but stopped and followed her.

The door to Einvarður's office was open and inside they could hear him and a woman discussing the formatting of a report, with which he seemed unhappy. Thóra peeked in but neither of them noticed her. He seemed irritated at how the woman was unable to do it like someone called Begga, and Thóra felt sorry for her for having to suffer this comparison. If this Begga was so good, why didn't he just get her to do it? She wondered how he'd like to have Bella as his assistant and briefly fantasised that the woman he was chastising would quit and he would hire Bella inadvertently. But rather than clear her throat or draw their attention some other way, she decided simply to wait. Thóra and Matthew listened quietly to their conversation about margins, fonts and colour schemes on bar graphs until the woman hurried past without glancing at them, her cheeks flushed, and joined the flow of people hurrying along the corridor. Thóra

466

knocked gently on the door. 'Hello, Einvarður, I see that you're very busy, but could you spare us a minute?'

He glanced up from the report and an involuntary look of panic flashed across his face before he regained his composure and assumed the expression of someone with all the time in the world. He stood up and motioned to them to sit. When Matthew shut the door behind them, Einvarður seemed surprised, but tried to maintain his nonchalance. 'Please excuse the commotion — we're finishing up a project that needs to be completed by tomorrow.' He sat down and smiled at them politely, his neatly combed hair and impeccably knotted tie suggesting that despite his earlier agitation, he was a man who handled pressure as easily as taking a drink of water.

'We'll try to be quick.' Thóra took a seat. 'Right, so since I took on Jakob's case, I've been receiving text messages from an anonymous individual who appears to have information about it.'

'What?' His shock seemed sincere.

'The source of the messages has been traced and the IP number of the computer they were sent from is registered here, at the ministry.'

'What?' His surprise hadn't diminished.

'Since the case involves your son, you're the obvious candidate. Other ministry employees are unlikely to know such in-depth details about the fire.'

'Yes, that's true.' Einvarður sat there silently. For the first time since they'd met him there was a trace of insecurity in his demeanour. His smooth, manicured hands trembled slightly on the desk. 'I don't know what to say. I didn't send any messages.'

'Then who did?' Matthew looked at the computer on the desk. 'Does anyone else have access to this computer, for instance?'

Einvarður shook his head. 'No, that's impossible. I access it with a login name and password that nobody else knows.' He grabbed the mouse and jiggled it nervously. 'It might be possible to log in to the machine under other names, but not to my account. I must confess, I'm not that clued up on how it works. And it's probably worth mentioning that my office isn't locked when I leave at the end of the day.'

'The messages weren't necessarily sent from your office or even from someone else's here in this building. I understand from the Telecom technician that there are actually two IP addresses involved; one is called an external IP address and is the same for all the computers connected to a particular network such as yours. The other is called the MAC address and is assigned to the network interface card itself. Just to reiterate, the access to the Internet that we're concerned with was not through the network in this building, but rather through a 3G Internet key that's registered at Telecom to the ministry. The man I spoke to didn't have any information about the MAC addresses so we don't know which computer it was. The Internet key is one of ten purchased by the ministry, and they weren't assigned to specific employees.'

'Then was it a laptop?'

'No, not necessarily, but it seems likely. It is possible to use this kind of key to access the Internet on a desktop computer, but I don't know who would, when desktops are generally connected to the Internet in the conventional way.' Thóra watched the man squirm and couldn't help feeling sorry for him. He didn't look at all as if he was involved in this, but maybe he was just a good actor. 'Do you have a laptop from the ministry or a key like the one I've just described?'

'Yes, I do.' Then he added hurriedly: 'But I never actually use the key. And I mean never, not for ages. I have a wireless connection at home and on trips abroad for the ministry I use the hotel networks. And besides, I'm so busy with work I hardly ever have time to look at the Internet. To tell you the truth I don't remember when I last used the key, but it's been quite a long time.'

'Who's your IT person? Would it be possible to compare MAC addresses with him or her and work out which computer was actually used?' asked Thóra. 'I have the number with me, as well as the external IP address.'

'Er . . . ' Einvarður reached for the phone and dialled, then got straight to the point without any preamble: 'Guðrún, who looks after our computers? We don't have a dedicated IT person in-house, do we?' He listened to the woman, scribbled something down on a sheet of paper, thanked her and said goodbye. 'We use a computer service in town. I have the name of the company, as well as the person responsible for

469

our network. Wouldn't it be best to talk to him about this?' He pushed the piece of paper towards Thóra. 'Definitely call him and figure this out. I have nothing to hide and I'd like this sorted out immediately.' He looked Thóra in the eye. 'Believe me, I haven't sent you any text messages.'

She called the computer company straight away and after a few moments she was put in touch with the right person, who acceded happily to her request and asked no questions. Perhaps they got a lot of odd enquiries and had stopped being surprised by them. He didn't question her calling on behalf of the ministry, but simply turned immediately to tracing the MAC address. 'It's an IBM laptop that we have registered to an employee at the ministry, Einvarður Tryggvason. At least the original request for its setup is registered to him. Of course that was some time ago — nearly five years.' Thóra wrote down the information about the make of the computer, then hung up.

'It is your computer. The laptop.' She looked from the paper to Einvarður. 'Where do you keep it? Could anyone else have had access to it? At your home, for instance?'

Einvarður stared open-mouthed at Thóra. Then he turned to Matthew, as if in search of support. 'This is absolute nonsense. I didn't send any messages.' He pushed his chair firmly back from the desk, and pulled out a black leather briefcase. 'This is the laptop. I usually take it home with me and of course both Fanndís and Lena have occasionally used it, but only very

rarely. My wife isn't that keen on computers and she's only used it to look up phone numbers from time to time. Lena uses it to upload photos from her camera, since the USB port on her desktop is so inaccessible. Otherwise they never touch it. They're just as unlikely to have sent the text messages as I am. As you can see, I have it with me at work, so someone here must have used it without my knowledge.'

'I received at least one message in the middle of the night.' Thóra pointed at the laptop. 'If you always take it home, then that message was sent from your house.' She thought about how busy the office seemed. 'Unless there's always work being done here at night.'

'Of course I occasionally leave it behind. That's what must have happened.' He opened the case and with fumbling hands pulled from it a silver laptop, marked *Dell*.

'Dell?' Thóra picked up the sheet of paper with the information the computer technician had given her. 'Here it says IBM. Do you have two laptops?'

Now it was Einvarður's turn to examine the paper. 'I only have this one. The IBM laptop must be my old computer. It's been out of order for ages.' He seemed relieved. 'This is just a mistake. It must be. It's been months since I stopped using it — at least six, I think.'

'And where is it now?' asked Matthew.

'No idea.' He looked stressed again. 'I don't have it, that's for certain.'

'I think I know where it is.' Thóra felt anger welling up inside her. 'Do you still have the key,

471

or could it have conceivably gone with the computer?'

'I still have it.' Einvarður hesitated. 'I think so, anyway.' He dug through the case's pockets one after the other. 'No, it's not here. I might have forgotten to take it out of the old case when the other computer crashed. I suppose it must still be there.'

'It looks like it.' Thóra's mind was racing. That bastard Jósteinn. 'Does the ministry send defective computers to Sogn?'

Einvarður paled. 'Yes, I imagine so.' He licked his lips, which suddenly felt dry. 'Are you suggesting that the computer is at the Psychiatric Secure Unit — and in working condition?'

Thóra nodded. 'I think it's highly likely.'

'Oh, God. I thought it was broken.' Einvarður was breathing unusually quickly. 'Oh, God.'

★　★　★

The snowfall hadn't subsided by the time they finally left the ministry, but the bustle in the corridors had diminished significantly. They could barely see across the street through the big, drifting snowflakes, which were turning the National Theatre into nothing more than a hazy silhouette behind a white curtain. Thóra felt as if they were figures in a snow globe that a giant had shaken as hard as he could. 'Look at the car,' said Matthew over the turned-up collar of his coat. 'How long were we in there?'

Thóra didn't know precisely, but a thick layer of snow now nearly covered the vehicle. After the

472

mystery of the computer was solved Einvarður had seemed distracted and anxious, and it was difficult to get him to focus on their questions. This did have an upside as well as a downside; for example he seemed less cautious, saying that of course it was perfectly natural that they would want to speak to his daughter, after Thóra had told him about the Facebook memorial page for Friðleifur. He seemed less concerned about there being a photo of Lena in that group than he was about the fate of the computer; he tried to play it down, saying that his daughter was a young woman and of course she went out and partied like other people her age. For her to have made friends with people of the same age at the residence just showed how sociable she was. She had a wide group of friends from all walks of life. Thóra decided not to press him about the nightlife at the care home, since he clearly didn't realize that it could have been connected to the fire. Thóra felt reasonably confident that his daughter hadn't had anything to do with the tragedy, but she was still certain that Lena would be able to shed some light on what had gone on there.

When she brought up his family connection to Ari, Einvarður grew wary, but he defended himself with the old tried and tested 'Iceland is a small country' line. Thóra didn't believe for a minute that this was sheer coincidence. But however much she questioned him about it, it got her nowhere; Einvarður wouldn't budge a millimetre. So Thóra changed tack and asked whether he knew anything about the case of

Jósteinn Karlsson, which she described in general terms. Einvarður said he vaguely remembered it, but only because of the media reports at the time. He hadn't been involved, either privately or through the ministry. He did know Jósteinn's name well, though, because the man had recently been under discussion at Prison Services in connection with where he and Jakob were now to be housed — though he didn't mention this until the end of their conversation, after they'd exhausted their list of questions. As they left, Thóra couldn't resist a parting shot: he could inform Prison Services that they no longer needed to concern themselves with Jakob's incarceration as in all likelihood he would be released from custody before long. This didn't appear to have any effect on Einvarður; it was as if he wasn't interested in knowing who had started the fire if it hadn't been Jakob. Perhaps he simply didn't understand the connection.

'Why isn't the scraper kept on the outside of the car?' Matthew stood next to the white hump covering the vehicle. 'If I open the door to fetch it, the seat will get covered with snow.'

Thóra stuffed her hands into her coat pockets and used her elbows to scrape as much snow as she could off the car above the passenger door. 'You just do it like this. You should know that, after all this time and all this snow.'

Matthew rolled his eyes but gave in and copied her. In the end they managed to clear enough snow from around the gap to be able to open the door and take out the much more effective scraper. 'Do you want to go back to the office or are you done for the day?' he asked as she scraped off the windscreen. 'Weren't you going to swap monitors with Bella?'

'No, that'll have to wait. We need to go and see Lena before her father comes to his senses and forbids her to speak to us.'

33

Wednesday, 20 January 2010

'I never suspected so many people had gone there. When I went there with my friends it was only the two of them. I thought they would have told me about it because I had a connection to the centre.' Lena spoke quickly, her voice trembling a little. 'I was really surprised when I saw all the photos on Facebook and maybe I should have told someone, but they'd already sentenced Jakob so I thought it was too late. How was I to know that it mattered?' She looked imploringly at Thóra and Matthew. When neither of them displayed any reaction she looked down, embarrassed. Turning an ornate ring several times around her finger she added in a low voice: 'But the damage is done and I would be very grateful if you could make sure that Mum and Dad don't hear about this.'

Thóra raised her eyebrows but didn't reply. Jakob's interests had to take priority. 'But are you sure you don't know this Bjarki Emil? Maybe he called himself Emil?'

Lena looked again at the printout of the photograph and shook her head slowly and hesitantly. 'I don't think so. Of course I might have met him, but I meet so many people, really. He does seem a tiny bit familiar though.'

Thóra watched the people streaming past the

476

café. This was one of those new places that catered to the younger crowd, and it sold organic coffee that was supposedly purchased directly from farmers. She was too old to fall for this spiel, but it did make her wonder whether other coffee was stolen from farmers at gunpoint. Still, the coffee tasted good — and who was she to say that wasn't partly because she could sip it with a clear conscience? Lena had suggested this place to Matthew when he called, as she was studying there at the time, and on Matthew and Thóra's arrival the average age of the café's patrons had risen significantly. Lena had been sitting at a small table with three of her friends, all hunched over their textbooks. When she spotted them in the doorway she left her friends and the three of them had taken seats by the window facing Laugavegur Avenue.

'Well, it would be good if you could try to remember,' said Thóra, turning back to Lena. She had a feeling that she knew more about this Bjarki than she wanted to admit. Of course it was possible that she was genuinely unsure whether she'd met him and therefore wanted to say as little as possible. 'Just keep thinking about it, would you? Sometimes once they've mulled it over, people remember a small detail.'

Matthew spoke up for the first time since Lena had given up lying about what had happened at the residence when Friðleifur and Margeir were on duty. 'How much did it cost per session?' He shifted in his chair, which was far too small for a fully grown man.

'I have no idea. They told me three thousand,

but as I said to you just now, I didn't know that it was something they did all the time. I actually thought it seemed a fair price. They could probably have charged much more — well, a bit more, anyway.'

'And what exactly was included?' It looked like Matthew hadn't understood this fully, which was to be expected. Perhaps he thought he'd mis-heard — it wouldn't have been the first time.

'Well, I don't know everything, of course — I can only say what they offered me and my friend.'

'Which was?' Matthew clearly wanted to get this sorted out.

'She was given intravenous sugar water, on a drip. That, and oxygen.'

'And she sobered up?' Thóra asked, unable to hide her scepticism. Lena's story was so different from everything she'd imagined that she found it nearly as difficult as Matthew to accept what the girl was saying.

'Absolutely.' Lena spread out her hands. 'It was unbelievable, like magic. Maybe she didn't sober up completely, but at least we could go downtown. She'd been totally wasted when we arrived and she certainly didn't regret spending the money.'

'So let me get this straight — you found out about this when Friðleifur mentioned it to you one morning?'

'I might not have explained this well enough, but I used to sit with him in his office on Sunday mornings when Mum was with Tryggvi. When I asked him about the beer cans in the rubbish bin, he said he'd been helping a friend of his who'd needed to sober up. The guy who'd come with him had been drinking beer. Then he told me how he'd gone about helping him and invited me to drop by if I ever got into trouble. When my friend got completely smashed I decided to try it. Another friend of ours drove us.' She seemed to be struggling to overcome her anger, but it still showed on her face. 'That's him in the photograph that was taken while my friend was on the oxygen, the one that ended up on Facebook. I still don't understand how you found me there, because I untagged it.' She saw that they weren't going to answer this, so she continued: 'It was a bit of a drag, because it took such a long time. Maybe that was why they didn't charge more. He said he could also cure hangovers using the same method but he did that less often because they were only there during the night and early in the morning on the weekends. Most people are hungover when they wake up around noon, but maybe people needed to go to work in the morning or something.'

'Where did this oxygen treatment take place, might I ask?'

'Oh.' Lena shut her eyes but opened them again immediately. Her face was scarlet. 'God, I just wish I'd never gone there. And you know what the worst thing is in all of this? We're not even friends any more. I'm in all this mess because of her.'

Thóra and Matthew's sympathy for the death of her friendship was limited. 'Where did the oxygen treatment take place, Lena?' repeated Thóra.

The young woman's cheeks turned even redder. She seemed to be aware that soon there would be no going back and she still believed she could persuade Thóra and Matthew to keep this information to themselves. 'Inside one of the apartments, where there was an oxygen supply in the wall.'

'An empty apartment?'

'Uh . . . no. My . . . ' She looked angry again. 'My ex-friend went into Lísa's apartment. I know because I saw Margeir go in with her and I knew exactly where each person lived.'

'And Lísa had nothing to say about this, or what?' Matthew didn't know as much about the residents as Thóra did and he obviously didn't remember what condition Lísa had been in.

'She wasn't conscious, so it didn't matter to her.' Lena didn't look Thóra in the eye when she said this. 'I don't think.'

'And did she sit in a chair during the treatment, this friend of yours?' Thóra was virtually crossing her fingers in the hope that this had been the case.

'I don't know, but I would think so. I didn't go in.' The hot flush in Lena's cheeks was nearly gone. 'You've got to believe me that I regret this massively and I do know it wasn't right. But it wasn't me who was most in the wrong. It was Friðleifur and Margeir. It's their fault.'

'We're not judging you, Lena. The only thing we're interested in is whether Jakob is innocent. However, I must admit that I don't quite understand why you wanted to meet Matthew and me. I'd have thought you'd want to avoid

480

drawing attention to yourself.'

Lena's friends were closing their books and putting them into their rucksacks. Lena watched them but didn't seem about to go anywhere. 'I was hoping to find out how your investigation was going. Mum and Dad never tell me anything and I was afraid that you'd suspect Tryggvi; I actually just wanted to find out whether you thought he was in the frame. Then I was afraid that you'd found this out and that you'd make a big deal out of it. I just wanted to get an idea of what was going on.'

'Why did you think that we would start suspecting Tryggvi?' Thóra saw that Lena's friends were just about to stand up; they turned round to try to make eye contact with her, but to no avail. 'We don't suspect any one person. Not yet.'

'I was just worried. Maybe it wasn't logical, but I was worried about Mum and Dad. They seemed really freaked out when this investigation started. I sort of confusedly connected it directly to Tryggvi; I got the feeling that they'd heard he was being investigated. I wanted to be involved and I thought I could get information from you. If I've wasted your time, I apologize. I wasn't thinking clearly.'

'You must have had some specific reason for believing your brother would end up under the microscope?' As Thóra said this, Lena's girl-friends stood up and appeared to be fussing about a bit with Lena's stuff. Things were doubtless complicated by the fact that it wasn't just her textbooks, but also a huge coat, a

481

rucksack and a sports bag that she'd left with them. Thóra hoped that it would take them plenty of time to find what they were looking for so that she could get an answer to her question.

Lena appeared to be thinking hard. 'No, not really. As I said, it was my mum and dad's reaction that stressed me out, not really anything to do with Tryggvi. They were acting so weirdly and I thought it was probably because of him. But now I think I know why they were behaving like that and it has nothing to do with Tryggvi or the fire.'

'Might I ask what it does have to do with?' Thóra spoke quickly because the girls had started to gather up Lena's things. Lena's expression grew fierce but her anger wasn't directed at Thóra.

'Yes, of course you can ask, it doesn't matter to me,' she said, although her expression suggested otherwise. 'Dad has a mistress. Or at least I think he does.'

'Oh?' Thóra certainly hadn't expected this. 'I'm sorry to hear that, but it's hardly relevant to the case, as you rightly said.' She added cautiously: 'Is he seeing a former employee of the residence, or someone at the Regional Office for the Disabled?'

'No. A woman at work. She's called Begga, I think.'

So the woman whose formatting skills Einvarður missed was good at other things besides word processing. 'How do you know this?'

Only now did Lena appear to pay attention to her girlfriends, but she answered Thóra nonetheless. 'I came across them arguing about her and

482

they started acting all sad when they saw me.' She did her best to appear detached and unconcerned about her parents' marital troubles. Her friends, wide-eyed and curious, had nearly reached the table where they were sitting. Lena stopped talking and her friends stood awkwardly next to them.

One of them said, 'We didn't know if you wanted this put in your folder, Lena, or just in the bag?' She handed Thóra, who was between her and Lena, two sheets of paper stapled at the corner. It appeared to be an exam or some homework. On the front was a large red '9.7', with a circle drawn around the score.

Thóra held the papers out to Lena. As she did so she caught sight of the girl's full name. 'Is your full name Helena?' She'd been an idiot. The cryptic text message she'd received before really had been meant for her: *how did Helena get burned as a child?*

'Yes, why?' Lena took the papers from Thóra's hand.

'I thought your name was Lena; I didn't realize it was a nickname.'

'No, no, my name is Helena, but I've always been called Lena.' She stood up and her friend handed her her coat. 'I've got to go now, I hope that you . . . you know, what I was talking about before. They don't need to hear about this . . . you understand.' These friends clearly weren't her closest confidantes.

'Could you possibly give us two minutes?' Thóra directed her words at the two other girls who left immediately, telling Lena they were going out for a cigarette. Thóra turned back to Lena. 'Do you have any scars? I know it might sound like a ridiculous question but someone told me you'd been burned, is that right?'

Lena opened and shut her mouth like a dying fish on dry land.

'What does that have to do with the case?'

'Do you have any burn scars, Lena? It's obvious what it has to do with the case.'

'Who told you that? Whoever it was is a complete idiot. Okay, if you really want to know, I was burned on one leg.' She lifted her trouser leg, revealing a shiny, whorled patch of skin that stretched up her calf and disappeared under the hem of the pulled-up fabric. Another customer's eyes widened. Lena dropped the trouser leg down again irritably, unaware of his shock, although Thóra suspected that she wouldn't have cared if she had seen him. 'It happened when I was a kid, it's not from starting the fire that night, if that's what you're thinking.'

'What happened?' asked Matthew calmly.

'Tryggvi accidentally set some ornaments on fire one Christmas and I was too little and too stupid to get away when the fire spread.' She turned angrily to Thóra. 'Did you know that even Christmas ornaments can catch fire? I bet no one else who's made that mistake is also suspected of having torched a community residence. But you can probably guess why I didn't tell you about it. You would have jumped on Tryggvi even though he had nothing to do with the fire.' She grabbed her bag and looked ready to storm out of the room, fire in her eyes.

Thóra stood up quickly and took her by the shoulder.

'Lena, trust me, the last thing we want is to free Jakob by pinning the guilt on another innocent person, alive or dead. Between you and me, I don't believe that your brother did start this fire — in fact, I strongly suspect one of Margeir and Friðleifur's night-time visitors. But I have to follow up on all leads, even though on closer inspection they might turn out to go nowhere.'

Lena breathed deeply, looking very relieved. She wiped a tear from the corner of her eye. 'I understand. I'm just upset about this and about Mum and Dad. You touched a nerve. I hate my scar — I can never wear short dresses like other girls do and if I want to dress up it's trousers or a long dress, which looks fucking lame. I do know it's ridiculous to get so pissed off; I've seen enough serious injuries and disabilities to know that this is nothing.'

Thóra squeezed Lena's shoulder gently before letting go. 'Do you know how I can get in touch with Margeir? The police need to speak to him regarding at least two serious matters, and I'm hoping he can shed some light on the cause of the fire at the same time. I have a hunch that he knows who started it.'

'I have no idea where he is. I used to run into him in town sometimes after the fire but I haven't seen him out for months. Maybe he's left the country. Otherwise, someone told me he had a radio show, but I don't know if that's true or whether it's still going. I think it was on a talk-radio station that I never listen to.'

The police already had this information; she recalled them describing him as a radio host in their first enquiry. 'I believe he did. OK, if you see him or hear from him, I advise you to behave as if everything is normal and then get away from him as quickly as possible. And you should inform the police about it immediately afterwards.'

Lena frowned. 'Why are the police looking for him?'

'I promise to tell you once the police have completed their preliminary investigation. For now I don't want to connect him to a case that might not have anything to do with him at all.' Despite saying this, Thóra was convinced that Margeir had ties both to the death of the man at Nauthólsvík Beach and to the violence against Lísa and Ragna. Maybe he wasn't the perpetrator, but he probably knew considerably more about these things than many others.

* * *

During the news that same evening, Thóra's mobile phone beeped. She grabbed it and saw that once again she'd received a message via ja.is. Instead of reading it immediately she called directory enquiries, requested the number at Sogn and then asked to be connected. Her call was answered on the fourth ring. Thóra asked the staff member to tell Jósteinn that she'd received his message. If he was uncertain about where Jósteinn might be, she considered it more

than likely that he'd find him in the computer workshop. Then she hung up without giving the man an opportunity to ask any further questions about this peculiar errand. Thóra was pleased with herself, although her mother gave her a strange look, obviously feeling that she'd dealt rather rudely with a public institution. She read the message.

Vesturlandsvegur Road, 8 December 2007

34

Thursday, 21 January 2010

'I don't need a scientific explanation for how it works, Hannes, I just need to know whether there's anything in it.' Thóra rolled her eyes, safe in the knowledge that her ex-husband couldn't see her on the other end of the line. She'd turned to him in his capacity as a doctor for clarification as to whether it were possible to reduce the effects of intoxication and hangovers through oxygen inhalation and intravenous nourishment. She found it all rather dubious and didn't want to include it in her report if Lena's claims turned out to be complete nonsense.

'It does work, yes.' Hannes sounded disappointed at not being allowed to continue bestowing on her the gift of his great wisdom. 'Medical students do it sometimes, and other people who work in places with access to oxygen tanks. I don't recommend it, especially if people have no idea what they're doing.'

'You knew about this when you were at medical school?' Thóra couldn't conceal her shock. 'And you never said anything?' If she hadn't already been divorced from Hannes, she would have started divorce proceedings immediately. In the early years of their marriage, when they were both at university, she'd spent countless mornings wishing her head could be wrapped in cotton wool to alleviate her terrible hangovers.

'Of course not. It never crossed my mind to do it. I was hardly going to drag you to a hospital and hide you in a linen cupboard with an IV stuck in one of your veins, hooked up to an oxygen tank. Very few people actually do this, and then hopefully only in moderation. It's much healthier for the body to wrestle with the effects of alcohol on its own, be it intoxication or a hangover.'

'You forgot to say that the healthiest thing of all is to drink sensibly.' Thóra stopped the discussion by thanking him for the information and then briefly asking him about what they would do with the children during the imminent winter holiday. Neither of them had anything planned, so the only conclusion they came to was that they'd both have a think about it and discuss it some more later.

Thóra was happy to have got her facts straight. It looked as if her report would be finished shortly and it would be so watertight that it would be difficult for the Supreme Court to reject the petition. But she was still going to wait until the results of the DNA test on Bjarki Emil, the man who had been found at Nauthólsvík Beach, were made available, since she was certain that they would show in black and white that he'd been the one who'd abused Lísa. Ragna's testimony was strong, but it would have to be verified nonetheless. Thóra's happiness was slightly diluted by this: even if she managed to prove Bjarki Emil's crime, it was unclear whether it would have any influence en the outcome of Jakob's case. The relationship between the rapes and the fire was unclear. In order to succeed she would need to be able to demonstrate that Bjarki Emil or someone else had set the residence on fire, and explain why. This was easier said than done, however. Even before she had to divine their possible motives for starting the fire, there were very few potential suspects. She'd gone over the main files in the case once more, weighed up which of the individuals she'd had contact with were most likely to be guilty, but the result was always the same: none of them had had the opportunity to start the fire, unless the various people providing each individual's alibi for the night in question were all lying.

Einvarður and Fanndís had been at an annual ball in the countryside east of Reykjavík, along with a large crowd of fellow partygoers. Of course none of them had been questioned, but the idea that the couple could have lied about this had obviously been considered absurd. If it had transpired that nobody recalled seeing them during the relevant window of time, they could simply have claimed to have been in their hotel room. Could Einvarður's peculiar behaviour be attributed to anxiety about concealing his part in the tragedy? For her part, Lena had been having a party at her place, and two stragglers — neither of whom had been named, but one male, one female — were both said to have been at Lena's home when the police turned up later that night, and had verified the girl's story.

The parents of the other residents had all been

either asleep at home, away from the city, or at parties, and Thóra had no particular reason to doubt their stories. Glódís had also been home asleep, but shortly before the fire started an old school friend of hers had woken her by calling to ask whether she wanted to meet up with her downtown. She'd been rather abrupt when the police had called to inform her about the fire, because she'd thought it was her friend calling back to persuade her. Margeir, too, had been asleep and it had been verified that he'd taken a call from Friðleifur on his mobile shortly before the fire started, at which point the phone was located at his home address. Of course Margeir could have gone to the residence immediately and started the fire, but he would have had to move very quickly. Plus it was hard to imagine what might have prompted a seriously unwell man to suddenly jump into a car and go to set a fire that would burn five people to death. According to the case files there was no doubt that Margeir had been ill that night. Others Thóra had spoken to — Sveinn, the filmmaker; Linda, the friendly therapist; Ægir, Tryggvi's therapist and Ari — were out of the question; it was simply absurd to think that any of these people would have had reason to want to kill either the residents or Friðleifur. Of course there was always a chance that Thóra had overlooked some possible motive in one of them, but it was an extremely slim one.

No, as far as Thóra was concerned there were only three possible scenarios: that Bjarki Emil had started the fire, to kill either Lísa, Friðleifur or both of them; that someone completely different who had not yet turned up in the investigation had done it in a moment of madness, probably a night-time visitor who'd come for the oxygen treatment; or that Tryggvi had attacked Friðleifur and set fire to the building for reasons that were impossible to determine. None of them could have known that the fire alarm system was disconnected, except possibly Tryggvi. Perhaps this was irrelevant to the case and the arsonist simply hadn't noticed the nozzles on the ceiling, which under normal circumstances would have extinguished the fire before it could spread. Thóra was finding it impossible to work out which of these three possibilities was most likely, but she was leaning more towards the idea that Tryggvi had been involved, based on the reactions of his parents and sister. They had all tried to keep information from her and concealed the fact that he had caused fires at least twice before, once with serious consequences for his sister. It was out of the question for Lísa Finnbjörnsdóttir or Ragna Sölvadóttir to have started the fire, and the same went for deafblind Sigrður Herdís Logadóttir. And Natan Úlfheiðarson had been heavily medicated, as the autopsy confirmed.

After going carefully over the points that she had gathered in her latest perusal of the files, there was nothing that particularly struck Thóra or made her inclined to change her opinion. So she decided her next step would be to find out about the text messages from Jósteinn. She'd been so furious with him when she'd worked out

492

it was him who was sending them that she hadn't been able to bring herself to do it straight away. It irritated her immensely to be manipulated by him and his strange impulses like this. She also found the way he'd chosen to do it particularly unpleasant. Admittedly, most of the bastard's messages had helped to propel the investigation forward. The one text that she couldn't work out was the one that said *02 short hose*. She suspected that o2 was supposed to be O2, the symbol for oxygen, but she hadn't come across anything that helped to explain the reference to a short hose. The only message left to deal with was the one about Vesturlandsvegur Road. It was nearly 10 p.m. and it was tempting to put it off until the morning, but then Thóra remembered the flickering monitor at work that she'd forgotten to swap with Bella's, and decided to try to figure out the message in the peace and quiet of home. She was also forced to admit that she was itching to know how it was connected to Jakob's case: the place and time didn't fit at all with the fire — the date was nearly a year before and the location was miles away.

It took Thóra a little while to find on Google what Jósteinn seemed to be referring to. The first entry was an old news story about how a section of Vesturlandsvegur Road had been closed due to a traffic accident, and the police were unsure when it would be reopened. Further details about the accident weren't available when the story was written, but a short time later a much more detailed article appeared. The article stated that a young girl had been hit by a car and had died. The driver had fled the scene and was being sought, and witnesses were asked to come forward. Thóra vaguely remembered this story as she continued perusing the articles. A huge investigation and a search for witnesses had yielded no result; the only thing that was known was that the girl had been hit by the car as she was crossing the road and had died of her injuries a short time afterwards. The driver had sped off but it seemed inconceivable that he hadn't been aware of the accident. The investigation appeared to have been extensive; among other things, all garages and car repair workshops had come under scrutiny. Police had hoped it would be possible to determine the make of the vehicle based on evidence at the scene and analysis of the girl's injuries, but this did not turn out to be the case. They discovered that the vehicle in question had been a medium-sized family car, but they found no further details. The driver failed to respond to repeated requests to turn himself in and no one had witnessed the accident. Gradually the story faded from the media. The girl's identity had been published: her name was Margrét Svandís Pétursdóttir, but that meant nothing to Thóra. She was sure she'd never seen this name mentioned in connection with Jakob's case.

Thóra was mainly interested in the next entry concerning the accident. Someone had blogged about a news item that appeared at first to be completely unrelated to this tragedy and had not shown up in the results of Thóra's Google search. In a short autobiographical description, the blogger said that he was a *self-appointed specialist on all things spiritual and supernatural.* The story that had inspired him to communicate with the outside world was brief, and described how the Icelandic Church had for the first time in more than a century undertaken to exorcise a ghost. Thóra had missed this tiny story completely at the time; it had probably slipped under the radar among the swarm of breaking stories about the bank collapse, much like the story about the fire. In fact the story had only appeared in one media outlet, and the blog entry was more detailed than the news article itself; it mentioned Vesturlandsvegur Road and the date given in the text message, which is why the search engine had listed it. In the text the blogger said that he knew the exorcism was related to the accident in question, and that when he had been called upon he had clearly sensed that the house was haunted. The girl had been on her way to this house to babysit a young boy when she was run over; since her death was unresolved, her soul had ended up in limbo between this world and eternity. As long as her death remained unresolved, the girl was unable to leave the here and now and she had anchored herself to the child she was due to babysit. Thóra couldn't make head or tail of most of the entry, which went on to describe the nature of limbo and to discuss other issues related to mediums.

Thóra saw that the names of those who lived in the house were given in the blog entry: Berglind and Haraldur; and although she only had their first names, it would be easy enough to find them in the town of Mosfellsbær. Thóra had to stop and think for a moment. It was undeniably important to find out how this tragedy was connected to Jakob's case, and she was sure it would help if she could do that before she next met up with that nutter Jósteinn, which she planned to do very soon. The danger was that although Thóra had decoded most of his text messages, and thus might have something of an upper hand in their relationship, the advantage might shift to him if she didn't stay on the alert. Given the chance, he would avoid her questions and instead continue to drip-feed her snippets of information. Of course she could contact the parents of the girl who'd died, but the thought of calling people who were very likely to still be consumed by grief, even though three years had passed since the accident, was less than appealing. No matter how she imagined starting such a conversation, she always came out sounding mad. *Yes, hello, my name is Thóra and I received a text message from a sociopath incarcerated at Sogn, suggesting that a multiple homicide by arson is related to the accidental death of your daughter. Would you be willing to meet up?* People who thought they were being haunted, however, were much less likely to hang up on her in mid-sentence. Without further ado, she looked up the number and called.

The conversation turned out to be much easier than Thóra had dared to hope. Berglind didn't seem remotely shocked when she explained why she was calling, with as much sensitivity as she could muster. It was easy to

496

hear from her gloomy voice and monotone replies that the woman had been having a tough time. When Thóra asked cautiously whether Berglind might be able to meet her, her reply was succinct. *Yes, just come now — my husband is at work and I'm not doing anything special.*

★ ★ ★

'This doesn't look much like a haunted house.' Thóra leaned forward to get a better view of the outside. The rectangular house was made of concrete and had two storeys, but it was unimposing. Even a quick lick of paint on the roof and window frames would have improved its appearance enormously. The front door was cheap plywood and looked almost temporary, and unlike the other gardens on the street the front garden was overgrown. But although the house appeared to have been built more cheaply and maintained less well than its neighbours, it was only superficially different to the others on the street. In fact it looked as if improvements were imminent, and it would only be a short time before the cracks in the concrete were repaired, the outside painted, and a new front door put on. A string of unlit Christmas lights lay along the edge of the roof, a reminder of the recent holiday.

'How do you imagine a haunted house looks?' asked Matthew, as he tried to decide where to park the car. Both spaces on the driveway were free but he didn't want to use either of them, since the husband was probably due home any

497

moment and the chances were they would choose his place. Matthew was very concerned about these things. 'Were you expecting an American wooden house with high gables and broken windows? Maybe a bat hanging upside down from the guttering?' Matthew parked the car next to the kerb in front of the house.

'Maybe not that exactly, but this is still different from what I expected.' Thóra stepped out onto the pavement and the new-fallen snow crunched beneath her feet. 'Damn, it's cold.' She waited while Matthew locked the car. She took a deep breath of the still winter air and noticed a faint but revolting odour that she couldn't place. 'Oh, yuck.' The metallic tang lingered in her mouth and nostrils and grew stronger with every breath. Immediately she felt a chill; she looked again at the house and suddenly it didn't seem as harmless as it had at first. The dark garden running alongside it seemed sinister somehow, and the building appeared to cast longer and darker shadows than the other houses on the block. She shook off the unpleasant feeling and headed towards the shabby-looking door. Lights were on in most of the windows; upstairs there was a flicker as if a bulb were about to go out, or was it just a television? It wasn't easy to tell, since all the curtains were drawn. Behind the ones drawn in the kitchen she caught a hazy glimpse of the outline of a person. Thóra couldn't see whether the person's face was turned towards them, but she was fairly certain that they were watching her and Matthew walk up the path. The silhouette disappeared just as

498

they reached the house. If it was Berglind, then she'd gone straight to the door, because it opened as soon as Matthew rang the doorbell. The noise of the bell didn't carry outside, making it seem as if the house had swallowed the sound.

'Come in. The doorbell's broken. I was afraid of missing you so I was keeping an eye out.' The woman was young, probably early thirties, perhaps slightly younger. Her straight, blonde shoulder-length hair looked dirty, and it fell across her face. Her worn jeans were obviously supposed to be skinny-fit, but they were baggy on her and her fleece hung loosely on her thin frame. Her eyes were large and expressive, and would have been beautiful but for the dull rings underneath. All of this fitted with Thóra's mental image of a woman who was being haunted.

'Hi, I'm Thóra and this is Matthew, who I mentioned earlier.' The woman's grip was slack and her palm cold and clammy. 'Thank you very much for agreeing to meet with us; we won't bother you for long. I realize it's getting late and tomorrow's a work day.'

'I'm on sick leave, so I don't have to get up. My husband is still at work; they're doing an inventory and he'll be there well into the night, so you aren't disturbing us.' She seemed to feel the need to go into this in detail, as if to excuse her husband's heavy workload in the midst of the recession: 'The company just changed owners, which means lots of changes and extra work — which is unpaid, but he's been promised additional leave in return.' Berglind showed them into the house. The hall was very tidy but devoid of all luxury. It could have done with a coat cupboard, but instead there was a coat rack on wheels. Shoes were arranged neatly against the wall in order of size, except for some fiery red boots in the middle that were decorated like mini fire engines. Thóra could see that Matthew was having trouble deciding where he should put his shoes; by the front door, in their correct place among the household's own pairs? Berglind also appeared to notice and announced, 'Don't worry about your shoes; there's not much to do here during the day so I try to keep the house ship-shape. There are only three of us so I've had to come up with various things to help fill the day.' She looked at the shoes, side by side as if in a shop. 'It's ridiculous, I know, but I hardly ever leave the house, so there's nothing to do but occupy myself somehow — no matter how strange it might seem.'

Thóra smiled. 'Well, I have to say I envy you your tidy hallway; you should see mine.' The hall in her house was always filled with shoes, left there by Sóley, Gylfi, Sigga, and now Orri as well, generally in a pile in the middle of the floor. Thóra was sure that they must fling them off on their way in, but without breaking their stride: they loosened the laces as they approached the door and then stepped out of them on the way in. The little space that was left on the floor was then heaped with the kids' coats; for some reason they never hung them on the hooks. When she and Matthew emerged from the hallway it always felt as if they'd just hopped from stone to stone over a river.

Berglind didn't smile back. 'Have a seat in the living room. I'm just going to check on Pési.' She pointed up at the Artex ceiling. 'He's upstairs watching a film. He doesn't have to get up tomorrow morning either because he's on a break from preschool. Actually a kind of mini-version of my circumstances.' The rings under her eyes seemed to darken and spread, probably because they'd left the brightly lit hall.

Matthew and Thóra sat down on a brown sectional sofa of the kind that had taken over the furniture market a few years earlier. It was as if the sofa wanted to show solidarity with the house and had decided to show signs of wear; the attached chaise longue had sunk in the middle and its colour had faded, making it look as though it belonged to an entirely different set. Like the hallway, the living room was excessively tidy, and Thóra thought she caught a whiff of cleaning fluid. She desperately wanted to stand up and have a look at the framed photographs on the wall to her right, but she was uncomfortable with the idea that Berglind might find her doing it. So she sat completely still and tried to examine them from a distance.

'Sorry — I had to find him some paper and crayons; he didn't want to stop watching the film.' Berglind sat down opposite Thóra. She smiled at them awkwardly and seemed to hope that they would do all the talking. 'Would you like some coffee or something?'

Thóra and Matthew both politely declined. 'We absolutely don't want to trouble you. You've got enough on your plate.' Thóra looked towards the stairs leading to the upper floor. 'Has your son been aware of this . . . spirit at all?' She didn't know how much she could trust the blogger's story; she would rather get her answers straight from the woman.

'Yes, very aware. He and I seem to be the most sensitive to it; my husband finds it easy to shut it out and act as though nothing's wrong.' She frowned. 'I can see that you don't believe a word of it. I've become an expert at recognizing that expression.'

Embarrassed, Thóra tried to hide her doubts. 'I certainly didn't intend to suggest that. I know less than nothing about ghosts and I don't really have an opinion on them either way. We're here for an entirely different reason, as I mentioned — a case that's connected to the accident here on Vesturlandsvegur Road somehow. I was hoping that the connection could be explained by speaking to you.'

At that the woman relaxed slightly. 'I understand. I've just become so sensitive about the subject; everyone around me has grown tired of it and their sympathy has worn a little thin.' She sat up straight. 'But that's life, I guess. Although one or two people have actually been extremely understanding; the couple next door have been very kind to us, as well as my boss at work. Other people just don't want to talk about it.'

'May I ask how the haunting manifests itself?' Matthew was clearly extremely curious. 'I've never met anyone who's been in this kind of situation.'

502

'Sure.' Berglind smiled unexpectedly, but then her face darkened as she began telling them the entire story. As the story went on, Thóra was glad that the curtains were all drawn — there was no denying it was powerful stuff.

When Berglind appeared to have reached the end of her account, Thóra was no closer to knowing how these events were related to the fire, and although every other message from Jósteinn had turned out to contain important information, it was conceivable that this time he had missed the mark. Thóra had the feeling that Berglind was telling the truth, and telling the story exactly as she saw it, but that didn't mean all her explanations reflected reality. 'Well now ... ' Thóra's throat was dry and she coughed gently. 'It all sounds rather frightening, but unfortunately I can't see how it has any connection to the case I'm working on. None of the names match; the dates don't ring any bells. The accident occurred almost a year before the fire. You don't remember anything special that happened here on 11 October 2008?'

'No, although it was actually around that time that the haunting grew significantly worse.' Berglind thought for a moment in silence and her expression turned to one of bewilderment. 'Did you say a fire? That occurred in October of that year?'

'Yes.'

'Are you referring to the fire at the community residence?' asked Berglind, sounding surprised. Light footsteps from upstairs indicated that Berglind's son was moving around and she started and looked up at the ceiling. She seemed to realize that her reaction might have appeared unnatural to her visitors and immediately turned her attention back to them.

'Yes,' said Thóra. 'Do you know anything about it?' Perhaps Jósteinn's message wasn't directly related to the accident on Vesturlandsvegur Road, but he had simply chosen it as a roundabout way of putting Thóra in touch with Berglind. 'Do you by any chance work at the Regional Office for the Disabled?'

She shook her head. 'No, at the Ministry of Justice. A colleague there lost his son in the fire.'

'I see.' Thóra was at a loss to come up with a sensible follow-up question to this unexpected information. There was in fact only one question burning on her lips, but she thought she'd better keep it to herself until she'd exhausted everything else that came to mind. 'Do people shorten your name to Begga?'

'Yes, they do.'

'Mummy.' In the doorway stood a little boy in Mickey Mouse pyjamas, clutching a picture with a serious expression. Berglind stood up, took him in her arms and sat back down. She stroked his blond hair and the child leaned his head against her chest. The picture lay in his lap, and its contents drew Thóra's attention.

'What a lovely picture you've drawn! Do you know the alphabet?' She leaned forward and reached for the picture. 'May I see?' The boy was shy and turned away from her, but he handed her the picture all the same. Large, clumsy characters were drawn in blue crayon. *NNI80.*

This was as disturbing as the string of characters with which Tryggvi had marked all of his drawings, and the chill that she'd felt outside the house now returned. 'Berglind, did you meet Tryggvi, or ever see any of *his* pictures?'

Berglind tightened her grip around the boy. 'Do you mean Einvarður's son? I never met him, and Pési certainly didn't. Why? Is it something to do with these characters?' She looked at the picture. 'I kind of recognize them, but definitely not in connection with Tryggvi.'

Thóra let the drawing fall into her lap. 'I know this is going to sound really impertinent, but . . . did you and Einvarður have a relationship outside work?' She half whispered the final part of the question even though the child in Berglind's arms wasn't mature enough to understand what she was implying.

'I'm sorry? Wherever did you get that idea?' Berglind didn't seem insulted, just extremely surprised. She adjusted Pési in her lap.

'I must have misunderstood something. Please, forgive me for being so rude.' Thóra wasn't certain she completely trusted the woman, but she didn't want to carry on making accusations that would only be denied. She knew nothing about this relationship that Lena had mentioned, but it was clear that if this woman had been having a secret affair then she was unlikely to admit it to a stranger. Thóra leaned down towards the little boy. 'Why did you choose these letters and numbers, Pési?' Thóra held up the picture. He had turned away from his mother and held his hands over his face. Then he peeked through his fingers.

'The window.' His answer was so low, it was barely audible. 'It was written on the window. Magga wrote it. She's outside.'

★ ★ ★

Matthew stood on the steps and stamped snow off his feet. 'It was definitely a man, and a young one, considering how fast he ran.' He tried to catch his breath. 'I would have caught him if I'd had better shoes and if he hadn't gone through the gardens and jumped over all these fences.' Thin clouds of vapour drifted up from his body, merged with the calm, frosty air and vanished. With Berglind's permission he had taken a look at the window to which Pési was referring, and while they were examining the characters in the frost on the balcony door that opened onto the kitchen, he had spied a man in the garden and set off after him in Berglind's husband's slippers, which had been standing by the door.

'It's a pity you don't ever run through people's gardens on your normal route.' Thóra stretched out to look over his shoulder, though she had no idea why she was bothering, since the man couldn't possibly be anywhere nearby considering how long Matthew had been gone. 'Dammit.'

'Who could it have been? Did you see his face?' Berglind stood behind Thóra with her son in her arms, his small body wrapped so tightly around his mother that she must have found it hard to breathe. The boy had taken the episode badly, and it was difficult to know how much more the poor little soul could endure. For him it might just as well have been the ogress Grýla coming into the garden to put him in her bag, drag him up to the mountains and eat him.

'No, he never turned around. He had dark hair, though.'

Thóra turned to Berglind. 'I think the best thing would be for you to contact the police. Of course it was probably just some loony, but in light of the case that I'm investigating it can't hurt to be careful, since you seem to be connected to it in some way. If this unexpected visit has something to do with the case, it would be much better and safer to place the matter in their hands. Maybe they'll want to keep an eye on the house.'

While Matthew had been practising long-distance running halfway across MosfellsbÆr, Thóra had continued speaking to Berglind, who at first shook like a leaf. No matter what she asked the woman, Thóra couldn't work out how she was connected to Jakob's case. No, she hadn't worked directly under Einvarður; no, she hadn't got involved in his affairs; no, she had nothing to do with the fire. She did say that Einvarður had been the only one at the ministry to show her any understanding when rumours of the haunting had spread, and he had worked hard to get her signed off from work when she could no longer sleep at night. Thóra didn't want to read too much into this at first; maybe the man was just being kind and understanding after experiencing great personal difficulties himself, what with his son's autism and tragic death. On the other hand, it bugged Thóra that until now, Jósteinn had always shared information that was relevant to the case, whereas here there was no apparent connection. She had even asked carefully whether Einvarður had had a close relationship with any other women at the ministry, but this had elicited merely a shocked look and an angry 'No.' In Berglind's eyes the man was an angel in human form and Thóra had immediately dropped all talk of possible adultery, since she wasn't keen to be thrown out and forced to wait for Matthew in the car in this cold. Maybe Jósteinn hadn't meant her to come here at all; maybe he'd been trying to direct her to the parents of the girl who'd died in the accident.

'My husband must be on his way home by now. I can wait until tomorrow to call them.'

'I think that's very unwise.' Matthew seemed to have got his breath back at last. 'You should call immediately; if you wait until tomorrow morning I bet you'll put it off again.' They could both tell from Berglind's expression that she wasn't going to take his advice. 'If you call tonight, you'll be glad you did. There's no way of knowing whether he's done this before or whether he plans to do it again. There are plenty of strange people involved in the case about the fire.'

'Do you think this guy has been here before?' Berglind adjusted Pési on her hip; his grip had slackened and his eyelids were drooping. 'I've sometimes felt as if someone were here in the garden.'

She reddened a tiny bit, so slightly that it was

barely noticeable. 'I thought it was just related to this . . . you know.' She fell silent, but the possibility lingered of there suddenly being a logical explanation for some of the things that she had previously thought were supernatural.

35

Friday, 22 January 2010

Sveinn held out the drawing; he didn't seem at all bothered about parting with it. 'Just take it. As you can see I'm not doing anything with it, and it's purely by chance that it didn't end up in the rubbish bin ages ago.'

Thóra took the drawing, thinking to herself that she seriously doubted the filmmaker ever threw anything away. The box from which he'd pulled the drawing looked as if it contained everything relating to his documentary for the Ministry of Welfare. Maybe he was still pissed off that the project had been shelved. 'That's great — thanks so much for making the effort to dig this out for me.'

'You're welcome. You could have had it sooner if I'd known you wanted it. As you said the other day, it's not exactly something you want hanging on the wall.'

'No, and that's not what I plan to do with it.' Thóra thanked him again and hurried out to her car. She couldn't disguise her joy as she hurried down the staircase of the block of flats. On her way back from Berglind's she'd been cursing the fact that she didn't have any of Tryggvi's drawings to compare with Pési's clumsy one, which Berglind had let them take. Matthew had then suggested that perhaps they could borrow the clip they'd watched at Sveinn's and take a close look at the wall in Tryggvi's room that was covered with his drawings, in the hope that they could enlarge a frame from the video recording. It was then that Thóra remembered that during the clip Tryggvi had handed the filmmaker one of his drawings, and wondered if he might still have it. She was fairly certain that the drawing would contain all the usual elements: the young woman lying down, who was probably Lísa; the person standing up, symbolizing his mother; the flames, the string of characters, and other little details that they hadn't been able to make out due to the resolution in which they'd viewed the video clip. In a brief phone call the next morning Sveinn had confirmed that he still had the drawing and that Thóra was welcome to drop by and get it.

She jumped into the car and slammed the door hard behind her. 'Bingo!'

Matthew drove off happily enough, although she knew he wasn't quite as pleased as her. The bank had given him a final deadline that morning regarding the new job; the offer would only stand until Monday. They couldn't wait any longer for an answer; he would have to make up his mind. Thóra tried to hide how much she hoped that he would take the job, confining herself to saying that her gut feeling was that he should. What she didn't say, and what bothered her, was that the likelihood of him finding another suitable job in Iceland in the next few years was extremely limited. And if he didn't have a job here, he would eventually drift away, whether or not her parents lived with them. For her it was Iceland or nothing; she had to stay here for her children, and her parents, and even for herself. If he moved away, their relationship would be over, whether it happened at a specific moment by mutual decision or whether it faded away slowly but surely. Any plans for keeping the relationship going long-distance would never work in reality. But it would be unfair of her to lay this at his door; it was his job and he would have to make the decision himself.

'Do you have time to look at this with me before you go and see them?' she asked. He had a meeting just before noon with the recruitment director; there was enough time, but he might want to have another shower, change his suit or put on a tie with stripes that sloped to the left rather than the right. He had the tendency to do such things after years of working in German banks. 'I mean, you don't need to do anything beforehand, do you?'

'No, nothing.' Matthew didn't elaborate and Thóra didn't know whether he thought it was useless to do any more preparation for the meeting, since he was going to say no, or whether he'd already decided to accept the job even though he'd told Thóra that he still had grave doubts about it. She decided not to question him any further; she would find out soon enough.

'Then let's go up to the office and have a look at the drawing. I've got instant coffee for you.'

★ ★ ★

'The characters are the same, just in reverse order — though obviously it's impossible to be completely certain about it, since the little boy isn't a particularly brilliant artist.' Thóra put down the magnifying glass between the two drawings. 'It's hard to determine whether this is the letter O or the number zero, and the same goes for this one — is it an 'i' or the number one?' She looked again at Pési's drawing. 'And then I can't see whether this is a B or an eight. And maybe it doesn't make any difference in the end, because no matter how you arrange these letters and numbers, they don't make any sense.'

Matthew leaned back and rubbed his eyes. 'There are some really intricate details in this picture — I don't know how he even managed to draw them. It hurts my eyes to look at it.' He reached for the magnifying glass. 'Do you think this is Lísa?' He examined the figure lying prone at the front of the drawing. 'Did she have any other disabilities besides being in a coma?'

'No.' Thóra understood why he was asking. Considering how well Tryggvi drew, there were details in the picture that seemed awkward, particularly where Lísa's body was concerned — if it was indeed meant to be her. One arm seemed to be turned backwards at the shoulder and her legs had two joints instead of a knee, one in the middle of the thigh and the other mid-calf. 'Maybe this is his interpretation of rape or something. Perhaps the rapist had to put her body in a strange position in order to be able to carry out the act. Tryggvi's sensory world was completely different to ours, of course, but that's what it could have looked like to him.'

'But she's screaming; or at least her mouth is wide open.' Matthew frowned at Thóra. 'Could he also have forced her into oral sex? There's something leaking from her mouth in the picture.'

'Is that even possible, if the person is unconscious?' Thóra took the magnifying glass from him and examined the gaping mouth. 'But you're quite right, it's as if something is leaking out of one of the corners of her mouth.'

'It's a real shame that he couldn't have drawn it just a tiny bit more clearly. Do you think that therapist, Ægir, could explain this any better?'

'Possibly. Mind you, I think he took a lot of poetic licence when he analysed the drawings before. I don't think you can force one specific interpretation on them.' Thóra pointed at the person standing upright. 'Why, for instance, should this be a peace symbol that the figure's holding, as he claimed? It certainly looks like one, but why would Tryggvi have been sticking a peace symbol in his drawings? People have to have some insight into human history in order to understand its meaning properly. At least that's what I would have thought.' She looked at the large ring that the figure was holding between its hands. 'Jesus. And here I was thinking we'd be so much closer with this.'

'But what if it isn't Lísa?' Matthew looked at Thóra. 'Aren't we focusing too hard on trying to see what we want to see? We don't actually know that he witnessed anything at all, and maybe it wasn't even possible to see her bed through the doorway of her apartment. We should maybe check all the facts before we go any further with this interpretation.' He looked at the clock and stood up. 'Well, I'd better get going.' He kissed her on the forehead. 'Don't you want to ask me what I'm going to say to them?'

She shook her head. 'Take me to dinner after the meeting and tell me about it then. Today is going to be a short one for me anyway because I can't meet Jósteinn until tomorrow, and I'm not going to write any more in this report until after I've seen him.' She blew him a kiss and wished him luck. Then she watched him walk out of the office and wondered whether this would be one of the last times that she did so.

To distract herself until he returned, Thóra decided to have a look at the Facebook page again. She'd had enough of the two drawings for the moment. Something was bothering her about Lena's story of her night-time visit to the care home, but she couldn't put her finger on what it was just by thinking about their conversation. Hopefully looking at the photos would inspire her. She particularly wanted to have a look at the photo of Bjarki Emil, in case that was what was bothering her. To her great surprise, several of the photos made her realize what it was that wasn't right.

★ ★ ★

'So, they did know each other after all?' Matthew dutifully stayed in the right-hand lane, though they were unlikely to meet another car as they

515

drove slowly through the convoluted grid of streets.

'I don't know whether they *knew* each other, necessarily, but they were certainly at the residence on the same night, and probably at the same time.' She pointed out a snowdrift in the middle of the roundabout that they were approaching, then continued: 'You remember she said she'd gone there with her drunk friend, along with another friend of theirs who drove? He was in the photo with Friðleifur and Margeir where Lena is visible in the background, which makes me want to know who actually took the photo. Hardly the dead-drunk girl if what Lena said is true — that the photo was taken while she was on oxygen. Which means there was someone else there, and I think it was this Bjarki Emil.'

'Just because Friðleifur and Margeir are in the same clothes in the photo with Lena as they were in the one with Bjarki Emil?' Matthew drove carefully past the snowdrift. 'Maybe neither of them had that many clothes, and it's just a coincidence that they were wearing the same both times.'

'You think it's likely both of them were wearing exactly the same clothing, and I mean *exactly*? Margeir's trousers were sagging on one side in both photos, and his shirt was hanging out in the same place. No, I think they either met there by accident or they went there together — and the latter seems more likely to me. In fact I discovered that they're both enrolled at the university, in the same department and the same year. That's too much of a coincidence, in my opinion. So she should have recognized him when we showed her the photograph of him. I don't know exactly what this means, but I think it's rather odd.'

'Yes, it certainly is that.' Matthew turned into the driveway that led to the charred remains of the residence. In front of the ruined building was a car that appeared to be abandoned. 'What's going on here?' Matthew stopped immediately, only a few metres up the driveway. 'Do you want me to drive up to the building or should we call the police? We can always come back later to check whether Lísa's bed was visible from her doorway.'

'No, let's find out what's going on.' Thóra tried to work out what the car could be doing there, but she didn't recognize it. No one she'd met in connection with the case drove a battered old banger like this.

Matthew inched forward again, this time with the headlights off so the visitor would be less likely to notice them. It could of course be a car that someone had left behind some time ago, but the snowless windscreen suggested otherwise. 'Maybe it's someone from the Regional Office monitoring the place?'

'I doubt it. Drive a little closer but not too close, so that whoever this is doesn't spot us. It can't hurt for us to keep quiet.'

Matthew parked the car a short distance away so that the crunching of the snow beneath the tyres wouldn't be audible. They opened their doors carefully, stepped as gently as they could to the ground and turned in the direction of the blackened building. Thóra felt as if she'd never been surrounded by such silence; they had the wind at their backs, so they couldn't hide behind the distant whine of traffic that was coming from the other direction.

By the time they'd finally inched their way up to the boarded-up door they'd first stood in front of several days ago, Thóra's heart had started to pound in her chest; the need for secrecy had made her nervous and the tension seemed to grow with each cautious step. Matthew had silently pointed out some tracks that led from the abandoned car alongside the house, disappearing at the door. She crossed her fingers in the hope that the driver wasn't waiting on the other side of the wall with a baseball bat. It was clear to her that if this person was the one who had started the fire, then he or she had already killed several people, meaning that two more corpses weren't going to make much difference — the sentence would be the same. There weren't many things worse than encountering a person who had nothing to lose and Thóra suddenly regretted not following Matthew's advice and turning back.

Matthew leaned over to her and whispered so quietly that she could barely hear him. 'Wait here. There's no reason for us both to go in. It just doubles our chances of being heard.' Thóra shook her head emphatically, despite her earlier doubts. She stretched up to his ear and tried to whisper just as softly as him: 'We'll stick together. It'll double our chances of restraining him, or her, if we end up in a fight.'

'Are you kidding?' Matthew was so offended

that he hissed in her ear: 'You add maybe thirty per cent, if that. Closer to twenty-five.'

They stopped making calculations when they heard footsteps inside the abandoned building. The floor must still be awash with water because at each step there was a splash. The sound was amplified in the empty concrete shell, creating a hollow echo. As far as Thóra's senses could tell her, someone was heading towards them. 'I'd forgotten the water,' she whispered. 'We'll be heard as soon as we set foot in there.'

Matthew nodded. He raised his hand to his ear and with a simple gesture motioned to Thóra to step aside and get ready to call the police. Thóra rummaged in her bag for her phone, hearing the footsteps approaching rapidly at the same time. They seemed to have reached the doorway before she could manage to hide. She and Matthew froze when the loose board was pushed away and a jeans-clad leg ending in a cheap trainer stepped out. This was followed by a man's torso, and finally his head. He saw them immediately, and for a moment he stood as motionless as them before suddenly scrambling back inside. Thóra was much too agitated to be able to think clearly, but the face was familiar even though it took her several seconds to place it — it was Margeir, who'd worked the night shift with Friðleifur. As this was sinking in Matthew disappeared into the blackened ruins behind him. The splashing inside suggested that a frantic pursuit was taking place, and Thóra hoped that it was Matthew chasing Margeir and not the other way round. After a brief deliberation she pushed her way in after them.

She'd forgotten about the smell of smoke. As soon as she stepped inside her nostrils stung. The darkness was total, since all the windows and doors were boarded up so the light from outside was negligible. There was a torch in Matthew's jacket pocket but he'd probably not had enough time to turn it on. She decided to follow the wall, for fear of stumbling over the rubbish that was probably still floating around on the floor. The concrete was icy and felt gritty with dirt, but Thóra didn't let that dissuade her, and she set off in the direction of the noise coming from deeper inside the building. When she'd gone far enough to meet a connecting wall she heard the situation change: there was a thud and a huge splash. One or both of them had crashed to the floor. She hoped it wasn't Matthew and hurried in the direction of the noise. It was impossible to say who was grunting louder, Matthew or Margeir, but she was glad she couldn't hear any screaming or cries of pain. Suddenly there was complete silence except for a panting sound. She sped up but slowed down again when she heard the men apparently coming back in her direction. They were moving much more slowly than when they'd rushed into the dark hole, then to Thóra's great relief she heard Matthew order the man to walk unless he wanted to be floated out. She sighed deeply and only then realized she'd been holding her breath the whole time. She called to Matthew, who told her to hurry outside. She picked her way slowly back along the same route, immensely grateful to escape the darkness and the suffocating smell of smoke. She held the board open to let in a bit of light.

Matthew appeared, dragging Margeir behind him, and it took their combined effort to get the young man out of the house. He put up a fierce resistance and when Thóra felt her index fingernail break to the quick she snapped: 'What's wrong with you?' Then she added, more calmly: 'You've got to come out. Were you planning on moving in there, maybe?' At that moment Matthew tugged at Margeir with all his might, causing him to fly out and land on his back in the snow between them. He was filthy and panting and held his upper arm as if he'd been injured. After catching his breath for a moment, Matthew bent down to the man and gripped his shoulder. 'Stand up. You'll die if you lie there much longer. We'll go to the car and wait there for the police.'

'I think I'd rather die, but thanks anyway.' The man didn't look at them, just lay there with his eyes closed.

'Stop being an idiot. Stand up.'

Thóra followed Matthew's lead and bent down to help him lift the man. 'Is your name Margeir?'

The man's eyes opened wide and he looked at her inquisitively. 'Did you send me those text messages?'

She shook her head. 'No. I've been trying to call you, that's all.' Jósteinn's texting thumb had obviously been busy.

'Who are you, then?' Margeir's breathing had

grown more regular and he let go of his arm and stood up. 'I haven't done anything to you.' He stared at Matthew. 'Aren't you the guy who chased me last night?'

'I guess I am; the back of your head looks familiar.' Matthew helped him to his feet, gripping him tightly in case he decided to run away. 'What were you doing in those people's garden? Do you know someone who lived there?'

Margeir shook his head and Thóra took the opportunity to ask: 'Did you set this place on fire, Margeir? We know exactly what went on here, and what sort of service you and Friðleifur were selling.'

'No, I didn't.' Margeir brushed the snow off himself with his uninjured arm; the other hung limply at his side. 'But I know who did.'

'You don't say.' Thóra assumed that he either meant Jakob or that he was going to falsely accuse someone else — probably one of the fire's victims.

'I'm not making it up, I know who started the fire.'

'That's just as well, since I'm Jakob's lawyer — you remember him, don't you? He's being held in a Psychiatric Secure Unit; did it never cross your mind to pass on this information?' She wanted to scream at the man. What was wrong with people?

Margeir said nothing, apparently pondering his situation. 'You're his lawyer? And you were trying to reach me?' Thóra nodded and he was silent for a moment. 'I had nothing to do with the fire. I wasn't here, I didn't start it and I didn't assist with any cover-up or anything like that. It's not my fault the police messed up the investigation, but you've got to admit that it doesn't make much difference to Jakob what kind of institution he lives in.'

Thóra was so offended by this that before she knew what she was doing she'd smacked the man hard on his injured arm. 'You arsehole! I'm going to do everything in my power to ensure that things go badly for you. Stupid, ignorant bastard.' Matthew looked at her in surprise, but said nothing.

Margeir stared at her and rubbed his upper arm, flabbergasted. Then suddenly it was as if all the wind were knocked out of him. He looked miserably at the snow and the wingless angel that had formed where he'd just been lying. 'That was a stupid thing to say. I know.' He sighed and shuffled his feet as if to keep himself warm. 'If I tell you what I know, he'll be released. Won't he? That's the most important thing.'

'It will help. Who started the fire?' Thóra knew how important it was to get this out of the man in case he changed his mind before the police arrived.

'Bjarki Emil.' Margeir looked from her to Matthew. 'I don't know his surname.'

'It's Jónasson.' He could be just trying to pin the blame on a dead man who can't defend himself, thought Thóra. 'The man found dead at Nauthólsvík. You know that the police are searching for you in connection with his death?'

'Yes. I know.' Margeir directed his attention

towards Matthew. 'He fell backwards onto the rocks, and the fall killed him. I didn't push him or anything. I just wanted to get him to turn himself in and confess everything. I didn't care what the consequences were for me.' Neither Matthew nor Thóra pointed out to him that if this were true then he would hardly have been on the run through the back gardens of Mosfellsbær or scurrying around the charred remains of a building in the middle of nowhere. 'It was an accident, but I panicked and tried to get rid of the body — I was afraid I'd be blamed. It didn't work, he didn't burn like I hoped he would. There wasn't enough petrol in the can in the boot of my car.'

'Did you think that he would disappear? Turn into ashes?' The tone of Matthew's voice had hardly changed and Thóra admired how calm he seemed.

'No, I was going to burn the flesh off so he'd be more likely to sink. I couldn't start dragging a body around trying to find a more sensible place to dump it.' His expression turned sheepish. 'And I was in a state of shock; I couldn't think straight. I guess I thought it was appropriate somehow, considering what he did.'

'Did you know from the outset that he'd started the fire?' Thóra tried to emulate Matthew's composure. The smell of smoke was having a bad effect on her mood; she couldn't shake off the images of the residents' blackened bodies.

'No, I didn't know it but I suspected it. I met him to find out for sure; I couldn't get any peace because of all the insane phone calls and text messages, and I wanted to do the right thing.'

'And he admitted to having started the fire?'

Margeir shook his head. 'No. Fucking idiot. But it was him. I know it was.'

'And how do you know that? Did someone else tell you?' Thóra was afraid that Jósteinn had perhaps believed he could play God and had put some sort of nonsense into this young, nervy man's head.

'I know what he was like. I caught him raping one of the girls at the residence. He was a monster, but we didn't know it to begin with; he came out several times drunk or really hungover to get the oxygen and nutrients treatment, but instead of leaving it at that, he . . . ' He fell silent.

'Didn't you find it odd for him to be lying in the residents' beds?'

'The oxygen hose wasn't long enough for people to sit in a chair, so it was the only way they could reach it. Ragna's apartment was usually empty, so the visitors would lie in her bed. The few times we needed a bed and Ragna was at home we used Lísa's. She was the least likely to tell on us, obviously. I guess we might have used Ragna's bed when she was in it, a few times. I can't really remember, we were drunk.' *o2 short hose.*

Thóra gathered her composure. 'Did he know that Lísa had become pregnant? Do you think he wanted to get rid of her by setting the place on fire?'

'They'd begun to suspect that something wasn't quite right and she was supposed to be examined by a doctor. But he didn't actually know that, because we threw him out when I discovered what he was up to and he wasn't allowed back. The night the place burned down I was sick at home, but Friðleifur called and said that Bjarki had been in touch and wanted to drop by to discuss something. He'd threatened to spill the beans about what we were doing if he wasn't allowed to come and speak to him. I lied to the police and in court about the reason for the phone call because I was afraid they'd find out what we'd been up to. I thought it didn't matter.'

Thóra was speechless. She remembered the references to the phone call to the residence that night, which had been thought to be a wrong number. The person who'd called, the anonymous young man, had been Bjarki. And there was a similar explanation for why so many drunk people had called on the weekends: they'd been trying to get in touch with Friðleifur and Margeir, but if someone else was on duty they simply said that they'd dialled the wrong number. 'What did Bjarki want to discuss, other than Lísa's condition?'

'Friðleifur didn't really know, but he said that Bjarki had made some vague mention of needing to give one of the residents a bit of a scare.'

'Ragna?' Thóra saw no real purpose in scaring Lísa, who had been comatose. 'Did he think she was there that night?'

'I have no idea. All I know is that he planned to come, and Friðleifur must have ended up arguing with him, which ended with Bjarki starting the fire. Maybe Friðleifur let it slip that there was some speculation about Lísa's condition.'

Thóra flipped her phone open to call the police. 'What were you doing here, and in those people's garden in MosfellsbÆr?'

'I came here to double check that there was nothing left of the money that belonged to me and Friðleifur. We hid it in boxes in our duty room and I've never dared to look for it until now in case it attracted attention. Now I'm in such deep shit that I was hoping the box had escaped the damage and I could use the money to get out of the country.' In other words, he was only worried about saving his own skin. 'It probably got burnt, or it's just gone, but I was so desperate that I had to check.'

'And MosfellsbÆr?' Thóra began to dial the police. 'What was that all about?'

'That address was in one of the text messages and I thought whoever lived there might be sending them. I've been trying to get in touch with the man because it was a man who called, not a woman, but I haven't managed to meet him. I've only seen a woman and a child in that house when I've been there.'

The police answered and after describing the situation briefly, Thóra asked them to send officers to the care home. Then she hung up. 'What is NNI80 supposed to mean? What you wrote in the frost on the window?'

'What? I wrote o8INN. It was in one of the texts and I hoped that the man would see it when he came home and realize I was there. The kid wasn't supposed to see it.'

Of course the writing had been in reverse on the window — Margeir had written it on the outside, while the child had seen it from the inside. Obviously Tryggvi must have intended to write NNI8O or something similar, since everything he drew was in mirror image. Thóra sighed. But how would Jósteinn know about this, except from having seen Tryggvi's drawings? And how would he have got to see those in the first place, and what exactly had he been up to? Perhaps Einvarður had scanned in the images and stored them on his laptop, even though that seemed a bit unlikely. 'Do you know anything about a hit-and-run accident on Vesturlandsvegur Road, in which a young woman died? Could that have had anything to do with Bjarki?'

He shook his head firmly. 'I don't know anything about that. All this stuff about the residence is enough drama for me.'

He had a point. While they were waiting for the police, Thóra couldn't help thinking that something was missing in all of this. Was Jakob's claim to have seen an angel really just nonsense, and why had Jósteinn got the poor woman and her son involved in the case through this nasty little game of his? Even though it now looked like Jakob would almost certainly be released, these niggles were destroying the sense of triumph she should be experiencing. She should be over-joyed: it was probably merely a matter of time before Jakob would be allowed to go home; Matthew had just informed her over pizza that he'd accepted the job — everything seemed to be

528

going as well as it could. And yet. She tried to shake off this negativity as she silently watched the flash of lights from the approaching patrol cars. The investigation had reached a reasonable outcome; you couldn't always expect to tie up every loose end. Maybe that bastard Jósteinn would answer some of the questions that were still bothering her when they met the next day. She didn't want the slightest doubt about Jakob's innocence to ruin the case.

What was really bothering her was not being able to see the link between these two cases. On the surface they seemed unrelated, save for the fact that in each of them innocent victims had died — but she was sure they must be connected, or why would the text have directed Margeir to Berglind's house? The phone call from Berglind that came as they drove away, following the police at a distance, confirmed it. '*I know where I've seen these letters and numbers . . .*'

36

Saturday, 23 January 2010

Thóra and Matthew had been sitting with the man for nearly an hour, but he had not looked up once. As a result, it was impossible for Thóra to fathom Jósteinn's reaction to her having found out about his computer activities; his averted face revealed nothing and everything he said was toneless. They were sitting as usual in the shabby living room at Sogn. Although it was quite spacious, being anywhere near this terrifying man always felt overwhelming. Although he didn't say much, and most of what he said was fairly innocuous, it was impossible to ignore the disgusting details he dropped into the conversation every now and again like little reminders of his wickedness. It was precisely the unpredictability of their appearance that meant neither Matthew nor Thóra were able to arm themselves against them. Every time Jósteinn said something vile it startled them. Thóra was convinced that he was behaving this way because he knew he would probably never see her again — nor anyone else from now on, apart from those who lived and worked there.

'We're not here to discuss your compulsions, Jósteinn.' Thóra moistened her dry lips. 'You should speak to a doctor about them, or someone who can help you. We're not interested in these things and we don't have the expertise to work through them with you. If you can't stick to the subject, then we'll just have to get the information we need from the police.'

'All right.' Jósteinn ran his hand through his thin, greasy black hair. A comb had left light stripes where the scalp shone through. Thóra wasn't sure what he meant by 'all right'; all right, they could go to the police or all right, he would stop his sickening digressions? She decided to assume the latter.

'Go over this again for me, just so that I'm clear on everything.' Jósteinn had refused to allow them to record the conversation, and fearing that he wouldn't open up, Thóra was limiting herself to only scribbling down the occasional word or two. 'Just start at the beginning and repeat what it is you think Ari has done to you.'

Jósteinn looked up now and stared out of the window, and Thóra and Matthew automatically followed his gaze. There was nothing to see but snow, the abandoned greenhouse and the bare branches swaying in the wind. 'He betrayed me. Maybe it's not that surprising, but nevertheless, he did. It couldn't have been anyone but him. He was the only one who knew about the pictures besides me.'

He let out a short, joyless laugh. 'I thought lawyers were supposed to protect their clients' interests, not run to the police with information.' Without turning from the window, he asked: 'What would you do if you had to defend a man and found there was more evidence against him?'

Thóra had no interest in making herself the topic of this man's conversation. 'Generally, lawyers aren't in the habit of handing over to the police evidence that is detrimental to their client's case.' She neglected to mention that the nature of Jósteinn's crimes was such that few would take pains to assure that he remained a part of society. 'But it isn't the lawyer's role to conceal evidence on behalf of his client. Are you certain you didn't ask him to get rid of them? You were in solitary confinement and I'm sure you were concerned that the photos would be found.'

'No. It wasn't like that. I merely warned him that the photos existed, and told him that I'd hidden them in a flowerpot on my grandfather's grave. No one else visited the grave, so they would be left alone there. It didn't take him long to fetch them and send them to the police, anonymously. No one else could have done it and though I've always known it was him, I haven't been able to verify it until recently.' Again Jósteinn laughed coldly. 'This computer came to me so that justice would be done, pure and simple.'

Thóra and Matthew were speechless. If justice always won out, this man wouldn't be sitting here, he'd be six feet under with his grandfather. Thóra was the first to regain her composure. 'How did you know the computer contained data concerning you? You've got a pile of machines here at the moment — surely you don't go through all of them that closely. Aren't most of them useless, anyway?'

'You can always retrieve data. It takes time and patience, but I've got enough of both. I do this with all the computers that come to my workshop. People think it's impossible to do anything with them but that's usually not the case. No one has any idea what I'm doing here; the staff know so little about computers that I can tell them anything. And in any case, they're all happy as long as I'm shut away in my little cubbyhole. When Einvarður's laptop landed on my table I hit the jackpot. Not just because it was his computer, but because he'd forgotten to take his 3G key out of the case. With that I was able to go online without anyone knowing, and even make phone calls all over town. The idiot had taped the password to the key.' He continued to stare at the snow outside. 'It was all most enjoyable, and what I found on the hard drive made it even better.'

Matthew cleared his throat. 'So you found e-mails sent between Ari and his cousin Einvarður, in which Ari offered the ministry evidence pertaining to your case, in exchange for his not being disbarred due to impending bankruptcy?'

'Oh, it was more than that.' Jósteinn stopped staring out of the window, directing his attention back at the embroidered cushion he'd put in his lap when he sat down. 'There were e-mail exchanges between Einvarður and other people in the ministry, including the person investigating the case. He's no idiot, that Einvarður, despite appearances to the contrary. He saved the e-mails because he was merely an intermediary. He worded them in such a way that even if they were made public he would have looked pretty much blameless. And he would probably even have become a hero.'

'And the police and prosecutor went along with it?'

'Oh, yes. Of course. How can temporarily disbarring one lawyer compare to putting me behind bars for the rest of my life? Less hassle for a much better outcome.' Jósteinn sounded triumphant. 'But the people involved in this had no idea that it would mean Ari would then owe Einvarður a favour — a favour that he then cashed in when the residence burned down and he needed an inside man in the investigation and the trial. There were e-mails about this too, and again I think that Einvarður wanted to shield his own position if these exchanges came to light. He words the messages so as to protect himself, puts some words into Ari's mouth and in doing so is able to hide behind bad legal advice, although it ought to be clear to anyone who reads them how he set things up.'

'If anyone actually does get to read them, at this point.' Following a visit from a Ministry of Justice representative, all the computers had been removed from Jósteinn's workshop, and Einvarður had almost certainly got his laptop back and subsequently destroyed it. He himself had been partly responsible for this, having put in a request to get it back after his meeting with Thóra and Matthew — although the ministry representative hadn't appeared immediately. Perhaps Einvarður hadn't wanted to come across as being too eager to get his computer back; or perhaps the matter simply had to go through the right channels before it was possible to take action. One thing was clear, in any case — the computer was gone.

Jósteinn tugged at a loose thread in the middle of the cushion's embroidered cover. 'It's up to you to prove who did it. And you should be able to, now that you know what you're looking for.'

'None of what you claim to have read proves anything about the fire. It's all very interesting, but if Einvarður doesn't admit straight out in an e-mail that he started the fire, there's no evidence pointing to him. There's another man under suspicion now, and he appears to be an extremely plausible candidate. Plus, Einvarður was at a ball in Selfoss that evening, along with his wife. It would be difficult to demonstrate that he'd driven to town in order to start the fire before driving back out there. His wife would surely have known about it and she would never have agreed to it.'

'You'll work it out.' Jósteinn tugged on the end of the thread, which he'd finally got a good grip on, and pulled it slowly from the cushion. The thread belonged to the largest of the roses and it was bright red. 'Have you ever pulled the guts out of a mouse?' He'd started again with his shock tactics.

'No, and we never will,' growled Matthew.

Jósteinn put the cushion down next to him but continued to stare at it. 'That's a shame.'

'Would you mind getting back to the computer and the files?' Thóra felt nauseous and couldn't bear any more of these deviations. 'Was there nothing there that could be considered concrete proof that he arranged the fire?'

Jósteinn shrugged. 'That's what I was telling you. You're not listening. His son, Tryggvi, had suddenly started to open up a bit and seemed to want to communicate a few things. Although they were ecstatic about his progress, they were very disturbed by what he wanted to communicate. Understandably.' He placed his hand back on the cushion and Thóra felt her gorge rise at the thought of him pulling another thread from it.

'How do you think it will look if it turns out his wife drove away after running over and killing that girl? Is that any better than what I did? I didn't kill anyone.' He fell silent and then added mournfully: 'More's the pity.'

Matthew shifted on the couch. 'And it turned out that his son was a witness? He was in the car?'

'Yes.' Jósteinn's voice was as emotionless as before. 'He was in the front seat and he saw everything. The daughter was also a passenger in the car. Tryggvi's violent reaction to the collision caused his mother to just keep driving, or so they say, although it might lead one to suspect that she'd simply had a bit too much to drink.'

Thóra sat silently. No doubt this was the reason why Tryggvi had hated being put in a car. It must have been a shock to Fanndís and Einvarður that when the treatment of their beloved son finally appeared to be producing results, it should also involve what they feared most. The boy had finally been able to interact with his surroundings, albeit to a limited degree, but when he tried to express himself it was to tell the world about the fatal accident on Vesturlandsvegur Road. The irony of it. The prone figure in the picture wasn't Lísa at all, but the young babysitter, and the peace sign must be the car's steering wheel. When the string of characters was viewed in reverse, it showed the licence-plate number of their family car, NN180, the car that Fanndís had been driving that evening. 'And Ari took on Jakob's case to make sure no incriminating evidence would get out during the trial?' He had already told her this, so it was a rhetorical question.

'All he knew was that he should keep everything concerning Tryggvi, his drawings and how fascinated he was with fire, out of the picture and prevent any suspicion from falling on him. Glódís, the director of the centre, was also drafted in to help Einvarður cover up a few things, without being told why. If she'd given it just a bit of thought, she would have realized that by doing so she was endangering an innocent man. Jakob. Actually, Einvarður never says anywhere that they started the fire; that's just what I inferred from some other things I found on the laptop.'

'Such as?' Matthew leaned forward but then jerked back immediately when he realized how close he'd got to Jósteinn.

'Some photos that were uploaded to the computer. I found several that were taken on the night of the fire. Einvarður thought he'd deleted them, but computer files aren't deleted completely unless the area where they're stored is written over. Laymen generally don't know this.'

Jósteinn gave a small, lazy yawn, as if he were bored with his visitors and the topic of conversation. 'Aren't you at all interested in knowing who started the fire? I still haven't told you. Well, since I can't send you helpful clues any more, I'll have to just come out with it.'

Now Thóra and Matthew's attention suddenly peaked. 'Weren't you suggesting that Einvarður started it?' Thóra hoped that he wasn't about to say something about guts or other internal organs.

'It wasn't him, it was his daughter. Lena.'

★ ★ ★

They barely spoke on the way home, lost in their own thoughts. Jósteinn's story fitted with everything that had already come out in the investigation as well as filling in the missing pieces. According to him, the photos from the party that Lena had held at home that evening showed her wearing a long white dress — the same dress Thóra had seen her wearing in a photo at her parents' house, taken the night before the fire. When she'd added a gold headband, she looked exactly like an angel, the 'angel' Jakob had seen. Jósteinn had got into all the case files Einvarður had saved on his computer, and had done his research into who was who and what was what. He'd discovered the Facebook page and realized what was in Lísa's autopsy report, in addition to finding the photograph of Friðleifur's burnt corpse, which he'd sent to Thóra by text message. He had

538

dutifully compared the photos on the Facebook page to those taken at the party at Lena's house that night, and had found some familiar faces. As the night wore on the number of guests in the photos diminished. Finally there were only three left, and of these, one was asleep on the sofa. The other guest was Bjarki, whom Jósteinn had recognized from the Facebook page.

The very last photo taken was of Lena. She was leaning forward on the kitchen table with a Bacardi Breezer in front of her, her hands and her white dress all sooty. It was no wonder her father had deleted the photos. There was absolutely no doubt about what she'd been up to.

Jósteinn had also found Margeir and started bombarding him with text messages and phone calls with the help of Skype; he had managed to steal a credit card number from a staff member at Sogn to purchase domestic credit. He was convinced that Margeir was more closely connected to the case than had yet been discovered, because he was in so many photos on the Facebook page and must at least have known what was going on. Jósteinn had sent him the sequence of characters from Tryggvi's drawings, which Ægir had mentioned submitting to Einvarður when he was dismissed. The report also mentioned the mirror imaging, which made Jósteinn realize that the characters needed to be read backwards. By searching the computer for various versions of the character sequence, in which he also tried exchanging numbers and letters, he found an electronic tax return that

Einvarður had also stored on his laptop. In it was the licence-plate number. No wonder he'd turned pale when he realized that the laptop was still in use. On closer inspection, Jósteinn noticed that the car had vanished from the following year's tax return without any mention of it having been sold, and another car had been added. Thóra found this quite ingenious, since it would always be possible to claim to have forgotten to delist the car, which had probably stood in the garage since the night of the hit-and-run. Tryggvi had written the licence-plate number on his drawings. He probably didn't actually understand its meaning, but he was able to connect it to the vehicle and the accident. Because he drew things in mirror image, no one had realized what he was trying to say when he drew his vague pictures of the accident again and again. When Margeir scribbled the number in the frost on the windowpane, the little boy had seen the reverse image. Jósteinn hadn't anticipated this coincidence. Thóra had been able to verify through Berglind, who had called her the previous evening, that this was the licence-plate number of a car that Einvarður had used two or three years ago. She'd assisted him in filling out the mileage log, so she had often entered the number over the years.

'Do you want to go straight to the police?' asked Matthew, as the lights of the city appeared on the horizon.

'No. Let's go down to the office; I need to make a copy of this.' She opened her hand and looked at the little USB stick. She hadn't wanted

to put it in her handbag in case it got damaged rattling around among all the other rubbish in there. On it were all the main files concerning the fire and the accident that Jósteinn had found on the laptop. He had hidden the key long before the computers were taken. He said he'd always assumed he'd be found out in the end.

She had to hand it to him, that bastard Jósteinn: he was cunning.

37

Tuesday, 9 March 2010

The sun was low in the sky and it shone in Jakob's eyes, but that didn't diminish the joy that radiated from his face. He was still wearing his Coke-bottle glasses, but the bandages were gone now and they sat much better on his ears, though one of the arms was still rather bent and would never be the same, any more than the eye in which he'd lost his sight. His ear was fine, but the blind eye was always pointing in a different direction to the other. This drew attention to the odd pupil, which had been oblong, rather like a cat's, since the attack.

'So the fire was accidental, if all of this is true and correct. Not that we'll ever be able to know for sure. When Jósteinn hired me for this investigation he said something like 'a child who's had their fingers burned might still want to play with fire', which is how it turned out.' Thóra was speaking to Jakob's mother. His attention had long turned to something else and he was now waiting excitedly to go out into the sunshine with Mummy. The investigation of the case was complete and a reopening of the case before the Supreme Court secured; the conclusion to the case was thought to be so likely to come out in Jakob's favour that a temporary decision regarding his release from Sogn would be hurried through the system. 'Lena says she met Bjarki at school and they'd been to several parties together along with some of her other friends, including the one at her house on the night of the fire. When only the two of them were left — apart from her best friend, who was passed out on the sofa — she got the idea of going over to the residence to sober up a bit. After they'd made sure that Friðleifur was on duty, they went over there with Bjarki at the wheel, smashed. Lena isn't sure whether she came up with the idea of getting Bjarki to scare her brother on the way there, or if it was after they arrived, but either way she asked him to do it. She remembers telling him that Tryggvi was simultaneously fascinated with fire and terrified of it. The theory behind her drunken plan was that Tryggvi would be frightened back into his shell, ensuring the accident remained unsolved.'

Jakob's mother sat there wide-eyed, nodding her head after every sentence Thóra uttered. 'How could these people let Jakob sit behind bars for this? I just don't understand it.'

'Her parents didn't know. Einvarður's only motivation was to ensure that the investigation didn't home in on Tryggvi because of his fascination with fire. That's why he got his cousin Ari to call you and offer his assistance when Jakob was arrested. He was afraid that otherwise the truth about the hit-and-run would come to light. Lena kept it completely secret; the photos on her father's laptop were hers but she deleted them immediately, so he never saw them. It doesn't explain how she was able to live with something so terrible, though; maybe she'd got used to it after keeping quiet about the death of the young girl. She was in the car with her mother and brother when the accident occurred.'

Thóra smiled at Jakob, who couldn't keep still in his chair. 'If she's telling the truth, then the fire was unintentional. She's probably been thinking that it would be unfair if she and Bjarki were made to pay for it. Everything in her story suggests that he was the one responsible, but that's hardly surprising; he's not exactly in a position to defend himself any more. Lena maintains that when they got to the residence, Friðleifur didn't want to let Bjarki in and the two men ended up having an argument that she couldn't make head or tail of. She had no idea about what Bjarki had done to the girls at the centre, or what had gone on between him and Friðleifur as a result. She persuaded Friðleifur to let them in and while she messed about with him, Bjarki went wandering through the building, found the petrol can in the storage shed that Lena had told him about and poured petrol all over the place. Lena says he was dead drunk and she'd forgotten to tell him what apartment Tryggvi lived in, so he poured petrol into all of them to be sure. He imagined that the petrol would ignite, form a carpet of fire along the corridor and in the apartments and would only last for a few minutes while the flammable liquid burned up. He'd noticed the sprinkler system on the ceiling and thought that that would save the day if things went wrong. He didn't know the system was disconnected.'

'Shouldn't we go now? It's almost the evening.' Jakob grabbed the arms of his chair and made an attempt to stand up, but his mother laid her hand on his shoulder and gently pushed him down again, saying that she'd be finished very soon.

Thóra continued, but started talking faster. 'While Bjarki was carrying out his plan, Friðleifur became agitated and gave Lena the slip to see what was happening; perhaps he'd smelled the petrol. He came across Bjarki just as he was emptying the can and went ballistic. He rushed to the duty room to call the police, but Bjarki hit him on the back of the head with the can, so hard that Friðleifur was knocked out. What happened next isn't entirely clear, but Lena says that they were horrified and planned to call an ambulance. To calm themselves down, they lit a cigarette that somehow caused a spark to fly into the petrol. This set off a sequence of events that two drunk kids were in no fit state to deal with. Lena says she ran in and tried to save the residents, but why she didn't manage to actually get anyone out is a mystery. However, I expect this will help to reduce her sentence. Jakob spoke of seeing an angel; no doubt that's what she looked like to him, in her long white dress and her gold headband, just like the angel on a poster in his room. But I suspect this wasn't quite as innocuous as it sounds — as you might remember, Jakob said the angel was holding a suitcase, which turned out to be the petrol can. Her excuse for this is that she was so panicked that she took the can with her. But the fact that she and Bjarki had enough sense to wipe their fingerprints off it suggests that they can't have panicked that much.'

'What will happen to her?' For the first time Jakob's mother's expression was severe; the soft lines of her face became sharp; the creases at the corners of her eyes deepened and her lips pressed into thin lines.

'I don't know. She'll be sentenced, but it's impossible to say whether the sentence will be suspended.'

'Suspended? Well, it's a shame Jakob wasn't that lucky when he was convicted. How can they discriminate against people like this?' She didn't need to add what was all too obvious: that Jakob had been discriminated against ever since his conception, even by his Creator.

'In her defence, she doesn't appear to have been the main perpetrator in the case, plus the fire does seem to have been accidental. The fact that she quit smoking afterwards gives credence to her story about the cigarettes.'

'I'm speechless.'

Thóra shook her head. The case was complicated. DNA tests had revealed that Bjarki had impregnated Lísa, and even though the justice system hadn't punished him, it was perhaps a comfort to Ragna to know that the sentence he had received was stringent, and not eligible for appeal. Margeir was still in custody, awaiting trial for the death of Bjarki. His defence was also based on the claim that Bjarki's death had been an accident, and in the end he was only convicted of trying to set fire to the body afterwards. Sentence had not yet been passed on Lena's mother for the hit-and-run. Fanndís had confessed to everything, but in Iceland there were few precedents of people being sentenced to prison for having knocked down and killed someone. There were even fewer where the driver had also fled the scene, although someone had been sentenced for this very crime only six months before. However, the driver in that case had had a colourful criminal record and his conviction was simultaneous with one for another crime, while Fanndís's record was spotless. Einvarður had been moved sideways to a similar position and news of his part in covering up a crime was not widely reported in the media. Jósteinn's case was mentioned nowhere at all, and nor was Einvarður's involvement in the handling of the evidence.

Glódís Tumadóttir was not as lucky as Einvarður. As far as Thóra could make out, the real reason for her dismissal wasn't cutbacks and optimization, as the media stated, but had more to do with her performance in Jakob's case and how she had acted as Einvarður's puppet in the hope that he would advance her career. When his position in the hierarchy weakened, she lost all her support. Apparently Glódís had informed the head of the Regional Office that Einvarður had got her to cover up additional costs associated with Tryggvi's special needs in terms of food and therapy; in effect, costs that Tryggvi's parents would normally have had to shoulder themselves had been paid for out of the limited funding due to other residents. When this was put to him, however, Einvarður feigned complete ignorance, claiming that he had believed it to be part of the residence's service and that he would of course repay the difference. E-mails that Glódís had submitted to back up her story proved nothing; Einvarður had taken great care not to say anything that could possibly implicate him in any way. Her desperate bid to have her dismissal rescinded was doomed from the start.

'You must try not to let it trouble you.' Thóra smiled again at Jakob. 'The most important thing is that you've come home, Jakob, and now you can start to get your life back to the way it was before. That's a pretty happy ending, isn't it?'

'Yes.' Jakob looked from her to his mother. 'But I would be even happier if we could go out now.'

Thóra laughed. 'You can go. There's no point in being free if you have to hang around a lawyer's office and listen to them saying lawyery things.' She escorted them out. They said their goodbyes in the firm's lobby and it seemed as if Jakob's mother would never stop thanking Thóra. When Jakob finally managed to get her out of the door, Thóra watched as they walked hand in hand down the steps. She was filled with satisfaction and had an overwhelming desire to go home. Home to her family. She was equally satisfied with her phone conversation with Berglind the day before, where Berglind had thanked Thóra for having solved the case of the hit-and-run accident and apologized modestly for having gone on at such length about the haunting, which now appeared to have been rooted in the unkempt state of the house and

Margeir's visits to their garden. All was well that ended well and Thóra really didn't want to turn around and see Bella painting her fingernails black at the reception desk, even though she knew she would have to. She had to get her handbag before going home, and on the way she had to stop for an appointment, for which she would need to have her credit card handy. A Brazilian wax in honour of Matthew's appointment at the bank, as well as her parents getting the keys to their apartment that evening. At this moment there was only one thing that bothered her more than her secretary and her anxiety about the pain she would soon be experiencing. Einvarður and his family would never be subjected to real justice, even though they had denied it to Jakob, Ragna, the girl who had been killed on Vesturlandsvegur Road and her parents, as well as all of those who died in the fire.

* * *

Fanndís rubbed her ear as she stared up into the starless night sky from the living room window. The silence was absolute. None of them was keen to turn on the television or the radio. News reporters had a tendency to ambush them when they least expected it, and if there was anything that really freaked them out, it was news stories about their affairs. She hated the reporters' singsong tone, characterized by an ever-increasing emphasis that reached its peak at the end of every sentence. It made her feel nauseous. She was aware of Einvarður on the couch behind her because she could still hear him rustling the pages of the book he was pretending to read.

'Would you like some coffee?' Fanndís did not turn around, but continued to stare out of the window and worry at her ear.

'What?' Her husband's voice was gruff. This was the first thing he'd said since thanking her for dinner.

'Coffee. Do you want some coffee?' Fanndís turned to him, letting her hand drop after arranging her hair to cover her inflamed red earlobe. 'It's so cold in here now. Did you call the plumber?'

Einvarður slammed the book shut and placed it on the coffee table. 'No, and no. I don't want coffee and I didn't call the plumber.' He stood up. 'I think I'm going up to bed.'

Fanndís stood in silence. Not because she had nothing to say, but because she couldn't get up the nerve to start. The life of this three-person family was in ruins. Everything they'd built up and strived for; all of it was gone, and they had fought for nothing. Einvarður was in a difficult position at the ministry and his dream of an exciting ambassadorial position had come to nought. Lena had dropped out of university and rarely came out of her room, and certainly never on her own initiative: It was as if they'd all been forgotten. The phone had stopped ringing. She couldn't even remember what the ring sounded like any more. It was sad how shallow friendship was when it came down to it — and family, too, even though Fanndís knew she only had herself to blame in that regard; she hadn't made much of an effort to keep in touch with her family in recent years. It also occurred to her that perhaps she'd exhausted her friends' sympathy quota a long time ago.

She watched her husband walk out of the living room without even looking at her or asking whether she was also going to bed early. It didn't particularly surprise her. Even though he hadn't said so explicitly, he blamed her for the way things were now. She was the one who'd run over the girl. She was the one who'd kept going, after only stopping long enough to see in the rear-view mirror that she was dead. At the time, Einvarður had said he understood why she'd reacted as she did: Tryggvi's screaming had confused her and Lena's crying hadn't exactly helped. He'd never breathed a word about the thing they both knew, that the other reason she hadn't stopped was the wine that she'd been drinking. Perhaps it was the reason he blamed himself. He had declined an invitation to dinner at his aunt's house that evening, but if he'd put his work aside then it would have been him at the wheel. The thought of his aunt made Fanndís even more uncomfortable. She'd contacted Einvarður yesterday and told him that the police were making enquiries about that evening, asking whether Fanndís had consumed any alcohol. The woman hadn't wanted to tell Einvarður what she answered, which meant that the police knew she'd had a few glasses.

Determined to make herself some coffee, even though she'd have to drink it alone, Fanndís went into the kitchen. Maybe she could persuade

Lena to come downstairs and join her for a cup. Otherwise she'd just drink it alone at the kitchen table — as she so often did nowadays. The aroma of the beans gave her a welcome feeling of anticipation and satisfaction; she brought the tin to her face and inhaled deeply. Then she poured a handful of beans into the mill and ground them — for rather too long, in fact. Once the coffee was in the coffeemaker and the water had started to boil, Fanndís felt a bit better again; the familiar sound of the bubbling water calmed her down and allowed her to forget for a moment how hopeless everything was. They would simply have to face the facts and make the best of their situation. Time would surely heal all wounds and their problems weren't any worse than those that other families had overcome. Perhaps it was the first step on the road to a better future to realize this simple fact. Although the ambassadorial position was out of the picture for Einvarður, that wasn't to say that a lower-level placement in an embassy abroad was out of the question; that or work for the Ministry for Foreign Affairs at NATO or another international institution. The situation couldn't get any worse — just better.

Suddenly the coffeemaker shut itself off. Fanndís looked in surprise at the machine, which now stood silent on the table in front of her; the water that had just been boiling was now still. She tried to restart the machine but nothing happened. She checked whether the cord at the back had come loose, but it turned out that wasn't the problem. Typical. Fanndís resisted picking up the coffeemaker and letting it fall to the tile-covered floor, and limited herself to imagining how the glass shards would fly in all directions and bits of plastic would skitter across the floor. Then she noticed that the clock on the oven was blinking as it did on the rare occasions that the power went off. Fanndís exhaled through her nose, then took a deep breath. But it didn't invigorate her — instead, her mouth was filled with a foul taste. It was as if she'd breathed in through a rusty pipe. She retched at the taste of iron and involuntarily turned to the sink. Thankfully, she didn't vomit, and felt herself getting used to the disgusting tang. She stretched out to the window to let in some fresh air, but jumped back when she thought she saw a person or a shadow right outside.

She grabbed at her chest as if to calm her rapid heartbeat and stood there like that, frozen, waiting for it to slow down. Then she noticed that frost had begun to creep slowly but surely over the windowpane, clouding her view out into the darkness.

Other titles published by
The House of Ulverscroft:

TRESPASSER

Paul Doiron

While on patrol one evening, game warden Mike Bowditch receives a call for help. A woman has reportedly struck a deer on a lonely coastal road. When he arrives, he finds blood on the road — but both the driver and deer have vanished. Her body is found the next day, brutalised in a way eerily similar to a case seven years ago, when a jury sentenced Erland Jefferts to life imprisonment for the rape and murder of a college student. So was Jefferts framed? When Bowditch begins to investigate, he receives a warning from state prosecutors to stop asking questions. But for Bowditch, doing nothing is not an option. And as he closes in on the truth, he suddenly discovers how far his opponents will go to prevent him from bringing a killer to justice . . .

POLICE

Jo Nesbø

The police urgently need Harry Hole. A killer is stalking Oslo's streets, and police officers are being slain at the scenes of crimes they once investigated but failed to solve. The murders are brutal, the media reaction hysterical. But this time, Harry Hole can't help anyone. For years, the detective has been at the centre of every major criminal investigation in Oslo. His dedication to his job and his brilliant insights have saved the lives of countless people. But now, with those he loves the most facing terrible danger, Harry can't protect anyone. Least of all, himself . . .

JUST WHAT KIND OF MOTHER ARE YOU?

Paula Daly

What if your best friend's child disappears — and it's all your fault? This is exactly what happens to Lisa Kallisto, overwhelmed working mother of three, one freezing December in the Lake District. She takes her eye off the ball for just a moment, and her whole world descends into nightmare. Her best friend's thirteen-year-old daughter Lucinda has gone missing and now, devastated by this and publicly blamed, Lisa sets out to right the wrong. But as she begins peeling away the layers surrounding Lucinda's disappearance, Lisa learns that the quiet town she lives in isn't what she thought it was, and her friends might not be who they appear to be, either . . .

UNDER YOUR SKIN

Sabine Durrant

Gaby Mortimer is a woman who has it all — and then everything changes when she finds a body on the common near her London home. After giving the police what information she has, she goes on her way. But very soon they are returning with more questions, and Gaby is horrified to find that she is being investigated as the possible murderer. Increasingly wary of those around her, she wonders how much her nanny can be trusted, and she is sure her husband is thinking of leaving her. Gaby makes contact with a sympathetic reporter, Jack, who he is keen to pursue areas of investigation to help her. But after a few days she wonders if she can actually trust him, or *anyone* . . .

MERRY CHRISTMAS, ALEX CROSS

James Patterson

It's a snowy Christmas Eve, and Detective Alex Cross is at home celebrating with his family. Nana Mama's famous pecan pie is in the oven, and the kids are hanging their favourite ornaments on the tree. Just as Alex's wife Bree emerges from the kitchen with a bowl of homemade eggnog, his phone rings with news that shatters the night: at a nearby home, a family has been taken hostage — and the situation is spiralling out of control fast. Alex rushes to the scene and confronts the unthinkable: a father is threatening to murder his own children and his ex-wife. Then, just as the insanity peaks, a second horrific situation explodes — one that no one could have foreseen, and that puts millions of people at risk . . .

SAINTS OF THE SHADOW BIBLE

Ian Rankin

John Rebus is back on the force, albeit with a big demotion and an even larger chip on his shoulder. A new law has been passed allowing the Scottish police to re-prosecute old crimes and a thirty-year-old case is being reopened, with Rebus and his team from back then suspected of corruption and worse. Known as 'the Saints', his colleagues swore a bond of mutual loyalty on something called the Shadow Bible. But with Malcolm Fox as the investigating officer — and determined to use Rebus for his own ends — the crimes of the past may not stay hidden much longer. With political turmoil threatening to envelop Scotland, who really are the saints, and who the sinners? And can one ever become the other?